THE SEARCH FOR
Zarahemla

(revised edition)

TERRY NEAL

© 2017 Terry Neal
All rights reserved.

ISBN: 1546822356
ISBN 13: 9781546822356

AUTHOR'S PREFACE

This is a work of fiction. However, the majority of the vignettes herein are true, or at least, as true as a fictional work will allow. The pull quotes from the Archeological Footnotes Paper, which appear throughout the second half of the text, are real. The document itself is also real, a construct of the author several decades ago. Much of the Mesoamerican historical data presented herein is not widely known. This may be due to intentional suppression.

Terry Neal

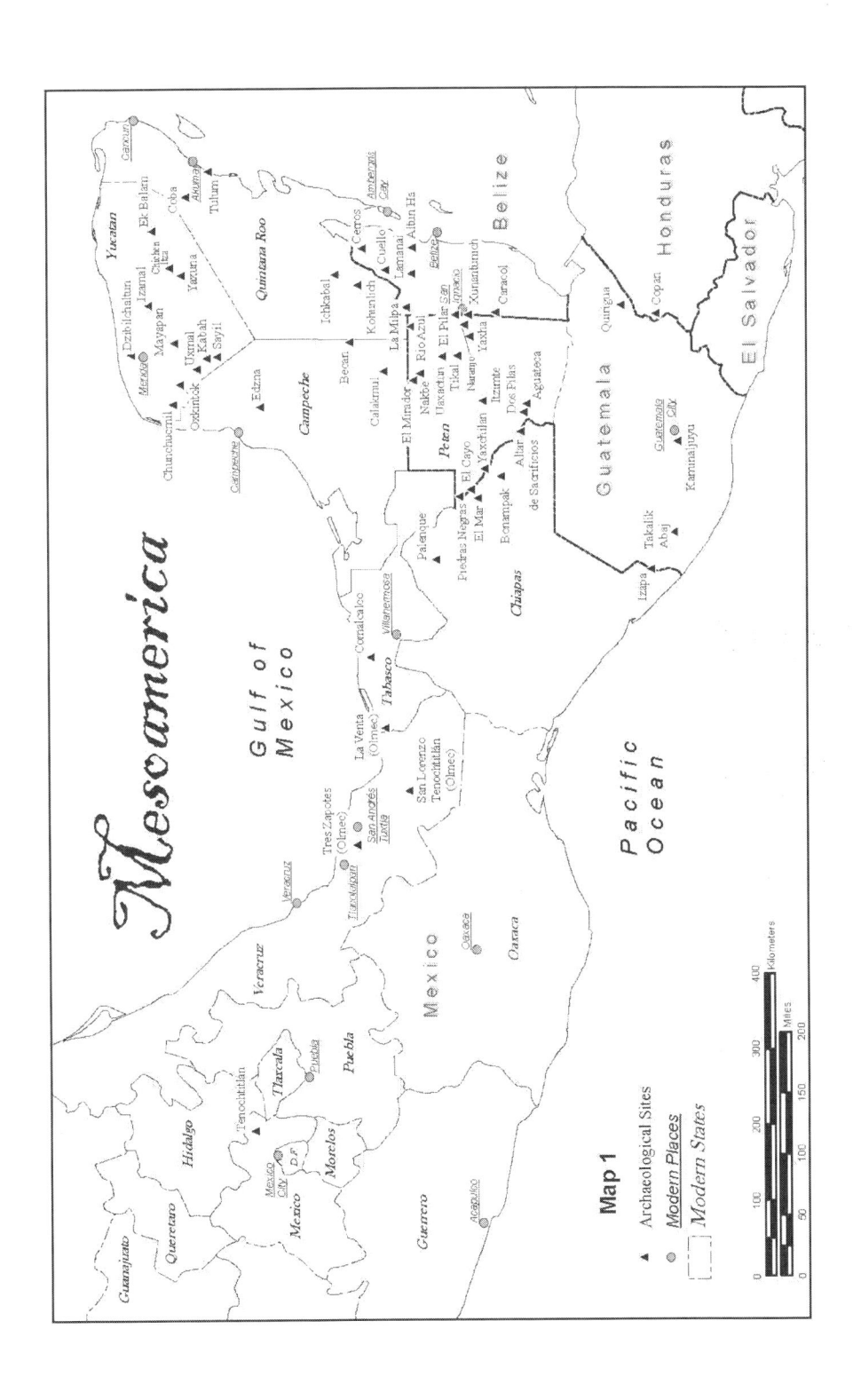

Mesoamerica

Map 1
- ▲ Archaeological Sites
- ◉ Modern Places
- ▢ Modern States

PROLOGUE

Present Day
Veracruz, Mexico

A middle-aged man of aristocratic bearing, lowered his head and whispered in heavily accented English, "Grant, you must leave."

The man addressed as Grant, pulled off his ball cap, wiped his brow, and replied quietly. "Pepe, I just flew in from Cabo San Lucas. There was a lot of weather up there. I'm tired and worn out. I'll check into a local hotel."

In an effort to look calm and unhurried, Pepe stretched and yawned, then whispered, "You do *not* understand. I'm being followed everywhere. I can only assume someone is watching us now. Get out of Mexico as fast as you can."

Grant Whitaker had never seen his long-time friend so jittery. He did not want to leave. The single engine aircraft he had just landed had been severely tossed about as he crossed the Valley of Mexico. Then he'd had to deal with the relentless chop of vertical updrafts caused by strong winds along the high coastal mountain range before dropping down to the sea-level City of Veracruz. Once Grant was down and on the ground, Pepe had shown up at the airport and told him an unbelievable tale, then insisted he leave Mexico immediately.

With a heavy sigh, Grant agreed to get back in the air, and head to Cancun. Tomorrow he would fly to Jamaica, and on to St. Kitts, West Indies. "Okay Pepe. I can be out of here in fifteen minutes."

CHAPTER ONE

Somewhere over the Gulf of Mexico

Rate of climb: *Dismal*. Engine heat: *Rising*. Turbine intake: *Red*. Cylinder head temperature: *Dangerous*.

What's going on?

Bleak and foreboding, the ocean stretched off in all directions. Angry clouds dropped low towards the churning sea. Dark grays punctuated by streaks of scattered light were all he could see. Grant Whitaker was one hour and twenty minutes out of Veracruz, Mexico, deep over the Gulf. The small aircraft's RPM had dropped suddenly. The engine was heating up for no apparent reason. At a little more than two miles high, he was too low, and too far out, for radio contact. With an overheated, underperforming engine, the plane would not climb.

No land in sight. There would not be for more than an hour in any direction. Worse, there were no airports even close to the nearest landfall. The critical decision was whether to turn back, or keep on course. If he turned around now, his plane would get a push from the gale-force headwinds that were slowing his progress towards the Yucatan. Time to choose...

Light flickered in the cockpit like an old-time news reel as hints of sun crept through broken clouds. The plane lurched violently. Wind shears spawned by the squall line he was transiting slammed the plane repeatedly.

Grant vaguely entertained going back. But, what Pepe had confided had shocked him. If the story he had heard was even partially true, the implications were huge. His whole life was in turmoil already, and now this new development.

A staccato jiggling ensued as the aircraft raced across the vertical updrafts that were pushing cumulous clouds into their dangerous cumulonimbus cousins. Grant twisted around to look over his left shoulder and watch the wildly thrashing ocean below. *What would it be like to ditch in the middle of that mess?* He caught a whiff of his own body odor. Fear and sweat. Chewing his lower lip, he decided to hold his heading and hope for the best.

Erratic engine noise kept Grant stiff and hyper-alert. More than once, he caught himself holding his breath, listening carefully for any sign the engine was faltering. *It must be fouled injectors. Maybe it's a magneto failure?* But this is a new aircraft, he thought. *Why?* Once again, he scanned all the gauges in the cockpit, trying hard to make sense of it. His mind drifted to the most recent weather update. A tropical depression loomed directly ahead. It extended all the way down the Maya Rivera. *Okay, better set down in the Yucatan for repairs, and wait out the weather.*

Forty minutes passed in frenzied tension. The headwinds began to ease. Grant dialed in the Chichen Itza airport. It was located in the middle of the Yucatan, close to the famous Mayan-Toltec ruins of the same name. GPS reported he was now sixty miles out. *Maybe I'm in range.*

"Cancun Center, November 4876 Delta, level 11.5, sixty miles east Chichen Itza."

Not for the first-time Grant considered his good fortune that international flight controllers were all required to speak English.

A static-laced voice came back through his headset, "Cessna 4876 Delta, Cancun Center, understand you are level at 11,500 feet, 60 miles east of Chichen Itza. Go ahead your request."

Letting out an audible sigh, he replied: "Center, 4876 Delta, request modify flight plan for unscheduled landing at Chichen Itza."

"November 4876 Delta, Cancun Center, understand you wish to land Chichen Itza. Request approved. Advise Chichen Approach, twenty miles out."

"Center, 4876 Delta, to contact Chichen Itza Approach. Thank you. Good day."

Landing checklists...go. Reduce manifold pressure to 14 inches. Open cowls...keep the engine cool.

"Chee-chen Approach, November 4876 Delta inbound for landing." No response.

"Chichen Itza Approach, November 4876 Delta, inbound for landing." There was still no response. *What is going on? There's no traffic chatter on this frequency. Maybe I've got a bad radio.*

Switching radios, Grant tried again. "Chichen Approach, November 4876 Delta, over." An eerie silence pressed in on him. *Okay, I'm tired and jumpy. There's a rational explanation.*

"Chichen approach, 4876 Delta, going to tower frequency." Toggling his secondary radio to the tower, Grant tried to raise someone there.

No response. Both approach control and the airport tower frequencies were silent.

"It's beginning to feel like the twilight zone," Grant said out loud to no one. He punched in a 700 foot per minute descent into the autopilot. Referring to the Jeppesen GPS database, he double-checked the local frequencies. Still talking to himself, he muttered: "It looks okay. So where is everybody?

Okay, I'm off the beaten track, dealing with a poorly performing engine, pushing into the middle of the Yucatan. I'm carrying the stress of harsh headwinds, and a shocking story from Pepe. Take a deep breath. Blow it out slowly.

Now too low on the horizon to raise Cancun Center, Grant would either have to climb back to a higher altitude on an overheated engine, or continue on his approach without radio contact. Easy choice, bad weather ahead; he was lucky to have gotten this far.

"Chichen Itza traffic, Cessna 4876 Delta, five miles west of field. Descending through 1500 feet for straight-in approach on runway 8."

The turbo-charged, single-engine aircraft, settled in from the west on an almost due east heading. It was much hotter at lower altitudes. At 11,500 feet, it had been a pleasant 72F. As he killed off altitude for the remote Chichen Itza airport, the temperature rose rapidly to 98F. It would likely go higher. "Warm day down there," he whispered to himself, still wondering what had gone wrong with the engine.

Low jungle canopy stretched out below. Ahead, building cumulus cells were becoming cumulonimbus thunderheads in an almost straight-line on the eastern horizon.

Pulling the throttle back, Grant advanced the fuel mixture too full rich, and pushed the manifold pressure to maximum. Ten degrees of flaps, and a few moments later his wing wheels kissed the tarmac right on the threshold stripes. He held the nose wheel off the ground, slowing the aircraft with natural wind resistance. Reducing back-pressure on the flight control, the nose wheel touched down softly. Grant braked to take the first taxiway to the parking apron.

On the ground, it was stiflingly hot. He quickly flipped open both side windows, as he taxied on. The cockpit cooled as the prop forced air through the interior of the plane.

"Chichen Itza traffic, 4876 Delta, down and clear the active runway," Grant signed off to no one discernable.

The single-engine aircraft turned off the runway, and taxied towards a squat tower and some scattered buildings. Painted stripes on the tarmac, worn and barely visible, indicated the approved aircraft parking for transients. Lining up at the parking tie-down, he moved mechanically through the aircraft shutdown procedure. The plane shuttered, the engine stopped.

Cramped and tired, Grant let out an exhausted sigh. *The airport looks deserted. Not a good place to have maintenance problems.*

The flight control lock secured, Grant unfolded an aviation chart to use as a sun block for the windshield. Cramming the extended chart across the dash, and tucking it up behind the top mounted compass, he pulled the sun visors down to hold the chart in place. A glimpse out the passenger window revealed a low-slung building with a palapa roof of palm fronds. *Maybe it's a restaurant.*

Climbing out of the aircraft into the late afternoon heat, Grant stretched. He bent forward to touch his toes, trying to restore circulation to the small of his back. Heavy shimmering air rose in gently swirling eddies over the black of the asphalt. The thick tang of jungle mixed with the smell of oil oozing up from an overheated tarmac, strong in the air. He took another deep breath and let it out with an audible moan. He was down and safe.

CHAPTER TWO

Two Weeks Earlier
Acapulco, Mexico

Jorge Ramon Garcia Peron, Assistant Director of the Museo Nacional de Antropologia, stood ramrod straight. His hands were clasped firmly behind his back. He was staring out the window of his winter office in Acapulco, seeing nothing. As a result of his position with the Museum of Anthropology, and his connections with a number of cabinet members, Ramon Garcia had become the titular head of the Department of Archeology for the United Mexican States. His authority in these regards, and his position of national import, were not widely known.

The labyrinth of the Mexican political machinery required that some counselors to the president, defacto cabinet members of a sort, should appear to be on the outside of the political process. It was believed that this would represent the best interests of Mexico rather than merely those holding current political office.

Ramon Garcia was a man of breeding and connections; he was the grand nephew of Alfonoso Caso, Minister of Archaeology under several consecutive Mexican presidents. Ramon Garcia knew his history, and he knew Mexico, and he had foreseen the political tide changing years earlier. In July of 2000, the Mexican populous had elected Vicente Fox president, voting out the Institutional Revolutionary Party, commonly known as the PRI. The PRI had been in power for 71 years. It had been an exciting time for Mexicans, who in a very real sense had voted to take the government out of the hands of the mutual-protection racket of bureaucrats, politicians, major corporations, and corrupt labor unions.

Ramon Garcia, like his great uncle before him, had served in his post through the changing of the presidencies of Mexico multiple times. He had been re-appointed to his position by the Harvard educated Felipe Calderon, the president of Mexico, prior to the current president, Enrique Peña Nieto.

Ramon Garcia, perhaps even more than his high-profile friends, was adept at multiple levels of subterfuge. Fashionably thin, he gave the appearance of being taller than his six-foot height. His hair, a silver gray, set off nicely with his tailored navy-blue suit. He wore only white starched long-sleeve shirts with gold cuff links, regardless of the occasion, or the heat. Ramon Garcia's appearance and grooming were impeccable; carefully calculated to convey confidence and an image of absolute aristocracy.

Imperial bearing or not, Senor Garcia was having stomach problems again. He held his abdomen with one hand as if the act would lessen the indigestion. It seemed to act up at the worst possible times. When problems arose, that were more bothersome than most, his insides seemed to revolt. Of course, he was careful to not allow any sign of this to others. Ramon controlled his exterior such that there was simply no opportunity to release his bottled emotions. Tamped down as he was, his emotional release was internal. Today he was suffering.

Starring out on the bay, his thoughts began to drift. Surely Mexico was the richest country in the world at the time of the Spanish Conquest. The accumulation of refined gold by the great civilizations of Mexico had been stolen and hauled off to Europe. In addition to being the world's wealthiest region, Mexico had also sustained one of the largest populations in the world prior the European invasion. Mexico had also boasted the world's largest city when Cortez arrived.

After the wholesale slaughter in the 1500's of the culture groups that constituted the Mexica nation, common European diseases, like measles, syphilis, and small pox, took hold, killing off entire communities. Like the American Indians to the north, the population of Mexico had been reduced by 95% before Britain had founded her first colony in the Americas.

Things were changing once again. Now, against all odds, the stolen gold was coming back. Notwithstanding the influence of Donald Trump disciples, Mexico was ready to replace China as North America's manufacturing and production floor. Archeological grants from European and U.S. universities were also enriching his homeland. In addition to the beaches and balmy weather, archeological tourism was attracting visitors from all over the globe. Large sums of money now flowed into Mexico. His country had become the leading tourist destination in the world.

Despite volcanic eruptions, destructive earthquakes, and yearly hurricanes, he was succeeding. Despite the scarcity of fresh water, the pollution explosion, and the inaccessible water resources in Central Mexico, things were improving. Despite the raw sewage and industrial effluents polluting rivers in urban areas, and the problems of deforestation, erosion, desertification, and air pollution in the national capital, his country was evolving. And, despite, and sometimes because of, the incredibly lucrative drug trade, the kidnappings, cartels, and human trafficking, Senor Jorge Ramon Garcia Peron, was enriching his beloved homeland.

CHAPTER THREE

Present Day
Chichen Itza, Yucatan, Mexico

Moving slowly in concert with the heat, Grant set chocks under the wing wheels with deliberate moves, stretching and holding, moving blood into stiff legs. Doing shoulder rotations, and turning his head from side to side to loosen tight neck muscles, he moved off towards the screen door of the hoped-for-restaurant.

It was cooler inside. Dark shadows in contrast to the bright light of the Mexican sun. Cheap wooden tables, rattan chairs, a bar with a dozen stools, and slow-moving ceiling fans, were his first impression. Black and white framed photos of old airplanes and Mexican bandits, the only wall decorations. There was a curious feeling to this place. It was as if he had stepped back in time. The smell of alcohol, cooking oil, and nachos permeated the air. The only color to an otherwise drab room of browns was the lavender Bougainvillea floating in the shallow bowls of table settings. Two men spoke quietly in a corner. A woman stood behind the bar.

"Buenos tardes, Senor," came an easy, almost sensuous greeting from the direction of the bar.

"No hablar Espanol," he responded, almost surprised to hear a pleasant voice.

Nodding as if she knew as much, she remarked in perfect English, "How may I help?"

"Something cold. Diet Coke if you have it. Chips and salsa would be nice."

Another slight nod as she gestured he find a table. A few moments later she moved around the bar carrying a serving tray containing a glass of ice, a can of soda, brown tortilla chips still moist with cooking oil, and a bowl of local salsa. Placing the contents on the table she asked if there was anything else he wanted.

Testing a chip, "Ah…yes. Is the airport closed or what?"

"The airport closes at five."

Shaking his head, he mumbled "But I only have 4:20…oh, I lost an hour coming further east, so it would be after five?"

Her voice low, "Yes, it is after five. It probably wouldn't have mattered. The airport staff leaves early if there are no scheduled flights."

Thoughtful for a moment he shook himself and managed: "Is there an aircraft mechanic on the field?"

"There is Moises. He works on the farmer's planes. He is usually here about now waiting for his brother-in-law to pick him up. If you miss him, he's always here in the mornings."

Grant was hot, tired, and worried, but he couldn't keep himself from noticing this was an attractive lady. *Thirties; she speaks with the ease of a more experienced woman. Her voice soothing and something more. She seems out of place.*

"So, I guess I'll be here for the night. Do you have a recommendation?" he asked.

She stood easily, hands on hips with a slightly quizzical look. "Things are pretty quiet right now. There are basically three places to choose from. They're all close to the ruins. There's the Hacienda Chichen Resort, your basic two stars. A no services kind of place.

There's the Hotel Mayaland, and the Villa Arqueologicas. Both of these are advertised as four star facilities." She paused looking at him. Then continued: "Have you been here before?"

"Yes, but I've pretty much stayed at the Villa Arqueologicas. I thought perhaps there might be some new facilities, with all the emphasis on the Mayan ruins these days. Years ago, I stayed at another place, probably the Mayaland. I remember it had monkeys and macaws in the courtyard. It was directly behind the temple of Kulkulcan at the back entrance to the ruins of new Chichen. It seemed the place had seen better days."

"That would be the Mayaland. It was built by Castilians from Merida. It's still run by family members. It has character, but it's a stretch to call it a four-star property. I hear the Villa is nice, but they don't encourage locals at their restaurant and bar. It's too expensive for locals anyway," she said thoughtfully, almost more to herself than to him. She paused a moment, then asked slowly, "Will you need a ride?"

Interesting woman, well-spoken, good Spanish, no accent speaking English, she's dark enough to be local, but her facial structure is definitely northern. The blondish hair says she's not from here.

"Guess so. Is there a taxi available?" he asked, managing a tired smile.

CHAPTER FOUR

One Week Earlier
Acapulco, Mexico

Ramon Garcia believed to his very core, that Estados Unidos Mexicanos, the United Mexican States, his beloved Mexico, needed him. Without him, he doubted that his country could bootstrap itself out of its grinding poverty. He had helped the Zedillo administration in privatizing state-owned enterprises. This was a significant benefit to Mexico. Not to mention his friends, who now controlled many of these businesses.

Mexico had become a free market economy. Or, at least one freer than it had been. The number of state-owned enterprises had fallen from more than 1,000 in 1982 to only a handful. Trade with the U.S. and Canada had grown four-fold since NAFTA was implemented in 1994. And, he reminded himself, that it was he, Ramon Garcia, that had led the charge on developing a free trade deal with the European Union in order to lessen Mexico's dependence on the U.S.

Mexico's landmass is about three times the size of Texas. It is roughly the size of Saudi Arabia. Mexico is blessed with almost

10,000 kilometers of coastline and beaches of incredible beauty. It is the perfect get-away for Canadians and Americans seeking relatively inexpensive sun-filled vacations. By the late 1990's tourism surpassed oil and mining as the country's largest source of income. By the mid 2000's, Europeans rivaled Americans as vacationers along the Maya Riviera, the 125-mile stretch of beach facing the Caribbean Sea that ran the length of the east coast of the Yucatan Peninsula.

Cancun, positioned at the top of the Maya Riviera, had become the world's most popular resort city outside the U.S. Cancun's only real rival was the fast-growing Cabo San Lucas at the tip of the Baja Peninsula on Mexico's west coast. By the close of 2016, Cabo had surpassed Cancun as the fastest growing employment state of the 32 Mexican states that constituted the country of Mexico.

The incredible success story of Mexican tourism was not just the beaches, Tequila, and the Spring break crowd. There was an underpinning of year-round visitors who came to sun and fun, but also came to learn and discover. These were the most valuable tourists. These are the visitors with money.

In America, school kids learn something about the Aztecs and the Conquest of New Spain (the name given Mexico by Hernando Cortez in 1517.) The same short unit of study in many U.S. schools typically included a short segment on the Conquest of the Incas. The Incas were an advanced culture based in what is now the country of Peru, but in the 1500s their culture extended the entire length of South America's west coast. The annihilation of the Incas took place directly after the Aztec empire was destroyed in Mexico. Spanish military opportunists, and the virulent diseases they inadvertently brought in from Europe, destroyed both empires completely. Unfortunately, most American kids were confused thereafter, thinking the Aztecs and the Incas were the same, or at the very least that they were both located in South America. Mexico is in North America, a fact ignored by most Americans, including much of the media.

The ancient Maya empire, followed in significance by the Olmecs, and Zapotecs, were the most significant high-cultures of the Americas during times prior to the arrival of Columbus. All three of these super-cultures were located in Mexico. The Maya empire was spread through Guatemala, Belize, El Salvador, and Honduras. But the glory of their incredible accomplishments had dimmed hundreds of years before the arrival of the Spaniards.

The Aztecs, a warrior society, and the Incas, best known for their dramatic engineering feats, were the only two nation builders fully functioning in the western hemisphere by the time the Europeans arrived. The Aztecs, and the Incas, were so incredibly wealthy, by European standards, that the looting of Mexico and Peru changed the course of Europe. The huge amounts of gold, silver, and precious gems, streaming out of the Americas, dramatically impacted the entire civilized world in multiple ways. The nouveau riche of Europe began to vie for finely crafted goods from India and China. They used the gold they grabbed from Mexico and Peru to pay for silks, translucent bone china, enameled furniture, porcelains, and finely carved woods. Mexico's wealth circulated the globe. But, it did not return home.

In addition to Ramon's influence in the world of archeological research, he had become the fair-haired child of the tourism industry.

His efforts had dramatically increased the number and quality of the visitors to Mexico. The booming archeological excursions industry had become the largest growing segment of Mexico's tourism cash cow.

Ramon Garcia was the final word on who received archeological fieldwork permits. Not unlike Dr. Zahi Hawass, the previous Secretary General of the Supreme Council of Antiquities for Egypt, Ramon Garcia alone determined to whom excavation permits would be provided in Mexico. Regardless of the country, or university footing the bill, without his approval there would be no dig. And also like Zahi Hawass of Egypt, Ramon Garcia was well positioned to organize and review new tomb discoveries *prior* to their official opening. As a result, and unknown by virtually anyone other than Garcia's closest confidents, he sat at the top of a booming multi-million-dollar business trafficking illicit Mesoamerican antiquities.

As so often is the case in conflicted governments, one person doing so much good for his country, was also doing much good for himself. For Ramon Garcia, there was no moral conflict. Without him, he reasoned, thousands of people working in the archeological research and tourism industries, would not be employed. Without him, many major ruins would not have been cleaned, cleared, and restored. And, without him, tens of thousands of visitors would not be streaming into Mexico to spend their Euros, their Sterling, their dollars. Ramon Garcia considered himself a distinguished, principled, and refined man. Those of the world who knew him, agreed.

He should be much happier he frequently thought. After all, he was easily one of the richer people in Mexico. But these days it seemed that just maintaining his position had become a full-time job. And now, there was this new problem, or perhaps he should consider it more of an opportunity, he reflected. A thin smile crossed his otherwise emotionless face. Yes, he had a problem that needed confinement. It also might represent the greatest potential score of his entire career. It was silly actually. It should never have got out of hand like this. He sighed deeply. It must be dealt with. His stomach roiled again.

Shaking himself from his thoughts, he became aware he was slumping. He stood to his full height, straightened his shoulders, and pressed the intercom button for his administrative assistant. Ms. Brun.

CHAPTER FIVE

**Present Day
Chichen Itza, Mexico**

She laughed gently, "Everyone who has a car in Chichen Itza is a cab driver." After a thoughtful pause she continued, "So, I gather you were not originally planning to spend the night here?"

Avoiding her question for the moment and responding to an earlier comment, he half-stated, half-asked, "You're not really a local, are you?"

Taking a chair opposite him and dropping into it with more grace than one might expect, she replied, "No. I'm from L.A. I came down with some archeology grads to do field work. I fell in love with the quiet, the peace, and the laid-back atmosphere. At the end of the season everyone went home, but me. And you…what are you doing in Mexico?"

"I was on my way to Cancun for a business meeting, then in a day or so I was planning to push on to Santo Domingo via Jamaica, then eventually down the eastern Caribbean to Saint Kitts & Nevis, West Indies."

"You do all that in the little plane out there?" she said in a slightly mocking tone.

"Yep, guilty as charged," he responded.

"So, what's in Saint Kitts?"

He shrugged his shoulders, smiled a crooked grin and said, "Well, you know, some business, some pleasure."

"Sounds exciting," she replied, without the emotion the word exciting usually conveyed. He was half-trying to be witty, but she noticed something going on just below the surface. Melancholy, she decided. It seemed out of place, for a guy who would fly a single-engine plane across a couple thousand miles of ocean to the eastern Caribbean islands.

"Where you from?" she asked, a bit more politely.

For some reason, her steady eye contact was slightly unnerving. He blinked and replied, "West coast. Up north. Oregon."

"You fly here from there? That's a long way for a small plane. Wouldn't it be easier to go commercial?"

Attempting mock bravado, he responded, "Sure, but where's the fun in that? This way I can stop where I want, go when and where I want." He finished off lamely, "You know, it's tough duty, but someone needs to do it."

A low gentle laugh. He'd said this before. "What do you do, to afford this kind of lifestyle? You running drugs, or selling antiquities?"

"I wouldn't know a drug if it was sitting on the table. Actually, I do company formations, offshore banking. Stuff like that."

A twin-engine aircraft taxied up to transient parking. The noise temporarily brought the conversation to a halt. They both paused, and looked out the shaded plate glass windows that faced onto the field.

It was a Cessna 310, no it must be a 320, he thought. The aircraft had been stretched to seat six, and was turbo-charged. He'd had a C320 twenty-five years earlier. For a light six-passenger twin it was fast, but unnecessarily complicated, and maintenance costs were pretty high. It occurred to him that red was the wrong color for the bright Mexican sun. The paint was sun-bleached and dull. The exterior won't last much longer outside a hangar, he decided.

Pulling her eyes away from the window she looked back at Grant, picking up the prior conversation with mock suspicion: "You a good guy or a bad guy?"

Trying to be clever he replied, "Depends on who you talk to." Then realizing it didn't come across the way he intended, he followed up with: "Well, not really. I'm a good guy. Bad doesn't work for me."

Behind them, three men shuffled through the half-opened screen door engaged in conversation. None of them were much more than five feet tall. Each wore the light-weight Mexican-style shirt famous in the tropics known as a Guayabera. Each of them had damp stains around their armpits. Beads of sweat on their foreheads reflected light. These were local workers. One was thin, the other two full-bellied. The darkest of the three waved to the waitress in recognition and boomed, "Tres cervezas por favor."

Without a word, she got up from the chair, smiled briefly, and moved back to the bar. A moment later she had collected the beers and with a slightly exaggerated gait, sauntered off towards her new customers. As she passed by Grant's table, she hesitated, turned back and said conspiratorially, "The skinny guy is Moises."

It took him a minute to realize what she'd said. This must be the aircraft mechanic, but her tone had conjectured a different set of emotions. He sat there momentarily shaken, saturated in sorrow. With some effort, he shook himself, and dragged his mind back into the present.

Speaking confidently in Spanish, she delivered beers to the new-arrivals. She seemed to tease them slightly, then turned around and headed back towards the bar.

Falling into the pattern of most men without an immediate mission to fulfill, Grant watched her. Nice figure; over tanned, an easy confidence, long slow strides, almost languid. *Hmmm, I wonder if she knows that all eyes in this place are focused on her. Of course, she does. Her movements are more exaggerated than before.*

The language at the table where the beers had just been served changed tempo and no longer sounded Spanish.

She materialized back to his table while he was lost in thought. "Will you be wanting anything else, or should I get you a ride into town?" The emphasis seemed to be on wanting. It was probably his imagination.

After a moment to collect his thoughts, "I think I need to visit with the aircraft mechanic. How do you pronounce his name again?"

"It's Moses in English, but pronounced Mo-we-sis," she said, offering him a dazzling smile.

"Is he Mayan?" he asked, knowing full well he was, just by looking at him. He was trying to keep her engaged in conversation. He wasn't sure why. "They sound like they're speaking Mayan," he stumbled on.

Slightly animated with mock surprise; she laughed: "I thought you didn't speak Spanish? Don't tell me you know Mayan?"

"No I don't. I've just been around them in the Yucatan and the Peten. I think there's about two million Mayans in the Yucatan and Guatemala."

"Probably more than that, but, most of the younger generation have lost their language and only speak Spanish. These guys drop into Mayan whenever they want some privacy. So, the Peten, huh? Sounds like you're involved in something more than banking. There's nothing in the Peten, but jaguars, howler monkeys, and jungle." With eyes twinkling, and a suggestive smile, she spoke with some exaggeration. "You sure you're not a treasure hunter searching for another ancient Mayan city lost in the tropical rain forest?"

Switching subjects, ignoring her last comment, he said: "I got the impression they were discussing you."

She was looking at him strangely now; aware he'd avoided her question. "Yeah, maybe...they're all married to short squat women, and it gives them a thrill to consider other options. They're not dangerous. And they'd probably never actually cheat on their wives, but like many men, they fantasize about what they can't, or won't, allow themselves to have."

She speaks her mind. She's brazen, and not at all reluctant to say what she thinks.

With a slightly crooked grin, he said, "Forgive me for the observation, but it didn't look like you were doing anything to reduce their interest."

"You think?" she said, with a toss of her head. "Perhaps I'm a little flirty. It's good for tips. Although in truth, Mexicans are lousy tippers. But I figure it makes their otherwise boring lives a bit more interesting. Other than the day-time tourists from Cancun, which the locals have little interaction with; these guys don't see many taller women. I mean, I'm only average height for an American girl, but here I tower over the guys. Makes them a little crazy, kinda-like Japanese men, they get all stirred up over taller women."

"Well, you seem to have that all worked out. Maybe we can continue the conversation after I've visited with Moses."

A slight acknowledgement and she turned to head off through a swinging door behind the bar. Probably the kitchen, he thought idly.

Grant walked to the table where the three Mayans were speaking Spanish once again. "Excuse me; I'm looking for an aircraft mechanic." There were puzzled looks all around, then the slender one lit up with a smile and responded in halting English: "My name Moises. I fix the planes aqui...no certi..fi." After a short pause, he continued, "Is your plane?" he asked, pointing through the window at the Cessna 182 Turbo.

Grant nodded agreement. Moises beamed. "Oh, is very nice. You want oil change?"

"No, well...I suppose." Starting over again, self-consciously realizing Moises was not following him. "The injectors are fouled. I think it may have been some bad gas."

"Si..si. Mexican gas is no bueno new aeroplanes. You want the (he stuck out his fingers trying to indicate injectors into cylinder heads) clean?"

"Yes, er...a si. Can you do this?" Grant asked tiredly.

"No problema...but no certify," he said, trying again to say he was not aircraft certified. This meant he could not do aircraft repairs in the States. More importantly, he could not record any work he did in the aircraft maintenance logbook. This was a legal requirement under U.S. law, and a new airplane warranty requirement.

Grant thought briefly on his predicament considering other options, but quickly came to the conclusion he really didn't have many choices. "Can you fix the plane in the morning?"

"Si...if no rain. No casa for plane," Moises replied while tenting his fingers to indicate a protective covering.

They have no hangars available, but he must have tools. This Moises guy seems confident enough. If the citrus farmers let him mess with their planes he is probably safe enough. I'd better be here through the whole process though. Grant continued, while pointing at his watch, "What time in the morning?"

"Nueve. Nine."

"Okay, see you in the morning at nine o'clock."

Pleased with making some progress, Grant walked back to his table looking around for the interesting waitress. Dropping into a chair he idly munched chips and salsa. A few minutes later she pushed through the kitchen door carrying a platter of roasted half chickens, just as a group of locals begin to arrive. Noisy prattle accompanied more new arrivals, and the place began to fill. Someone stepped behind the bar and turned on music and began to pour a line of Tequila shooters. In just minutes a deserted sleepy restaurant was transformed into a raucous bar.

The smell of roasted chicken began to filter through the room. The scent reminded him he hadn't eaten much today. *Perhaps I ought to have a real meal before leaving.* Several of the newcomers, impatient for service, began to call out: "Alex, Alex, pollo por favor."

So, her name is Alex. It seems like an odd name for a girl. Maybe they're mispronouncing it? Walking to the bar, Grant watched her for a moment making up plates. *It smells good. She must have known these folks were coming.*

"Alex?"

Looking up from preparing a dozen plates at the same time, she swept back a lock of hair. "Yes, pilot man. What do you need?"

Raising his voice to be heard above the music, "I forgot to introduce myself, I'm Grant, ah…Grant Whitaker."

Looking busy and distracted, "Okay, Grant, what do you need?" There was heavy emphasis on his name.

"Maybe some of that chicken if it's available. I'd like another Coca Light, and some more chips, and then a ride to the hotel."

"Hold your horses. I've got a bunch of folks to handle. Take your seat before someone grabs it. Oops, too late. Take a stool here at the bar I'll be back in a minute."

She hustled off, laughing and poking fun at newcomers, while delivering plates of chicken with some kind of slaw that had coconut and raisins in it. Other plates were piled with chopped potatoes, black beans and avocado slices. Everyone was getting baskets of those oily chips, along with trays of different types of salsas.

Lying on the bar within easy reach was one of the numerous brochures promoting tours of Mayan and Toltec ruins. Idly he picked one up and read:

> In the high civilizations of ancient America, the state organized its citizenry for the building of

massive pyramids, temples, and palaces. In Mexico alone, there may be as much as 100,000 pyramids still waiting to be uncovered. The number of ceremonial centers shrouded by forest in other parts of Mesoamerica must surely be large. Mexico's Cholula pyramid is the largest in the world.

The quote was credited to a Reader's Digest book, entitled *Mysteries of the Ancient Americas*. I wonder how many people have any idea the size and scope of the archeological ruins in Mexico and Central America, he thought absentmindedly. *Although it seems like 100,000 undiscovered pyramids and temples is awfully high, the density and size of the jungle in northern Guatemala would be hard to convey to someone who didn't have a background on this kind of thing.*

The Mexican gentlemen that had turned on the music materialized from somewhere, and began to open beer bottles, setting them along the bar. He glanced at Grant, nodded his head and held up a beer in his direction. Grant shook his head no, while saying, "Coca Light, con hielo por favor."

Without a word, the barman reached into an old-style open top refrigerator, brought out a can, and opened it with one swift move of the same hand. With his other hand, he scooped a glass through a bucket of ice and deposited the can and the glass on the bar. Grant nodded a thank you and poured. The air was still warm, but more pleasant than when he arrived. The iced soda was cooling him down. The caffeine was helping overcome his tiredness. He looked idly around the room trying to block out the volume of the music.

Alex had picked up her pace, moving back and forth delivering plates of the strange chicken dinner. Her Mexican skirt was cut well below the knee. It swayed rhythmically as she walked. The third trip back to the counter he caught her eye. Some slight recognition passed between them. Once more she moved on past him, balancing a tray of beers and dinner plates. That conspiratorial tone, low and melodious, came out again: "Hang on Cap-e-tan, I'm all yours in just a minute."

He watched her walk away, recording somewhere in the back of his mind that her movements were captivating, both coming and going. Then with a flush of embarrassment he realized he was staring at the sway of her hips. Looking quickly around to see who might have noticed his tired fixation, he caught the eyes of a man watching him, watch her.

He must have just come in, Grant thought. He wasn't there earlier. For a moment, their eyes locked; the watcher of uncharacteristically quiet demeanor, notwithstanding the rising decibel level in the room. Even sitting, Grant could tell he was too tall to be Mayan. He was probably a Mexican of European decent, he decided. The man did not avert his eyes. He just gazed steadily straight at him. *Rather unnerving actually.*

Grant swiveled back around on his bar stool, reflecting for a moment on why this guy was staring at him so intently? He could literally feel his eyes at his back. Grant's thoughts slipped back to his unsettling conversation in Veracruz, with Pepe earlier in the day. Jose Robles was known as Pepe to his friends, a common nickname. Grant was more than a friend. The Robles considered Grant part of their family.

CHAPTER SIX

Four Days Earlier
Acapulco, Mexico

General Jose Diego Botia Gill was waiting for Ramon Garcia in the outer reception area. Ramon was going to have to tell him something. Diego Botia had served his country long and well. He had held many important posts during his military career. Among others, he had served as: Aide to the President of Mexico; Assistant Chief of Section Five (Strategic Plans) of the General Staff of the Secretariat of Defense; Military and Air Attaché to the Mexican embassies in Costa Rica, Commander of the 56th Infantry Battalion in Acapulco, Chief of Staff of the 8th Military Zone in Tamaulipas; General Staff of the Secretariat of National Defense; and on it went. This was a man to be reckoned with. He would not broach much intrigue. Botia was from the old school, but he had supported the change in government under Vincente Fox. Now he was in President Enrique Peña Nieto's good graces.

Ramon Garcia walked swiftly to his desk and buzzed his administrative assistant, the strikingly attractive Claudia Brun, and asked her to see the general into his office.

Ramon Garcia's office was on the top floor of a modern building of glass and steel. It had panoramic views of Acapulco on two sides. It was expansive, large enough to host private cocktail parties and meetings of various boards. Notwithstanding, it was not artistically overdone. At one end of the room was a conference table with sixteen blood-red leather chairs, styled after the traditional wing-back of the past century. Each was mounted on rollers for easy movement. There were three conversation centers, widely spaced, each with a couch, two chairs, and coffee table. They were strategically located to facilitate breakout meetings for semi-private conferencing during larger sessions. On two walls were hung large paintings of historic landscapes. A full-sized grand piano adorned a corner of the room, where wall and paintings met the glass that faced on to the beach and bay. Centered in the extreme corner, where the two walls of glass came together, was Ramon Garcia's executive desk.

"General Botia is here to see you, Senor Garcia," the words clear, but somehow seductive. Claudia Brun opened the double doors to his office. She inclined her head ever so slightly, and stepped to one side to let the esteemed general pass. Botia's shoulders were held rigid, his eyes straightforward. Botia picked up the tastefully applied scent of expensive perfume as he passed by Claudia Brun. He showed no sign of his notice.

With arms open wide, and a gratuitous smile, Ramon Garcia welcomed his guest. Garcia walked towards Botia in a manner that he hoped would infer equality. "I hope you have not been waiting long," he said smoothly. I must apologize, I was on the phone and Senora Brun was afraid to interrupt me," he lied just as smoothly. Ramon Garcia had not been on the phone. He had kept the general waiting on purpose. And Senora Brun was not married therefore she was actually Senorita Brun. Ramon Garcia was the consummate politician. The truth was not particularly important to him. What *was* important was how people perceived a situation.

"I came as you requested," was Botia's straightforward reply. "You have not asked me to meet with you privately before, so I assumed it was something of a sensitive nature and needed my immediate attention."

"You are correct general. We have a problem associated with the Museo Nacional de Antropologia. You will be aware that Mexico is blessed with one of the largest and best known museums in the world. You may also recall the devastating robbery of the museum, back in 1985?"

"Certainly. It was a national disaster. It embarrassed Mexico in front of the entire world. Are you suggesting that there is another such conspiracy about?"

Ramon decided to risk over familiarity with general Botia by switching to his given name. He hoped this would heighten the air of confidentiality. "I do not know Diego, but I have some indications that there are things not right. I could use your assistance in helping me outside normal channels." Ramon continued in a hushed tone, "You will understand that anything said within my Ministry will be on the lips of many within an hour of the time I broach such a subject. Perhaps we might sit and visit a little and discuss the situation confidentially?"

"Yes, yes, of course," Botia replied.

Ramon walked to his private bar and mixed fruit juice and dark rum. The sweet combination seemed to agree with his stomach more than other liquors. "What would you like, Diego," he asked in a gentlemanly tone.

The general declined a drink, taking a straight-backed chair while setting his hat carefully on one knee. Ramon joined him and sat in an over-stuffed chair next to a white couch that faced towards the bay. Sipping his drink Ramon sat for a moment in quiet contemplation. "Hmmm, where to begin... Well, it seems that Esteban Morelos has in his possession, or knows the whereabouts of, a rather explosive archeological find."

"Esteban Morelos? You refer to the former governor of the State of Veracruz three elections back?" Botia asked in some confusion.

"Yes, I do. Esteban Morelos, the former governor of Veracruz. The two since him were deeply involved in the drug trade. Well, as I said, he seems to have been involved in the black market for Mesoamerican antiquities, along with his brother-in-law Miguel Ramirez. Of course, that's illegal. But I suppose if we were honest with each other, the trade in antiquities has probably brought billions into the Mexican economy. And, by and large, it really isn't hurting the gathering of quality pieces for the museum. I say this because I am not overly concerned that Morelos has occasionally traded in artifacts. After all, we have more legitimate archeological material here, than anywhere else in the entire world. However, I am deeply disturbed about the unusual characteristics of the find Morelos apparently has in his possession."

Ramon watched Botia carefully, trying to gage his level of interest. Then continued: "According to the law, any Mexican citizen may keep a private collection of artifacts, provided the Museo Nacional de Antropologia has been apprised of its findings, and assuming the Ministry has no objection to leaving the pieces in the finder's possession. Of course, the museum is empowered to assert control over any new find. You understand this is so, do you not?"

"Antiquities are not my expertise, Senor Garcia. But what you've said, agrees with my recollection of the law." Botia shifted uncomfortably. "However, I do not see how this involves the military. A situation, such as you have described would normally be considered a federal police matter."

"Of course, but the problem that presents itself is that Esteban has broken the law inasmuch as he has a very valuable antiquity not registered with the Ministry, *and* he is apparently trying to move it beyond our ability to secure it. Only the military can quickly get roadblocks into place, and search vehicles effectively in certain areas. I fear we are going to need this type of action rather quickly."

"All of this effort for an artifact?" Botia asked, his upward-turned chin indicating an incredulous attitude. "You said yourself that the trade in antiquities was, shall we say, all too normal? So, forgive me Senor Garcia, but I fail to see the urgency."

Ramon Garcia turned slowly away from the window. He looked directly into Botia's eyes without the slightest indication of irritation. "You are correct, but it is the special characteristics of this new discovery that are so important. If it is, as I have been led to believe, it is a discovery of such magnitude that it could dramatically impact Mexico and the entire tourism industry virtually overnight. And as you surely know, tourism is our largest and most important source of foreign exchange. Anything that affects it, affects us all. Mexico has much to lose if this particular antiquity is not recovered with great haste."

"What kind of artifact might be so valuable as to seriously impact the tourism industry?" Botia said sternly. "After all, even the Narcos and their constant string of murders have not impacted tourism overly much." Botia's mannerism calculated to make it obvious he did not accept this line of reasoning.

Ramon Garcia gave momentary thought to the current predicament he found himself in. He decided it best that he appear to provide a complete and candid explanation.

"General Botia, I have it on good authority that what has been discovered is a stone box, containing an important record, inscribed on plates of a gold alloy. I have reason to believe it was discovered deep within a natural cave in the Santiago Tuxla mountain chain in Veracruz. Apparently, the plates have been bound together with metal rings, not unlike a large notebook. The script is neither Olmec, nor Mayan, and yet it may date back to a time before the close of the Olmeca period. Perhaps to that age we think of as the inception of pre-classic Maya."

"I see," was all the response Botia was ready to provide.

"My dear general, you may recall that in 2006, a pyramid complex in the Guatemalan jungle was uncovered. It was but a few miles from our southern border. This discovery contained the earliest known example of Mayan writing. It caused a great sensation worldwide. And yet, it only included ten hieroglyphs painted on plaster. These ten glyphs dated to about 300 B.C. What we are now talking about is something of much greater significance. It may have hundreds, perhaps thousands of glyphs, recording events reaching back to 600 B.C."

His interest peaked, Botia exclaimed, "Is it written in the original Nahuatl?"

"It may be. Documentation on the mysterious Nahuatl language, the tongue of the ancient Toltecs and their predecessors, seems to be directly associated with their belief system. This is the first place we are confronted with the prophesied coming of the fair god. This mythology was known throughout all of the high cultures of ancient America. Of course, the Tulteca, are almost mythological themselves, but they appear to have been instrumental in the formation of the mother culture from whence the major languages of ancient Mexico were derived."

Botia endeavored to contain himself. His practiced formal, and mostly emotionless demeanor, had been thoroughly overtaken by what Ramon Garcia was sharing. It showed.

Warming to his subject, Garcia continued, "I am told that the metal plates contain original writings from multiple authors, and cover a period of almost a thousand years. That is surely reaching, but still, nothing like this has ever been found in all of world history. Even the Dead Sea Scrolls, which were a series of separate writings brought together by ecclesiastical authorities of their day, pale in comparison. This golden notebook may be the lost record referred to by so many Mexica scholars at the time of the Spanish invasion. I have heard that the script has Egyptian overtones, mixed with early Mayan glyphs. That remains to be seen. However, the record, if it truly exists, is priceless. More importantly, it is our history."

Stunned by what he had just heard, the general rocked back in his chair unable to mask his fascination. "So, the myths are true'"' he breathed out loud.

Pleased that he had captured Botia's interest, Garcia replied, "Perhaps. Ah, I presume you are referring to the persistent belief of an ancient transfer of culture from Mesopotamia, Egypt and the Mediterranean, the so-called old world, to Mesoamerica, the so-called new world?"

Having gained control over his initial reaction, Botia responded solemnly, "Yes I am. However, I thought it was inappropriate to acknowledge such a possibility. Everyone knows the stories. It is the learned professors that scoff at such beliefs."

"True enough. It is an unpopular concept with the university intelligencia. They are terrified of validating any particular group's political or religious persuasion. Until recently, they have insisted that Mexico has never had any contact with the old world, for a whole host of reasons. Most of which were political. Once scholars had committed their careers and credentials to such a notion, it became almost impossible for them to recant. Even in light of massive amounts of current information gleaned from fieldwork that supports just such a thesis. But now, the existence of the records, if true in all respects, could bear significant impact on world history, politics and religion. This single discovery will put Mexico at the center of worldwide attention."

"How so?" was all the general could manage.

"The records of gold would surely capture the imaginations of people throughout the world. It would be Mexico's equivalent to Israel's Dead Sea Scrolls. I gather you are aware of the significance of the Dead Sea Scrolls?" Ramon did not wait for an answer. He was in form, speaking with authority. He was captivating, inspiring, bigger than life, his stomach problems temporarily forgotten.

"The impact of the Dead Sea Scrolls has been almost beyond assessment in virtually all respects, financially, politically, and religiously. There were a number of religious and political groups that would have preferred they were never discovered. Several organizations were quick to invest large sums to assure the scroll's contents were not translated and released before damage control devises could be thoroughly implemented. It was only a dozen years ago that the Huntington Library in California, stunned the world by providing photos of the Dead Sea Scrolls over the Internet. Only since then, were scholars worldwide able to see copies of original materials. For fifty years, original scroll contents had been closely guarded. Translations only trickled out over long periods of time. Even today, less than half of the translated materials have been released to the public."

Continuing his saga, Ramon emphasized the economic implications of the find. "The amounts invested in the scrolls, their study, publication, and the construction of a museum in Israel to hold them, was immense. Couple this with the impact on tourism to Israel, and it totals in the multiple billions of dollars. All of this happened, notwithstanding the constant threat of terrorism, and the warfare that has always overhung Israeli terrain."

"Ultimately, the direct value of the inscribed plates of gold could easily exceed several billion U.S. dollars on the open market. The multiplier effect on our economy, as the world rushes to examine this wondrous new discovery, would be many times that number. It could easily erode the political power of some, and endorse others. I tell you general, it would be hard to overestimate the value that such a find might have for Mexico."

Not one to waste words, Botia responded simply, "I see. What would you have me do?"

Ramon's voice hushed to infer continued confidentiality. He began again, "Let me share with you what we know and what we suspect."

CHAPTER SEVEN

Present Day
Chichen Itza, Yucatan, Mexico

Grant sensed the lone man still staring at him. After a moment, he realized he'd done the same thing before…noticed some guy watching a woman so intently he didn't realize he was dumb obvious. Actually, I suppose it's pretty normal, he thought, men watching women. On the other hand, this guy might be somehow attached to Alex.

Stepping around the bar, Alex turned to face him: "Chicken?"

Slightly embarrassed, as if she had known of his indiscretion, he mumbled "Sure."

Somewhat slyly, she whispered: "Anything else?"

Trying to find his mental balance, and feeling a little self-conscious, he muttered, "More chips and salsa, another diet coke with ice."

"That stuff will kill ya."

Catching his equilibrium, "The chicken dinner, or those oily chips?"

"Ouch. Snarky." Moments later, "Seriously, you'd be better off drinking beer."

"Not the water," he said with a slight smirk.

"Definitely not the water, but it's probably not as bad for you as that aspartame sweetener in diet soda," she said half seriously.

The chips had taken the edge off his appetite, but the chicken was good. The slaw was different, but also good, and with enough salt, pepper and Tabasco sauce, the beans were agreeable. Scrapping his plate, he looked up to see Alex had returned. She stood behind the bar watching him. Clearly, she was more comfortable than he, with the pregnant silence between them.

"Cat got your tongue, Captain?"

"Tired I guess.

"You about ready for that ride?"

"Yep, but I need to get back to the plane and get my bag."

"Okay. I'll find someone to drive you."

"I appreciate your help."

Returning to the plane, it was now dark. He reminded himself that the closer one got to the equator, the more quickly the sun set. In the Leeward Islands of the eastern Caribbean, twilight was more like a dimmer switch, not more than a few minutes. Out here on the tarmac, it was still warm, but cooling fast. There will be ground fog soon, he thought idly.

Without light pollution, the night sky was ablaze with stars. The Milky-Way was brilliant overhead, the moon rising in the east. He could hear the music from the bar; it was silent nonetheless. Unzipping his pants, he urinated on the asphalt just back of the baggage compartment door. Two cokes away, he mused, one to go. Unlocking the pilot's door, he looked carefully around and considered the security risk of a new plane left out in the open and unattended. His eye caught movement off the left wing. About a hundred meters back in the shadows, the glow of a cigarette. Someone was leaning against the building watching him. *Why?* He felt a creepy sensation move right up his back. *What is wrong with me? Scared of someone having a smoke? I must be seriously worn-out to be this jittery.*

It had been a tough day. A bumpy flight from Guadalajara across the Valley of Mexico, then the flight over the coastal mountains peppered with vertical drafts causing a nasty chop. Couple that to the unsettling news from Pepe, followed by an unplanned flight, disconcerting engine problems, and the foul weather. A long hard day, plus I'm hot and dehydrated, he reasoned. *I need to get to a hotel and get some rest.*

He grabbed his overnight bag, relocked the plane, and walked briskly back to the restaurant with a tingling at the back of his neck. He was certain someone was watching his every move.

It felt awkward pulling a travel bag into a bar atmosphere, so he left it just inside the door. It hardly mattered, several people noticed him come in anyway. "Capitan, Capitan," Moises said, as he staggered towards him. "I fix your aero plane manana." It was more of a statement than a question.

As Grant looked around for Alex, right over the top of Moises, he responded: "Si…manana." It then dawned on him that Moises was showing off his American customer with the new airplane. Grant smiled weakly, nodded, and then smiled with greater emphasis to endorse Moises stature. He walked towards the bar wondering where Alex had gone.

A teasing voice came from somewhere behind him, "Hi, sailor, looking to show a girl a good time?"

He smiled and turned around. "Yep. Let's go."

"Come on, I'll drive you to town. Mario says I should take you."

"Thanks. Which way to your car?"

"Don't forget your luggage…we're taking Mario's pickup."

"Ah…who's Mario?"

"Oh, I thought you met him. He runs the place. He's the guy behind the bar. I work from 11:00 in the morning through lunch and dinner. We overlap in the evening for a while. He's a good guy, always looking after me."

"Your boyfriend?" Grant ventured in a neutral tone.

"Nah, he's a big brother type."

Changing the subject abruptly, Grant said, "Alex is the plane safe here? I saw someone hanging around on the tarmac. It makes me a bit nervous."

"It's probably one of the night guards. There are actually two of them here all night keeping an eye on the place. I think your plane is safe enough."

Relieved, he followed Alex through what he thought was the door to the kitchen and was surprised to discover he was standing outside. A 55-gallon drum had been cut in half length-wise. Both halves had been placed on metal supporting structures to serve as outdoor barbeques. Fifty steps further, an unpaved parking area. A single bulb hung from a ceramic socket mounted on a battered post. Insects buzzed noisily about it. The insect armada was so thick he had to wave his free arm to move through their mass. Alex didn't seem to notice. She ducked her head and walked straight on through the insect swarm to an old model Nissan pickup. It had definitely seen better days.

"Throw your bag in the back. There's no room for it in the cab," she said as she climbed into the driver's seat. "There's probably no room in the back either, but wedge it in the junk."

The night air was sticky and close, but measurably cooler than it had been. Everywhere, insects buzzed, clicked and chirped. Their collective noise was so loud it reminded him of the hum of an electrical transformer on a cold morning. When Alex started the engine, and turned on the headlamps, insects formed a fog in front.

Grant tried to roll up the passenger side window. No luck. The window stuck half way up.

"You're better off to leave it all the way down," she said. They'll thin out, as we get moving. Keep your mouth shut for a bit. You get used to it after a while." Even in the poor light he noticed her left leg work the clutch as she shifted through the gears. By the time she was in fourth, the hem of her skirt had worked well up above her knees. Nice legs.

Now that he was clear of the smell of alcohol and nachos, he picked up the smell of her. Clean sweat and some kind of floral scent…probably her shampoo, maybe something more. His mind drifted off to the movie, "The Scent of a Woman." He couldn't really remember the movie, but the title stuck in his head. Watching her in profile he began to feel that familiar biological tug, masculine neuropeptides striving to seize control. They drove on, the silence palatable.

The ride to town was quiet, a little eerie; a bit surreal. The light from the headlamps was sucked up by the night, casting strange shadows against the jungled forest. The little Nissan truck the only audible noise.

"You okay over there?" she asked.

"Yeah, but sleepy."

"You sure you're okay? You got awfully quiet all of a sudden," she continued.

"Long day. Not very nice flying weather. I haven't been sleeping well."

"Where'd you come from today?" Alex asked curiously.

He yawned and stretched. "This morning I left Cabo San Lucas for Guadalajara, then flew to Veracruz where I was planning on spending the night, but something weird came up, and now I'm here." It felt almost delicious to stretch and let the road go by, not worrying about driving or flying. He could feel himself sinking into a dreamlike state.

"That's a long way to go in a little single-engine Cessna. That a 182 Turbo?"

He looked at her in surprise. Not many people could give the precise designation of a plane. He smiled, more alert now, and asked, "And how would you know that?"

"Not hard really, I work next to an airport. It's larger and heavier than a 172, smaller than a 206. The airplane looks new, no paint peeling, it has a three-blade prop indicating a turbo."

"You would be a pilot then?"

"Yes. My daddy taught me. When I was little, he'd have me take the stick in his old Piper Cub. I got my license twenty-five years ago, but I haven't flown for the last two years. I still love to hang out around airports. I guess that's why I took the job here."

News flash…twenty-five years a pilot…how is that possible? Grant turned perceptively towards her again, trying not to stare. No, that's not possible…twenty-five years…nah.

"You must have been five when you got your license," he teased half-heartedly.

"Yeah sure." A few moments later she added, "There's no minimum age limit to get your pilot's license, I got mine before I could drive. Daddy was proud of his little flying princess. He showed me off at pilot fly-ins all over central California."

"How old were you when you got your license?" As soon as he asked, he realized it wasn't very subtle. What he was really doing was asking how old she was.

Laughing that soft chuckle, he had heard several times this evening, she said, "Well Grant, I'm 41. I got my private certificate when I was 16, multi-engine rating at 17, commercial rating by my 18th birthday. I got sidetracked and never finished my instrument rating."

Grant looked at her with renewed interest. He smiled. She noticed it even in the dark. He drifted off in thought.

"There you go again getting quiet on me. You're a little spooky, Captain Grant." A moment later she offered, "Peso for your thoughts?"

He began quietly, gaining momentum as he picked up the conversation. "Well, I'm thinking that here before me is a woman who is confident, secure, and obviously accomplished, and how strange it is to meet someone like you in a place like this. And, I'm wondering what your real story is."

She didn't answer, but smiled. Then adroitly downshifted to handle a sharp curve in the road. Some unidentified items in the back of the truck banged against each other and then settled down. For a moment. he worried about his bag then decided it was heavy fabric so it should be okay.

"Sorry, I didn't mean to pry. I'll be less intrusive in the morning," he mumbled.

"Is that an offer for breakfast?"

"Well…ah sure, that would be nice. There's a pleasant restaurant next to the pool in the hotel as I remember. It's a beautiful setting in a mass of vegetation."

"Everything here is surrounded by a mass of vegetation. When did you stay here last?"

"Oh, a year or so ago, I think. My oldest son and I dropped out of the sky to visit some old haunts. We had driven here twice when he was in high school."

"You drove here? From where?" she asked in surprise.

"Beaverton, Oregon, it's a suburb of Portland." *Whoops, there I go again being a dog.* He was feeling groggy and not making sense even to himself.

"What'd you say?"

"Ah, I'm not sure."

"Right after Portland, Oregon. It sounded like you mumbled something about being a dog. You really drove all the way from Portland, Oregon? You must be a little crazy."

"Sorry, when I get really tired, I think out loud. My wife used to say I didn't know what I was thinking until I heard what I said." He drifted off in thought once more.

"What did you mean… about being a dog?"

"Oh yeah, I attended a privacy conference once in Vancouver, Canada. One of the speakers made a curious statement that stuck with me. He said that all people fall into one of two categories when it came to privacy issues. His position was that you're either a dog, or a cat, by nature. You know, a cat will peer around a corner before entering a room, a dog runs straight in with tail wagging and tongue hanging out, wanting to play. You get the idea."

"So you're a dog then?"

With a shrug of his shoulders: "Guilty."

"Interesting; I guess I'm a dog too. But dogs can still have secrets I suppose. The analogy is about your basic nature," she mused. "Curious concept, rather simple, but sounds about right. I suppose we're all victims of our nature. Of course, there are those old arguments of Nurture Verses Nature," she drifted off, captured in her thoughts.

The area began to look familiar. Another turn, and then one more, and they drove into the gravel parking lot of the Villa Arqueologicas. It was a five-minute walk from the back entrance to the pyramid of Quetzalcoatl, the Aztec Mexica's name for the Mayan Creator-god Kulkulcan. This famous stepped pyramid, one of the most photographed in the world, now loomed as a high black shadow in the moonlight. When the Spaniards first saw this hauntingly beautiful, long-deserted pyramid, they called it El Castillo; it reminded them of a castle.

"Well, here you are," she said matter-of-factly. "Maybe I'd better wait until you're sure you've got a room. We can settle up in the morning."

He pushed open the squeaking rusted door of the pickup, "Thanks so much…hang on for a minute, and I'll be right back."

There was a slight hesitation while he tried to decide whether to take his overnight bag or leave it with the truck. He decided to take it, and reached back and lifted it out from amongst the wooden pallets, wire cages, rope, buckets, and the other miscellaneous junk piled in the bed of the pickup. He carried his case across the gravel and into the hotel designed for archeology groupies. He set the case down, lifted the handle, and pulled it behind him.

Around the corner and past a stone fountain gurgling water over a replica of an ancient Mayan nobleman, the registration counter sat silent. The click, clicking from the wheels of his travel bag over tiles ringed by pebbles in a cement-grout, echoed throughout the foyer. By the time he reached the counter, a sleepy-looking man appeared, blinking and yawning a "Como esta."

"Muy bien, y usted?" Grant replied, straining his limited Spanish.

It took less than three minutes to complete the registration, see his card imprinted on an old-fashioned, hand levered credit card machine, and receive the keys to his room. No. He didn't need assistance. Yes. He was familiar with the layout.

Walking back into the dark, now growing heavy with moisture, he could just make out a number of swooping bats. The sounds of night contrasted with the Nissan's idling motor. Fog was forming against the green foliage of banana plants, bamboo, fig trees, and the blossoms of bougainvillea, yellow bells, and hibiscus.

The window down, she waved, "You set?"

"Yep, all set. Are you going to meet me here for breakfast?" Grant asked.

"Si Capitan. Nine?" she replied.

"Maybe a bit earlier, say 8:00?"

She rolled up her window against the damp night and mouthed, "See you."

Collecting his bag, he stumbled along the wide tiled corridor to where it opened around the pool. Two floors of hotel units faced the gardens surrounding the water. A strong feeling of intimacy enveloped him. This was a romantic place. Memories of Marianna came flooding back.

He was on the bottom floor, last room against a back corner. The room was smallish, but clean with good bathroom facilities.

The air conditioner was on cold; within minutes he was chilled by the contrast from outside.

Bottled water sat next to the sink. Thank heaven. A warm shower, the air now turned off, he toweled dry and fell on the bed. He was tired. Not just tired, disturbed. Something was eating at him. It must be the story Pepe had told him. *Was it just today? It seemed like a week ago.* Pepe had been scared.

Staring at the ceiling, just barely visible from outside light that filtered through a curtained window, Grant lay quietly waiting for sleep to overtake him.

CHAPTER EIGHT

Present Day
Chichen Itza, Yucatan

Grant slept and dreamed of Marianna. A memory drifted up from his subconscious. He was in the islands writing in his journal:

> Sorting mixed feelings, I sit down to write and await Marianna's morning company. Dull, and unable to think enough to capture the flood of feelings that wash over me, I wander into the guestroom where Marianna sleeps quietly and stare at the woman I've loved for as long as I can remember. The last two nights we've talked until very late. She is not well, and is overly tired. It may be depression. Whatever it is, she's convinced it is real. Marianna wants to return to Oregon and see her doctor.
>
> It's a long uncomfortable trip from St. Kitts, West Indies to Oregon. Ever since 9-11 it takes two days each way by commercial carriers. Marianna would like me to cancel my

incoming business guests and go home with her and leave our plane on island. I've spent a good deal of time working with some clients regarding their arrival. They've already bought their tickets and organized their schedules. It seems unwise to simply abandon carefully coordinated plans, and tell customers I'm not going to be available. In an emergency, people would understand. There is no crisis, so we are at something of an impasse.

We've agreed. Marianna will leave without me. I'll be left alone in our tropical paradise; lost until I can hurry back to the gray and rain of western Oregon in the wintertime. I love the islands, especially in the winter, but if Marianna is not here, I am simply marking time until we are together again.

Turning over fitfully, another memory arises to the surface and plays out its movie narrative during sleep. They were in the air, flying direct to San Juan, Puerto Rico from the island of St. Kitts. Grant's journal-style narration in full play:

> We decided to change course slightly, adding about twenty minutes to our trip. We dropped altitude and flew up the length of the Caribbean island of St. Croix, then continued on over the island of Isla de Vieques, Puerto Rico.
>
> Vieques was remarkably beautiful, with pristine beaches and wonderful inlet bays. One could immediately see why so many Puerto Ricans had wanted the island turned into a nature preserve.
>
> Flying across the channel that separates Vieques from Puerto Rico, we gained the extreme east end of the island nation,

and crossed Roosevelt Roads airport at center field. Dodging low lying clouds, we climbed just enough to top a mountainous ridge then homed directly on for Isla Grande airport. Approach control gave us a new squawk code for the transponder and asked us to Ident. We were cleared through the traffic control area towards San Juan International. Over flying the tower at 2,200 feet we looped out over the Caribbean, and tacked back in for a left base approach past the Capitol Building. Turning final at the west end of the bay we set down on runway 9 of Isle Grande airport. It had been a perfect flight and a perfect day. Cleared to customs by ground control, we walked into a nightmare of U.S. bureaucracy.

We had originally planned to simply refuel, and then take off for our final destination on the island of Hispaniola, the capital airport of Santo Domingo. It was just another 90 minutes' flight time from San Juan. But, the incredibly absurd, three-hour delay, caused by U.S. immigration, forced us to rethink the process. We decided to spend the night in Puerto Rico. A taxi picked us up from the private terminal, and drove us to the Caribe Hilton, a newly refurbished property we could see from where our plane was tied down.

Marianna dressed up and we dined at Morton's steak house on the Hilton premises. She looked simply terrific, a result of her confidence, a recent diet and exercise routine, and the flush of excitement that seems to follow a new adventure. It was an incredible evening, the moon shone bright on the ocean, a pleasant breeze played gently through the palms. White foam swirled around the rocks and reefs that defined the beach area directly in front of the hotel. I was in love all over again.

The next morning was one of those amazingly beautiful days with which the Caribbean is so often blessed. After a breakfast buffet at the shoreline, we caught a taxi back to the airfield. A short time later, we took off using the Tango departure guidelines for the Isle Grande airport area. It required that we angle out the gap of the inlet bay at 070 degrees so as not to disturb residents in Old Town, the culture core of old San Juan. About a mile out over the Atlantic, we banked left and proceeded to track the north coast almost due west. One gorgeous resort after another passed under our left wing as we flew at low altitude, mesmerized by the magnificent line of white sand beaches, cresting waves, golf courses and coral reefs.

Eventually we came to the west end of Puerto Rico, and climbed out over the Mona channel, in route to the Dominican Republic. Thirty minutes later at 9,500 feet we made the transition from sea to land at the eastern end of the island of Hispaniola. Continuing to fly due west, we proceeded up the southern side of the island, and were once more greeted by one fabulous resort after another. Looking inland was a huge patchwork of rich green agriculture. It extended as far as the eye could see. Odd, how much the inland looked like Ireland. The view, stunning in its own right, was interspersed with lazy rivers flowing to the sea from their beginnings high up in the mountain chain that runs east to west down the back of Hispaniola.

Grant awoke suddenly! *What was that? The door? The window? Something outside?* He lay there willing his heart rate to subside, listening, waiting, straining, to sense what awakened him. A deep sadness began to ache inside. He'd been dreaming of things from many years past. Now, slammed back into the present, he felt profoundly alone.

Something stirred outside the window. He tensed once more. Then he heard it again. He relaxed somewhat. It was a cat. A cat in season. That distinctive yowl, it was frightening in the black of night, but nothing to do with him. He stumbled to the toilet feeling drugged. On the way back, he weaved and walked into the corner wall that separated the bed from the bath. He didn't hit the wall hard. But his lack of grace was irritating. He fell back in bed and slept again, deeply.

A knocking at the door, something mumbled in Spanish. Grant felt as though he were deep underwater and couldn't make it to the surface. The knocking again, then a key turned in the lock. He jerked his right arm in a defensive motion that a moment before had been covering his eyes. Awake! It was light.

"Be right there," he managed to croak.

Grabbing his shorts, he held them in front of him, trying to be modest, as the housekeeper peeked through the chain on his door. She babbled something rapidly in Spanish.

"Okay, okay, I'm coming," he responded half-heartedly. Balancing on one leg he shoved the other into his shorts, catching his foot in the waistband, stumbling in the process. He was being watched through the partially opened door. He pushed the door shut then removed the chain, and reopened it to a blast of bright light. It was so bright he immediately began to squint and reflexively crooked his arm across his face.

A little Mayan woman stood with a mop and bucket, mumbling to herself. Oh wait; she was actually saying something about mujer. *I know that word. Let's see, oh yes, Isle de Mujeres, the isle of women. A woman must be waiting for me. Damn! What time is it anyway?*

Putting on his native leather sandals, and pulling a polo shirt over his head, he leaned into the sink to get a look at his face.

Whoa, scary. You need a shave, and you need to comb your hair, not to mention brush your teeth.

A glance at his watch, 8:25, he was late for his breakfast date. It would be his first private meal with a woman since his wife had died. Cold water in the face with wet hands drawn over his head he rumbled his hair a couple of times, decided it was going to be too hot for a ball cap, and set out the door. Blinded once again by the sunlight, he ducked back in and rummaged around to find his sunglasses then set out once more to see if Alex had waited for him.

He looked around; there was a woman that might be Alex standing by a Palapa-covered concrete bench that projected into the swimming pool. The entire area was bordered by an explosion of growing things. Blossoms were everywhere.

She wore a large floppy hat, dark glasses, and, what he thought of as a spring dress, hem above the knees, sleeveless, light and cool, with paisley-type flowers on a white background. Not entirely certain it was Alex, he walked towards her, but not directly so, until he was close enough to make a decision.

No guests appeared to be about. There were two small Mayan women in traditional white dresses, cleaning around the outside restaurant tables. She was standing under a long palm-covered awning just back from the pool. Still a little stunned by his sudden awakening, and definitely underdressed, especially if this lady was Alex, he felt unusually off balance. Grant waved, what he hoped was a casual good morning, and waited for a response. A broad smile, and return wave. It must be her.

Now, what to do? In the islands I would immediately greet a woman with a kiss to the cheek, and that's the custom here, at least in Mexico central, but she's an American. Everything is culture....

"Alex?"

"Good morning Capitan. Sleep well?"

"Sorry, I overslept. How are you this bright, very bright, sunny morning?"

"Doing just swimmingly, thank you," she said grinning at his attire.

He looked down at his swim shorts. "Yeah, I just woke up... sorry."

"You seemed pretty gone last night. I thought you might sleep longer than you expected. That's probably a good thing."

She seemed taller than he recalled. In fact, he felt like he had shrunk. There was an awkward moment while he chose how to proceed. "Here, let's take a seat," he said, while gesturing towards a glass table that allowed a view of the garden and pool.

They sat. She removed her hat. Light-brown hair framed her face and fell to her shoulders. Through the glass table top he could see long tanned legs...something else he didn't recall. *Ah, but yesterday's dress was long, and today...well, today was another matter entirely.* Painted toenails in stacked high heel sandals. *And that would account for why he felt shorter.*

Feeling more confident sitting down, he took her left hand and kissed it with mock chivalry. Looking up to her eyes with his lips still lightly on the back of her hand, he gushed: "What a vision of beauty, and so early in the day." He was clowning. There followed, a gentle, captivating laugh, as if she knew the joke, but kept it to herself.

Smiling, he let go of her hand and said gallantly, "What would you like for breakfast? Whatever you would like, I would like also."

"Hmmm, let me talk with the server."

Small talk ensued, mostly about private aircraft, the pros and cons of various planes, their maneuverability, performance, and general characteristics. Talking planes was like talking sports, it was safe, and gave one a starting place for real communication. A waiter provided bottled water, tea for the lady, soda for Grant. Alex frowned disapprovingly when he ordered the Coca Light, causing him to remember her little discourse the night before about aspartame.

Breakfast came and went, mixed breads, scrambled eggs, and strips of peppered sirloin, beans refried three times. Lost in the first semi-intimate conversation he'd had with a woman in a very long time, he entirely forgot he was supposed to meet Moises at 9:00 with the key to the plane. When Alex excused herself to go to the ladies' room, Grant stood and walked over to look at some of the hotel displays featuring locally discovered artifacts. An interesting sign introduced the displays:

> Deep within the jungles of Mexico and Guatemala and extending into the limestone shelf of the Yucatan peninsula lay the mysterious temples and pyramids of the Maya. While Europe was still in the midst of the Dark Ages, these amazing people had mapped the heavens, evolved the only true writing system native to the Americas, and were masters of mathematics. The Maya constructed vast cities across a huge jungle landscape with an amazing degree of architectural perfection.

It seemed strange that folks from the States knew so little about the incredible structures that lay south of their borders. Americans would fly to Egypt to visit the fabulous pyramids, but generally had no idea that the largest pyramids in the world were in Mexico, not in Egypt. There were hundreds more of them in Mesoamerica, than there were in the Nile Valley and the Sudan combined.

Alex came up behind as he stood deep in thought. "I hate to interrupt, but its five till ten and you need to get to the airport, and I need to get ready for work."

Looking at his watch reflexively he said, "Seems I'm hell-bent on running late today,"

"Well, I enjoyed myself. It's been a pleasant morning. I trust I will see you in the restaurant? After all, you left without paying last night."

"I did? Oh, I did! How embarrassing. I'm so sorry. I can hardly remember anything of last night. Well, that is, except you, of course. Do you mind giving me a lift to the airport? It will just take a minute for me to check out."

"You sure you want to check out? You don't even know what the problem with your plane is yet."

"Well assuming it's something simple like varnish residue in the injectors from poor avgas, it shouldn't take more than a few hours to get them cleaned. I need to get back in the air and scoot over to Cancun."

A momentary look of sadness passed through her eyes, quickly covered with a cheery, "Well better get moving then."

CHAPTER NINE

Chichen Itza. Mexico

Driving to the airport in the morning was an entirely different experience than the trip to the hotel of the night before. The road looked nothing like the ghostly route through the fog-shrouded forest he remembered. It was surprising to see how close and thick the jungle appeared in places. In some areas, the work of a bulldozer had cleared ground to reveal haphazard soil deposits dispersed amongst boulders and football-sized rocks. The contrast between the deep green of the jungle, and the sparse soil from which it grew, was shocking.

With the windows rolled down and warm air blowing through the cab, they talked over the noise of the truck. Alex was pleasant enough, but a little subdued. She finally brought up the conversation about Grant's driving from Oregon to the Yucatan. "You mentioned you were here last year with your oldest son. How many children do you have? And what on earth caused you to drive all the way from Oregon? Didn't you say you'd done that more than once?"

She doesn't ask single questions, he mused.

"Mesoamerican archeology is my hobby," Grant responded. "It eventually became of some interest to Marianna and the kids. Most of our children did private foreign exchanges with a wonderful family in Veracruz. They all love Mexico. Several of the kids speak excellent Spanish. Two summers in a row, I outfitted a van and drove to virtually every major ruin in Mexico and a couple in Belize. We even managed that horrible dirt track through the jungle from the Belizean border crossing of San Ignatius, into Guatemala, to visit Tikal. At one point, we had quite an experience with Communist rebels. Later we had a similar experience with the Guatemala military. Scary stuff. Over the years, I've made about fifty trips down here banging around in the outback."

"Whoa, so you *DO* know something about the neighborhood!" Alex exclaimed. "You didn't mention your wife earlier. If I'm butting in, just say so." She continued right on without waiting for an answer. "Your wife's name is Marianna? And, how many children did you say you have?

"Marianna is a tough subject for me right now." he replied, sadness apparent in his voice. "She died fourteen months ago. Esophageal cancer. We had seven children. They're all grown, lots of grandkids."

"You're a grandfather?" Alex blurted in surprise. "And, you thought I was young when I got my pilot's license! You must have been married as children."

"Not too far off. We were just out of high school. Somehow, we stuck out our immaturity and made it work. We did the night school routine at college. I… uh…" His voice faltered. Alex changed the subject to cover his embarrassment.

"Why don't you speak Spanish? Seems like your hobby would demand it?"

"I thought I was too busy trying to afford a large family to take the time to learn another language. It's a bit late now. Not so easy to learn another language at my age. I pick up words here and there, but as my friend Pepe says, "If you speak English, and have American dollars, you can go anywhere and do anything."

"There's truth to that," she mumbled. "Well, we're just about there. See that construction?" she asked, while pointing with two fingers extended like an over-under two-barreled handgun. "The Mexican government is funding the installation of a VORTAC and ILS approach for this place. They hope to pull passenger charters, and eventually scheduled flights, directly in from the States to visit the ruins. They're extending the runway, and have plans to do all kinds of development. You probably know that tourism is Mexico's most important business?"

"Yeah, I was at a meeting in Acapulco some years ago, when Salinas told us that tourism had just surpassed the oil industry as the country's largest source of hard currency."

She turned into the parking lot, tires crunching on the gravel. "Salinas! You mean the former president about four terms back? You know the guy? He was pretty controversial."

"Once upon a time my oldest son kept close ties with the Minister of Tourism. Apparently, it was through him that Salinas heard of my interest in ancient Mexico. Salinas sent me an autographed, limited edition photo essay on the ancient cultures of Mexico. It's kind of a long story, friend of friends, that kind of thing."

"Curiouser and curiouser, Alice said in Wonderland," she mumbled.

"Alice, or Alex?" Grant quipped.

She smiled weakly, deciding to ignore the implications of falling down a rabbit hole and disappearing from home. A moment later she brought the little truck to a stop. "Alright the best way on to the field from here is to head down to the Quonset hut. I'm sure you know the drill? Mexican aviation authority, base commandant, customs, your plane's clearance, proof of ownership, aircraft insurance documents, etc. The penchant for official-looking paperwork in Mexico is pervasive. You can leave your luggage with me until you're done if you like."

"Isn't that risky? Won't customs want to go through it?" he asked.

"If it's with you, sure they will. Otherwise they'll ignore it," Alex replied, "There's practically no chance anyone will go out and look through your plane. Not here."

"Thanks for the ride then. I'll see you in a while."

Once through the bureaucratic paper shuffle and onto the field it turned out that Moises had not waited for him. The plane had been pulled off the tarmac and was now on the grass perimeter about fifty feet from where it had been. Moises was working away. The engine cowling was removed. Someone had evidently helped him lift it off. He wasn't tall enough to even reach the engine, much less lift the cowling.

Moises was busy disassembling the fuel injection system when Grant reached the aircraft. The plugs were removed. They had been laid out carefully on an old piece of newsprint on the edge of the grass. Grant could see a large bucket turned upside down next to the engine. Evidently, this was the step stool that allowed Moises to reach the cowl fasteners.

Moises was respectful and pleasant, but he seemed slightly concerned with his findings. "Capitan, the plugs muy bueno. The injector's bueno." Further conversation was attempted without either one of them confident they were understood. Grant interpreted their attempt at communication to mean that something else may have been the cause of the drop in power and rise in engine heat of yesterday. Moises would clean the injectors, just in case there was some minor blockage he hadn't spotted. Sometimes pollution in the fuel would accumulate and cause uneven fuel disbursement.

Moises was also concerned about the weather forecast. A line of large dark clouds was not far off in the distance. He would have to cover up the engine compartment of the airplane, and any unassembled parts.

Unhappy with the prospect of staying in Chichen Itza much longer, yet secretly pleased to have an excuse to spend a bit more time with Alex, Grant headed off towards the restaurant. There was no cell service here. Not for the first time, he wondered why he hadn't purchased a satellite phone for circumstances such as these. He made a mental note to consider this option with more gravity, as he pushed through the half-opened screen door and looked around for Alex.

There were already several customers focused on lunch and their own various conversations. He wandered over to the bar and sat, waiting, lost in thought. He couldn't keep from thinking about her; his self-talk eroded into a mental debate.

You just met this gal yesterday. Obviously, you're lonely. Make a friend, and if she's here when you fly back in a couple of months, there will be someone to talk too. You've got your wife's memory, and your children's reactions, to consider. This line of reasoning seemed to settle the matter for the moment. Then came the yes-but argument. *It was Marianna who had said I shouldn't wait longer than was socially necessary to find a companion. She used to say I wouldn't be able to last a year. She just laughed when I worried about what the kids might think.*

Hello Grant? Are you hearing yourself? This is a woman you met yesterday. You know absolutely nothing about her.

A local girl, probably early twenties, with pouty lips, and a surprisingly forward attitude, demanded he tell her what he wanted. Startled out of his head game, it took a moment for him to realize she was speaking English, albeit with a serious accent.

"Diet Coke," he managed.

"No more Coca Light. Pepsi only."

"Okay, that will be fine…con hielo por favor."

It appeared unusually fast for a Mexican café. The waitress looked vaguely familiar. He watched as she sacheted off to handle another customer.

Got it, she has some of Alex's mannerisms. Makes sense, they work together, Alex's personality must be rubbing off on this girl. Or, maybe it's some kind of local culturalism? No, the bold confidence of a woman very sure of herself, is not often seen in rural Mexico.

Looking around the restaurant, he caught the young waitress's eye and raised a couple of fingers in the universal way of asking for assistance. She moved boldly over and raised her eyebrows in the form of a question.

"I had dinner here last night and forgot to pay the bill. Can I take care of this with you? I also owe for a ride into town, and back in this morning. Alex used Mario's truck."

Her eyebrows arched higher as if she'd caught him doing something slightly wicked. "What did you drink, Sir?" The "Sir" drawn out with emphasis, her dark eyes twinkling.

"Coke…three or four of them, I think four. I also had the chicken dinner."

"The ride into town for the visitors is American $10 dolars each way. The dinner is $8 dolars, plus $4 dolars for the sodas. Ah…

Before she could figure the math he simply said: "Thirty-two dollars plus tip?"

Si, Senor, ah, yes sir. Drawing out the emphasis on both "yes" and "sir" with a mischievous upturned curl to the edge of her mouth.

He handed her a hundred-dollar bill. "See that Alex gets it, will you?" He vaguely wondered why he'd given the large tip. *Am I playing into this young woman's expectation, or paying Alex for being nice to me?* Walking out to the tarmac he saw Moises sitting in the grass eating some kind of taco looking affair. He was studying the injector assemblies. He smelled of gas. When Moises saw Grant, he nodded his head as he finished chewing, "Cap-e-tan…the injectors clean."

Another conversation ensued. Each person said his piece in his own language, using hand signals and pointing at parts. Grant sensed a change in the light, and looked up to see dark clouds moving fast towards the airport. They would soon be overhead. Moises had noted this too, and made it clear through various gestures and a slightly formal speech that the reason he was still working was to beat the coming storm clouds for the Capitan importante. Or, at least that's what Grant thought he was saying. While standing there thinking about what this might mean for the immediate future, two helpers arrived carrying a large blue plastic tarp.

Using the overturned bucket as a stepping stool, Moises placed the canvas tarp over the engine compartment and one helper stood on each side of the plane holding it in place like a tent so that Moises could work under it.

After straightening out the baggage compartment, Grant pulled out a plastic garbage bag and began to clean the plane's interior. He removed a large Gatorade bottle, half-full of a slightly yellow liquid, and walked about thirty steps away in the grass where he emptied it. You wouldn't do this with a women's urine, he thought. It's stronger than a man's, more caustic and it will kill the grass. *And, there we have it, more useless trivia from the mind of Grant Whitaker.*

Shaking himself from his musings, he looked around for a place to deposit the trash. He noticed rain was already coming down across the field. *Oops, better get moving.* With his hands full, it somehow reminded him of his luggage. He hadn't thought of it before. His travel bag was still with Alex. It would be necessary to see her again, regardless of having set himself up to slip away.

First the down draft hit, then the rain. Both were in full force before he got to the screen door. He turned around and saw the Mayan men stoically holding the flapping blue canvas with Moises underneath.

With hands full, he pushed into the restaurant and looked for a trash can. Nothing was in sight. Probably out the back door, he thought. Moving swiftly across the room he shoved the back door open with his foot. He walked straight through, catching the waitress he had seen earlier completely by surprise. She had been running in to escape the downpour, just as he was headed out looking for a trash can. She squealed and fell backwards coming down in a puddle just as the rain really broke loose. At the same time, and as surprised as she, Grant dropped the trash bag. Without thinking, he automatically leaned forward to pick it up. The door swung back and hit him in the head.

Putting both hands over her mouth, the young waitress began to laugh uncontrollably. A down draft caught the bag sending it careening off towards the parking lot.

Offering the waitress his hand, he pulled her up, and together they stumbled back through the door and out of the deluge.

A few steps into the restaurant and she slipped in a puddle of her own making. Grant reached for her putting himself off balance. She went down pulling him right on top of her. His fall and slide to her left scrunched her dress above her waistline. For an awkward moment, she was trapped with him on top, her dress raised to her waist on one side, and the white cotton of her top soaked through and no longer opaque.

The gods and goddesses of confusion must have choreographed the entire scene, as no sooner had they found themselves on the floor in a public place than Alex ran through the broken screen door from the tarmac side holding a scarf over her head. Stunned at seeing the two of them lying there in such an unlikely and intimate position, Alex froze. The young waitress erupted in laughter once again.

Somewhere in the back of his mind, Grant realized he'd just been in a more intimate position with this young woman than anyone he'd known since Marianna had taken ill. Funny, he didn't even know her name. Apparently, their little skit had been performed with an audience. Four men sat slack-jawed at a table nearby watching as Alex stood there trying to put it all together.

The rolls of laughter from Lupe put at ease the concerns of those having watched the episode. Moments later the entire dining room chimed in. Pulling her wet dress down to a more modest level, Lupe tried to explain the event to Alex in high-speed Spanish, while waving her arms in all directions. This made the entire affair somehow even more humorous. *Marianna would be pleased, she loved to laugh.*

The three of them stumbled to a table and sat down to catch their breath. Pragmatism finally seized the day. Alex told Lupe her top had become transparent. She immediately stood up and hurried behind the bar to find a large towel, which she wore for the next half-hour like a fur stole. One of her customers must have made a remark about her new fashion statement. She stepped back from his table abruptly and stuck her tongue out.

The emotional release and spontaneity of the event, was a healing balm for Grant. His disposition immediately improved. He forgot for a moment why he was there, that he had pressing matters to attend, that serious forces were combining against him, that his friend in Veracruz was terrified of something, and that his airplane was grounded in a place where cell phones didn't work.

The rain stopped as quickly as it had begun. A short time later Moises came in to discuss developments. This time Grant had Alex with him to interpret. Things went better. The injectors were re-installed, so were the plugs. Grant was needed to start the engine and do a run-up. He excused himself and followed Moises out on the tarmac where he and his two assistants had already moved the aircraft.

Map 2

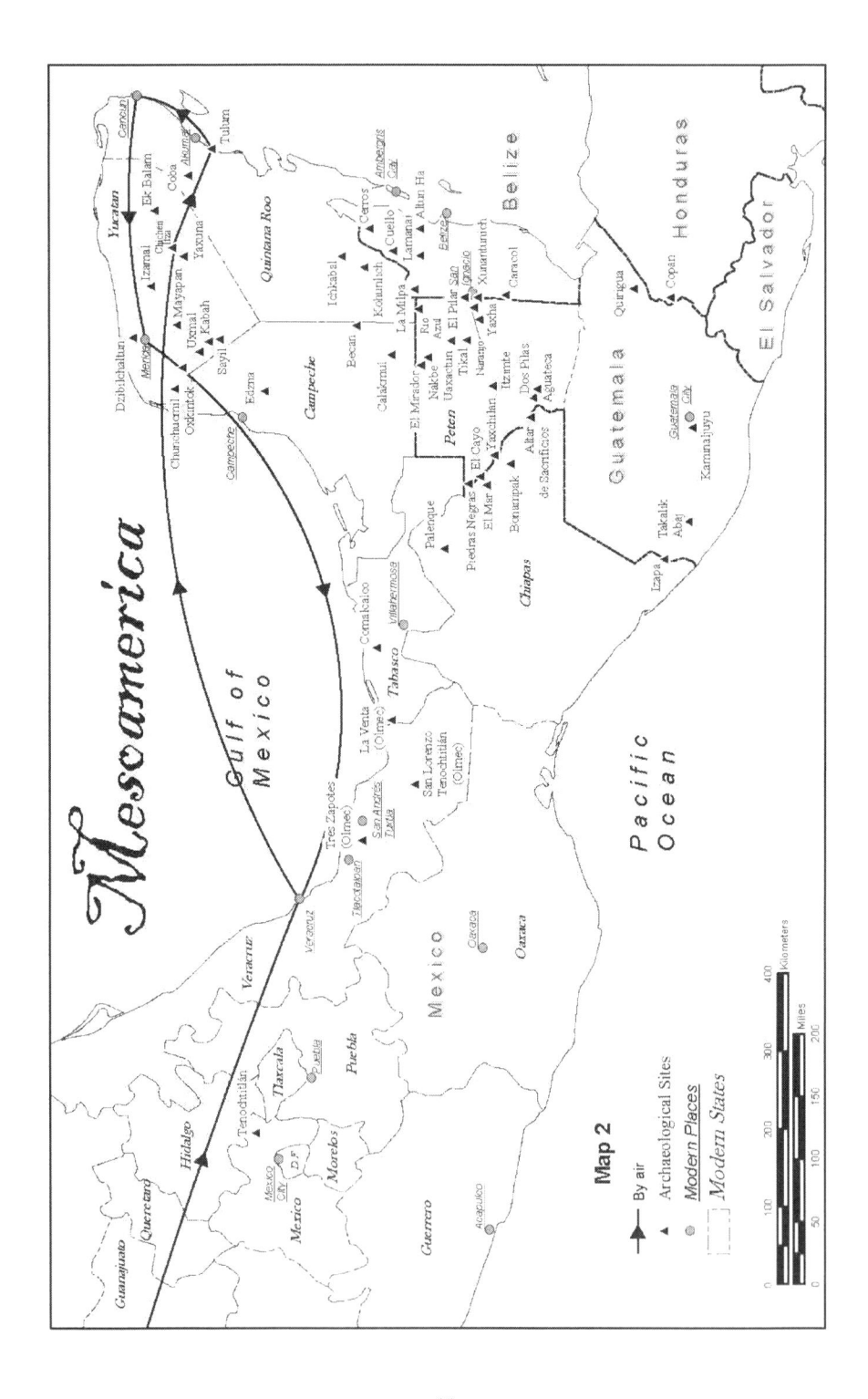

CHAPTER TEN

Chichen Itza, Yucatan

The plane started smoothly. Grant paid Moises and returned to the restaurant to get his luggage. Alex was gone.

Filing a flight plan was quick and easy. The payment for landing fees and the completion of a number of forms went smoothly, mainly due to the grease of a few U.S. dollars provided the two different officers with which he was required to clear.

In order to clean up the graft that plagued all Mexican governmental operations, President Vincente Fox had placed cameras and recorders in the offices of public servants. Now when a public servant sought a propina, "tip, or gratuity," he or she (the latter rarely), would simply move out of line of the camera, and hold their hand out low, saying nothing. Experience had taught Grant that it was immensely easier to slip a few dollars in the paperwork. It was less stressful for everyone.

When he returned to the aircraft, Alex was wistfully gazing at the cockpit controls through the pilot's window. She was holding a shoulder bag made of what could only be carpet. "Got room for me?" she said brightly.

"Well sure, where do you want to go?" he joked back, not for a minute thinking she was serious.

"Cancun for a couple of days. Lupe can handle things here, and I can catch a bus back," she said with growing enthusiasm.

Seeing his hesitation, Alex quickly added, "Lupe's mother lives in Akumal, about an hour's drive south of Cancun. We all go there from time to time to look after her. She's a wonderful woman."

More at ease with this new information, he responded, "Guess I'd better amend the flight plan."

"Oh, don't bother. Nobody really cares. Let's just get out of here before it gets dark. She smiled broadly, as she walked around to the passenger side of the plane.

Grant and Alex climbed in, and buckled down, Grant yelling the obligatory "Clear," as he cranked the engine. Once running smoothly, he flipped on the master electronics switch and powered up the radios.

"Chichen Itza tower Cessna Skylane November 4876 Delta on the tarmac, taxi to takeoff."

"November 4876 Delta clear to back taxi runway 26."

After a quick run-up to check the instruments, and setting the GPS for the Cancun airport, he taxied back on runway 26, circled about and keyed the mike. "Tower, 4876 Delta, ready for takeoff."

"Cessna 4876 Delta, cleared for takeoff, straight out departure, report 10 miles east of field."

"Copy tower, 4876 Delta rolling, report 10 miles out."

Moving the throttle smoothly the plane gained speed. Grant eased back on the flight control at 60 knots lifting off the ground, "rotating" in the vernacular of pilot-speak. They flew straight down the runway to gain speed. He eased back on the flight control and watched the vertical speed indicator register 1,500 feet per minute climb. A full color electronic map in the dash showed a miniature airplane constantly centered, as the map moved underneath.

Building cues coming off the Caribbean were once again moving westward across the Yucatan. Today they were scattered and easy to avoid. They leveled off at 5,500 feet. Close enough to the ground to enjoy the view, and high enough to see fifty miles in every direction. They dog-legged to fly over Coba, Tulum, Xel-ha, and Akumal, then called up Cancun approach, and were cleared into a righthand pattern for landing.

As they taxied up to the private FBO terminal, Grant said, "I'll be renting a car here. Would you like me to drive you to Akumal? It's one of my favorite spots. We've had a couple of family vacations there."

"Oh, so you know the place? Why didn't you say so?" she asked with a puzzled look on her face.

"Mind somewhere else I guess," he replied, wondering why he was making the offer.

"Well, if it wouldn't be too much trouble, I'd really appreciate it," she said flashing him a radiant smile.

Cancun's FBO terminal, like its sister FBO in Cabo San Lucas, are two of the best private aircraft terminals in all of Mexico. Personal service is automatic, follow through is good, and the car rental facility for pilots is professional and expeditious. In just minutes, Grant and Alex were in a late model rental car, headed for Akumal.

He felt good. It was nice to be driving this familiar stretch of road. His mind wandered to loving memories. "Have you eaten at the rotunda at the Akumal hotel? Marianna and I stayed at the hotel once with five of our children for a few days. We were eating dinner one night when a lightning storm out over the Caribbean was so dramatic we were spell bound. Well, that is, until the building was struck. The power was out for the entire night, which isn't such a big deal for a couple, but it complicates things exponentially when there are rambunctious teenagers involved. The kids still talk about it."

Glancing sideways, he noticed that she smiled softly, almost wistfully. He drove on. It was quiet for a moment. The silence itself seemed to convey something. Alex visibly relaxed into the car, bringing her legs up and crossing them underneath her. "You sound like you are very close to your children."

"There is nothing in the world more important to me. They are great parents, and good uncles and aunts to their siblings' kids. It's hard to imagine them any better."

"It's so nice to hear a father speak well of his children. No wayward kids?"

"Well, they're all different, and some have gone down paths I wouldn't have chosen for them, but they've all turned out incredibly well. Besides, I have an abiding belief in free agency. So, it's up to them to decide what to do, and when."

"Free agency, what's that?"

"Well, I suppose, that at its most fundamental level, the term simply means the freedom to choose. Personal liberty is all about the power of choice. In other words, an individual's right to freely choose between various paths and lifestyles, is greater than any right granted by government. Actually, the concept was beautifully set forth in the Constitution of the United States. Its entire ethos is about individual rights, liberty and the right to own property."

Grant continued, "One of the most dramatic notions expressed by early prophets and philosophers was the principle of free agency. In fact, the ancients argued convincingly that "imagination" or "creativity" and its correlative, the "power to choose," were the only things that separated mankind from animals. This philosophical position makes a lot of sense. It seems that the ability to imagine an outcome, then to consciously choose a process in advance, is only well-developed in humans." Grant paused for a moment, sounding slightly embarrassed, "Ah, sorry, I fell into lecture mode."

"No, don't stop, I find this interesting. It's just like being back in school."

He couldn't tell whether she meant it, or was just being polite, but he went on anyway. "Well, from my perspective, simple observation indicates that we appear to be the only living things on planet earth that can imagine something clearly in our mind, and then do it. For example, look around. Everything you see, in this car, on your person, on the highway, the signs along the road, everything, was first a thought in someone's mind."

"Okay. I get that, so?"

"So, everything created by humans is first mentally considered, a choice is made, after which it is designed, which involves a myriad of choices, and finally constructed, this requires even more choices. What other living creature has imagined and chose to do something new, something none of their predecessors have done? What has a chipmunk, a whale, or an ape, done for the next generation of chipmunks, whales, or apes? They can be trained to use tools, or accomplish tasks, but they do not seem to have the power of creative choice. In order to choose, you must be able to imagine the effects of your choice.

"Our ability to imagine multiple outcomes, and choose to pursue the one we feel is best suited to our situation, is the essence of freedom. There is no greater power on earth. It is the source of all of our accomplishment. It is the source of most of our misery. As far back as the beginning of civilized society, we can observe that thinking man concluded there was no greater gift."

Alex stared out the passenger window captured in her own history. "Yeah, I hear the part of it being the source of most of our misery. I have the scars to prove it."

"I suspect we all do," Grant replied thoughtfully.

"So as this relates to your children, you're saying they have the right to choose their direction and destiny, and you do not have the right to interfere?"

"Perhaps it's not that simple. Parents have the responsibility to train and educate, in addition to providing love and security, but essentially that's right. By the time our children were ready for college our role as parents was that of counselors, not directors. It can be rather painful, but I believe that each of us have the inalienable right to be as wrong as we want to be."

"I'll give that some thought," she said quietly. "My folks were a little more controlling, but certainly good parents. My dad adored me, and was always hauling me out to do things with the guys. That's really how I got my name. My full name is April Alexandria Jardine. April is pretty girlish, and I grew up mostly a tomboy, so I became Alex, a contraction of my middle name."

The traffic was heavy in the late afternoon. They found themselves caught behind a string of buses heading to the Playa del Carmen turn-off where the hydrofoil embarks for the island of Cozumel. Conversation sustained them. At one point, they pulled over to a roadside vendor. They bought bottled water and Peguinos (Mexico's Hostess-style cupcakes), and sat in the rental car with the windows down talking and watching the traffic stream by. Time passed. It eventually began to feel awkward. Grant started the car and they continued on.

"Curiously enough, I have a niece named Alexsondra, she goes by Alex, too," he said resuming an earlier string of conversation. "So, tell me Alex, why here, why now? What's in your future?"

She let out a nervous laugh: "I'd tell you, but I'd have to kill you."

"Come on, you're no spook," he said laughingly.

Having made a snap decision to trust him, she blurted: "No. The truth is I'm hiding out. I had a short-lived fling with a really handsome guy. He turned out to be some kind of Narco. In thinking back about it, I guess I was pretty vulnerable at the time."

She shook her head grimly, and continued. "You see, I had just come off a broken marriage. Eight years. Can you believe it? I returned to school to pursue my interest in archeology. That's when I met Jose Antonio at a "Religions of the World" class at the University of California at Long Beach. His family seemed to be respected art dealers. They specialized in ancient American antiquities. Strictly legal stuff, I was told. Hello, wake up and smell the coffee, Alex," she said in distress. "Ms. Gullible, that's me.

So, anyway, at the time all I could think about was how I'd met this incredible guy with the same interest in ancient cultures, and he was interested in me, and wasn't it all terrific?" With an edge of sarcasm, she finished as if talking to herself, "You know, the tall, dark, handsome, mysterious guy that knocks you off your feet?"

She fell silent again, realizing she'd said more than she intended. After a few minutes, Grant replied, "Sounds like we have two things in common?"

"Huh?"

"I'm thinking we both love airplanes and Mesoamerican archeology."

"Oh. Yeah. Right. Ah, I guess I kind of dumped my bucket, sorry," she fumbled.

"My guess is you haven't begun to dump your bucket. But, for the whatever-it's-worth department, I'm dodging bullets too. And, on a professional level, I'm used to knowing lots of private things about a lot of people. It's been my job really, helping the wealthy with asset protection structures."

"So, you're an accountant? Or, are you a lawyer?" Alex adopted a neutral tone.

"Neither. But I work, or rather use to work, with accountants and lawyers in developing asset protection strategies for affluent individuals and their families. The core of my business was in providing structures for people to use in implementing their legal strategies."

"What? Okay, so I'm lost. Strategies, structures... What's it all about Alfie?" she said, laughing at an old movie line.

"Is that a rhetorical question, or do you want to know? It can switch off your brain if you're not in a position to need my kind of help," Grant said calmly.

"Oh, I need help alright. But, there's probably nothing you can do for me. Give me the dumbed-down version. You know, a thumbnail sketch," she said with a wave of her hand.

"Okay, first some background: Roughly five percent of the world's population reside in the U.S. About thirty-two percent of the world's total economy is developed within the U.S. Seventy percent of the world's lawyers reside in the U.S. Ninety-four percent of all the lawsuits in the entire world, are filed in the U.S."

She looked genuinely surprised. "Come on, are you kidding? Ninety-four percent of all the lawsuits in the entire world are in America? I'll bet some politician would have a field day spinning that one." Alex paused for a moment, "Yeah, but then most politicians are lawyers, aren't they?"

"Yep, that's right."

"So, getting back to what you do," she continued. "What is an asset protection structure? Don't explain the whole thing just put it in some perspective."

"Well, basically, they consist of corporations, limited liability companies, sometimes charitable remainder trusts, asset protection trusts, and educational foundations. It's the kind of stuff that makes most people yawn. Yet, without asset protection characteristics, none of these legal structures would be of much value. The essence of an asset protection strategy is to divide goods into separate legal units in order to protect them more effectively. It's the ancient equivalent of separating treasure amongst various castles."

"Really? That's all there is to it?"

"Yes, that is basically it, but as always, the devil is in the details. John D. Rockefeller was purported to have told his children on his death bed: "Own nothing. Control everything." You can do that with trusts that maintain the controlling stock in various corporations, etc. The essence of it all, is that one can be in a position to influence the use of resources, without being their sole, or logical, beneficial owner. This kind of strategy provides a veneer of additional protection, and drives predatory lawyers nuts."

"Alright, I admit I'm sorta lost here. So that's what you do? It sounds rather mysterious."

"Yes," Grant replied. "This is what I used to do. I'm winding down my operations. It's become way too controversial. For all the wrong reasons, I might add. The business of Asset Protection is generated primarily by lawyers. However, the multi-jurisdictional trust in English common law dates back over 800 years. However, the concepts at play here are at least three thousand years old. But, I'll spare you the history lesson."

They drove on in silence. The turquoise on blue seascapes that materialized every mile or so on their left, were achingly beautiful. Neither of them seemed to notice. Alex was thinking feverishly. She was trying to put something into words. Eventually, she asked, "So you know something about how federal agencies operate?"

"Well, yes, to some degree. I used to write a bi-weekly report on governmental abuse of power. It certainly didn't make me popular with them. As a general rule, U.S. federal agencies are complex and deeply entrenched in their own culture. Some have annual budgets greater than the total GNP of small countries. Not well known is that they each tend to have their own political agendas. And frequently, those agendas have little to do with the president's plan for America. Presidents come and go, but the bureaucracies that administer the country are firmly established. It's very difficult for a president to redirect an agency's self-serving agenda. In fact, a number of agencies have their own version of international diplomacy. Some actually have great influence on other countries."

"You're not just making this stuff up?"

"Speaking as an American who has lived in small island nations for many years, I can tell you that it is maddeningly apparent that some U.S. agencies are continuously involved in manipulating small democratic countries in order to achieve their own political agendas. I suspect that much of the time, the White House is essentially unaware of these activities. It is pervasive nonetheless. Some politically motivated groups in Washington are so adroit at meddling in other countries' affairs, that in some respects they're almost running them," Grant mused.

"You get this kind of stuff in movie plots, but we don't really hear about this in the news," Alex offered.

"Occasionally things like this get some press in international media. The U.S. media rarely covers things of this nature. American media is very careful about taking on entrenched agencies. Basically, the media carries the government's spin. Around election times, multiple points of view are debated, but the elephant in the living room is rarely discussed. The thing to realize is that government media releases are always self-serving. Their intent is to create public support for bureaucratic initiatives. For example, after the invasions of Afghanistan and Iraq, offshore investments, including vacation homes, investment properties, and other types of business activities, for rank and file Americans, were branded by aggressive three-letter agencies as sinister plots to undermine the U.S. economy."

"Of course, it is absolutely okay for corporate America to aggressively pursue offshore interests. It is no longer okay for the rank and file. Incredible resources were provided to investigative agencies to stop individual Americans from investing offshore. After all, the Congress had given huge tax incentives to large corporate donors who were pursuing this kind of business. They certainly didn't want the average American having access to these same incentives."

"Eventually, the agencies charged with limiting American's access to various resources, had to justify their huge, and frequently absurd, expenditures. I know this personally, as I am in their crosshairs. And it isn't a stun gun they're aiming at me."

"You're serious! You're a target of the U.S. government?" Alex erupted. It was not a question.

"Yes, I am. It's very unsettling. I find myself spending an inordinate amount of time looking over my shoulder, as it were."

"Whoa, I had no idea. It gives me a little more balance to know that someone like you is on the government's shit list. They're after me too. The U.S. District Attorney's office in San Francisco is looking for me in association with a drug smuggling sting against Jose Antonio. That's the guy I was telling you about that I met at university. I don't know what is the greater risk, being arrested and dragged through the justice system, or having Jose Antonio Vilchez put a hit on me."

The car fell silent as they each considered their individual predicaments. Five kilometers north of Akumal, Alex suddenly exclaimed, "Oh, maybe that was about you and not me!"

"What do you mean?" Grant asked quietly.

Slowly, picking her words carefully, Alex replied. "Remember when I was speaking with Moises earlier today about the plane? Grant nodded. "Well, he told me there was an official-looking guy asking questions about you and me out on the field. Moises said the guy was writing stuff down. Apparently, he is an investigator of some kind. He flashed an official ID. The guy was in the restaurant last night. He saw us leave together."

With sudden insight Grant exclaimed. "I saw that guy! Steady gaze, sitting at a back table by himself watching the room. I actually thought he was watching me when…" His sentence hung unfinished in the air.

"What?" Alex exclaimed.

He laughed uncomfortably for a moment. "I was pretty tired last night. I got fixated watching you do your waitress thing. So, I realized I was starring when I looked around and saw this guy studying me. I thought he was just catching me paying too close attention to you."

Alex gave him a sidelong look. "Got caught, did ya?"

"Guess so. It's not my usual conduct. I was just too tired to exercise much control," Grant said, slightly embarrassed.

"You need to turn left here," Alex pointed. "This is the first road to the beach at Akumal, the second goes down to the hotel."

"Still a sand road I see," Grant observed. Ignoring the alarms going off in the back of his head, he continued, "Alex, would you like to have dinner?"

"Yes, I would. Let's go to the restaurant at the hotel. The one you were telling me about. I've seen it from the beach, but never actually been inside."

The packed sand road was crowded. A group of primary age children, all wearing smart white shirts and navy blue pants, were headed home from school. Grant carefully turned the car around and headed back to the highway. They made small talk while waiting to make a left turn. "A lot of traffic for this time of day. It looks like they're widening the road though," he commented, without much emotion. Then he plunged back into their prior conversation.

"It sounds like we're both living our own personal nightmares right now. Not knowing any of the details of your situation, I'd say your chances are lot better with the DA's office. They're not in the habit of killing people. After all, the federal prison system is a growth industry. I read somewhere that America has 7.3 times more people in prison per capita, than the average of all the other first world countries combined. It seems to me you're worth a lot more to the system in prison than you are dead." He had meant it as a joke. It didn't play well.

Alex shot back with more sarcasm than she intended, "What do you know about the drug trade anyway?"

Ignoring the fire in her reply, he responded evenly. "I've read some. You know, follow the money, and all that. The truth is, I wouldn't know an illegal drug if it was starring me in the face."

"Even with my limited exposure to the drug trade, it became very obvious that there are federal types in the game. Some are paid to look the other way. Some to give early warning signals. There are others that are actually suppliers. Sometimes agents resell Blow from dealers they've hit. Jose Antonio does business with at least two of them. I do not know them. But, I do know *of* them. I'm afraid that makes me a target, both from within and without."

Grappling with confusion, Grant said weakly: "Is "Blow" a drug?"

With an affected sneer, Alex replied. "Boy, you weren't kidding. You are naïve. Snow, Blow, White, Yahoo, Yeah, the Lady, all these are names for Cocaine Hydrochloride. It's a salt. That means you can shoot it, but not smoke it."

Grant parked the car in the hotel parking lot. He wondered seriously if dinner was a good idea. He'd never known anyone to speak about drugs with this familiarity. *She seems sort of innocent, and then she comes up with this stuff.* •

CHAPTER ELEVEN

Acapulco, Mexico
Present Day

Business women in Mexico, tend to dress more formally than their American counterparts. As a general rule, they also tend to exaggerate their femininity, at least by U.S. standards. A Latin woman in a corporate setting would rarely wear slacks, modest necklines, or flats. The Hispanic ideal of femininity requires low necklines, dresses that dramatize the swing of a woman's hips, and very high heels. This was especially true of Claudia Brun, a former model of good education and high birth.

Claudia had conscientiously developed a cultured voice and sensuous presence. When she was in the room, it was hard for most men to concentrate. Although simply a distraction to the more centered, she was a vital component in the carefully orchestrated setting that comprised Ramon Garcia's lair.

Claudia Brun was keenly aware of why she was so well-paid. Her responsibilities went well beyond sexual favors for Senor Garcia. It was her explicit responsibility to distract and destabilize male visitors in general. Her physical beauty was apparent enough.

But her ability to make a man believe she was somehow enamored with him personally, had many times been the critical component in a delicately choreographed plan to gain the upper hand in a vital negotiation. From Ms. Brun's perspective, men were clearly the weaker of the sexes.

General Jose Diego Botia Gill was a challenge. He had arrived without notice, and was standing in Claudia Brun's tastefully appointed outer office. He sought immediate audience with Ramon Garcia. The general seemed impervious to her sensually widened eyes as she looked directly up to him. As he stood in front of her desk she made a point to push back slightly so he could catch a glimpse of her legs. He didn't even glance. Botia was a tough one all right. She smiled seductively and leaned innocently forward to adjust something on her desk, the subtle movement of her blouse ensuring he was able to catch more than a glimpse of her breasts.

Is this guy alive, she thought? In her experience men were incapable of resisting that many opportunities. Claudia Brun was not just a practiced seductress, she had degrees in both business and psychology, and she was definitely street-smart. Claudia innately recognized what worked, and when. But, this guy was a hard nut to crack. She switched strategies and decided to play the busy professional.

"General Botia, would you please have a seat," she said using her most professional voice. "Senor Garcia is on a private call. He will be available shortly. May I get you something? Coffee perhaps? Something stronger?"

"Thank you no Senora," he stated without emotion. He stepped back and selected a firm straight-backed chair, avoiding the more comfortable overstuffed pieces.

Botia was tense. Claudia Brun sensed his irritation. Perhaps I need to be more obvious she decided. She stepped around to the front of her desk and stood between the general and the double-door access to Ramon Garcia's executive offices. She paused for a moment forcing him to look towards her to see what she intended. Every man had a weakness. She would discover his.

Claudia Brun walked around to the front of her desk. She struck an innocent poise. It wasn't working. Or, if it was, he was a master at controlling his emotions. She finally chose to be absolutely direct. "Please, Senor Botia, let me be of service. Senor Garcia will be very unhappy with me, if I have not put you at ease."

The general was equally direct, "Senora Brun, you are disturbingly distracting. I do not understand how Senor Garcia is able to work with you nearby."

"Why thank you, Senor Garcia," she demurred with her head tilted down, her eyes cast up. She did not understand. He had not meant it as a compliment.

General Botia continued, "You may indeed do something for me," he declared in his monotone voice.

"Anything," she said batting her eyes at him.

"Interrupt Senor Garcia and explain I have a tight schedule and do not have the time to play games with his assistant." He had called her out. This was a man she could not move.

Gracefully she bowed slightly towards him, as if granting him the game. Without any apparent irritation, she said, "Why of course, general Botia." I clearly did not understand the urgency of the situation." With that she returned to her desk, pressed the intercom and said formerly, "Senor Garcia, general Botia is here to see you."

Instantly Ramon knew there was a problem. Rather than let Claudia escort the general into his office, he walked straight to the doors and opened them himself. He immediately stepped into the reception area to greet Botia without further ceremony. "My dear general, what a pleasure it is to see you. What brings you to Acapulco?"

"I felt it better to meet with you face to face," he stated flatly.

"But of course, please," said Ramon Garcia as he gestured the general into the privacy of his spacious inner sanctum. The dour faced Diego Botia marched in holding his hat in the crook of his arm as if he were on military parade.

After the doors were shut, and while Botia yet stood, he commenced his speech, "Senor Garcia, I have done as we discussed, but I am dissatisfied with the results. The matter you requested of me can hardly be kept confidential much longer. There are too many people now involved in the hunt to keep this issue quiet."

"Yes, yes, of course. I was hopeful that with the internment of Esteban Morelos this affair could be addressed in short order. Would you be so kind as to provide me with an update," Ramon said smoothly. "Please do take a seat," he said gesturing to one of the sitting areas.

Botia was used to giving and receiving reports. He was comfortable in this mode. He launched immediately into it. "As you suggested, a small military contingent picked up Esteban Morelos from his home in Veracruz. He was taken to the prison in Xalapa. Morelos was isolated there, and interrogated by one of my more persuasive captains. He has not provided much useful information. He cannot be kept much longer without attracting undue attention. The story we've released is that he has been detained regarding issues of political corruption, which took place while he was Governor of the State of Veracruz."

This was old information, and although Ramon Garcia showed no sign of his impatience with Botia, he was peeved that the general would waste time in review. Ramon felt his stomach roll and knew he was going to need something shortly to contain the reflux.

Botia continued, "You were correct that Esteban Morelos is married to the sister of Gualu Robles, and that they have homes next door to one another in the city of Veracruz. You were also correct that Miguel Ramirez is the brother to both Senora Morelos, and Gualu Robles. And, it appears that your source of information was correct, regarding Miguel Ramirez's high-profile restaurant in Veracruz. It is, or at least was, a cover for an antiquities smuggling operation. However, it would appear that Ramirez had advance notice of our arrival. He has disappeared. We were able to effectively interrogate certain persons working in the administration of his affairs. It was eventually confirmed that Mesoamerican artifacts were frequently held for outbound shipment in the restaurant's bodega."

Struggling to control his growing impatience with Botia's seeming need to state the obvious, Ramon Garcia said with ultimate quiescence, "Yes, thank you, but what else have you to share?"

"As you suggested, we endeavored to learn more about the American friend of the Robles. The one who authored the inflammatory paper, *In Defense of an Obsession*. It makes the case for a transfer of high culture from Mesopotamia to Mesoamerica hundreds of years before the Christian era. Have you read it?"

Ramon could not believe Botia's officious attitude. He must be purposefully drawing this out to test his composure. "Ah, yes general, I have read Mr. Whitaker's paper. It is, of course, not widely distributed, and let us hope that it shall not be. Am I to assume that you have seen this controversial work?"

"Yes, I have seen it." The general was not at all convinced that Whitaker's paper was so controversial. In fact, he was, by and large, in agreement with the bullets of information contained in the Archeological Notes section. However, this was not the time to cross swords with the hugely influential and well-connected Ramon Garcia.

"And how is it that you came across this paper?" Ramon asked calmly.

"A copy was in Senor Morelos' home. There was also a copy in Miguel Ramirez's home. In both cases the paper sat out in the open," Botia reported.

"Ah. Well then, that explains that. Please continue," Ramon offered, in a subdued voice.

"After searching both residences, we placed an agent outside the Robles home to observe activities. We assumed that there might be some effort on the part of Miguel Ramirez to contact them. Two days later, Jose Robles was followed to the Veracruz airport where he met with an American pilot who had just flown a small plane in from Guadalajara. Senor Robles visited with him at the airport. Our agent was not able to get close enough to listen to their conversation. However, he did catch the name of Morelos as he was walking past the table where they were talking quietly. We assumed then, that the pilot was somehow involved in the scheme to smuggle antiquities out of the country."

"And what did you learn from the pilot?" Ramon inquired gracefully.

"I am getting to that... Senor Robles did not appear to give anything to the pilot, but based upon the pilot's subsequent actions, Robles must have advised him to leave the area. Jose Robles returned to his home with Special Agent Armando Vargas following. Vargas is the agent in charge of this investigation. Upon taking up position outside the Robles home once more, Vargas called in to check on the private aircraft, only to discover it had just departed for Cancun. Agent Vargas made a snap decision that it was important that he follow the pilot. He immediately made arrangements to charter a faster aircraft and fly to Cancun, expecting to arrive at close to the same time, or perhaps even earlier. Vargas returned to the airport with speed, and called in an associate to accompany him. The local command center sent out a replacement to watch the Robles home."

Ramon Garcia's mind was spinning. He may have to eliminate these agents, and possibly organize an accident for the general at some point. Botia was a wily old fox. He was not likely to be exposed for any length of time. "Excuse me, but what is the name of the other agent?"

"That would be Special Agent Roberto Soria. He works in military intelligence and is permanently assigned to the Veracruz station."

"And the pilot?"

"Adrian Oliveros. We have chartered his aircraft several times, running drug interdiction and reconnaissance flights. His aircraft is a turbo-charged light twin. His response time is good, and much less expensive than other flight options. Using Oliveros is also faster than requisitioning a military jet transport."

"Thank you general. Please continue." Ramon Garcia stood up and walked matter-of-factly to the bar. He fixed himself a drink after surreptitiously self-administering his second doze of antacid. Raising the drink and his eyebrows, he hung the unspoken question in the air for the general to affirm or decline.

"Hmmm, yes, I believe I will have something. Whatever you are having," Botia said, continuing with his report. "Adrian Oliveros is a dependable sort; he already had a flight plan filed and was ready to go when my agents arrived. They pressed hard for Cancun, and arrived when the single-engine aircraft should have been on approach."

"Ah...did you say --- should have?" Ramon inquired quietly, his stomach acid increasing.

"Yes. It seems that Robles friend, oh, ...did I mention it was Grant Whitaker?" he inquired mid-sentence, "the author of *In Defense of an Obsession?*"

Another hit of acid squirted into the bubbling cauldron masquerading as Ramon Garcia's stomach. He tried to smile and act as if nothing was wrong, but the acid was churning up his esophagus. "Excuse me a moment. Nature calls," he chuckled lightly. Garcia carefully controlled his pace as he walked to his private toilet. The only thing that was going to help instantly was several swallows of Mylanta, which he aggressively consumed the moment he was inside his washroom. Sipping only enough water to wash the taste from his mouth, he chased the Mylanta with two double Tagaments. There was no sense taking more Nexium, it worked well, but took too long to respond for an instant need. He washed his face, and pulled himself back under control. He returned to Botia as if nothing untoward had taken place.

"You were saying," he said politely.

"Yes…well it seems that Whitaker changed his flight plan in route, and landed in Chichen Itza. Apparently, he had some engine difficulty as a local mechanic was contracted to do some minor work. When my agents discovered where Whitaker had gone, they flew to Chichen Itza. By then it was early evening and the tower was closed so they could get no information on Whitaker's whereabouts. Agent Vargas, in company with the pilot Adrian Oliveros, commandeered a car and made an immediate scan of the local hotels. Roberto Soria stayed at the airport to keep an eye on the plane and watch to see if anyone showed up that was interested in Senor Whitaker's aircraft."

"Your report seems to be taking longer than I would have expected. Might we hurry it along?"

"Certainly, but there are things you should know so you might better understand our current dilemma," he responded neutrally.

"Ah. Well then. Proceed as you deem best," Ramon said with a smile painted on his face.

"As it turned out, Senor Whitaker was in a bar just off the airport and had not left the area, which explained why Agent Vargas was unsuccessful in determining his whereabouts. Agent Soria actually saw him, but having never seen him before, was not sure who he was observing. The curious thing was that Whitaker left the bar in company with a waitress. It seemed to Soria that they were very friendly and surely had known one another for some time. He discounted this particular man as Whitaker initially, for that very reason. When Soria came to the conclusion that it might have been

Whitaker, he assumed that he had gone to the woman's home and not to a hotel."

"And where is he now?" Ramon Garcia broke in.

Botia continued as if the question had not been asked. "Agent Vargas interviewed various persons at the airport the next day including the mechanic who was more than happy to explain what he was doing to Whitaker's plane. The mechanic assumed the aircraft would be grounded at least another two days, as he believed the maintenance issue was a magneto failure, which would require a replacement to be flown in from the U.S. There did not appear to be anything of interest in the aircraft, so Vargas had just about decided there was nothing unusual, when he called central command in Veracruz to discover that the entire Robles family had disappeared."

"Agent Vargas returned to the hotel room where he had spent the prior night. From there he began to coordinate the detainment of other Robles family members. He was thus engaged when he got a call from Agent Soria saying Whitaker had returned to the airport and taken off for Cancun. The waitress he had been with the night before was in company with him. She was not included on his flight plan. This was highly unusual. When they checked further on this woman, it turns out she is a field archeologist. The connection was obvious. It appeared Whitaker had been directed to her. The investigation team regrouped and flew to Cancun."

Again, Ramon Garcia broke into Botia's report. "So, you have Mr. Whitaker in custody?"

"They missed Whitaker, and Senorita April Jardine's arrival in Cancun. Jardine was Whitaker's unregistered passenger. We assume someone by prior arrangement picked them up when they arrived in Cancun.

There was a firm warning knock at the door and Claudia Brun stepped into the room, showing appropriate deference, "Excuse me gentlemen. Senor Garcia, the Ambassador is on the phone."

"Whose?"

"Ours," she said, with a slight forward nod of her head. "Hacier Jesus Derbez, our Ambassador to the United States. He is calling from his embassy in Washington D.C."

"Please excuse me a moment, general Botia," Ramon said as he crossed the room to his desk as the call was rung in. "Senor Derbez, how nice to hear from you."

Garcia is a cagey one, Botia observed to himself. He is listening and not talking. He could give lessons to our agents.

As promised the conversation ended shortly. "Thank you, Jesus. I will use your information judiciously. Ramon Garcia was smiling broadly as he hung the phone up. He pushed the intercom button to access Senora Brun. "Hold all calls until we are finished."

Normally unfathomable, Ramon Garcia seemed pleased with himself, as he crossed back to Diego Botia nodding at him to continue.

CHAPTER TWELVE

Akumal, Quintana Roo, Mexico

The view was breath-taking. The day was done. The moon reflected on dark open water. The night was warm, the seafood fresh and delicious. They sat and talked. Alex spoke of her childhood, and her interest in anthropology and archeology. She had a keen interest in the Mayans, Toltecs, the Mixteca, Zapotecs, and the Teotihuacan cultures. She had even studied the not-so-well-known Izapa culture, located on the southwest Pacific coast of Mexico. Grant listened with intelligent understanding. He refrained from saying much about the subject. He wondered at their shared enthusiasm. In his experience, few people found this stuff interesting enough to sustain an evening of conversation.

Grant's thoughts drifted back to his unscheduled departure from Veracruz. So much had happened since then. Could it really have been only yesterday? His closest friend in Mexico had rushed to the airport just after Grant had landed. In hushed tones, he told Grant of an incredible discovery; a find of immense significance. There were frightening overtones to the conversation. Grant was asked to leave immediately, rather than get caught up in what might become a serious affair.

Alex was put-off. She had caught him drifting again. He recovered by saying that Akumal reminded him of his late wife, their lives together, their children and grandchildren. She expressed sympathy. By unspoken mutual assent, they had avoided the discussions from their drive. Neither of them wanted to waste the view, the food, and the setting, on more sordid subjects.

At 10:20 Alex remembered she needed to call Pepe's mother. Grant's Mexican cell phone had good signal so he passed it over. She spoke in rapid Spanish and rang off. Alex had been surprised that Grant carried three phones, one for the islands, one for Mexico, one for the States and everywhere else. When she pressed him on the subject he reminded her that he had a home in Cabo San Lucas. He explained that if you needed to receive calls from Mexicans while in Mexico, it was necessary to have a local phone. Locals would refuse to call a non-Mexican number. It was absurdly expensive. The same was true in the islands.

Grant excused himself to use the men's room. When he returned, Alex reported, "Loreto left the door unlocked for me, so I ordered another glass of wine. You sure you won't join me?"

"No thanks. I'm not much of a drinker," Grant said quietly.

He was worried. Could it be true that the investigator at Chichen Itza was there because of him? It was certainly possible. Federal agents had frozen his primary brokerage and bank accounts. They had been tracking him all over, judging from texts and emails incoming from friends. Business associates, family, and friends alike, had all been alarmed at government agents showing up unannounced. It seemed that everyone he knew had been interrogated.

Grant was aware that a grand jury had been convened over a year ago. That option provided expanded powers to investigators so that they could pursue what they wanted to believe were his nefarious activities. The DA's office had not contacted him, and refused to admit, even to his lawyer, that he was the subject of an extensive investigation that had agents flying all over the western hemisphere endeavoring to obtain condemning evidence of some sort.

Government agents had thoroughly shaken close to a hundred friends, business acquaintances, and relatives. All but one of his children had been subpoenaed to a grand jury hearing. All of their personal banking records for the prior five years had been obtained, including all their credit card purchases. Two of his daughters-in-law, and three sons-in-law, had been twice interrogated and then called before the grand jury.

Originally, the concept of the grand jury was to function as a layer of protection for the accused. It had eventually become a tool for the district attorney to advance their case. The entire process had become a Star Chamber inquisition of self-validating prophesies. Today's grand jury functions solely to empower the government. Anyone holding good feelings towards the accused is subjected to an excruciatingly painful ordeal. This process causes potential witnesses for the defense considerable pause. If they stick up for what they deem is right, it is suggested that they must be implicated in some form of criminal activity. Witness intimidation by the prosecution is usually sufficient to eliminate potential witnesses for the defense.

Grant had learned to his amazement that no one was allowed to say anything positive about the accused in a grand jury setting. The moment someone tried, they were cut-off by the district attorney. There was no defense counsel permitted, not even legal counsel for witnesses was allowed. No offer of evidence to contradict the message of the prosecutor was permitted. Witnesses were, with few exceptions, frightened into saying anything the district attorney wanted. After all, weren't the prosecutors supposed to be the good guys? Unbiased witnesses were routinely threatened and bullied into believing that if they did not help the prosecution's case, they would come under investigation themselves.

All those exposed to the extreme behavior displayed by the untouchable U.S. prosecutors, and their special agents, had been deeply affected. Good, honorable people had been thoroughly intimidated for even knowing him. Everyone that had dared to contact him recently had said they had the horrible feeling that they too were now under suspicion for something.

Governmental pressure had begun several years earlier as a result of four books Grant had written. He had been outspoken in his criticism of three specific federal agencies. After he appeared on a number of national radio talk shows, sharing his views on federal abuse of power, things swung into high gear. Eventually, he had reconciled himself to the fact the government did not care about the truth. The entire matter was about neutralizing his influence and winning the war of spin. At this point, he could only ride out the process and hope for the best.

Now there was this new twist. A Mexican investigator checking up on him at the Chichen Itza airport would mean they were aware of his flight plan from Veracruz. That meant they may have been waiting for him in Cancun. It must have thrown someone a real curve when he didn't show up. Either these investigators had driven in from Cancun, or an agent in Merida was sent out to see what was going on.

He was still struggling with his thoughts when Alex demanded: "Grant...Am I boring you?"

"Uh no...just thinking again. You're right; the Mayans are the least understood major old world civilization. And, I agree, there are probably hundreds more ruins waiting to be discovered in the jungles south of here."

A bit more relaxed, she said, "Oh you *were* listening. I thought I was just babbling to myself. You had such a distant look."

Embarrassed that she would think he was such a horrible bore, he decided to tell her some of what he had heard in Veracruz. She was seriously interested in the mysteries of the Mayan culture, and would probably find the story more than just curious. Admitting to himself that the real reason he wanted to tell her was simply because he didn't want the evening to end badly. He launched in.

"You're familiar with the ancient Mesoamerican texts, The Annals of the Cakchiquels, The Title of the Lords of Totonicapan, the Popol Vuh, and the Books of Chilam Balam?"

"Yes. Every student of Mesoamerica has read translation excerpts from these manuscripts. Advanced students will also read the works of Bernal Diaz del Castillo, *The Discovery and Conquest of New Spain*, and the writings of San Bartolommeo, Father Diego Duran, Fray Juan de Torquemada, Bishop Diego de Landa, Fray Bernardino de Sahagun, and of course, Ixtlilxochitl."

Grant was impressed. Trapped inside that trim figure and sweet face, was a real brain. It was funny how guys tended to underestimate attractive women. Obviously, he'd been doing just that. As he thought about it further he was reminded that she also seemed to have a rather frightening understanding about subjects he knew nothing about.

"It's a treat to visit with someone studied on these subjects. Someone not stuck in a class room regurgitating the works of Eric Thompson, or Sylvanias Morley."

"The classic Mayanists," she observed.

"So, two days ago I visited Veracruz. I'd flown in from Guadalajara," he began.

She raised her eyebrows suggesting this was nothing new and that he continue.

"While there, Pepe, my "Mexican brother," well sort of…I mean, he calls me his American brother so I guess I can call him my Mexican brother. Anyway, he met me at the Veracruz airport just after I arrived, and told me the most incredible story. His brother-in-law, Esteban Morelos, lives next door to him. He was formerly the Governor of the State of Veracruz, before that he was the Mayor of the City of Veracruz. It seems Morelos had just been arrested, and taken to Xalapa, the state capital. The official news release says his incarceration had to do with political corruption stemming back from when he held political office.

"Go on," she said mildly, not at all sure where the conversation was headed.

"Some years ago, when Esteban Morelos was the mayor of Veracruz, he allowed me *unofficially* to do some *unlicensed* archeological research at Cerro Vigia. Vigia is a prominent hill, really a small mountain, in the Santiago Tuxla area. That's a couple of hours drive south of the city. You may be familiar with the Olmeca archeological site of Tres Zapotes? It's located on the opposite side of Vigia, from where the highway that runs from the city of Veracruz, takes you south to the Coatzacoalcos River. This is the road that continues on to the State of Tabasco, and finally to the Yucatan."

Alex interrupted with renewed interest. "I know the area. When I first came down as a field student I was working at the Palenque ruins in Chiapas, we flew into Villahermosa, the capital of Tabasco, and took a bus right down the same road until the turn-off to Palenque." She suddenly stopped and glared him. "You were looting!" She exclaimed almost in amazement.

He waved his hands dismissively. "No. Not right at all. And where I was working was north of Villahermosa, not south. At the time, I was following up a theory about ancient rituals associated with records, and caves. This idea suggested there might be an historical record hidden in the large hill of Vigia. The hill is really the final outcropping of an entire mountain line. It's a long story, but the point is, I did some work there three summers in a row. It was an interesting time."

He paused to collect his thoughts. She encouraged him to continue.

"While in the city of Veracruz, Pepe – remember that's Jose Robles, my closest friend in Mexico. Well, anyway, he introduced me to some very interesting folks. They were all upper-class relatives of his. A couple of them, as it turned out, were dealing in artifacts."

Interrupting again, Alex asked suspiciously, "How do you know Pepe?"

Sidetracked for the moment he stalled. "Oh, ah…his oldest son Jorge stayed in our home as part of a school exchange program when we lived in Washington. We became great friends of the Robles family and over the years we traded kids nine times. Last year four of my grandchildren spent a few weeks during the summer in the homes of Pepe's now grown children. These are the families of the children who had formerly been exchange students with us. We have all become very close over the years, and attended each other's university graduations, weddings, and so forth."

"State or D.C.?" Alex responded.

It took a moment for Grant to realize what she was asking. "Oh, that would be Washington State. We lived in Washington State," Grant stalled again trying to pick-up on the story.

Alex prompted with, "Artifact dealers." She didn't comment further, so Grant continued. "Right, so I met some interesting people under curious circumstances. It happened after I had been nosing around Cerro Vigia for a while. One evening the Robles invited my oldest son and me to dinner, after which Pepe asked if I would like to see some very special artifacts. Pepe and his immediate family didn't have much interest in pre-Columbian history prior to our families becoming friends. He got interested in the subject because I was so absorbed by it. Each time one of his children came to stay with us, they brought two or three pieces of pre-Columbian art. Collecting gifts for me got him interested in the subject, and he ended up with a fair collection of his own."

"You were receiving stolen merchandise," she stated flatly, irritated, but interested.

Ignoring her outburst, he went on. "Well, anyway, when Pepe asked us if we would like to see some historical stuff, which I assumed were minor artifact, we did not hesitate to say yes. Then things got a little mysterious. After dinner, he drove Matthew and me around in the city of Veracruz, until we were hopelessly lost.

She seemed slightly confused. "Oh, sorry, Matthew is my oldest son. He was staying with the Robles on a private exchange at the time."

It was obvious to Alex, that Grant had fond memories of this experience, or at least his relationship with the Robles and his son. His face had relaxed, and he was smiling thoughtfully. "Go on," she prompted.

"Well, there we were, driving around in circles when Pepe stopped and gave us blindfolds. We were to wear them the balance of the trip. This was a really weird development, which I actually took for something of a joke, or at least overkill. Matthew and I took it in stride sniggering to ourselves. A short time later, we arrived in a fashionable neighborhood where the blindfolds were removed. We went directly into an upper middle-class, modern-looking Mexican home.

Once inside we were introduced to the man and woman of the house. After perhaps an hour of general discussion about Aztecan art, which doesn't much interest me, I was asked my opinions about certain Teotihuacan artifacts. We talked about ancient Mexican cultures for a bit. Eventually, we were to learn that the fellow I was visiting with was one of Pepe's brothers-in-law. In the midst of our conversation he walked up to the dining room hutch, a rather large and elaborate affair. He fooled around with some kind of release mechanism, and the whole thing turned sideways to reveal a hidden room of artifacts stacked on mirrored shelves, literally floor to ceiling."

As Grant paused to take a breath, Alex jumped in to make the point that these were the kind of artifact dealers that all archeology students are trained to despise. Theft of national treasures, barred from public museums, etc. etc. Nodding his head, as if he understood her point of view, but not necessarily agreeing with her, he continued. "Miguel, that was his name, brought out some amazing things. They were of better quality and more compelling, than many of the things I'd seen in the Museum of Anthropology in Mexico City, the largest museum of its kind in the world."

Alex stammered, "Yes, yes, I know, I know. Where is all this going?"

"Well, several of these items demonstrated there had been an intimate relationship between cultures that were, archeologically-speaking, considered completely separate and distinct. At least that was the opinion of Sir Eric Thompson. You probably know that Eric Thompson, and his scholastic disciples, ruled all of Mayan archeology for decades. No one dared mention anything that might conflict with his published theories. To do so could cost one not just creditability, but their professorships. Very much in the same way that Freudians controlled the psychology departments in all major universities until fifty years after Freud died."

A waiter interrupted to tell them the restaurant was closing. They would need to handle the check. Grant fumbled around and finally produced a credit card.

"We'd better get you a room before they're closed at the front desk," Alex suggested. "It's too late for you to head back to Cancun, and start looking for a room."

"I suppose you're right," Grant said, while settling the bill. A moment later they walked out comfortably together, looking like just another couple on vacation. At the registration desk, they discovered no one was there. They made an increasing amount of noise until the night clerk came sleepily out from an office in a back area. "I need a room for the night," Grant said.

"I'm sorry sir, there are no rooms available."

"Come on, you've got to have something," Grant insisted.

"I am so sorry sir. There is nothing available tonight."

Alex jumped into the conversation and rattled off some quick Spanish. She slid him three U.S. $20 bills.

Looking around surreptiously the clerk winked, and handed her an old fashion room key. He explained where they should go. No registration was required. Grant was not officially staying there.

It was almost midnight as she walked him to his room. It was not a half mile walk to Loreto's, but at this hour Alex should be driven. He'd have to drive the mile or so back to the highway, then turn towards Cancun, and take the next turn back to the beach. Then repeat the process in reverse.

The room was fine. In fact, better than he expected. Both of them stared for a moment at the two double beds and considered the options.

"Listen Grant don't leave me hanging on that story. I'll sleep here and walk over to Loreto's in the morning."

"You sure that won't worry her?"

"I doubt it. She'll probably think I am in Cancun, and will come down in the morning. Let's go to the car, and get our stuff before we're too tired to walk."

The ground floor room faced towards the gravel parking lot. It was not a prize location for vacationers. It appeared to be the only room of its kind. It had been built out from an otherwise dead space designed to anchor the north end of the building and support an upstairs suite facing the other way, out on to the bay. All the other rooms in the complex were faced out on the Caribbean. This was an overflow room, not part of the normal rental pool.

The brief walk to the car was stunning. The clear night sky was brilliant with stars. The dim yellow night-lights that marked the perimeter of the parking area were not bright enough to diffuse the effect of the black night and starlight. There was a major difference here, in comparison with Chichen Itza. No flying insects. The ocean breeze seemed to sweep the area clean of them.

Back in the room, he picked up the story. "There were hundreds of smaller statues and shards wrapped in newspaper and stored in buckets. These were in addition to the much nicer pieces we saw on the shelves. One particular item, a funerary amulet, was apparently found in a sarcophagus at Palenque. Probably, not unlike the one you would have seen in the main temple structure at the bottom of the steps within..."

Jumping into the story she exclaimed with enthusiasm: "You mean the Temple of the Inscriptions! It has nine tiers to the top of the temple pyramid, and seventy-two steps down to the burial chamber deep inside."

"Yes, that's it. Well anyway, this particular amulet was made of polished mother-of-pearl, turquoise, and jade. It was set in a carved wood backing. We hung it around my son's neck with a piece of leather cord. They even allowed me take pictures of him sporting this elegant piece of ancient workmanship. Mind you, this was a long time ago, but I still remember that on the back of the amulet was some writing that did not seem to be classic Mayan. I was so impressed with the things they kept unwrapping and showing us, I could hardly contain myself."

"As it turned out, Miguel had worked at secret excavations at Teotihuacan, El Tajin, Tula, Palenque, La Venta, Bonampak, and a number of other well-known archeological sites. At first, I simply did not believe what he was telling me. But knowing the way Mexico worked, especially so many years ago, a major paradigm shift began to take place in my thinking."

"What are you saying," she muttered.

According to Miguel, all of the really special artifacts were in private collections. No great news flash. He also told me he was an "approved" artifact dealer. One permitted by the State, to participate in the pre-opening of tombs, palaces and other archeological places of interest, *before* their "official" openings. He told me that he had multiple times, attended pre-openings of burial chambers in order to assess and bid on funerary goods. These openings would take place before a photo op at the burial chambers was held by the supervisory archeologists at a dig. The goods that remained at the site for the official opening, would be the only ones cataloged.

Alex looked skeptical. "I don't believe that fairy-tale. You're describing a pervasive governmental conspiracy to traffic in stolen artifacts."

"It's not my story. I'm simply giving you the gist of an entire evening of evidence. Evidence I might add, I saw with my own eyes and handled with my own hands. In fact, I still have original photos of the evening. No people appear in them other than my son, but there are some remarkable works. Some didn't turn out very well. This was before digital cameras. The age of the photos is pretty easy to demonstrate because my son was only eleven at the time."

Shifting emphasis, Grant asked, "You must be aware that in the mid 1980's some of the most valuable pieces in the National Museum of Anthropology in Mexico City were stolen in a single night?"

"Everyone knows that story," Alex said, her lips pursed. "The press has never let Mexico forget it either. The thieves had to have had protection from someone up the governmental ladder. No one was ever prosecuted."

"Listen Grant, I'm going to fall asleep on you, and we're off the point again. Do you always ramble like this?"

"Yes," he admitted sheepishly. "Okay, the point I was leading up to is that Esteban Morelos, remember he is another brother-in-law of Pepe's, was just recently arrested. Supposedly it was for political corruption, but according to Pepe, the real reason had to do with the discovery and cover-up of a major find. He told me that someone had discovered metal plates containing historical and religious commentary, right where I had been working years before at Cerro Vigia.

"Metal plates! I've never heard of such a thing! Metal would hardly hold up in these climates. All you'd ever find would be rust stains," Alex pointed out aggressively.

"That might be true if the metal were iron or even steel," Grant replied blandly. "Copper or brass wouldn't hold up much better. However, if the metal was some kind of gold alloy, like electrum, it would easily survive the elements. Electrum is essentially a gold and silver alloy. It occurs naturally in the earth. Most early civilizations learned how to make it with raw gold, silver, and occasionally some copper. Electrum was used by the Egyptians at least 5,000 years ago. It was used by both the Aztecs and the Incas, along with earlier Mesoamerican civilizations."

Most people are completely unaware that gold and silver alloys, made into thin plates, were anciently designed to preserve important political and religious pronouncements. Most recently, they have been discovered in Turkey. In fact, in the last twenty years, ancient metal plates have been found in several places around the world. Each time they were inscribed with what the writers clearly believed to be information of great value to future generations."

"I hadn't heard that before," Alex said sleepily. "Regardless, I can hardly believe that thin sheets of metal, of any kind, would survive the weather of this region. Look at the cars along the coast. Unless they are constantly cared for, the doors will rust out in a couple of years."   "Actually Alex, gold is the only substance known that does not rust. It simply does not dissolve over time. Silver comes close, but gold is impervious to rust. That characteristic is probably why ancient religions identified so closely with gold. It was considered the *eternal* metal. It really doesn't matter whether it was mined thousands of years ago, or yesterday afternoon. Gold is gold is gold. It does not deteriorate."

"Why do I suspect you have more than a passing background in gold?" Alex grumbled. Expecting no real response, she continued, "What you say may be true. But gold is rare and was, and may still be, the final measure of wealth. So, I suspect religions collected gold and silver because it conveyed the concepts of power and wealth, rather than for its beauty and durability."

"Agreed," Grant said, nodding his head. "It also makes sense that some kind of gold alloy would have been just about the only portable substance available to preserve writings of great value. Even the ubiquitous steles of the Mayan empire, aside from their non-portability, were frequently defaced of characters by marauding kingdoms intent upon political overthrow. So, if there are significant records preserved from ancient times in this kind of climate, they've got to be on gold. Nothing else except stone will stand the test of time."

Alex didn't respond immediately, she seemed to be taking it all in.

Grant continued. "Another interesting characteristic of inscriptions found on metal plates, is that they seem to be carefully preserved inside stone boxes. These things have turned up in Iraq, Syria, India, and Greece, just in the last two dozen years."

"Hmmm," Alex began. "As I recall, Jill Furst translated the ancient *Mixtec Codex Nuttall* of Oaxaca, Mexico. I'm sure you've heard of it, because it caused such a ruckus. All the hoopla was due to its connection to Jesus Christ and the theory that Christ appeared in the Americas because it records a crucifixion of Quetzalcoatl and his resurrection three days later. But my point is, this codex pre-dated Columbus, and it was written on bark paper, similar to the papyrus paper developed by the Egyptians. So, your argument that important records need to be preserved on some kind of gold alloy doesn't hold."

"Good point," Grant began, "Ancient records around the world were prepared and saved on inexpensive media. Things like clay tablets in Sumer and Mesopotamia, papyrus in Egypt, etc. But what I am saying is, there is no material we know of, that has the staying power of gold."

"As I recall," Grant continued, "There are only four ancient books left from all the developed cultures of the Americas. The rest were destroyed in the Spanish Conquest. Huge burnings of these ancient texts (codices if you prefer), were mandated by the church. The people were forced to bring them to the missions for destruction. Anyone caught with "pagan" written materials after a certain deadline, was put to death."

"Yes, that's common knowledge," she agreed. "Virtually everything was lost. It's amazing how complete the devastation was. Early Spanish chroniclers, primarily the Catholic clergy, suggest that every Mayan city had libraries of historical and religious books at one time."

They were tired. Alex was yawning. It was contagious. Grant struggled on, "If really important information were to be preserved on gold, it would allow for an essentially "eternal" media that could be both storable and portable. There is really no other way. In Israel, where it is dry, there have been discoveries of brass and copper books. The famous Copper Scroll, from the Dead Sea comes to mind. But in Qumran, where the Dead Sea scrolls were stored in caves, many were found in large jars sealed up to come forth in the last days."

Alex and Grant had been sitting on the edges of the two beds facing one another for hours. "Grant, I've got to get some sleep," she groaned. "Finish in the morning." With that said she lay down and rolled away from him. Grant was still fired up with his story, but hearing her steady breathing he lay back and fell asleep, dreaming fitfully of ancient warriors, caves, government agents, and metal plates.

CHAPTER THIRTEEN

Mexico City, Mexico

After receiving the latest field report, general Botia called Ramon Garcia on his home phone.

A maid answered and carried the phone to Senor Garcia. Botia commenced without preamble. "Early this morning we were able to track the credit card Whitaker used at a hotel in Chichen Itza. He had dinner in Akumal late last night. We assume the woman is still with him."

"I thought you told me he didn't stay in a hotel in Chichen Itza," Ramon said, his voice slightly on edge.

Botia ignored Garcia's irritation. "Yes, that is correct. Agent Vargas was not able to find him on the night of his arrival in Chichen Itza, but the next day Agent Soria re-checked the local hotels. There are only three in the area, you see?" Ramon Garcia did not see. Wasn't this an admission of incompetence?

Botia continued, "Soria determined that Whitaker did check into a hotel, but not until late, or at least not until after agent Vargas had already canvassed the hotels. He discovered this the next day. Vargas got Whitaker's credit card number from the hotel. An issuing bank in Mexico put a trace on his card, and we were able to spot his next charge. He was at a restaurant in Akumal late last night. We are only hours behind him, and we have reason to believe he is staying in Akumal."

Ramon Garcia spoke quietly into the phone. "Is he aware that he is being pursued?"

"I rather doubt it. In any event, it would be very hard for him to evade us even if he were."

"General, I trust you will detain Mr. Whitaker shortly?"

"That is our intention," he replied without hesitation.

* * *

Akumal, Quintana Roo

He got up twice during the night, the curse of getting older, he assumed. But somehow, he managed to sleep right through Alex's departure in the morning. When he awoke, Alex was gone. A deep loneliness settled in on him.

Since his unplanned landing in Chichen Itza, he had felt some respite from the immediate pressures of his life. There had been relief from the constant knowledge that forces were gathering against him; a break from the worry for friends, employees and clients. Most of all, there had been relief from the ever-present foreboding that his family was at risk due to a capricious and unjust judicial system.

The reprieve was now gone. The worries came crashing back with such intensity he staggered back and sat down heavily on the bed. His head fell into his hands. He felt desperately sorry for himself.

Grant understood that he could ill afford to think this way. It was a sure slide into depression. I cannot become a victim, he thought. *Do something. Do something now. Take some sort of action. Go outside.*

What he wanted to do was lie back down and continue to feel sorry for himself. What he did, was get up and shower. He had to admit, he felt better after shaving and cleaning up. And, even though he had already showered, he dropped to the floor and did his thrice-weekly regime of 100 push-ups. It was harder than usual. He almost quit. By the time he was back up and standing, his arms felt like lead and his shoulders were quivering. Pulling on a clean shirt and pair of shorts, he stepped into his sandals and headed out the door. Walking around the north end of the room, he ducked under a large sea grape, and came out at the back of a dive shop. Skirting the dive shack he stood and looked out on the bay.

Akumal is comprised of a coastal cove and two bays. The bays have been designated an underwater national park. The beaches lie inside a protecting reef. It is located about an hour and ten minutes' drive just south of Cancun, on Mexico's Caribbean coastline. Akumal has long been a secret getaway, discovered only by those who bother to travel down the coastline in search of something different. It is a small community with white sand beaches, swaying palms, two reefs, and clear water. Taken together it is the quintessential tropical paradise.

His mind drifted back to what had brought him here so many years before. It was the history of the area; it was the fascinating and mysterious culture of the Maya. It was his belief that something truly fantastic had happened here.

Mesoamerica is the name archaeologists call the area of Mexico, Belize, Guatemala, El Salvador, and Honduras. But, Mesoamerica also refers to the time *prior* to the arrival of Europeans. Grant's interest in Mesoamerica was because it was the only known place in the western hemisphere with a fully developed written language prior to Columbus. If there were records that dealt with the ancient history of the western continents, they would have to be in Mesoamerica.

The sun was well up in the eastern sky. A few sun worshippers were already staking claims on beachfront. When he had first come here, sunbathers were unheard of. You came to either fish or dive. Towels on the beach were the providence of places like Cancun. No more. The setting was still beautiful nonetheless, and wonderfully peaceful. It was no surprise that the tourist industry had begun to promote Akumal as an escape from the pressures of the outside world.

Standing there lost in thought, he idly watched a single runner moving swiftly down the beach. Barely covered in an athletic bikini, she was fit, strong, and evenly tanned. A ponytail, threaded through a Nike baseball cap swayed from side to side as she ran. Her strides splashed the thin film of water at wave's end, just where it turned to race back to the ocean. The perfect photo-op for the healthy life, he mused.

Slowly Grant walked out to the edge of the water and stood in the surf. He moved further, feeling the wash of the clean salt water around his legs, rising almost to his knees. A small charter fishing boat raised anchor and headed out through a break in the reef. Grant's mind flitted back to the heady days of his youth, when at fourteen he got a summer job working on an offshore fishing boat. Life was simple then. Time stood still.

"Hi Grant, you finally up, I see," Alex said playfully from behind him.

Hearing her voice brought him instantly back to the present. "Hey. I thought you just up and left me," he said, as he turned and came face to face with the girl in the Nike cap. "Whoa. That was you running down the beach?" he asked in amazement. "I didn't even recognize you."

"You're just used to seeing me with my clothes on," she teased. "I saw you standing there gazing out into never, never land. Pretty full of yourself today, yeah?"

"Perhaps you're right. But that's going to change right now. Had breakfast?"

"Is that an invitation?" she said flirtatiously.

"Indeed. Where do you suggest we dine?" he said grinning broadly.

"Just a minute, I've got to grab my bag." There it was, sitting right at the edge of the dive shop. Not ten feet from where he had stood under the sea grape.

Sea grape is one of the few plants that grow well in salty sand. It tends to hold sand dunes in place while it provides ground cover for a host of small animals and birds. If left to grow, it can become a substantial bush, and eventually a shade tree. Sea grape is a warm weather plant encouraged wherever sand needs the anchor of their roots. It was perfectly placed.

Opening her bag, she grabbed a T-shirt and pulled it over her head. It struck him that she was a good deal more athletic-looking than he expected. Somehow that was slightly unnerving. Not for the first time he felt himself drawn to her, but then backed off mentally scolding himself. *Give it a rest. You're fifteen years older than she is.* It did seem strange though. It felt like they had known each other for a long time. For some reason, he instinctively trusted her. And yet, he knew little about her.

Alex led Grant with long energetic steps to a simple beach bar. The barkeep sliced fresh oranges and made juice. It was amazingly good. "Wow, so much for Florida oranges. I had forgotten how good they are down here," he said, with genuine enthusiasm.

"You gonna finish that story from last night?" she asked. "I just flat ran out of gas."

"Sure, but I need to make a couple of calls first. Did you check in with Loreto?"

"Yes, and happy she was to see me. She didn't ask, but her eyes were twinkling. She seems to think I have a boyfriend locked up somewhere."

"What is your relationship with her anyway? Isn't she the mother of your boss or something?"

"Well, sort of. Mario doesn't actually own the place, but he *is* the boss. Lupe is Mario's sister. We're roommates. We met through a friend at the dig, and I came home with her. Loreto has treated me like a surrogate daughter. These are really good people. They're as honest as they get. I am lucky to know them. They treat me like family."

"You are fortunate then. I couldn't imagine dealing with the stress of looking over your shoulder all the time, and not have someone close to lean on."

Her eyes drifted up, as they did when she was lost in thought. Snapping out of it, she refocused, and looked straight at him. "So, Grant, who do you have to lean on?" The question was simple, direct, and spoke volumes. Or at least he thought it might. In fact, he hoped it did, all the time knowing it was not a reasonable wish. His logical mind kept reminding him that a relationship beyond temporary was not plausible. They were both in harm's way. That kind of mutual experience tended to bond people temporarily, but it was not the stuff of serious commitment. Of course, they did share a mutual interest in ancient history and airplanes. But, beyond these things, there was practically nothing to interest them in one another. Except physical attraction and conversation. And that might not cut both ways. And, lest he forget, there was also the matter of him being older, and certainly not nearly as fit.

He briefly argued with himself that age might not be as big an issue as he thought. *What do you really know about her anyway? She's cute, she's fit, and she's running from the DEA, or FBI or somebody. Oh yes, and her old boyfriend apparently has guns, and plays for keeps. You share the same enthusiasm for archeology, but that's pretty thin stuff to build on.* Be cautious, very cautious, he told himself.

"You're drifting again. Do you always do that or is it just me?" she teased.

"Sorry, I get trapped in my thoughts. You know, I've got my children, friends, a dog and a cat when I'm in Oregon. My oldest daughter cares for my animals when I'm gone. The kids miss me, or at least they tell me they do. Anyway, I miss them a great deal."

"No romantic attachments?"

She just doesn't let things drop. Straight ahead... "Mark Antony," he muttered.

"Mark Anthony?" she asked.

"Oh, sorry, that's twice I've done that with you. Signs of my age abound. I was just thinking that your way of asking questions is straight up the middle. You know, the way Marcus Antonius, i.e. Mark Antony, fought his battles?" Realizing she might not know who he was talking about, he added: "The Roman Mark Antony, Julius Caesar's right hand man, Cleopatra and all that?"

Looking away towards the bay, she said, "I got it, Geez. Sorry if I make you feel uncomfortable. Just nosey I guess."

"No, I didn't mean to sound critical. I'm not used to direct questioning about such things. You see, I was married for most of my life. I've never had any romantic involvement with anyone since Marianna and I met in high school. It's a little strange for me. I mean, you are a very attractive woman, and it's a bit unnerving just to be visiting with you alone. But in answer to your question: No romantic involvements. It just wouldn't be fair I suppose. I am definitely not over my wife's passing, and sometimes I wish something swift and deadly would descend upon me so I could be with her again."

They fell silent for a moment. After which, Alex said quietly, "Okay, I understand. Don't get too close. Yet, it's kind of odd our being out here watching this beautiful, sleepy, piece of beachfront, and talking like we've known each other for years. I guess that's because neither of us represents a risk to the other. We don't know each other's friends, family, business dealings, involvements, anything. We just know something about each other. That's rather nice. No history problems. It seems somehow safe."

It was not much of an intellectual argument, but what she said felt right. "I agree," he said softly, searching her eyes for insight.

Breaking away from the melancholy that had descended upon them, Grant said brightly: "I need to make some calls. Its two hours later in the islands. After that I'm headed to Cancun to check out an option on a boat. It's for sale by an old friend. I'm already two days late arriving. I may have missed my window of opportunity," he chuckled knowingly. Actually, it's not in Cancun proper. It's in Puerto Aventuras, south of Playa del Carmen. You probably know the area. So, if you're looking to do some shopping in Cancun, I'm your ride."

"That works for me," she replied lightly. "While you're making your calls, I'll head over to Loreto's and see if she wants me to pick something up for her while I'm in Cancun."

Reluctantly they moved away from the perfect setting for a leisurely morning conversation, and set about dealing with life. "I'll meet you in the room within the hour. That work for you?" she asked as she got up to walk away. He nodded.

She is so alive. I want to run away with her and not look back. A moment later he was chiding himself again. *You're lonely. See it for what it is. You're emotionally vulnerable. Enjoy the company, but DO NOT let yourself get involved. It would make things worse for both of you.*

He headed to the hotel room in the same unorthodox way he had left. Ducking behind the dive shop, he moved under the shade tree and froze. There was a man at the end of the parking area closest to the west entrance of the hotel about 200 feet away. The man looked suspiciously like the guy in the bar in Chichen Itza. This was apparently the same guy Alex reported that the aircraft mechanic claimed was asking questions about them.

Stepping back slightly he watched the interaction between the man, he thought of as the "watcher," and another man. The one responding shrugged his shoulders in the universal way of saying he didn't know. If this was the same man, then it was surely no coincidence. *How could anyone have known where I stayed? Could it have been Alex?* He abandoned the thought as soon as it occurred to him.

The two men climbed into a nondescript late model car and sped off towards the highway, kicking up a cloud of sand and dust.

Steeped in thought, Grant opened the door and stepped into the cool of the room. *Something else is going on. Perhaps they're looking for Alex, and they knew she was headed to see Loreto. If that's the case she is in immediate danger.*

With that single thought, he spun around and hurried back to where he had last seen her walking. He had no idea where Loreto's house was, except that it was near the other beach access road coming down from the main highway. Alex said it was close to the hotel, so he needed to find the other access road where it terminated at the beach. He would follow it until he spotted Alex. It was not much of a plan, but his immediate anxiety for her pressed him on.

He walked quickly north up the beach until he spotted another parking area. It was also packed sand. Here was another dive shop, outdoor bar, and a couple of free-standing shops selling bathing suits, sun tan lotion, and cold drinks. These were small wooden structures built right on the sand. Some biblical verse ran through his head about building houses on sand, but it didn't stick as his mind raced.

If there were other bad guys here they might not recognize just another attractive woman in a bathing suit, t-shirt, and ball cap. Well, they might notice her, but like him, they probably wouldn't recognize her even if they knew her. Unless of course, they'd seen her like this before; whew, who knows? From what she had said, these guys must be either government types, or possibly worse. Either way, it was a scary scenario. His mind drifted to another unpleasant thought. He'd heard a number of times that Mexican jails were not where anyone wants to spend time, especially a woman. Rape and physical abuse were common. The thought spurred him on.

Grant hurried across the parking lot, trying not to attract attention, all the time knowing that anyone in a rush did not fit in.

He could see a sand-packed road winding out from the back of the parking area. He broke into a jog moving between the occasional parked cars and trucks that had arrived early in the day. Gaining the road, he moved swiftly ahead. There were a number of cul-de-sacs positioned at ninety degree angles off the road. The cul-de-sacs ran north and south. The road ran roughly east and west.

His left knee was aching, as it so often did when he moved too quickly, or for very long. He fleetingly remembered his doctor's comment. "You can ski for all I care; it's just pain. If you can manage the pain of bone impacting bone, then okay. Otherwise get the knee replacement." The cartilage was gone on his left knee, the result of old athletic injuries coupled with later antics, stupid even for a younger man. It caused him a good deal of discomfort. But he'd come to the conclusion that now was not the time to be doing knee replacement surgery. He grimaced and sped on.

Grant was now in some kind of lot development. The north-running side roads looked longer than those running back to the south. Remembering that Alex had said it was a short distance from the hotel, he stopped, turned around and looked in all directions. Arbitrarily he chose the 2nd sand road running back to the south. This was back in the general direction of the hotel.

His pace slowed, of necessity more than desire. He was well back of the beach on a flat sandy patch of scrub brush. There were some occasional trees. It occurred to him that wherever there was an abundance of greenery, there was also some sort of building. Local houses he supposed. They seemed too small for American-style homes, but he was in Mexico after all. The size of these vacation homes was on the order of those found throughout the West Indies.

Breathing more deeply now, he kept up a steady pace moving south along one of the local roads. He could see that sand paths were laid out in a standard grid fashion. People evidently bought a sandlot here, and did what they wanted with it. Water had to be brought in, power was your own problem, but you could build something on your lot, and it was within walking distance of the beach. Not bad.

Look for a newer model car, it will stand out here. There were no fences and little to obstruct the view. He kept turning around scanning in all directions. Nothing. How was he supposed to know Loreto's house from any other structure? He headed back in a circuitous route towards where the hotel should be. There were sheets of what appeared to be corrugated metal standing vertically between the beach area and the lot development. Trees grew on both sides of the corrugated fencing, indicating someone watered them.

He kept on. Then suddenly stopped to watch movement by two men coming out of a small comfortable-looking house about hundred yards south and east of where he stood. They were talking rapidly, their actions aggressive. They did not look as though they belonged. Their dress was not local, nor the beach garb of visitors. Grant immediately turned in the opposite direction trying to avoid attention. He probably looked more like a beach-tourist who had simply taken a walk off the beaten track. *Surely, he blended more than they.* Daring to glance around, he saw the two men get in a late model car. He was just too far away to be certain. But, he wasn't about to stand there and stare. The car took off and sped down the roadway, leaving a blur of dust in its wake. It could have been the car he'd seen at the hotel. He couldn't be sure. Perhaps these were the same men. If so, the place they had just left would likely be Loreto's house.

Grant jogged towards the house the car had just come from. It was quiet, at least from the outside. There were bushes that needed water, two shade trees, and a rock garden. A statute of the Madonna stood about four feet tall in the middle of a white rock circle and some planted cactus. An empty bench and two buckets of seashells were close by. Suddenly he felt awkward. His Spanish was not even close to passable, and he was standing in someone else's space. *How would he explain himself?* His trepidation gave way to anxiety for Alex. He went to the front door and knocked on the screen. There was no response. He knocked again. Nothing.

He decided to call out. "Loreto? Loreto? I am looking for Alex." Still no response. He waited for a few minutes longer, undecided as to how to proceed. He headed towards the vertical metal sheets that seemed to shield the beach from the development.

The corrugated fencing was about ten feet high. It ran for some distance separating the beach from the area where he had been walking. As he reached the barrier he turned south, and walked until he found a bottom corner of one piece of metal that had been purposely turned up as an access point. He stooped down and passed through. Just ahead through a number of sea grape, he spotted the backside of a dive shop. Its universal diving symbol painted in red. He'd seen two dive shops on the beach earlier, there were probably more, but he couldn't have walked back past the hotel without intersecting the second roadway from the highway, so this had to be one of the two he had already seen.

Slowing down and picking his way carefully amongst the dry plants, he spotted the corner of the hotel. His room would be just off to his right. Standing back in the planted area amongst some yellow bells, he scanned the area before moving towards the hotel. The vegetation had been planted thickly in this place. Apparently, it was so that no one would spot the metal sheeting that separated the hotel area from the lot development.

Once again, he stopped and carefully scanned the area. When it seemed safe, he stepped out and crossed the forty feet to his room. Moving swiftly, he fumbled the key into the door, opened it and stepped inside. Nothing looked unusual. It was just as he left it. Breathing heavily, he scolded himself. *I've told myself a story. It's probably not true. There is nothing wrong here. Have I imagined this entire scenario because I saw someone that looked like the fellow in the restaurant the night before last?* Not for the first time on this trip he told himself to get a grip.

Collecting a phone from his valise he dialed the 13 digits required of Mexican cell phones. After several rings, it was answered by a distinctly Texan drawl. "Jackson P. Morgan here."

"Jack, this is Grant. Sorry I missed our meeting. My plane developed engine trouble and I had to put down in the outback. No phone service."

"You okay buddy?" came the concerned reply.

"I'm about an hour from you, but it may take me a while to get some things together before I can head your way. Will you be available mid afternoon?"

"For you good buddy I'd wait till evening," he said with quiet laughter.

"I'd love to talk, but best get moving for now. How do I find you?" Grant asked.

After writing the instructions down, he rang off. *Now where is that girl?* Listening to himself, he realized he had already adopted the drawl of Jackson Porter Morgan, aka J.P. Morgan or simply J.P. to most. Grant was just about the only person J.P. would allow to call him Jack. It irked Grant that Jack's embellished Texas drawl was so contagious. After all, Jack was really a Canadian, a fact unknown to most.

Tempted to walk around and look for Alex, but still a bit shaken by the events of earlier, he decided to stay put. He couldn't remember the exact time they'd parted, but it seemed as though it had been more than an hour by now. With his heart still racing and anxiety over Alex heavy on his mind, every minute seemed like fifteen. When there was a soft knock at the door he literally jumped. "Yes" he replied. A man's voice speaking Spanish; no, he was speaking heavily accented English. He opened the door to see the man they'd met the night before. It was the desk clerk that had given them the room for a bribe.

Looking furtively around, he said: "The Senorita is in the office. Get your things and come." Knowing instantly that something indeed was wrong, he grabbed his roller bag and computer valise and followed him to the registration desk. A section of the counter lifted up. Grant followed the clerk on through, and into a back office. There was Alex, heavy worry lines apparent on her face. She was biting her lower lip. "Oh," she gasped. "I was so worried." Taking three quick steps she threw her arms around him and started to sob. Feeling awkward standing there holding the luggage and a computer, but knowing the right thing to do was hold on to her, he led go of the luggage handle. He was afraid to drop the computer so he stood there with one arm around her until she gained some control.

"Grant, there were men here, they were looking for you," she blurted. "How did you get away from them?"

"Looking for me? No, they couldn't have been," he said in confusion. "No one knew I was here. No one but you, and we spent the night together." As soon as he'd said it he realized the desk clerk was watching and listening carefully. Thinking quickly, he turned to the man and said, "Thanks so much for looking after us. Let me show my appreciation." He reached in his front left pocket where he kept a clutch of folded US dollars and handed him a $100 dollar bill. The fellow looked at it for a moment, smiled broadly, and stepped out of the office.

Turning back, he could tell that Alex was still visibly shaken. Her shoulders slumped. The bright-faced, athletic-looking lady was gone.

"I thought they caught you, she started to sob. They were at Loreto's before I got there. I stayed low until they left, when I snuck in through the back door she told me they had been grilling her about someone named Grant Whitaker who I had taken up with."

Grant was clearly confused, but before he could muster his thoughts, Alex went on. "She said she'd never heard of you. Apparently, she also told them I had not spent the night with her, but walked to the house earlier this morning. I guess they figured we must be in the hotel, or somewhere close by, so they came here and rousted a woman at the front desk and insisted she show them a list of all the registered guests. I had just headed out the back door of Loreto's when I could see a car speeding down her road. I moved back away and dropped flat in the sand behind some scrub trees. When they went in I headed back to the hotel. I ran into the night clerk, he pulled me aside and told me that men with badges and guns had just been here looking for a man and a woman who fit our description. Fortunately, the day clerk was unaware we were in the overflow room. Grant we've got to get out of here now!"

Grant was stunned. Why him, why not her? Was she telling the truth? Was it him they were after, or was it really Alex? Things were getting complicated.

CHAPTER FOURTEEN

Acapulco, Mexico

Ramon Garcia sat back and turned slowly towards the bay. His elbows were on the arms of his executive chair. The fingers of both hands tented as he thought through developments.

Claudia Brun walked softly to his desk and raised her tight, short dress above her hips so she could sit on the desktop. The narrow isosceles triangle of a thong was clearly visible. Ramon Garcia swiveled slowly in his chair, and looked into her dark eyes.

"Yes, my dear, you are stunning, but this is not the time." She slid off the desk smoothing her dress. She took a chair opposite him without any sense of rejection. "What did the Ambassador want?" she asked with feigned innocence.

"He had some interesting information about our Mr. Whitaker. It seems he is under a federal grand jury investigation, and about to be indicted." Ramon smiled thinly.

She returned the smile openly, perhaps too much so. "Did you tell general Botia to quit worrying about Whitaker being a U.S. person? This pretty much clinches it, doesn't it? The military can eliminate him if necessary, with essentially no questions. Once he has been indicted, they can justify their actions by claiming he was resisting arrest."

Ramon listened to Claudia's observations with pensive interest. She really doesn't have many scruples, he mused. True, *she is quite valuable, but if she has no resistance to an act of violence against someone she doesn't even know, what would she be prepared to do towards someone she was angry with?*

"I did not tell Botia about this development. It is sometimes wise to hold back information, and Whitaker has not yet been indicted, so we are not in a position to arrest him on behalf of the U.S. government. We don't need an excuse to arrest him in any event. Although I am assured that Whitaker will be indicted soon, the situation merely gives us greater latitude."

"How can you be certain he will be indicted?" she asked curiously.

"Claudia, you are bright and beautiful and you know a great deal about a lot of things. But, if you have to ask this kind of question you have a lot to learn about the U.S. justice system." He relaxed and laughed out loud.

"Please enlighten me, Ramon," she oozed sweetly.

"In the U.S., a federal grand jury consists of twenty-three citizens who sit in secret session. The person under investigation is not present, and neither is his or her attorney. So, hearing only one side of the case, the grand jury votes to indict. The percentage of those not indicted when the U.S. government considers itself the victim, is statistically negligible. They have a saying in U.S. criminal law: "Any federal prosecutor can indict a ham sandwich.""

Claudia Brun had a puzzled look on her face. She clearly didn't understand the metaphor. "What does that mean, Ramon? Are you sure he will go to prison?" she asked with growing interest."

"He will be indicted. The grand jury is simply a tool of the federal prosecutor to expand his or her powers of investigation. It also provides a winning edge for the prosecutor in the remote event that the indicted actually goes to trial. Once indicted, Whitaker will have to plead guilty, or run the kind of risk virtually no one is willing to take."

"So, you are saying that there is no chance that he will not be convicted," she said in some amazement.

"Not convicted my dear, indicted. Yes, he will be indicted if the U.S. government wants it so, and apparently, they do. And, guess why? For the same reasons, we want him. For the things he writes, and the things he knows. It seems he has published a number of articles, and several books, deeply critical of U.S. federal agencies. Plus, he was a guest on over a hundred talk shows venting his spleen about governmental abuse of power. What kind of fool would do that? You simply do not challenge the U.S. bureaucracy. They are incredibly vindictive. It's the first rule of governance. Bureaucracy will always find a way to protect itself. It will thoroughly discredit anyone who raises serious questions about their activities."

Claudia was still struggling to understand. "So, when he is indicted then he goes to trial?"

"That is theoretically correct," Ramon said pleasantly, as the corners of his lips turned into a wicked smirk. "And, the moment he is indicted there will be a warrant issued for his arrest."

"Yes, but he does have an opportunity to present his defense at trial. Is this not so?" she said in confusion.

"Yes, in principal. But the federal prosecution system is thoroughly rigged in the government's favor. In the few cases where a trial actually follows an indictment, then a jury is convened. Now remember, we are talking about the U.S. federal government prosecuting someone on their own behalf. This is not about a state, county or city prosecution. Anyway, jurors come to trial presuming the indicted person must be guilty, because he or she was already convicted by a grand jury, which supposedly already reviewed the facts. Of course, that is untrue. The grand jury saw only information the prosecutor wanted them to see. And they heard only the conclusions the prosecutor had already drawn. The whole thing is circular logic, giving ever increasing power to the U.S. District Attorney."

Ramon was quiet for a time staring off into space, his mind pursuing some corollary thought process. After a full two minutes, he resumed his explanation as if no time had passed. "In practice, rarely does anyone escape final conviction in the U.S. federal system. The statistics vary slightly from year to year, but the conviction rates at the federal level are close to 100%. That is why over 97% of the accused, simply plead guilty, rather than be subjected to a system where there is almost no hope to prevail. Those charged with crimes against the U.S. government are going to go down, one way or the other. In fact, it is considered mal-practice in the U.S. for a criminal justice lawyer to not insist that their innocent client take a plea."

"Federal prosecutors have all the cards Claudia. And, they have an unlimited war chest. They are also experts at keeping information from the courts that might prove useful to the accused. It is VERY RARE that anyone is able to escape government traps, once laid."

"That's unbelievable," she said, her eyes widened in amazement. "How is it that Americans do not know this about their own system?"

"Americans believe what they're told in the media. The media sensationalizes things until they are no longer meaningful. The average American has no understanding of the difference between civil and criminal courts, lower and higher courts, state and federal systems."

Ramon paused, then turned and pointed to a framed quotation hanging on his wall. It was a frightening statement he had hung there to remind him of the realities of government. It was entitled "REALITY." It was a statement taken under oath at the

Nuremberg trials from Reichsmarschall Hermann Goering of Nazi Germany. It said:

> "It is the leaders of the country who determine the policy and it is always a simple matter to drag the people along, whether it is a democracy, or a fascist dictatorship, or a parliament, or a communist dictatorship. Voice or no voice, the people can always be brought to the bidding of the leaders. That is easy. All you have to do is tell them they are being attacked, and denounce the peacemakers for lack of patriotism and exposing the country to danger. It works the same in any country."

Claudia had seen the framed statement before, but not really given it much thought. Sobered and contemplative, she tried to understand it in terms of their conversation.

"So, no matter what happens, Whitaker loses? Do you suppose he knows this? Because if he does, it sounds like it would make him a more dangerous adversary."

CHAPTER FIFTEEN

Akumal, Quintana Roo

Grant stood in the administrative office of the hotel. His mind was swimming with theories. He was having trouble focusing. Why would someone be in Akumal looking for him?

"Alex, let's stop and think a moment. If these guys knew we were here, wouldn't they also know the car that we are driving? And, therefore wouldn't they have spotted it in the parking lot? Instead of looking for us, it seems reasonable that all they would have to do is sit down the road a short way, and wait for us to drive out. In fact, whether they knew we'd rented a car or not, which should be easy to determine, they would probably assume so. Either way, the thing for them to do is simply to wait for us to leave the area."

He thought for another moment then continued. "On the other hand, if there were only two of them with one car, and they didn't know which car was ours, how would they watch both access roads to the highway?"

"They'd probably scan the beach area then return to the highway, and park to watch the cars that turned out from either of the two Akumal roadways," Alex offered.

"Exactly, but they would only need to pay attention to the cars turning north towards Cancun."

"Why wouldn't they be concerned we were heading south," she questioned.

"If this is about me, they'll know my plane is at the FBO private terminal. It seems logical they would assume I wouldn't just up and leave it. So, all they have to do is wait for me to return, and that means I'd turn north out of Akumal," he replied thoughtfully.

His mind wouldn't let go of inconsistencies in what was happening. Every air terminal in Mexico had armed military guards around the place. If the men chasing them had governmental blessing, they need merely warn the staff at FBO, or tell the guards assigned to the terminal. Wouldn't it be easier to not let them out onto the tarmac? Besides, the tower could simply stop them from taking off, he thought.

"If they are tracking us so closely that they've figured out we spent the night together, they may also know I have an appointment between here and Cancun," he reflected.

"How could they possibly know that?" she growled, looking thoroughly distressed.

"Because I just made a call, and tracking a phone number is an easy matter, assuming they know my cell number. Depending on how important I am to them, they could have allocated sufficient resources to actually listen to my calls, although that doesn't make much sense. And, now that I think about it, they probably don't know I have a Mexican cell phone. Not many people do. The only reason I have it is so that locals can contact me on a Mexico number when I am in the country."

Alex whimpered, "Grant, I'm scared. What are we going to do?"

After considering her frame of mind for a moment, he replied: "We're going to think. We're going to think out loud, so we both know what the other is thinking."

Continuing on, he asked, "Now, are you sure this is about me, and not about you? Couldn't my involvement be only as it relates to you? It seems much more logical. If the CID was looking for me, they'd just put out a border watch, or have the Mexican military stop me when I reach any point on a flight plan. My movements are pretty transparent. Why would they try and chase me down at a hotel in Akumal? Flying in Mexico is not like in the States. You can't even take-off without clearance and a flight plan. In the U.S., you can fly anywhere you want without telling a soul where you're headed, unless of course the weather is bad, or you're leaving from, or heading into, a terminal control area."

"What's the CID?" Alex asked.

Oh, sorry, that's the Criminal Investigation Division of the IRS," he responded.

Returning to his earlier point, "In Mexico, or any of the Caribbean countries, you can't take off, or land, anywhere without an approved flight plan. And, you're not permitted to fly at night unless you're a commercial pilot on a scheduled route," he said.

"So, what's up with Mexico and the Caribbean?" Alex asked.

"Mexico and the Caribbean have been forced by U.S. policy to implement stricter flight regulations on their airspace than is required within American airspace. The U.S. government insists this is a necessary step to interdict the narco-terrorism trade. No aircraft can lift off from any airport south of the U.S. border, extending down through the northern part of South America, and maybe even further south, for all I know, without a pre-approved flight plan. Private VFR flights are not permitted, even with a flight plan, if you are south of the U.S. border at night for any reason. Our government has taken the position that any private flight during the evening, anywhere in the Caribbean, Central America, or Mexico, must be involved in doing something illegal, and somehow it must have something to do with the United States. Anyway, my point is, why would somebody be looking for me down here, when all they have to do is pick me up when I file a flight plan?"

"That's absurd! How can the U.S. government force other sovereign nations to do anything?"

"Let's not go there. It is what it is. Right now, we've got more to worry about than U.S. policy. My thinking is that we ought to reconnoiter the parking lot, and get the car. If it seems clear, we'll creep towards the highway, double checking to make sure we don't have someone following us."

"Okay, but what happens if they're right down the road waiting?" she asked nervously.

He shrugged in frustration. "I don't know. Maybe you should jog down the road with my local phone, and call me back on my U.S. number if you spot trouble ahead. This morning I didn't recognize you even though I watched you running down the beach. Just act like a tourist taking a jog."

"Yes sir, Capitan Grant," she said with attempted bravado and her signature mock salute. "But what if they come after me," she said with a frown.

"I suppose that's possible. Are you sure it is me these guys are after?" he said, revealing his growing suspicion.

"That's what Loreto said. They were asking after a Grant Whitaker. They told her they had reason to believe that you were with me," she replied in a neutral tone.

"It doesn't make sense. Why me, why now? Why not wait until I'm at the airport or someplace easy to track me. It just seems like a lot of unnecessary effort. I'd be such an easy target at the airport. Or, even a Cancun hotel, or when I return the rental car," he muttered, trying to cover up the inkling of disbelief that had shown through in his voice a moment earlier.

Alex interrupted impatiently, "Grant, you don't always have to know *why*. Isn't it enough to know *what*? I mean, think about it. It is happening, and you need to decide how to respond!"

"Okay, okay. Does plan A work for you?"

"Do we have a plan B? Oh, never mind. What you said works for me. Let's go," she said with more force than she felt.

Together they looked over the parking area from the inside windows of the lobby. There were places a person could conceal themselves out there, but the need to get moving and do something, rather than be stalled and trapped inside, made Grant antsy. Moving towards the door he said "Wait here, I'll get the car."

No one seemed interested, as he started the car and drove around to the lobby entrance. Whoever had been looking for them didn't seem to be here now. Alex jumped in. They drove around the inside circle of the drop-off area, and headed back out to the highway. After pulling clear of the tree line, and the dense shrubbery planted around the entrance to the hotel parking area, he stopped the car and looked ahead. There were small rolling hills of scrub brush between them and the main road, but probably not large enough to park a car without being seen. He slowly drove ahead a quarter mile. He stopped for a vehicle coming down the road towards them. "Better just stay in the car for now," Grant said. The car coming at them was kicking up a rooster tail of dirt. "Give me your hat" he spoke quickly, "and duck down to the floor."

Alex unclipped her ball cap in the back so her ponytail could fall out. She handed it to him as she squeezed down on the floor in front of the seat. It was a good thing the adjustable band was unclasped or it would never have fit on his much larger head. He pulled the hat on with the brim angled down over his face. A white battered pickup drove by, two more cars following at a modest pace, slowing as needed to keep from breathing the dust from the car ahead.

So much for plan A he thought. I'm not stopping now. As he approached the highway, there was a dark car, similar to the one he'd seen earlier. It was stopped at the intersection ahead. It was parked about thirty meters north of the shoulder on the main road. He could see the backs of two heads. "Alex, keep your head down," he said quietly, as if being soft-spoken would not alert their attention.

Gaining the intersection, he forced himself to not look at the car parked to his right, just a few car lengths north on the highway. He waited for traffic to clear in both directions, and turned south. Several times he glanced in the rearview mirror, keeping track of the dark car faced in the opposite direction behind him. It did not move.

"Okay, you can get up now."

"Where are we going?" she blurted. "You're heading the wrong way."

"I know, but there was a suspicious looking car just north of the intersection, on the shoulder. I thought it wise to turn south."

"Was it a dark colored late model Nissan or something like that?" she asked.

"Yes," Grant replied simply.

As Alex climbed back up into the seat, she said nervously, "Those are local cars. Nissan manufactures them in Cuernavaca, south of Mexico City. Just down the road from the Nissan plant they still make the original Volkswagen beetles." She was making small talk trying to overcome her jitters.

They drove on in silence hardly noticing the spectacular ocean views. The jungle had been cut away along the east side of the road leaving sand and scrub brush, and an occasional pasture that supported a few cows. The west side of the road was primarily brush and limestone outcroppings.

"What do we do now?" Alex mumbled. "There is no other road back north to Cancun. The only road possible is to take a right at the Tulum highway and drive to the Coba ruins, and follow the loop highway around to the toll road from Chichen Itza to Cancun. That would take at least three hours," Alex said sullenly.

"If we stay moving in this direction the turn-off past Coba is almost to Chetumal, the southeast corner of the Mexican border with Belize."

"I keep forgetting you know the area," she said dully. "What would going that way accomplish?"

"Not sure. Just thinking," he said. "There has got to be an explanation for all this. Things don't make sense. If they were looking for you they could have picked you off at the restaurant back in Chichen Itza, if me, the same. I suppose it's possible they were intending to pick you up, but perhaps you fooled them by jumping a ride with me." He let the comment hang. She did not respond.

"How about it Alex, were you ducking out?"

"She seemed to shrink in her seat. "In a manner of speaking," she stammered. "Yeah, I suppose so. I got concerned when Moises told me someone was asking about the two of us. My first reaction was it had to be about me. So, I ran home, changed, and got my shoulder bag."

Grant's tone had shifted again, revealing his doubt. "And let's see, that would be why you didn't want me to report you as a passenger before taking off?"

"Something like that," she said miserably.

"This isn't about me at all. This is about you," he said, irritation clear in his voice.

"No, no, I'm telling you, Loreto said those men were looking for you, not me," she fired back.

"Sorry Alex. It simply doesn't make sense. I'm going to turn around at Xel-ha, and drive back. If those guys are still parked alongside the highway when we go by, we should blend into the traffic going north. It will probably never occur to them it is us. Unless of course they have the license number of the car, but if they did, it seems they would have simply waited by the car in the first place."

Alex was upset. He couldn't tell whether it was because she felt she was headed back into danger, or because she was angry that he did not trust her. Probably both, he thought. At Xel-ha, he stopped the car for something to drink. When he asked Alex what she wanted, she just shook her head and didn't look up. Glancing at the keys in the ignition he removed them as he got out. It was an instinctive reaction, but also a sign he did not trust her.

He bought a couple of bottles of water and a tan baseball cap that said Xel-ha. It was warm outside, but not yet hot, so he decided to walk around for a few minutes, trying to work out the next best move and consider the implications of what was happening. Alex stayed in the car with the window down, staring out into space.

Walking a short distance, he stopped in front of a sign that marked the beginning of a circular educational pathway. It was designed to teach visitors about the ancient Mayan civilization. The first sign caught his attention:

> They had letters. Each letter was a syllable, and with them they were understood. They had a year consisting of 365 days. They had knowledge of a Creator of all things... and of the fall of Lucifer, and of the creation of man, and of the immortality of the soul, and of Heaven and Hell, and of the Flood. Those who anciently came to people this land.... did not worship idols....
>
> Bishop Diego de Landa -1531

He tried to focus on what he had just read. It was amazing that this information had been suppressed for so long. It was just now coming out. He couldn't hold the thought. He knew his relationship with Alex had just taken another radical turn. His mind kept returning to her. *I wonder what she's thinking. She must know more than she is saying. What do I do now, and do I dare do it with her?*

Confused, he continued to walk along the trail, trying to distract himself from the logical conclusion that Alex had been lying to him. There were large stone carvings scattered along the path amidst the signs. He stopped and read another sign:

> Calendars of significant precision, based upon identical astronomical observations and calculations are found in both the Fertile Crescent (Bible lands) and Mexico. The true solar year was worked out in both areas to the 7th decimal point, 365.2421987 days. In both Mexico, and the Fertile Crescent, the precise timing of the cycles around Venus and Mercury had been calculated. This was not accomplished in Europe until Kepler's work in the 17th century A.D.

People were now openly commenting on the similarities between the old world and pre-Columbian new world. For years, even mentioning something like that had been dismissed as the lunatic fringe. The concept was something of an anthropological Monroe Doctrine. It was political and intellectual isolationism, regardless of data to the contrary. Hmmm…the Fertile Crescent, he had never actually thought of that area as Bible lands per se. He supposed that was fundamentally accurate. The Fertile Crescent was the term anthropologists had given to ancient Iraq, Assyria, Syria, and the area south through Israel into Egypt. The fertile areas of the ancient cradle of civilization seemed to form something of a crescent on the map. All of it, except Egypt, was known as Mesopotamia. Perhaps the term "crescent" was popularized because it was the symbol of Islam, which dominated the entire area for the last thousand years.

Returning to the car, he opened the door, and laid the hat and bottles of water on the seat between them. As he settled into the car, he said "Water?" It was a question. Alex did not respond. She seemed to shrink towards the door and stare out the window, making no attempt at conversation. After the constant dialog between them the last two days, the absence of conversation was deafening. A half-hour later, as they closed on the Akumal intersection, Grant broke the silence, "Time to slide down."

Lying between them, the Xel-Ha cap had become an almost tangible barrier marking the space that separated them. He picked up the cap, put it on, and pulled the brim low over his eyes.

Trapped in slower moving traffic he maneuvered in behind a tour bus returning to Cancun from the ancient Mayan seaport of Tulum. Behind him was a heavily loaded truck hauling limestone. He dared not look at the parked car on the shoulder as they passed by, but did glance quickly in the passenger side mirror. Two men. One was turned in his seat so he could study the cars coming up the connecting road from the hotel.

His mind racing again, he reflected on what had just happened. *They are probably looking for a car with two people, turning right from the hotel roadway, headed north to the airport, or on to Cancun. There is virtually nothing south of here, but the daytime tourist attractions of Xel-ha and Tulum, so under normal circumstances their thinking would be accurate. I was right to have Alex down and out-of-sight. Now what? What's really going on here? Why all this effort for me? Or is this really about Alex? It's for sure I'm a target of the IRS, but why would the Mexican government go out of their way to help the U.S. track down an outspoken author who simply writes stuff three-letter agencies don't like? There is something going on here I do not understand.*

"Okay Alex, we're past them. It's pretty clear those guys in the car are looking for somebody." She did not respond. "Here, take my cell and call your boss, and see what you can learn."

Quietly, without comment, she dialed the restaurant.

Could this really have something to do with me? Could it have something to do with the story Pepe told me as I left Veracruz? It seemed pretty far-fetched. The most logical conclusion is that someone is after Alex, and I'm simply an innocent by-stander that gave her a ride.

He was lost in his mind, thinking furiously. He realized that to an outside observer it would look like they were a couple. Especially, once they knew Alex and he had spent the night together. *Maybe these guys are private investigators hired by her ex-boyfriend. Maybe they're trying to figure out if she is connected to anyone else that's a possible threat. How did I get myself into this?*

Alex was on the phone with someone. Sitting more erect, her voice went up an octave. She used her free hand to screen the road noise. "What," she gasped. She quieted down for a moment then spoke again in rapid Spanish. He could not understand much of what she said, but it was obvious something was wrong. A moment later she rang off and sank back into the seat.

"What's wrong," he asked gently. He waited. She began to cry. Then started to speak, choked, and began to gasp for air trying to control her sobbing. Finally, she managed, "Mario is in the hospital. Someone beat him badly. Lupe is panicked. She says someone is after you, and she is afraid for my life. She's worried you are a killer, or something. I tried to reason with her, but she kept saying why else would such bad people be after you."

Stunned, he did not know how to respond. Worse, he did not know what to believe. Sensing his dilemma, she said in sober tones, "Believe whatever you want. I don't care anymore. Please let me out at Playa del Carman, I'll catch a bus back." She didn't say back to where.

After a long silence, Grant decided to be upfront. "Alex, I don't know what to say. The fact is I don't know what is going on. I am confused and shaken by all that seems to be happening. I really have no idea, well, maybe just an inkling of an idea. The only thing I can come up with is so absurd it's hard to give it any credence." Feeling guilty for not asking after Mario before blurting out his thoughts, he recovered and said, "What is the prognosis for Mario?"

She didn't answer. Whether she was just exhausted from adrenaline release, lost in her own thoughts, angry with him, or frightened silly about what was happening, he couldn't tell. He started to say something then thought wiser of it.

The silence dragged out between them as they both struggled to grasp the situation. Finally, she said carefully, "All I know is he is badly hurt. I'm not sure what that means. He's in the hospital, and that must mean something, because people down here don't end up in the hospital for minor issues."

"I'm deeply sorry," he said. He meant it.

They were silent for a few miles further. Alex eventually stammered, "I believe this isn't making sense to you. It isn't making any sense to me either. The thing is I'm not the problem. No matter what you think. This is about you. And, my guess is, it has nothing to do with the IRS. The IRS can be awful; everyone has heard stories. Apparently, they're an agency answering to no one but themselves, but they don't go around having people beaten up, or at least I'm not ready to believe that right now."

There was a certain palpable relief in the car, simply because they were speaking again. It was strained, but they were beginning to open up and talk. "What did you mean when you said you had an "inkling" of an idea," she continued.

Even though the car was air conditioned and the temperature balmy, his hands were sweating on the wheel. "I agree with you. Nothing makes much sense. You know, the story I was telling you last night? The one where Pepe (my Jose) told me about Esteban Morelos, the prior Governor of Veracruz? Well, he was arrested."

"Yes, you said," she replied.

"Pepe told me that the situation was so serious everyone in the family was afraid. I had planned on spending the night with them when I flew in from Guadalajara, but when I called, Pepe told me that I was to stay right where I was, and he would come to me. When we met at the airport, he insisted I leave as soon as possible. Thinking it was probably more awkward for me to have arrived without telling him in advance, I offered to stay at the Emporio

Veracruz. It's right down the street from his place on Insurgentes and Veracruzanos, at the harbor's edge.

Grant realized he was beginning to ramble. Things were moving towards the surreal. "In the past, I've stayed there many times. It's only a dozen blocks from their house." Spacing off for a moment he caught himself again, trying to work things out. "Pepe was insistent that I not stay in Veracruz. He said that I should leave right then. He was insistent. This was pretty strange, but then I've always thought he took some things more seriously than he should. He and his wife strike me as slightly superstitious at times although they are both well-educated. They are wonderful people, great parents, and true friends. He and his wife teach marriage encounter classes. They are dedicated Catholics," he trailed off.

"Grant, will you please get to the point?" Alex said; irritation evident in her voice.

"I'm sorry, just rattled I guess. I've been trying to decide how to tell you this. I'm not saying I believe it, mind you, I'm just going to tell you what Pepe told me. He was certain that some ancient pre-Columbian writings had been found. He told me they were inscribed on sheets of gold. The remarkable thing was that the writing style was something not seen before. It was baffling to those trying to determine their source. Frankly, I didn't give the story much credibility, Pepe couldn't tell Coptic from Old Slavonic."

Alex cut in, "And you could," she blurted in frustration. "What's Coptic and Old Slavonic got to do with anything?"

"Nothing really, it was just a comment," he mumbled.

Her voice laced with stress, she continued, "Why do I think these engraving are in a private collection being held for resale? Probably the man you told me about last night."

"I promised not to say," he mumbled uselessly. "But you have the general idea. Pepe told me the engravings could not be placed by traditional archeological methods. They didn't appear to be a part of any known Mesoamerican culture. They were considered something of an anomaly." His voice gained in strength as he focused on telling Alex the story. "According to him, they are authentically old; but that is not the real issue. Apparently, the writing style has some pictographic glyphs in common with ancient Mayan, but also has what appear to be ancient Egyptian markings, or something similar."

He paused in thought, and then continued. "The theory is that it may be a mother-culture script, existing before the modification that takes place with all written languages over time. You know, like what's happened to written English. It is quite hard to read early Colonial documents and understand them, and that wasn't all that long ago, and it's our own language."

Showing interest in this line of thought, and rising to the discussion, she interrupted. "I took a class in ancient languages. There is a standard formula at the rate that word meanings are modified over time and new symbols are incorporated. I don't remember the formula, but I do remember how surprised I was to hear it. Most of us in class thought it was a silly exaggeration, until we started working through word-meaning changes over hundred year sequences."

Nodding agreement, Grant continued. "Some of these sheets of thin metal are bound together with rings and inscribed on both sides. This alone makes it extremely valuable and an absolutely unique find. But, some of the symbols seem to be in common with stories from much later Mayan works. You know the stuff we discussed last night. The *Popol Vuh, The Annals of the Cakchiquels, The Title of the Lords of Totonicapan,* or maybe the *Books of Chilam Balam.* All of these were written to preserve the lost writings, traditions, and history, of their predecessors, i.e. the mother-culture of American high civilization."

"Yes, yes, so?" Alex exhaled.

"Pepe says these newly discovered writings are America's equivalent to the Dead Sea scrolls, or perhaps something much greater. You know what a ruckus those things have caused over the years. Aside from being absolutely priceless, they have been at the center of continued political conflict, and become the source of philosophical and religious wars since they were discovered in 1948. Had it not been for the Huntington Library in San Marino, California, the majority of the Dead Sea material would still be under wraps. It's really unimaginable that the vast majority of these priceless pieces of ancient religious history were kept from the public for fifty years after their discovery."

"Grant, what's all this got to do with you, or with me, for that matter?" Alex barked.

"I don't know, but it is the only other thing I can think of that might cause someone maneuvering to control these materials to try and track me down and stay on my tail. I told you it was a crazy idea, but if the story Pepe told me was even partially correct, an incredible fortune is at stake, plus the impact on world affairs could be dramatic."

"That's pretty thin Grant. Especially the world affairs part, but I do get the economic implications. A document like you described, one in good condition, even without its special metal characteristics, would make it essentially priceless."

"Oh! I just remembered," Grant interrupted. "In 2005 in Iran, the police in Tehran recovered a number of artifacts that a farmer had found while plowing a field. He had sold them to smugglers. Among the objects was a book consisting of eight gold sheets. They were inscribed in cuneiform script. The sheets were bound by four small rings passing through holes in the sheets. It was in the same fashion as an ancient Etruscan gold book found in Bulgaria in 2003. That gold book dated back to 600 years before Christ!"

Alex sighed. "You're really caught up in this stuff, aren't you? I mean really, how does this affect us?" She carried on as if she had not asked the question. "Of course, you'd have a huge battle on your hands just getting it out of the country, not to mention keeping it under wraps until you were able to find a buyer. Alex tended to look up when she was trying to remember things. After a moment's pause, she went on. "Let's see, there is *The Dresden Codex* in Vienna, which was damaged in bombings during the Second World War. It was a gift from Carlos V of Spain. And, there is *The Paris Codex*, which was returned to Mexico. It is incomplete, and in a severely frayed condition. There is *The Madrid Codex*, which was divided in two pieces, it's the largest Mayan book, totaling 112 pages, but much of it is indistinguishable. Oh, and there is *The Grolier Codex*, which is only 11 or so pages. It might not be Mayan anyway; it's argued that it has a heavy Mixteca influence."

"Recently I read something about a Mixtec book, *The Codex Sheldon*. Seems there is another book written underneath it," Grant mused quietly. "Researchers from both the Netherlands and England using some high-tech imaging equipment were able to reveal an entire beautifully painted book just beneath the manuscript already on display in a European museum. It is a palimpsest: an older document that was covered up and reused. It is about sixteen feet long folded up into 20 large pages."

She hesitated a moment then replied, "I heard that. Pretty amazing stuff. It revealed the genealogies of a whole host of formerly unknown kings and rulers. Speaking of the Mixteca, have you ever seen the cut stones in those incredible designs in Mitla? I have seen photographs, but have never been there."

Caught off guard by the sudden change of direction, Grant stammered, "Ah, yes. On a road trip from the Yucatan with a bunch of teenagers, I decided to cross the Isthmus of Tehuantapec. When we got to the city of Tehuantapec, on the Pacific side, we took the switchback mountain road inland. It was a pretty dangerous, but a beautiful drive up into the mountains and back down into the Oaxaca Valley where we saw Mitla. I remember the mountain passes were cluttered with wild burros and goats. That was definitely more interesting to the kids than the Mitla ruins. Actually, there is nothing really to see of Mitla except some standing walls, with the designs you are referring to, but if you head on up to the mountain-top city of the ancient Zapotecs that is truly spectacular."

"You mean Monte Alban? Is it really as dramatic as the photos?" Alex pined.

"Yes, it is. I'm sure you've tried to explain the main palace of Palenque, or the Pyramids of the Inscriptions, to someone who has not been there. Even with photos you can't do it justice. Monte Alban is like that. You must *see* it to appreciate it. The Zapotecs whacked off the top of a mountain and built an amazing fortress city up there. It was pretty much impregnable, and ensured the survival of their people for hundreds of years. Even through the Aztec period. From my perspective, it is almost as impressive as the Inca fortress city in Peru, but it probably doesn't get one percent of the attention that Machu Picchu does."

Turning to face him, she replied, "In my opinion Mexico is pretty much about booze, beaches and bums. You know, *Party-Time*. The tourism department promotes Chichen Itza, Tulum, and Uxmal, because they are within driving distance from Cancun. Other than Teotihuacan, now within the city limits of Mexico City, the rest of the major ruins are virtually ignored."

With disappointment clear in her voice, she continued. "There are more ruins from ancient civilizations in Mexico than in Egypt and Iraq, put together. It amazes me that Americans know so little, of how truly advanced civilization was prior to the arrival of Columbus."

They were talking about what they knew. Subconsciously, they were distracting themselves from the concern and fear that accompanied their current circumstances. Grant lowered his voice and spoke thoughtfully, "You know, there is good evidence that Tenochtitlan, the Aztec capital, was the largest ancient city in the world in its time. It was way larger than London, Madrid, or Paris, for example. Of course, today it is the foundation of modern Mexico City."

Alex responded reflexively, "The Valley of Mexico is a hugely productive agricultural area. It has always supported a large population."

Grant continued, "My point is that nothing really has changed. It's still one of the largest cities in the world, with a population greater than the entire country of Canada. And Canada is the second largest country in the world geographically." After a moment's pause he finished his thought. "It's really staggering to contemplate."

"You know," Alex said, as she ruminated on his comments, "It just occurred to me that *The Nuttal Codex* that we discussed last night, is the only other ancient book in all the Americas. It is a Mixteca document from the Oaxaca Valley. So that means there are five codices, not four as we concluded last night."

"You're right, that would be five, or at least five that we know of, because these five are all in museums. But the Nuttal document, is not Mayan."

Feigning continued interest in their mutual obsession, which was not hard for either of them, they talked on, hitchhiking off each other's speculations. Progressively, the walls of distrust began to diminish. Shortly, they arrived at the private marina and gated community of Puerto Adventuras.

Just as they pulled up to the gate, Alex said, "If those two guys back there are tracking you, because of something they think you may know about the Cerro Viejo plates, how did one of them find you in my restaurant, within a couple of hours of the time you made an unscheduled landing in Chichen Itza?"

"I have no idea." Stopping at the gatehouse entrance to Puerto Adventuras, he turned and looked at Alex quizzically, "You've named the plates?"

"Well, what else would you call them?" she shrugged. "If they were found where you said they were, the name seems logical."

"Hola Senor, how may I help you?" a uniformed guard asked, as he stepped out of the guardhouse built in the middle of the divided roadway.

"Here to see Jackson Morgan and the vessel Zarahemla," Grant said carefully.

After checking some records, they were waved in with instructions as to how to locate the appropriate access gate down to Zarahemla's dock. As they drove around the inside harbor, Alex said thoughtfully, "Maybe you should call your friend in Veracruz, and see how things are going at his end. It might be worthwhile to tell him you think someone is following you, and hear his response."

Everywhere they looked there were Yachties. These are the people with the money and resources to own their own private docks and maintain boats in Puerto Adventuras. Even Grant was impressed with how much things had improved since his last trip here. He thought back about how he and Marianna had reviewed the entire development prospectus before the first channel was dug. At one point, they had put a down payment on a lot, which was to face on to a finger inlet from the main inside harbor. Once upon a time they had plans to retire here, at least for the winters. The plan was to permanently moor their 54-foot pilothouse Symbol, the motor yacht Zarahemla, right at the back door of a home planned for the lot. Now it was Jack's dream fulfilled.

Coming out of his reflective mood he responded to Alex's earlier question. "Yes. A good idea. Remind me later. Right now, I've got to meet someone for a bit. I may be a while. Would you like to come?" Grant offered.

"No, not unless you want me to," she said, as she looked about taking the place in. "Geez Grant, this is really an amazing place. I think I'll do a little exploring and then grab one of those lounges by the pool over there." She pointed to the first of three pools close by. The projection of land they were on was built inside a seawall where floating docks to either side had magnificent private yachts moored.

Grant left the car unlocked with the windows open, and walked down the ramp to the dock where Zarahemla was secured. "Permission to come aboard," he called out.

"Permission granted, you-old pirate!" came a booming drawl.

Grant stepped aboard. He smelled the salt, and the slight odor of a clean bilge. He felt the gentle rocking underneath. A stab of nostalgia arced through him. He missed this life. He missed the esprit-de-corps, the companionship of blue-water sailors, and the exhilaration of a boat underway. He missed the beauty of the open ocean at sunset, and the peace of a gently rocking vessel at anchor.

Jack stepped out from the main salon and threw his arms around him. "Hey, buddy, I understand you're having hard times. How you holding up?"

CHAPTER SIXTEEN

Mexico City, Mexico

"Ramon, General Botia is on the line," Claudia Brun spoke softly into the intercom.

"Give me the call," Garcia snapped.

Without ceremony Botia began speaking. "We've temporarily lost track of them, but found Whitaker's airplane at FBO in Cancun. We have instructed Cancun tower to keep watch on the aircraft. We have also determined that Whitaker rented a car at the private terminal building. He apparently carries more than one cell phone. We do not have the equipment in place, to triangulate the phone signal. However, we can tell what cell tower picks up his signal when he calls someone. We will find him soon."

The general abruptly rang off. He was getting increasingly frustrated for having been drawn into this operation. *How did he get into the position of reporting to Ramon Garcia, as if he were his lackey?* Shaking his head in disgust, he decided to finish this business quickly and disengage.

* * *

Puerto Adventuras, Quintana Roo

Stepping back from J.P. Morgan's embrace, Grant said soberly, "It's good to see you Jack. It's been pretty crazy lately."

Jack nodded his head in understanding. He motioned Grant to an overstuffed chair in the main salon. "Drink? Diet coke, I suppose? Now tell me what's going on."

J.P. was an old and reliable friend. Grant and he had met more than twenty years earlier in a church parking lot in Canada. Both of them had large families, and were struggling with the logistics of moving a pack of kids around. Grant and Marianna had just moved to the area, and were living in an oceanfront home in Sidney, a small boating community on Vancouver Island, just north of Victoria, the capital of British Columbia. The move to Canada for the Whitaker's was to last only two years, while their youngest child attended a program for the pre-school aged handicap. Their youngest son was legally-deaf; hearing impaired was the PC term.

Immediately after meeting the Morgan clan, something special had developed between the families. That was particularly true of Grant and Jack. There was really no way to explain it. They became more like brothers than just friends. The bond that connected them continued to strengthen over the years. No matter how far away they were from one another, they were always interacting. They wrote, phoned, faxed, and once the internet became a reality, they emailed, facebooked, and texted. They shared family stories, personal adventures, business deals, everything.

Jack was a "recovering lawyer," one that had put in his thirty-plus years and decided it was really not for him. Smart, and incredibly kind, the legal profession seemed to be at cross-purposes with his primary goals in life, which were basically exploring new ways to have fun. In spite of his gray hair, he was a boy at heart. Jack was almost always with his family, and generally doing nutty things. Things like setting sail from Victoria, Canada for Tahiti with no previous sailing experience.

One day on a whim, and with little warning, Jack sold his legal practice to a mutual friend, and bought an old 65-foot steel-hulled sailing yacht that had been in dry dock for ten years. He named it *Dreamweaver* and commenced to outfit it with intentions to sail the world with seven of his children on board. This was both amazing and slightly aggravating to Grant. It had been Grant's much discussed plan for many years. And, besides, Jack did not know how to sail. J.P. had listened to Grant's yearnings for such a life, and decided it was a wonderful idea and simply did it, rather than talk about it. By then, Jack's oldest daughter was away at college, a roommate of one of Grant's daughters.

After constructing new bunks, a galley and other amenities, then outfitting *Dreamweaver* for an ocean voyage, Jack still had no sailing experience. The day before he was scheduled to leave Victoria, he had the vessel lowered into the harbor where it immediately began to take on water. He had incorrectly installed two through-hull fittings backwards. The boat almost sank before it ever left the dock. Thankfully, Dreamweaver was still in the lift rigging, and they were able to pull her clear. Back in dry dock, Jack reversed the fittings, which act like check-valves allowing water to flow only one way. The very next day, he put her back in the water.

The boat looked water tight to Jack, so he simply fired up the diesel engine, aimed his steel sailing vessel towards open water, cleared the harbor, and turned right. He motored for the next thirteen hours to the opening of the Straits of Juan de Fuca. There he made a left turn around Cape Flattery, the northwest corner of the State of Washington, and drew a course between Jones Rocks and Tatoosh Island, heading south straight down the Pacific west coast. His sixteen-year-old son, Tyson, was the only other person on board. Tyson had taken a four-hour sailing class the day before they left Victoria. He was all excited about his newfound knowledge. Jack, who thought he could learn anything from a book, had several sailing magazines and various cruising publications on board, and lots of time to read them.

After two grueling weeks enduring gale force winds, they made safe harbor in San Francisco. Jack now had a swagger in his step, having lived through a Pacific Northwest storm at sea. The truth was that neither Jack, nor his son Tyson, understood much about sailing. In fact, they had never figured out how to actually handle the sails. They had motored the entire way. One could call them offshore cruisers, but certainly not sailors.

After vessel repairs and re-outfitting, a necessary requirement due to the heavy seas and storm winds they had endured, they set out again. Their next landfall, eleven days later, was the San Diego yacht club where Jack's wife Lynn, with their kids in tow, met Jack and Tyson at the dock. They did the live aboard thing for several months, fixing up the boat, home schooling, learning boating skills, and celestial navigation. They were simply waiting for the end of hurricane season, so they could cruise to points south.

As it happens, the boating season for southbound vessels is heralded by the Halloween holiday on the West Coast. The day after Halloween, the first of November of each year, the Archbishop of San Diego performs a blessing on the fleet of private yachts staged to San Diego from ports north. All of them have been waiting to leave for southern destinations. As an excuse for an all-out party, cruisers tend to gather around the docks, and act as though they have known each other for half their lives. Many leave on the 2nd of November in spite of severe hangovers.

Jack and his entire brood, save a daughter who fell in love with a pre-med student while they were in San Diego, embarked for Cabo San Lucas, Mexico, on November 2nd. They would motor their sailing yacht over a thousand miles south to the end of one of the longest peninsulas in the world where sits the famous arch of San Lucas bay. Arriving safely, but just barely, they lived on the hook (at anchor), aboard Dreamweaver, for a full year. The boat needed some serious enhancements by the time they actually got to Cabo, so Jack bought a Volkswagen bus, an old hippy-mobile, and made the thousand plus mile trek each way, back and forth to San Diego three times over the next year buying parts and picking up gear he couldn't find in Cabo.

They set sail the next year, crossing the equator at mid Pacific, and spent the next six years in various island destinations. They sailed from Nuki Hiva in the Marquesas Islands, to the Tuamotu Archipelago, the Society Islands, French Polynesia, then on to Fiji. Eventually, they sailed back up hill to American Samoa, where they found their "hurricane hole," to hunker down and sit out the typhoon season.

Jack sent lengthy letters to Grant wherever there was a place he could get one mailed. Grant kept them all, threatening to write their story someday, if Jack didn't get around to it. J.P. finally sold Dreamweaver to an Australian, who lost the main mast on his maiden voyage from Samoa to Sidney. The boat rolled and sank. The buyer was fortunate to be rescued floating around in a yellow-inflatable, somewhere in the middle of the South Pacific.

After selling his boat, Jack had gathered together what was left of his nuclear family living in Samoa, as by then, two were married and three were at university in Hawaii. After bidding their tropical life good-bye, they returned to Victoria, Canada. A few years later, missing the sea, but not wanting to mess with sails, or deal with cramped quarters, he bought the motor yacht Zarahemla from Grant. It was then moored at Point Roberts on the 49th parallel, north of Bellingham, Washington, right on the border with Canada.

After cruising the U.S. and Canadian San Juan Islands, Jack shipped Zarahemla by ocean-going barge through the Panama Canal, and had it delivered to Miami, Florida. Once there Lynn and J.P. began motor-cruising the Caribbean during the winter months.

In due course, they made safe harbor in Cancun, bought a home in the gated boating community of Puerto Adventuras, and moored Zarahemla at their own dock, in what was essentially the backyard.

Grant and Jack had history, lots of it. And, both of them, at one time, had owned Zarahemla. Some years earlier, Grant and Marianna had cruised Zarahemla from Portland, Oregon down the Columbia River and across the Columbia River bar. The Columbia River bar is considered the most treacherous major river-to-ocean transition in the world. Here lie over 2,400 sunken vessels from the last hundred years.

After crossing the bar, they had cruised up the outside of Washington State, staying about twenty miles offshore. They had made the run through the Straits of Juan de Fuca, and cruised north up the famous Inside Passage to Alaska. This is surely one of the most scenic voyages in the entire world. Grant and Marianna made the entire round trip to Alaska and back, three separate times in the next five years.

Grant and Jack both had a lot of water time. They shared more experiences than most men of similar friendship. It was with this underpinning of soul, heart, and experience that Jack had inquired after Grant's struggle.

"Where's Lynn?" Grant asked, avoiding the "Now tell me what's going on," question for the moment.

"She headed off to Toronto, Shira is having another baby and grandma can't control her anxiety. I'll be following shortly as soon as I batten down Casa Liahona, and the Zarahemla," he replied, recognizing Grant's reluctance to answer his question.

Casa Liahona was the name Lynn and J.P. had given their winter home. It sat right above the dock where Zarahemla was moored. Liahona was an ancient mythological name meaning "sacred director or compass," recorded several places in the *Book of Mormon*, and Zarahemla was the name for an equally ancient, pre-Columbian city speculated, but not yet discovered. It was believed by some, to be in the jungles in northern Guatemala, close to the Usumacinta River. Other seekers were quite certain the ruins lay at the bottom of an artificial lake, created after the damming by Mexico, of the Grijalva River in Chiapas.

The people that shared an interest in this subject were fairly sure it was on one, or the other, of two primary river networks. Both the rivers had their origins in the tops of a high mountain range stretching from the Pacific Coast to the Atlantic, just north of Guatemala City. As explorers were to discover, Guatemala City was built on the ancient archeological site of Kaminaljuyu, which had been continuously occupied from the sixth century before Christ. The narrow mountain range that is the source of both river networks also provides a boundary line separating Highland Guatemala from Lowland Guatemala, and the Central Depression of Chiapas, Mexico. This mountainous region is called Sierras Cuchumatenes; it is a part of the great Sierra Madre Mountain Range.

J.P. shared Grant's enthusiasm for pre-Columbian archeology. However, his interest was purely intellectual, in the sense that he had not spent time in digs, or slogging through jungles. Jack was an adventurer to be sure; he was just focused on different things. Probably, as a tribute to his friend Grant, or perhaps because of the old superstition not to rename a boat, Jack had kept the name Zarahemla after he had purchased her.

Jack was aware of Grant's high-profile IRS problems. Everyone that knew Grant was being visited by agents, and several had been subpoenaed to appear before a grand jury. Jack was spared because he was really a Canadian. He had been called by agent's exuding intimidation, but Jack had simply laughed and said, "Some other time, maybe." J.P. knew the situation was bad, and like Grant, he received numerous calls from terrified friends that had been visited. Now he needed to hear from Grant, face-to-face without the danger of wiretaps, emails being captured, or faxes being electronically snitched.

In American Samoa, Jack had once been the legal advisor to the governor. He had learned firsthand that information garnered through electronic eavesdropping could be twisted beyond recognition, in order to fit the claims, the Fed made. He was cautious, and wise. He wanted straight information, and he wanted to know how to help.

Unfortunately, everything Grant knew about what was going on was coming from the same sources as the information Jack was getting. The government had not spoken to Grant directly. They had not questioned him, and had not served him with any form of interrogatories. What they had done was file an affidavit with the court, saying he was guilty of virtually every crime government agents could think up regarding tax evasion, conspiracy to defraud the government of taxes, etc.

Things were coming to a head. The ugliest element was that the U.S. District Attorney's office was now threatening to trump up reasons to indict all of Grant's children. This was simply an effort to gain leverage over the situation. Knowing Grant's dedication to family, the prosecutor expected Grant would have to "fall on his sword," and plea to whatever Washington D.C. decided to charge him with. Were he not to do so, it would expose his children and grandchildren to further harassment. Grant's kids would be dragged through the most excruciating process, along with being placed under constant surveillance. The emotional strain could literally be life-threatening. In fact, Marianna had been diagnosed with cancer after the government's smear campaigns had hit full throttle. She finally had succumbed eight months after her diagnosis.

In response to Jack's questions, Grant did a virtual core dump. Jack occasionally interrupted to clarify a point, or ask a question. He was a professional listener, and good at it. Masked by his disarming smile, he could ferret out nuance, and grasp the essence of most situations. For Grant, just letting it out in a safe place, was somehow cleansing. The two of them discussed the U.S. Justice system and the IRS for almost three hours, when Grant suddenly jumped, and said, "Oh, I forgot, I have a woman up at the pool waiting for me." That comment got more reaction from Jack than just about anything Grant had thus far said.

"What! You've got a woman along with you? What's this all about?" Both Grant and Jack were the adventurous sort. Both were men of action. And both were subject to the same inclinations as all men. But as they had discussed many times, one of the things that separated man from beast was that humankind could rise above their animal instincts, and make decisions for the higher good. Although understandable enough, Jack was not prepared to think of Grant traveling around Mexico with a woman, especial under these circumstances. Jack was struggling to reconcile this new piece of information. What else did he not know about his lifetime friend?

Grant blurted, "Take it easy Jack. It's a pretty strange story, but before it gets dark I need to find her and bring her back for you to meet."

"No, you don't. You will tell me what this is all about before you walk out of here, and drag someone back I'm supposed to be nice too. Give it to me straight, and give it to me now," Jack said with emphasis.

With a sheepish look, Grant mumbled, "Okay. I'll try and be brief, but this is a bit weird, and I still don't know what to make of it." Grant proceeded to outline the story of the last three days.

When he was done, Jack probed and prodded, asking some questions two and three times in different ways. He finally said in some amazement, "You're not kidding; this is all happening right now?"

"Afraid so," Grant muttered, almost as if to himself.

"And you really believe this might not be connected to either you, or this Alexa woman?" Jack queried.

"Her name is Alex. I had the same problem for a while, sounds like a guy's name, but she is definitely not a guy," Grant had said it reflexively without thinking.

The comment was not lost on Jack. "Okay, this young lady you've taken up with…"

Jack was trying to finish, but Grant interrupted before he could complete his sentence. "Jack, I have not taken up with her, I was merely giving her a ride to Cancun, and when we got here I offered to drive her to Akumal."

"Yes, and then spent the night together," Jack retorted. "And then you drove all over hell's creation dodging spooks, and now you're at my place where you're going to spend another night together. Am I missing something, or is that not correct? You know that puts me in an awkward situation. I'll have to tell Lynn, and then it will move immediately through both our families."

"Yeah, I guess that's right. But it sounds different than it is. Look Jack, I've got troubles enough without taking on extras. I am simply at a loss right now. Things seem to have moved way out of my control. If I ever had any control to begin with. Maybe I should call Pepe and see what's up at his end, and put this into some perspective," Grant trailed off, his mind already drifting.

With a shadow of reconciliation in his voice Jack said: "Listen buddy, I may have come across a little harsh, but man you're scaring me. I agree you should call Pepe, but you'd better go out there and find your lady friend first. It's going to be dark soon, and she must be wondering what the heck you're doing."

The two men quietly discussed choices and resources as they stepped off Zarahemla on to the dock. They walked up the ramp, and took the stone steps up to the back door of Casa Liahona. Jack walked through the house turning on lights, while they continued to talk. "Grant, go get her and bring her in through the front door, please. I'll get a bedroom ready for each of you. Then, let's go get some dinner and figure out what to do next."

Grant found Alex asleep in the car. She was still wearing a T-shirt over a bikini. When he brought her back to the house, he was more than a little self-conscious about the way she was dressed.

Jack may have been worried about his friend, but you couldn't tell it by the grace with which he welcomed Alex. He immediately made her feel at home. Within a few minutes, they were gabbing around the kitchen table like old friends. They whispered to one another in conspiratorial tones, and then laughed out loud about Grant's tendency to wax philosophical on any subject he deemed worthy of his attention. When Jack set out some sliced vegetables as snacks, and made a comment about eating smart, Alex and he discovered they had something else in common besides poking fun at Grant. They were both health-food nuts.

The conversation took an abrupt detour while Jack and Alex exchanged ideas on the value of a number of natural foods and remedies for virtually everything that ailed you. Realizing he was a third wheel to this two-wheeled carriage, Grant excused himself and stepped into the next room to call Jose Robles, his friend Pepe.

There was no answer at the Robles phone, and no answer to Pepe's back up private line located in his study. There was also no answer on his mobile phone, and Grant began to worry. Grant called Pepe's younger of two daughters, Josefina. Josie was married to a graduate engineer who had become a building contractor.

Josie had twice come to live in the Whitaker's home as a teenager. By the time. she was in high school, she was very smart, remarkably attractive, and graced with both poise, and confidence. By the time, she had graduated from high school she was earning a significant income as a model. Eventually, she made it to the cover of a top-rated woman's magazine in Mexico City. The Robles family, who were radical about higher education, put their foot down, and recanted on having supported her in a modeling career.

Off to university she went. Josie graduated from dental school near the top of her class, but only worked as a dentist for two years before getting married. After giving birth to their first child, she decided to stay home as a full-time mom. Her husband was doing quite well by then. A woman of her cultural background in

Mexico found it more socially upward to stay home with a full-time maid, cook, driver, and a grounds-keeper. By this time, she was twenty-five.

Grant called Josefina, rather than her older sister Guadalupe, for no particular reason. Both had been exchange students in his home. As he was dialing the number, he realized that Guadalupe's English was actually easier to understand, but he was committed, and let the phone ring ten times before hanging up. Strange, both homes had full-time maids that would normally have answered, even if no one else was home. He quickly followed up by dialing Guadalupe's home, and got voice mail. As is common in upper-middle class Mexico, she too, had three or four domestics. None of them were apparently available to take a call. Strange that…

Grant left J.P.'s phone number on voice mail and rang off. It would do no good to call the Robles boys; all three of them were outside of Mexico, one in Europe, two in the States. All three had received advanced degrees from U.S. universities, mathematics, engineering, and business, respectively. Grant had a mental argument with himself, ending up with don't jump to conclusions. *There is most likely a perfectly legitimate explanation for all this. The Robles are very close, and like our family, they are constantly involved in each other's lives. They're probably at a social event they are attending together. Perhaps they sent their domestics home while they were gone.* He wasn't convinced, but it was just too much to dwell on other possibilities.

Feeling only slightly better after the self-talk, he went back to the kitchen where Jack and Alex were knee-deep in a conversation about the value of iodine for the thyroid. Jack paused and looked up, showing some concern, "Grant, is everything alright? You don't look so good."

"Probably everything is okay. But, I couldn't raise Pepe, or either of his daughters, nor anyone, at any of their homes. It seems strange. Anyway, I struck out, and have no new information."

Alex chimed in, "I should call Lupe and find out how Mario is doing." Changing the subject mid-stream, she said, "My best bet is to catch one of the tour buses out to Chichen early in the morning from a Cancun hotel on the seven." The seven was a local term for English-speaking expats who'd permanently moved to the area. They used the expression to describe Cancun's upscale hotel strip. Cancun was actually an island right next to the mainland. On a map, it looked like a backwards seven, with bridges connecting it at both ends. Visitors to Cancun's finer hotels rarely even knew they were actually on an island.

"With Mario gone, Lupe will need help, she can't carry the place by herself," Alex continued.

"Excuse me, ah...who is Lupe?" asked Jack somewhat bewildered. Alex quickly filled him in. However, it was clear Jack was having trouble keeping the players straight. Having met and spent a good hour talking to Alex, he was reassured that Grant hadn't taken complete leave of his senses. He seemed content to drift along with the conversation.

"Your turn to make calls," Grant said to Alex. She agreed and retired to the next room.

"You didn't say she was a knock-out Grant," was the first thing out of Jack's mouth. "And don't tell me you didn't notice, because I'll call you a liar to your face."

"Okay, I agree she's easy to look at, but to be honest I didn't really notice how much so, until this morning when I saw her jogging down the beach. Actually, I didn't know it was her, and then..." Grant drifted off without finishing his sentence.

"Yeah, I can see that," came back Jack's mildly sarcastic reply. "Tell me. Are you in the habit of giving just anybody a lift in Mexico? Ever done it before?"

"You're killing me here, Jack. The way it happened seemed, well natural, and it wasn't like it was a big deal. I was headed to

Cancun anyway, and she was headed here to go shopping, and well, then things started to go weird on us, and here we are."

"Yes sir. Here you are!" Changing the subject abruptly, Jack asked, "What do you want to do for dinner?"

Alex returned to the kitchen ashen-faced. "Lupe closed the restaurant so she could visit Mario at the hospital in Merida. She'll be back in the morning. I called the hospital. They wouldn't let me talk to him. The police are there. I have no idea what that means. Why they are there? What's going on? Basically, I got nothing."

Jack cut in. "Look Grant, I think you better put-off your business in the islands. Fly this girl back to Merida, and figure out what's going on. I'd say you should get on this at first light, and not waste any more time debating things. Something is up. You're not going to know sitting around here talking about it."

That's one of the things Grant loved about Jack. He listened carefully, came to a conclusion and spoke his mind; simple and straightforward.

Grant looked over at Alex. She starred back at him for a moment, then said carefully, "Grant if it isn't too much trouble it would sure help us get to the bottom of this." Then, almost as an afterthought, she added, "and it would help me."

Grant was not the kind of guy that liked to change plans midstream. He had business to attend to in the islands, and it was going to cost him to delay. But sometimes you had to set things aside, and deal with the problems at hand. Besides, he was worried about the Robles family, and slightly concerned about his plane. It was agreed. They would leave together in the morning.

They decided to eat at a hotel close by rather than driving in to Cancun. After sharing more concerns, and back tracking their experiences for Jack to better understand, the conversation turned to other things. They all quite forgot about the strange activities of the day, and lost themselves in telling stories, and sharing pieces of wisdom gained from past errors. It was agreed all around that some of their most difficult and trying times came from just downright dumb choices. However, with age, some of their earlier bad choices seemed to provide the best story fodder. And sometimes, perhaps more than not, what seemed horrible at the time, turned out to be a benefit in disguise. On that note, they headed back to Casa Liahona.

Map 2

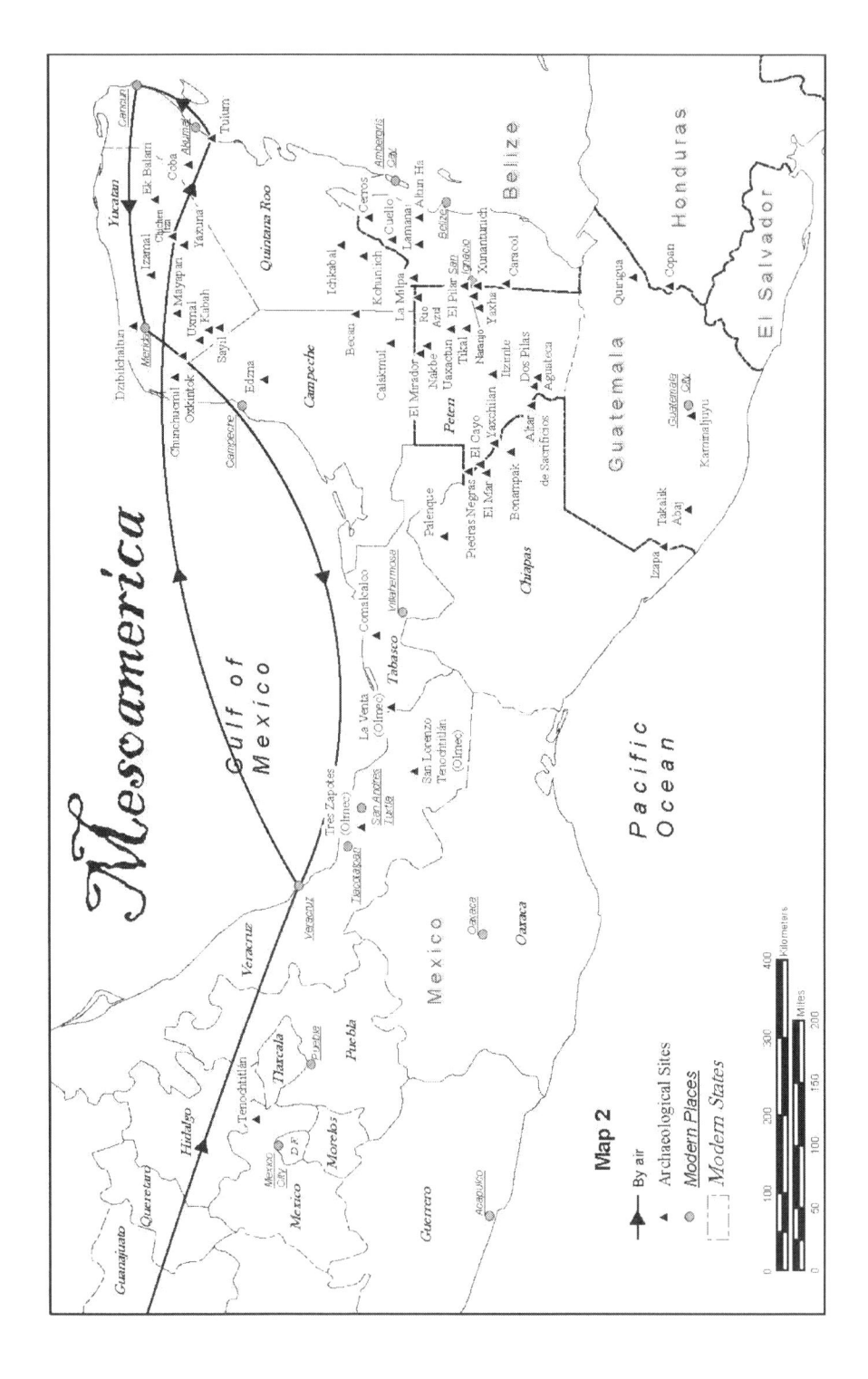

CHAPTER SEVENTEEN

Puerto Adventuras, Quintana Roo

Jack woke Grant early. It was well before dawn. During the night, Jack had come awake remembering that Grant told him he had left the phone number for Casa Liahona on either Josefina's or Guadalupe's voice mail. Alex may have done the same with Lupe. They visited quietly, and agreed it was better that they leave early, just in case the agente de policia was backtracking phone numbers.

Grant took a badly needed shower while Jack woke Alex and explained the situation. She had showered before bed, so she merely brushed her hair, pulled on shorts, a T-shirt, running shoes, and a ball cap. Grant wore jeans, a white button-down casual travel shirt, and Ecco walking shoes. Although it promised to be hot, he felt slightly insecure in shorts and sandals. He supposed that was because he was not sure what he might be confronting today.

Jack laid out fruit and some not-very-sweet pastries. He also had a bottle of multi-vitamins sitting conspicuously in the middle of the table, along with a couple of bottles of water that Grant and Alex were clearly intended to take with them. Alex graciously accepted an herbal tea, and casually took a seat on a high stool at the kitchen counter, rather than sitting down at the table where Jack and Grant sat. Both men self-consciously tried to avoid staring at her legs. Alex seemed not to notice. It was either that, or she was simply used to men's eyes lingering on her while she went about the most mundane tasks.

Not for the first time in the last few days, Grant considered what Marianna had been saying for years. Men were handicapped by their hormones. He glanced up towards the ceiling. He could almost see his deceased wife laughing at him.

In the early dawn, just as the sun was coming up over the Caribbean, they left. The traffic was light. The trip to the Cancun airport was less than thirty minutes. They were early, too early to depart. At the private FBO terminal the immigration officer was not due to arrive until 7:00. They had an hour to kill.

Seeing that Grant was holding the key to his aircraft, the guard at the departure door allowed them on the field. He did a quick scan of their bags and let them go. Quiet and nervous they found themselves constantly looking around for signs of danger. They went through a pre-flight check of the plane, so they could leave on a moment's notice. Returning to the FBO terminal, Grant filed a flight plan for Merida, naming Alex as the co-pilot. This kept her from having to pay a passenger departure tax. The base commandant maintained an office in the private terminal, so the paper chase was confined to within a single building. Grant settled up the outstanding fees, which included topping the tanks with fuel, tie-down fees for two nights, an aircraft departure tax, and an initial landing fee.

The grumpy immigration officer arrived, had them push a button on what looked like a four-foot tall traffic signal. It flashed green and they were free to go. The signal, now used throughout Mexico, was a random inspection device. The sign said, in English, that if it flashed red, your luggage was to be examined completely. It wouldn't have mattered; their luggage was already on the plane.

Clearing back through the gate to transient aircraft parking they walked the 150 meters to the plane, gave it a quick visual once again, tipped a uniformed attendant, who pulled the chocks from the wing wheels, got in the aircraft, and cranked the prop.

"Cancun clearance delivery, November 4876 Delta at FBO, VFR, GPS direct Merida."

A tired voice came back from the tower: "November 4876 Delta, cleared to Merida VFR, squawk 1203, right turn out approved at 1,500 feet, tower 119.8, five miles out contact departure on 125.6."

Grant read back the clearance receiving the "Read back correct," response, then dialed in ground control advising he had clearance, and was approved to taxi to runway 09. After run-up and systems checks, he called the tower.

"Cancun tower, November 4876 Delta, ready for take-off."

There was no arriving traffic at this hour, so with no delay they were cleared onto the active runway. All aircraft perform better in cool air so the take-off was clean and smooth. The tower turned them over to departure control just as they broke ground. They made a climbing right turn and flew back parallel to the runway. Cancun approach cleared them to their requested flight altitude of 6,500 feet. Thirty miles out they were dropped by flight-following, with the message: "November 4876 Delta, frequency change approved, have a nice day."

They were now on their own, moving direct for Merida. On the way, they flew over Chichen Itza. The airport was clearly visible from the air. Alex wanted to fly the plane until they began their descent into Merida. It only took her a few minutes to get the feel of the aircraft. She did a good job of holding heading, and maintaining altitude. It had been more than two years since she was functioning as a pilot. Grant mused that private flying was a lot like riding a bike. You never really forgot. It was more an art form than a science. At least that was true for light aircraft. The technical pilots never seemed to have the grace of someone who treated the plane like an extension of themselves. The best pilots seemed to "wear their plane."

The landing at Merida went smoothly. They taxied to parking, sped through the shutdown, quickly handled their arrival paperwork, and were flagging a cab within a few minutes of landing. Ten more minutes and they were at the single-story hospital where Pepe was recovering. Grant took a seat in the outdoor-indoor waiting room. The waiting area was covered on top, with one side open to the air, two solid walls, and a cinder block wall with open designs cut through for additional airflow.

Alex went to the front desk and spoke quietly with a woman that seemed to be in charge. She was dressed in traditional white starched nursing garb. The place smelled like a hospital, even in the outdoor waiting area. It reminded Grant of his wife when she was struggling with cancer. The smells triggered memories of sadness, melancholy, love, and affection.

Alex walked to where Grant was seated. She sat down beside him and whispered, "They'll let me see him, although it's not visiting hours. They are pretty picky about when one is allowed to visit a patient. I told her I was Mario's half-sister on our mother's side, and that I had flown in to see him, but must catch a plane back out by noon. I was told to wait, that someone would escort me."

The administrative nurse from the main desk returned to the waiting area with a shy young woman. The nurse directed the younger woman to Alex by simply pointing at her, then turned and walked away. Grant stood up with Alex, an act that seemed to intimidate the poor girl unnecessarily. Alex spoke softly to her in Spanish, she nodded her head. Alex put her hand inside the crook of Grant's arm and together they followed her through a single large door into a long hallway. One wall of the hall was constructed of the same concrete block used in the waiting room. It allowed airflow from the outside, and some light to pass through. The other side of the corridor was a solid wall with regularly spaced doors accessing wards. It reminded Grant of classrooms in an elementary school when he was a kid.

The hospital was much larger than it looked from the outside. It seemed to be an accumulation of freestanding one-story buildings with a single corridor connecting them. After three-turns around as many bungalow structures, they were issued into a ward with eight beds. Two walls were made of the porous concrete block. It permitted limited privacy. However, this type of construction provided natural air circulation through the heavily shaded buildings. Air conditioners were apparently an unaffordable luxury for a remote medical facility.

The smell of ether and antiseptic, and the slightly sweet odor of decayed flesh, hung heavy the air. The room was warm and dry, no jungle moisture here. Five beds stood empty.

A shadow of the man that had served Grant just three days earlier lay asleep. He wore a pale yellow and white vertically striped smock. Idly it occurred to Grant that the smocks were probably donated from somewhere in the States. They were not the kind of thing one would expect to see in Mexico. A moment later he realized he had never been in a Mexican hospital before, and the smocks could just as easily be the norm. Not for the first time, he reminded himself, that our unconscious judgment is shaded by our cultural lens. Our cultural lens generate prejudice. Conclusions based on what we like to think of as common sense, is essentially an assessment derived from reflection of events in the mirror of our experience. *Slow down. Don't be so quick to judge.*

Alex bit her lower lip in a futile attempt to keep from crying. Grant was at a loss of how to act. He didn't know this man. He felt sorry for him to be sure. But, Grant felt strangely off balance, and wasn't quite certain how to act. He looked at him with what he hoped was appropriate concern. It was a bit depressing to admit to himself that he was more interested in how Alex responded to his conduct, than he was concerned about Mario. The thought triggered feelings of guilt. *It's likely this guy is lying here because of me. And, I'm more concerned with how Alex will react? What does that say? Damn Grant, get a grip.*

Self-talk was characteristic of Grant. He tended to work out his thoughts through internal dialog. On occasion, when he had been caught thinking out loud, he would explain by saying something like, "How do I know what I'm thinking until I hear what I say?" Sometimes people would laugh, other times they just looked at him oddly. These self-analytical sessions frequently ended with a quiet prayer for personal improvement, and the integrity to do the right thing for the right reason.

Mario sensed their presence. His eyes fluttered open. He tried to focus on the two of them standing there. He starred at Grant, a dull expression on his face. After a few moments, his eyes shifted to Alex. Slowly a glimmer of recognition registered. He managed a weak smile as she picked up his hand and squeezed it tight. She was afraid to hug or kiss him, not knowing where he was hurt and what to expect. He murmured something inaudible.

Alex bent forward and leaned in with her face close to his. She kissed him ever so lightly on the forehead, trying to avoid an unbandaged gash with heavy black thread stitches. She whispered something in his ear. He smiled with greater strength and almost managed a laugh. A glass of water served to clear his throat, and before long he was able to speak, albeit with difficulty.

Much of Mario's slowed response must be due to heavy sedation, Grant thought. That's probably an indication he's had more damage than the obvious scar on his head.

Alex and Mario talked for a while. The entire conversation was in Spanish, leaving Grant catching a few words from time to time, but still not getting the gist of the discussion. Mario spoke his name. A short time later the young woman, who had escorted them in, returned and motioned to them that they must leave. Alex said her good-byes. Mario looked deep into Grant's eyes then nodded and gave him a weak smile. That was it. They turned and left.

Once outside, Alex said quietly but firmly, tension evident in her voice, "We must leave!" They walked out past the hospital parking area and down the street. They continued on past two intersecting unpaved cross roads. Grant could feel the anxiety locking up his neck and upper back muscles. He willed himself to relax.

"What did you find out?"

Alex took a deep breath and started in. "The local police were called in originally. He was brought to the hospital by some friends from Chichen. They found him lying in the parking lot behind the restaurant in a pool of blood. He had been beaten badly. It seems he is having some trouble remembering what happened. This much he knows: two guys jumped him when he closed the restaurant the night we were in Akumal. They kept insisting that he tell them what he knew about Grant Whitaker. He had never heard your name before. They would not accept his explanation. They beat him senseless, trying to get him to admit to something. Finally, he figured out that you must be the guy they were looking for, when the thugs said the waitress left with Whitaker in a plane."

Alex began to hyperventilate. They stopped walking. Alex stood still, trying to catch her breath and ease her anxiety. "Mario said he told them we did not really know one another. You had just offered me a lift to Cancun. He also told them I would be staying the night with his mother in Akumal. They knew that we had left together the night before. That didn't seem to wash with Mario's claim that we didn't know one another. He thinks he may have told them his mother's name. The rest is foggy. They left him lying in the parking lot. He had never seen them before."

"How is Mario doing?" Grant asked.

"The nurse said he was being kept for observation, in case of continued internal bleeding. He was passing blood in his urine, but apparently, that has stopped. It seems they kicked him in the kidneys. He has three broken ribs and the gash on his forehead. He should be okay."

Grant nodded, and uttered a prayer of thanks. Then speaking thoughtfully, almost to himself, "So, what have we learned? Are we any closer to knowing what these guys are about? Why are they asking about me? And, what part does Alex play in this tangled web?"

Alex blurted in frustration, "Grant are you asking me, or talking to yourself?"

He continued with an unfocused look. "Both I guess. I'm still confused, but it seems we can draw some conclusions. Whoever these guys are, they don't appear to have the resources we feared. It appears there are only two of them. They did not show up at the Cancun airport this morning, and we flew here without delay. No one intercepted us at the Merida airport, and no one apparently followed us to the hospital. And, finally, only the local police seem to be involved, and that's because of a beating and robbery, not because of you or me. Does this sound right to you?" he asked.

"I suppose so, except for the part about the police. They knew something about you. They asked Mario about you by name. They didn't say why. It was Mario's impression that you have something they are looking for."

"What!" Grant exclaimed. "I have something? What on earth could that be?" Then a thought forced its way to the surface. "You know Alex, when Pepe, that would be Jose Robles, came to see me at the Veracruz airport we discussed a number of things. He seemed frightened for his family, but he was in a reflective mood. He gave me what he called his "book." It's a journal, or perhaps a manuscript of sorts. It looks to be about 40 pages stapled together. He said it took him two years to write. I'd forgotten about it. I'm pretty sure it's in a pocket of my computer valise, back at the plane."

Waving to a passing taxi, Alex said, "What's it about, Grant?" The taxi went on by without stopping. They continued to walk along the road somewhat aimlessly.

"Well, I'm not sure. He wanted me to give it to one of my boys so they could translate it for me. He told me it was about his relationship with God. You remember I told you the other night that he was a dedicated Catholic?" Well, about three years ago, Pepe took quite ill. He was told he only had a few months to live. Subsequently, he had a triple by-pass, and recovered beyond all reasonable hope. Thereafter, he became quite contemplative. He wondered why he had lived, and returned to full health, when others of his condition died. In the end, he decided it was his responsibility to write of his struggle with developing a personal testimony of God. From what I gathered, the pages reveal his story with spiritual challenges. Or, perhaps it is about his religious upbringing, or the conclusions he has drawn about God, or something along those lines. It was clearly important to him, but essentially unreadable to me. I just put it away and forgot about it."

Missing the second drive-by taxi, they wandered into a typical old-style, Mexican market square. A large Cathedral faced on to a plaza. A government building faced the cathedral from the opposite side of the park. Shops and outdoor restaurants cluttered the other two sides of the square. A fountain bubbled in the center of the plaza, surrounded by flowers, plants, and trees. The borders of the square were cluttered with vendors offering their wares to everyone walking by.

They had stepped back in time. Little girls with ribbons in their hair, and boys all cleaned up, were walking hand and hand with their mothers. Restaurateurs waved white starched linens to attract customers. It was right out of a movie set. Alex and Grant joined the walk-about for a while before sitting down at a shaded table that faced onto the square.

"This isn't making sense, Grant. Why would anyone consider Pepe Robles' personal journal something worthy of interest? I don't mean to be rude, but really, why would thugs, and the police, want with a personal record of Jose Robles' religious experience?"

"I don't have any idea. It's just that I cannot fathom what is really going on here. I suppose I'm grasping at straws. When we get back to the plane, take a look at it," Grant said carefully.

Alex forced an issue in the back of both of their minds, out into the open. "Where do we go from here? Will you just turn around and fly to St. Kitts and forget the whole incident, or is there more going on we should look into?"

Her use of the "we" word, as though they were a couple, was both unsettling and satisfying. Grant was stuck. He simply did not know what to do. Lost in thought he starred into the plaza, seeing very little. "I think we should organize ourselves. Let's make sure we're not missing something. Let's make a list of things that need doing." Materializing a pen from his pants pocket, he asked Alex to ask the waiter for paper.

"Let's get writing. What do we need to do first?"

Alex jumped in, "I'm not sure what's first, but I think you ought to show me that manuscript of Jose Robles. You need to follow up with him and see if there is anyone home yet. Call Jack, or should I say, "J.P." and check in. And something tells me you forgot to call your staff in the islands to reorganize your schedules. How often do you check in with your kids? Do you need to contact some of them? What am I missing? Oh yes, and another thing," she stalled. "We'll get to that later."

"You forgot any action items on your part. I think you need to check in with Lupe, and determine how to proceed with the restaurant. You should probably let Loreto know you're okay. And, there's something else bothering me Alex. If the police have your name, and they decide to run it against a U.S. database, you could be exposed. Did you ever apply for an FM-3?"

"I have an FM-2," Alex said matter-of-factly, "I can work here legally. I get it renewed each year, but no one seems to be paying much attention. The FM-3 allows you residency, but does not allow you to work for anyone other than yourself. You know, Immigration no longer uses the FM nomenclature, now its Temporary Residency, or Permanent Residency, with either the right to work, or not. Getting the right to work is now a big issue."

"Yeah, I guess I had heard that, but our residency begs another question. In that both of us have official status in Mexico, and considering both of us are apparently in trouble with U.S. federal agencies, why is it so darn hard for them to find us? Assuming they really want us?"

Wrinkling her brow, as if giving the subject serious thought, Alex responded, "The only thing I can think of is that my FM-2 application was cleared before Antonio was arrested. The annual renewal of residency is pretty much automatic. Immigration only runs a police report for problems inside of Mexico, and then only in the state of your residence."

"Makes sense," Grant replied. "Listen, I need to handle some email. The stuff is piling up on my phone. Maybe, it wouldn't be wise to use my own computer through a local Wi-Fi connection."

They moved off to track down an Internet cafe. Some still existed in Mexico. As he feared, his mailbox was overloaded. It took ninety minutes for him to clear his email and send needed communications, including updates to his grown children. He committed to his West Indies office that he would check back within 24 hours on several items. A call and update to Jack was next. Jack answered on the first ring. He was very interested in Grant's report regarding Mario. Things were quiet at Casa Liahona.

Alex reached Lupe, and told her they were in Merida; that they had seen Mario, and he was improving. This helped. Although Lupe had seen him the day before, she was still worried sick. Lupe had made arrangements with two local girls to step in and help out while Mario and Alex were gone. The restaurant would be reopening that evening. Lupe had spoken with Loreto and told her there was an incident involving Mario, but pitched it as a common robbery, and left it at that. She didn't want her mother worrying about everyone at the same time.

They caught a taxi and headed to the airport. Grant did not feel comfortable calling Jose Robles from a cell phone from within the taxi, so he waited until after getting to the airport. They rode in silence, each wondering what their next move should be. Breaking the quiet, Grant said, "Look Alex, considering this mess seems to be about me, and not you, maybe the best thing is for us to fly back to Chichen, and let you resume your life before running into me." The moment was pregnant with tension. He had said the right thing. Even though he knew something else was developing between them. Grant had said the logical thing, but had phrased it such that there was really no way for Alex to respond other than, "Yes, I suppose you're right."

As they got to the airport, Alex suggested she review Pepe's journal before making plans to fly to Chichen. This would give Grant an opportunity to call the Robles. They were cleared on to the field, retrieved the manuscript and returned to the terminal. Finding a small open-air restaurant directly across the street, they ordered drinks. Grant munched idly on chips and salsa Mexicana, the ubiquitous Pico de Gallo, staring out into space. Something was dead wrong. He knew it. But, he couldn't quite get the sense of it. Alex immersed herself in Pepe's journal. A few minutes later Grant placed a call to Veracruz.

Marilia answered on the fourth ring. She was one of two maids in the Robles home. She was also the impromptu nanny when grandchildren were over to visit. Marilia recognized Grant's voice, but they were not able to communicate effectively. He handed the phone to Alex.

Alex was animated. Even though she was on the phone she made exaggerated expressions, and used her free hand to make explanatory gestures. She rung off, and reported to Grant that Senor Robles was in Mexico City on business. He was also visiting family. Grant reflected on this information for a few moments and decided it was reasonable. But something still didn't seem quite right. Alex returned to the manuscript. Grant tried to quiet the internal voice that seemed to be warning him. Something was there, just below his conscious. He tried mediation techniques he'd learned from a Qigong Master.

A deep-pitched twin-engine aircraft flew the downwind leg of a left-hand landing pattern, engines slightly out of sync. Grant looked up and idly watched the red plane bank for the crosswind leg before turning final. Curious, he thought, it looks like that same red Cessna 320 he'd seen taxi up in Chichen through the restaurant window, just after he arrived from Veracruz.

He stood up and walked about thirty steps away from where they were seated. He tried to get a better view of the plane as it turned on final approach. Surely it was the same plane. It was too far away to read the V number, indicating it was a Mexican registered aircraft. All U.S. aircraft began with the letter N, pronounced November phonetically over the radio. When traveling outside the U.S. it was important to begin radio communication with the word November, so the controllers knew it was a U.S. registered aircraft. When flying within the states, the November protocol was rarely used.

Grant looked back at Alex who was engrossed with her reading. She didn't seem to notice he'd left. Thinking back about his experience on the first night in Chichen, he remembered the guy that had been watching him. It was one of the men he thought he had seen in Akumal two days later. Perhaps he was the pilot of the Cessna 320. It would be strange indeed for there to be two C-320's in the local area, especially both of them red. The Cessna 320 was a limited model upgrade of the immensely popular Cessna 310 light twin of many years prior. The 320 was stretched to provide for six passengers. The engines were turbo-charged to give better efficiency at higher altitudes, and deliver enhanced overall performance. There were still a lot of 310's around, but darn few 320's. It had to be the same plane.

So what, Grant? The Chichen Itza airport and the Merida airport are not 30 minutes away from each other by air. It stands to reason that this airplane would be circulating the area. Still...

Walking back to Alex he asked, "Do you remember the red twin that landed at Chichen Itza the other day?" She was so deeply engrossed in reading she gave a little jump when he first began to talk.

"Uh...what?" Alex managed.

He tried again: "The day I met you. A red Cessna 320, a turbo-charged stretch 310, taxied up and tied down about 50 meters away from the restaurant. Do you recall?"

She thought for a moment, and then said, "Sure, I think we saw it at the same time. Must not be from around here, I've never seen it before."

"Well, for whatever its worth, I'm pretty sure it just landed. I was wondering if the guy I saw watching me that night in the restaurant was its pilot. That might explain why the men who beat-up Mario were sure you and I had gone somewhere together. I was slightly captivated by you, and from a distance it probably looked like we were flirting. When we left through the back door together...well you can see why a third-party unfamiliar with the turf might come to the conclusion we were a couple." He trailed off, slightly embarrassed.

Alex sat up a little straighter, angled her head slightly down with her eyes cast upwards and her eyebrows arched, and said: "slightly captivated?"

"I suppose it must have looked like that," he responded weakly.

After a pause, with eyes twinkling she said: "Is that all you can say Capitan?"

Her playfulness had caught him off guard. He blinked, and gave her a lecherous grin. "Well, maybe more than slightly." His mood swung to somber. "Alex, I think we need to see who's flying that bird, and determine if there are passengers aboard. And I don't think we want to be seen doing it."

Dropping money on the table, they headed across the street into the terminal building. Walking to the extreme end of the small facility, they stopped at a large window facing on to the field where they had a clear view of the red twin just then parking on the transient ramp. Three men got out of the plane, one looked vaguely familiar. At this distance, he couldn't be sure.

The two passengers moved immediately towards the terminal, the other, presumably the pilot, walked towards Grant's 182 turbo. The pilot paused, looked around the field slowly, and then walked up to the passenger rear window. He looked in. Grant was not going to take his eyes off that pilot until he was sure he didn't do something to his aircraft. The other two men, both large of stature, and too tall to be locals, were by then almost to the terminal. Both men had dark blue baseball caps pulled down tightly on their heads. Their eyes downcast, they seemed to be focused about twenty feet ahead of them. They walked with a certain serious determination. There was no way he'd know if he recognized one of them until they looked up. Alex whispered with an edge of desperation obvious, "What are we going to do?"

CHAPTER EIGHTEEN

Merida, Yucatan

Looking around for somewhere to appear inconspicuous, Grant whispered, "I don't know, but I've got to keep my eye on that pilot until he leaves my plane."

Alex whispered back, "I'm headed to the lady's room. It's right behind you. I'll wait five minutes then step out long enough to make sure you're okay. You signal me when it's clear." She spun around and entered the women's room just seconds before the two men reached the door to the terminal. The door was about forty feet to his right. Pulling his Xel-ha cap low over his face, and turning slightly away from where they were entering, he felt like a blinking light. There were few Norte Americanos in the terminal, and he was sure he stood out like a sore thumb.

Remembering he was to signal Alex in five minutes, he glanced at his watch, hoping he looked like a passenger waiting for a plane. The pilot left off looking into Grant's plane, turned around and headed to the commandant's office at the base of the tower. Nervous, and desperately wanting to turn and see where the two men were, Grant held his ground with his back in the direction of where he assumed they would be waiting for their pilot. He checked his watch again…surely it had been five minutes. He glanced over his shoulder in casual fashion. They weren't there. Perhaps they'd taken a seat, or stepped outside the terminal. His mind raced. He was afraid to turn around and search for them for fear they were seated and watching any gringos in the terminal.

Five minutes were up. It was time to check out the Ladies room, but that would make his face clearly visible from the seating area. Instead he turned his body further to the left while lifting his left hand up to adjust his hat. This way he could cover the side of his face with the crook of his arm. He glanced at the Ladies room door. Alex was standing three feet inside with the door held open waiting for his signal. He moved his head slightly back and forth as he adjusted his hat, and turned back around the same way to look back out the window.

Several more minutes he stood there frozen. Grant hated to stand on concrete surfaces for very long. It seemed to exacerbate the problems with his knees. He wanted to sit down or get moving, or turn around and determine where those men had gone…anything but just stand there.

The pilot came back into view. He was headed toward the field access door. Grant held his position and waited until the pilot was just coming through the door before he chanced a glance over his right shoulder once more. No one greeted him. He walked right through the small waiting area of the terminal and out the front door. Grant signaled Alex the all clear.

They crossed the room slowly looking at the hundred or so people packed into the waiting area. Grant ventured around the corner to the glass door facing onto the roadway. Looking out, he spotted the pilot just then taking a seat at the outdoor restaurant directly across the street. He was at the very same table Alex and he had been sitting at just minutes before. Alex approached cautiously and looked around. "Where did they go?" she whispered.

"The pilot is that guy across the street at the table we were sitting at earlier. I don't know where the other men went. If I were going to guess, I'd say they grabbed a taxi, or met someone out front. They probably intend to be back soon. The pilot appears to be waiting."

"Lots of speculation, no real information," she mumbled. "What was the pilot doing at your plane?"

"He was looking in the cockpit. It's not all that unusual. Lots of pilots will stop and checkout the avionics package in a new plane. It's entirely possible this whole little scenario was completely innocent," Grant replied unconvincingly.

"Well then, we could always go join him at the table for lunch, and talk pilot stuff," she growled back flippantly.

With a small laugh, "Guess we could, he probably wouldn't know us even if the other guys are tracking us. My guess is he's a charter pilot hauling those two muscle-bound guys around." After a slight pause, he added, "Alex, why not call the hospital and tell them no one is to see Mario…that you fear the men who beat up on him are headed there now."

"Good idea," she said sharply. She stepped away to a quieter area. He could see her with one hand over her uncovered ear. Alex returned a couple minutes later. "Done."

"Let's go to the commandant's office and file a flight plan," Grant said.

"A flight plan to where?" she countered.

"Oh…probably Chichen Itza, it's the logical place." He turned and headed towards the door.

She caught up with him just as the security guard at the door to the tarmac decided to check Grant's pilot's license before letting him on the field. She rattled off some Spanish and the guard opened the door without comment.

"You're pretty good at getting people to do stuff," Grant observed.

She smiled brightly. "Yep, that's why you need me along."

Just before entering the commandant's office, Grant said, "Find out where that aircraft came from, who the pilot is, and anything else you can finagle."

"Si, si, Capitan," she smirked, giving her silly mock salute.

There were two men, and one woman working in the office. Alex caught one of the men's eyes. He gave her an appraising look and sauntered up to the counter with his chest expanded in typical machismo style. He addressed her in Spanish. She immediately responded. As Grant turned to fill out a flight plan form, it was clear she was doing just fine. The flight plan process took only a few minutes and he was back out the door walking to the plane. A few minutes into his pre-flight, Alex came strutting up with a pleased look on her face.

"First officer reporting in," she said, with yet another of her nutty salutes. "The pilot's name is Adrian Oliveros. His home address is in Veracruz. He is a charter pilot. They just flew in from Cancun. The passengers are Armando Vargas, and Roberto Soria. They do not expect to spend the night."

"I am not going to ask how you got all that…, it is pretty impressive though," he acknowledged. "If that plane is from Veracruz, and just came in from Cancun…and was obviously in Chichen Itza the other day, it narrows the possibility of this being a coincidence. Your thoughts?"

"I agree completely," she replied. "I suggest we go to Veracruz, and check-in on the Robles family. However, I think you should take-off for Chichen, and then change the flight plan in the air with Center, rather than the local tower."

Smart girl. Makes sense all the way around. I'm not going to get to the bottom of this without seeing Pepe. She's including herself in the process, even though this isn't really about her. Her looks, attitude, and language skills, are obviously valuable, and she's a delight to be around.

"Cat got your tongue," she said brightly. "I'm user friendly. You know you need me. And, once we're in the air, I get to fly the plane. I'm having so much fun, even though you're a bit stuffy."

Grant turned and looked straight into her large brown eyes. He was searching for something, not sure what it was. He grinned, "Okay, let's getting going."

Alex held the co-pilot's flight control lightly, following through as Grant took-off and handled the radio work. Speaking through the headsets, she said, "I've got the stick. Now, don't go getting picky with me, it's been a while." Climbing out was different from the straight and level heading she had been holding on the way to Merida from Cancun. She wrestled with the flight control for a while, until Grant pointed at the electric trim tab. She nodded and immediately brought the aircraft under control.

"Keep the manifold pressure, RPM, and fuel at the top of the green on climb-out. Reduce manifold pressure to 25 inches for cruise; bring the RPM back to 2400, and fuel flow to 12 gallons per hour. Once you're straight and level tinker with the fuel flow, keeping your eye over here on the TIT," he said.

Looking slyly at him for a moment, while trying to maintain tight control of the aircraft, she said easily, "Did you say what I thought you said? You know, in the U.S. that comment could get you a sexual harassment suit."

"Oh yeah, the TIT gauge," he said, while pointing at a display instrument to the left of the pilot's yoke. It was hard for the co-pilot to see without leaning right into the pilot's lap. She leaned in, as he continued, "See there, it says TIT right on it. It stands for turbine intake temperature. It's like an EGT, exhaust gas temperature gauge, on a normally aspirated aircraft. You dial back the fuel mixture at cruise until the engine starts to get rough then increase fuel flow ¼ turn. Don't let it red line."

"Give me some space to fly. You handle the communications and navigation equipment," she instructed. "Who will you call to amend the flight plan? When these guys come back, and see the plane missing, they'll pull something like I did, and immediately learn where we're headed," Alex said carefully. "And, when they do, they'll discover I was asking after the pilot. I told the flight plan guy that I thought the 320 pilot was someone I used to date. If that gets back to him, they're sure to know we're on to them."

"Got it," Grant said as he scrambled through his paper charts looking for the frequency for the controlling flight center in the area. "Turn to a heading of one-nine-five and hold your altitude until I figure this out," he said.

On the GPS screen, they could clearly see their location as the colored flight map passed underneath the figure of a little plane in the center of the monitor. The triangular tip of a red-colored no flight zone, was straight ahead…a military operations area. "Come about to a heading of two-six-zero," he said.

"You sound like you're afloat Capitan," she mused.

Venturing a small laugh, he responded, "Lots of hours in both environments. Sometimes I get my terminology a little mixed up."

She did a solid job of bringing the aircraft around to a heading of almost due west, while holding altitude. Grant called Cancun Center, but could not raise them. "We're too low. Alright take her up to 12,500 feet and stand by. To accommodate the climb, screw the nose trim to the right about three turns so you're not fighting the prop torque … then adjust as needed. The nose trim works similar to the elevator trim, but it's designed to take turning pressure off the wheel. Okay…now, increase fuel first, then RPM, then Manifold pressure all three to tops of the green for climb. Climb out at 500 fpm."

Grant continued to fiddle with frequency settings looking for someone to talk with that was not located at the Merida airport. As they gained altitude, and radio reach, he picked up Campeche airport approach and asked what frequency they could use to modify a flight plan in the air. Campeche approach gave him frequency information with the caveat that if he could not reach Center he should return to their frequency. They would handle flight plan changes, and forward them via land line to Center. A few minutes later, Grant amended his flight plan with the Campeche tower. "That ought to keep those guys on the wrong track for a while," he said. Twenty minutes after take-off they could see the Gulf of Mexico coming up straight ahead. There was a long green-blue strip of water as far as the eye could see looking north and south.

They crossed the shoreline, level at 12.5 thousand, holding a GPS direct course for Veracruz. Technically it was illegal for a single-engine aircraft in Mexico to be more than 25 miles over water. No such rule existed in the U.S. or Canada, as single-engine planes tended to be safer than twins. At least that's what the aircraft incident statistics reflect. However, in Mexico, where aircraft may not be maintained like those of their northern neighbors, it was their aviation administration's wisdom that single engine aircraft should not be allowed to fly over the gulf. In the several years Grant had been flying Mexico in a small plane; only one Mexican flight briefer had given him static for filing to fly over water. Mostly, no one cared.

Alex looked happy. There is a certain pleasure that goes with flying private aircraft that is not easy to explain. A twenty-knot push was scooting them right along, making for an easy flight. Personally, Grant considered himself a lazy pilot. There was no way he would be flying right now. Auto does a better job, and allows the pilot to read, eat and, fool around without micro-managing the flight control. Whereas he made fun of himself for being lazy, Grant was actually a good pilot. He had poked holes in the sky for 30 years, and been in and out of strips that hardly qualified for landing model airplanes, much less real ones. His experience was varied and broad. It held him in good stead with pilots whose living was made flying.

Grant had both brass and brains. And that was trumped by years of solid experience. Alex on the other hand, was not used to flying with an auto-pilot, and its GPS interface. Although once you got the hang of it, they were much simpler to operate than the VOR stuff she had learned on. Alex was adaptable however, and a quick study. It was obvious from the start that she had once been a competent pilot.

"How long do you think it will be before those guys get back to the airport, and buzz over to Chichen looking for us?" Alex asked. She continued on without expecting an immediate answer. "They should be gone less than an hour to the hospital, assuming that's where they were headed. When they return, and discover the plane is gone, they'll probably fly to Chichen Itza. That gives us about a 2.5 to 3 hours jump on them. It could be more, if they aren't able to figure out where we went right away."

"That sounds about right," Grant replied. "If we're lucky, and they don't have any serious connections with air traffic control, they may not figure out where we've gone anyway. Campeche may be slow in forwarding information. They may not forward it at all. That would be ideal. On the other hand, if they do have solid connections, their aircraft is about 40 knots faster than ours. They could be right on top of us by the end of this flight."

Long before Europeans arrived in Mexico, at the landing site that eventually became the port city of Veracruz, the area was occupied by the Olmecas. These were the common cultural forebears of many Mesoamerican ethnic groups. The Olmecs were the oldest known high cultures in the Americas. The Huastecs and the Totonacs Indians still live in the area, and are famous for their cultivation of vanilla and other culinary specialties. These last were the first allies of Hernando Cortez during the period known as the Conquest. They provided tens of thousands of warriors to join the march on Tenochtitlan, the Aztec Capital. They marched right alongside the Spaniards. To Grant, Veracruz always seemed somehow exotic. It stretched along the Gulf Coast like the graceful tentacle of a sea creature.

The landing at Veracruz was uneventful. The entire trip was just under three hours. They decided Alex should rent the car, in case they were following Grant's credit cards. It occurred to them that Grant had used the same card at the hotel in Chichen, and at the Rotunda restaurant at Akumal. These guys, whoever they were, might be zeroing in on them through his card purchases. It was incredibly easy to track someone through use of a credit card, assuming you had access to the clearing system.

During the flight, Grant shared the story of two year's prior, when he flew from St. Kitts to Grenada on a Friday night, for a brief one-hour meeting hastily scheduled for Saturday morning. Virtually no one knew he had flown there. He had made the decision at the last minute. He had just arrived when the phone rang in his hotel room at the Rex Grenadian. It was Erik Johansson from Sweden. He had just arrived in St Lucia, an island located between St. Kitts and Grenada. Erik wanted to know if Grant would fly to St. Lucia the next day, and drop in and see him. Erik was the president of the issuing bank for Grant's credit card. He had simply checked the last charge on the card, which had been registered within the hour at the Rex in Grenada. Grant never forgot it. It was downright spooky. Later, when he told the story to his financial controller, she told him that she always knew where he was by simply calling up his credit card charges on the Internet. Apparently, she did this all the time, thus keeping constant track of his whereabouts. Surprise!

Alex drove. The traffic was bad and road construction pervasive, so the route into town required flexibility. The Robles lived just two blocks off the beach highway on Xicontencatl, and only ten blocks from the harbor. The beach highway was a well-designed six lane affair. It had green belts, benches, gazebos and vendor areas. All were laid out between the road and the steps that lead down to the beach. It was landscaped for several miles right along the waterfront.

The Robles home was one of several extended family houses along the same block of highly coveted real estate. Their homes and courtyards were separated by large stucco walls. From the front, it was nondescript. A white-washed stucco wall, ten feet high ran the length of the property along the street. A large gate, the width of a three-car garage door, stood closed. A door in the stucco wall just next to the large gate was also closed. Alex pulled the car to the curb in front of the house, they got out together. Grant rang the gate bell. The buzzer was a standard doorbell, but the door would open onto the front courtyard and driveway. There was no answer. He rang again, no answer.

Grant reoriented his face to one of the cameras. A few moments later, a woman addressed them through the speaker at the gateway door. The upstairs maid recognized Senor Whitaker from his visits, but she did not speak English. Alex immediately began to speak for him. The dialogue continued, but they were not buzzed in.

Grant turned to Alex and asked her to tell the maid that it was very important they be admitted to the house. They must speak with her in private. The gate lock buzzed. Alex and Grant stepped through into the outer courtyard, closing the door carefully behind them.

The driveway and outer courtyard were tiled in a soft red brick color. Trees and plants had been carefully manicured inside tiled planters. A fountain splashed to one side of the front door. Grant opened the door and walked in. Directly inside on the left, was a large semi-circular marble stairway running up to the second floor. To the right, across a modest entry area, was a spacious great room that contained beautifully appointed chairs and couches. All were done in rich silk fabrics. Dark, intricately carved wooden tables, held heavy silver, and cut crystal service. Persian carpets covered much of the polished marble floors. A hallway led forward around the stairway to a dining area that faced opposite an aviary that reached about 30 feet high. At least a hundred small colorful birds fluttered and sang directly across from the dining room table.

Grant walked straight back to the table. He took a seat, waiting for either the cook, or one of the maids to wait on him. Alex stood for a moment seeming uncomfortable, until Grant indicated she should sit. No one immediately arrived, so Grant suggested Alex stay where she was. He walked through to the kitchen, got himself a soda and poured Alex water from the purified water bottle mounted on the kitchen wall. When he returned, the younger of the two maids, a petite dark-skinned girl, whose features suggested she was almost certainly of pure Indian bloodline, bowed towards them, looking perfectly miserable. She asked what they would like to eat. Alex looked surprised. She asked Grant how to respond.

"Tell her we'll have whatever is easy for her to prepare. And, tell her we will be eating on the patio, and would she please join us."

Alex explained Senor Whitaker's wishes. The girl had a stricken look; she starred at the ground in complete deference. Alex advised Grant that the young girl had said it would not be permitted for her to sit at table with them. Grant immediately realized his mistake, even before Alex was able to translate. He quickly asked Alex to tell her to go ahead with the food and return for a discussion later.

"What was that all about?" Alex asked.

"The Robles are wonderful people. They are very good to their staff, but they draw a clear line between staff and family. That line is never to be crossed. I stepped into a cultural quagmire many years ago, because I asked Anna Gonzales, the family cook, to join me at the dining room table. Anna had been with the family for over thirty years. She was treated very well. I thought of her as an extension of the Robles family," Grant explained.

Alex followed Grant out to a large round table located under a covered patio that faced onto a pool. Large stucco walls stained a dark dusty rose, provided privacy from the neighbors on either side, both of which were families related to the Robles. The rear wall was fronted by a gardener's shed, pool house, and an outdoor changing facility. All around were trestles with red and purple bougainvillea in full bloom.

Seated at pool front, Grant continued. "Two summers in a row, I stayed in the house for three to four weeks. That's when I was working at my "unofficial" dig at Cerro Vigia. Anna Gonzales took great delight in preparing me special dishes when I would come to visit. My approach was to show appreciation to her by complimenting her with extreme gestures. You know, putting my hands together like I was praying, and nodding acknowledgement, patting my heart with both hands, smiling a lot, rubbing my stomach. That kinda stuff. Anna was thrilled. So, one day I asked her to sit at the table and visit with me using one of the kids whose dual language skills were quite good. It was the one, and only time, Pepe and Gualu got upset with me. At least, it was the only time, of which I'm aware.

The Robles told me right away that what I had done was not acceptable. It was not my place to extend this privilege to hired help. I was surprised. But, quickly realized I was viewing the situation through my own cultural eyes. I immediately acquiesced to their household rules. At the time, it seemed inconsistent with their real love for her. They maintained a staff of two maids, a cook, groundskeeper, and a driver, as did their relatives along the block. Evidently, the crossing of familial lines was strictly forbidden in all these households. I suppose the implications were much greater than I could understand, but it still seemed strange. In my world, you put people at ease by dining with them. Here, that is not to be done with working staff."

"I learned something rather significant from this experience," Grant continued. After rethinking my initial reactions, and considering my personal predispositions, which I suppose, are really my personal prejudices, I wrote a note to myself that went something like this:

> Am I able to consider new possibilities to my already entrenched beliefs? Can I allow myself to explore something that may threaten my religious, political, or cultural predispositions? Am I able to assume a position of mental neutrality? Without knowing it, my "belief-filters" reduce expansiveness. I need to suspend unneeded judgments. I resolve to let things be."

Alex was looking at him strangely. With her head turned slightly askew, as if she was seeing something for the first time, she said simply, "You're a philosopher."

The late afternoon sun would soon be down. For now, the air was warm and pleasant. The setting was peaceful, and the pool inviting. "Nice pool," Alex offered, letting her voice trail off as if she were suggesting something.

"Go ahead. There is a changing room right behind the pool," he said pointing in that direction.

"You really think it would be okay?" she said hopefully.

"Of course. Swim and cool down. Dinner will be here when you're done."

"Join me," she said with an upward lilt to her voice, making it more a question than a statement."

"I'd rather think for the moment. And watch you," he added.

Alex went back through the house and out to the car. She got her travel bag and returned. She used the bathroom off the dining room to change. A few minutes later she walked boldly from the house in the bikini she had been wearing on her beach run at Akumal. Without any hesitation, she walked the twenty feet past Grant, and dove in the pool. Surprised to see her back so quickly, and already in her swimsuit, he did not even have the presence of mind to say something. Alex surfaced and swam to the end of the pool. She performed the underwater turn of a competition swimmer, and swam gracefully back to where she had begun. Standing up in waist high water, she smoothed her hair back, smiling broadly. Alex seemed to radiate a childlike happiness with her immediate lot in life.

Grant sat there reflecting on what seemed to be happening. It was not easy to find a quiet space in his heart. He was under assault from so many directions. Apparently Alex was in a similar situation, yet here she was, relishing the moment, beaming an almost naive innocence. *I need to rethink my happiness paradigm,* he thought.

Happiness is an unfolding process. It is not a destination. We either decide to live in a happy space, or we do not. That place is in our heart, mind, and soul. Happiness is an inside job. There is very little external to it.

Emerging from the kitchen, Marilia carried freshly cut fruits to the table. She brought a flower vase with multiple sprigs of color. Seeing Alex in the pool, she set the serving platter down and hurried off. Towels, and a terry-cloth robe, were shortly draped on a chair near the pool.

Alex stood dripping at pool's edge. With her head cocked to one side she tried to clear water from an ear. *She's beautiful,* he thought. *She's fresh, lovely, and desirable. If I were a younger man, or my life was not turned so upside down...* Reluctantly he changed the direction his mind was headed.

Donning the terry-cloth robe, she walked to the table's edge where she picked up a piece of melon, and drew it slowly into her mouth. She flashed him a bright smile and said, "You simply do not know what you're missing. That was wonderful."

Perhaps I have forgotten how to enjoy myself. The pleasure she seems to have with simple things is something I must relearn.

She sat down at an angle in front of him, propping the heels of her feet on the edge of his chair. "Okay, mister business guy. What's next?" she said with a playful grin.

Struggling not to stare, he offered: "You are a very attractive woman Alex. Maybe distractive is a better term." She blinked her eyes innocently, pulled the robe together, and tied it around her waist. She stared straight at him. Her eyes widened indicating her question was still hanging there.

"As soon as the maid returns we'll ask her some pointed questions," Grant offered. "See if you can get her to at least sit down." A platter of gordos and picaditas were on their way to the table, along with table settings, and drinks.

They sat quietly as the young Indian girl served them. She seemed overly self-conscious, and was extra careful in her conduct. Alex asked Grant about her, but the only things he remembered were that she lived upstairs adjacent to the laundry area, that she had been with the Robles for only a few years, and that she was playful with the Robles grandchildren when they were visiting.

Alex seemed puzzled by the dish. She recognized the ingredients, but had never seen it served this way. Noting her look Grant commented, "This is a typical dish from Veracruz. I've not seen it anywhere else in Mexico. When I've asked for it in other places, people give me a blank look."

The dish consisted of a corn tortilla split on the side and stuffed with a black bean paste, then deep fried. It was accompanied by a flour tortilla stuffed with powered white cheese, also deep fried. A sauce of onions, sweet peppers, local herbs and mild spices, were served on the side. The stuffed tortillas were stacked alternatively on a plate like pancakes, and then the sauce was poured over the top like syrup. "It does not contain any of the hot peppers we associate with the Indian-Mexican food we call TexMex, in the States," Grant offered. "The Robles don't eat spicy food. They are much more European by nature. Pepe is actually Castilian Spanish. Many sophisticated Mexicans seem to relate hot pepper dishes with Indian culture and border towns." As an afterthought, he added, "I think you'll be pleasantly surprised."

The plan to ask questions of the young maid was abandoned in favor of the food. Noises of delight and smiles of appreciation produced the first shy grin from Marilia. She stood quietly by, doing her very best to anticipate their needs. Several times, she returned to the kitchen to bring other tidbits, including chips and pecante for Senor Whitaker who it was known to be eccentric about such things.

Around a mouthful of food, Grant asked Alex to find out where Anna was today. As Alex asked the question he could see Marilia's uneasy response. Alex looked at Grant strangely and then said, "She died two months ago."

"What!" he exploded. "That's not possible. I was just here and Pepe never mentioned it." Grant was struggling with this new information. After calming himself, he began to speak again, "Anna worked for years next door." He pointed to the wall perhaps a hundred feet behind Alex. "She was Gualu's mother's cook. When Gualu's father passed, they reduced their staff and she came here. Anna literally raised the kids. She was a fixture here."

Alex ate quietly, taking pains not to look directly at Grant. He began again, "When my boys lived here during exchanges, Anna would chase them around the house with a mop because they had a habit of roller skating down the marble staircase and around the inside of the house. I couldn't tell you how many stories the kids have about her." He fell quiet once again, pensive, thoughtful. "She seemed so healthy last trip through. She was teasing me about my having gained weight. She told me she was going to quit feeding me," he mumbled on.

Marilia could also see that Senor Whitaker was upset. She quickly went and got tissues and offered them to him. He took one, nodding his appreciation.

Alex tried to engage Marilia in conversation. Marilia was not going to do much more than answer direct questions. After discussing the problem with Grant, Alex began again. This time she explained that she was Senor Whitaker's associate on the study of ancient Indian cultures. Alex reminded Marilia, that Senor Whitaker's passion was his obsession with the accomplishments of those who lived in Mexico before the Europeans arrived. A small flicker of interest seemed to show in her eyes. Alex spent some time expanding upon this subject, noting that Mr. Whitaker's late wife Marianna, had also enjoyed learning of these things. Before her death, Marianna had encouraged Grant to share with the world, the great accomplishments of Marilia's forbearers.

Marilia was clearly more interested now. Personal pride in her heritage may have been part of it, but the comment that Alex had respect for the late Marianna Whitaker, seemed to be of evener greater importance. Alex turned to Grant and said, "Did you know this young lady has been to your home in Oregon?"

"Ah, no, well, I suppose it makes sense. Each time one of our kids got married the Robles family would come to Oregon to attend their weddings. The married children brought their young children along, in company with their nannies. Now that you mention it, I believe I do remember her being in our home for a few days."

"It appears your wife made a big impression on her. Seems the smartest thing I've done so far was to speak highly of Marianna. Marilia seems more willing to talk now."

"Good thinking. It never occurred to me that our being together might be misinterpreted, especially by the maid." Just as he said it, he realized the implications of his comment. "Guess I'm guilty of some class smugness. I suppose I'll have to work on that."

"You sure seem to worry about stuff like that; kinda surprising actually," Alex said as she turned to question Marilia. They spoke for some time. It was not really a conversation, but the maid had at least opened up enough to answer uncomfortable questions. At one point, Alex turned to Grant and asked if they were planning on spending the night. Marilia was concerned she should be preparing rooms for them. Grant thought about the aircraft in possible pursuit, but finally said, "I think it is safe to stay here one night. But, tell her we must find Senor Robles quickly, as he may be in some danger."

Marilia excused herself to make up separate rooms for her guests. Alex turned to Grant and began her report. "Marilia knew you had arrived at the airport the other day, because she was the one who answered the phone. She overheard the conversation between Senor, and Senora Robles about your arrival. She made a point of saying she was not eavesdropping, she was merely trying to determine whether to make up a room for you. It seems they were deeply concerned about your unscheduled arrival. Apparently, they were then headed out of town. Marilia says they were trying to avoid contact with someone. Directly after Pepe met with you, they loaded up the Combe, and drove off."

"Right after the Robles left, the police came to the house. Marilia says they asked many questions. She had no answers, only to say that the Robles had said they were going to Mexico City. The next day more police came, these without uniforms, but having official badges. She told them the same."

Alex paused. She seemed genuinely concerned for these people she had never met. "Yesterday, a distinguished looking well-dressed older man came to the gate. She watched him on the closed-circuit monitor, but did not let him in. She did speak with him through the intercom. Evidently this person had been to the house previously. But, in her words, "he was not a family-member." She didn't recognize him as a family friend either, so she was unhelpful. Marilia was clear that Senor Robles had instructed her to not let anyone in the house during their absence. She is a bit concerned that she let the police in twice, but is not concerned about us, because you are regarded as family. No one seems to trust the police here. She is afraid that what has happened to Senor Esteban Morelos may also happen to Senor Robles. She was quite disturbed that Morelos was arrested. Did you know Marilia's sister is a maid with the Morelos family?"

"No, but it makes perfect sense. Many of the professional help here are related. It's rather like families whose role in life is to be the caretakers of other families. The Morelos live just there" he said, pointing.

"You said," she said reflexively.

"Yeah, that's right. Get changed, I'll show you something."

CHAPTER NINETEEN

Veracruz, Mexico

Alex was given Josies' old room. It was a delightfully feminine apartment that included a powder room and separate bathing facilities. It faced out on the street from the second floor. From its windows and balcony, one could see the sidewalk on the opposite side of the street, but not the walk directly next to the large front courtyard wall. Grant got Manuel and Eduardo's old room. It too included a private bath and separate shower.

After a long shower, Grant lay down, intending to collect his thoughts. He stared up at the ceiling, and was shortly mesmerized by the slowly turning fan. Two hours later a quiet knock at the door woke him. Marilia wanted to know if she should plan to prepare dinner for her guests. Grant said no. He looked at his watch and realized he'd been asleep.

Walking out to the second floor common area, he saw Alex quietly reading Pepe's manuscript. She looked up and said: "Are we feeling rested?"

Slightly chagrined, Grant nodded in the affirmative, adding: "Hey, I'm ready to go, if you are." They left the Robles home, walked the two blocks to the highway, crossed over to the beach, and joined a cadre of others strolling along the esplanade. It was a warm, clear night. The view and the surroundings were inspiring.

Alex filled Grant in on what she had learned from Pepe's journal. "Really, it is quite interesting, but strictly personal stuff, it's almost a little embarrassing at times. The bottom-line is that there is nothing I've seen so far that would give any clue as to what is going on. However, I admit that written Spanish is not my strong suit. I can speak well, but I am not usually faced with a written document of this complexity."

"What is he writing about?" Grant inquired.

"As you said, it's something of a personal journal. It starts with his parents sending him away to finish college in the U.S. He was distraught and very depressed, and felt he was completely alone. One particular priest helped him get through the tough times. I suppose this was written for his children and grandchildren, although he does explain some things they would probably automatically know. So perhaps he was hoping to use his writing for something more than a family journal. It's a bit hard for me to follow at times. Anyway, I'm almost done. There is nothing strange or unusual that I could spot. Your family is mentioned three times so far. Evidently you met with some Jesuits many years ago in company with Pepe, regarding archeological stuff. He was quite proud of your knowledge and your love for Mexico's culture. He was equally pleased with their acceptance of you, non-Catholic that you are," she laughed softly.

"Oh yeah, I remember. We got involved in the legends of Quetzalcoatl. I was surprised at the depth of their knowledge, and what they believed. In Veracruz, the Jesuit order is committed to assisting the poor, and improving the lot of the common people. They eschew outward signs of wealth and power, almost like Franciscans. I was impressed, not just with their knowledge of ancient Mesoamerican history, but their sincerity of purpose. Those with whom I was privileged to visit, were convinced that Jesus had visited the Americas after his resurrection in Israel. The Jesuits were reluctant to share these beliefs initially, but once the conversation shifted to Quetzalcoatl, they were quick to point out the mystery of the Fair God. This legend has a lot of traction down here. After all, it has existed in the Americas since well before Columbus.

"So, you're speaking of the classic Mayan, plus the Olmec, Zapotec, Teotihuacan, Mixteca? What else?" Alex asked.

"Technically, not the Olmecs, as it seems their civilization self-destructed about 200 years before the time of Christ. However, their writings seem to have prophesied the coming of the Central American version of the Son of God. They even prophesied their own destruction," Grant explained.

"Yes, it is one of the larger mysteries of Mesoamerica; what happened to the Olmecs? The current theory is they killed themselves off in constant war. Evidently, they experienced a series of civil wars," Alex remembered.

"What the Jesuits shared with me, was not an official Catholic position. In fact, the Catholic church had specifically forbidden they discuss their beliefs about Christ having visited the Americas in ancient times. However, early reports from the 1500 and 1600's, both in Toledo, Spain, and in Rome, still exist. Information was recorded by early Spanish conquistadors, and the Catholic clergy. The early bishops of this area believed that Jesus himself had visited here directly after his death and resurrection in the old world. It actually became a significant political problem in Europe, because it was well established and reported by scholars and respected bishops that every major indigenous group of Mesoamericans believed things in common with Christianity. Early padres reported that the natives, and their documents, spoke of an initial confusion of tongues at a great tower. These people also believed that the Son of God had been born of a virgin, came to earth in a land across the sea, and had died and was resurrected. There is the concept of pre-existence in their belief system as they claimed that Jesus held court in a council in heaven, before the foundation of the earth."

"Wasn't it Father Diego Duran, in the mid 1500's, who was convinced that the native Mexicans were part of the lost tribes of Israel? In my university studies, he was classified as one of the elite Spanish chroniclers of his time. However, professors give no credence to his conclusions surrounding the lost tribes," Alex mused.

"Torquemada, likely the most respected historian of New Spain, and the author of the *History of Mexico,* came to the same conclusions as Father Duran," Grant added.

"I believe you're speaking of *Monarquia Indiana*," Alex remarked.

"What did you say?" Grant said absently.

"The name of Torquemada's historical work," she replied.

"Very impressive," Grant exclaimed. I'm not used to people having an interest in this kind of thing, and especially someone with your knowledge."

"Yeah, well, my major was anthropology with a degree in archeology. My specialty is Mesoamerican archeology. I was completing my Ph.D. when everything went to hell," she said with a tinge of bitterness in her voice."

It made no sense, he thought. It was as if he'd known her for years. And yet, he didn't even know her last week. Ever since meeting Alex, he had felt relief from the crushing loneliness that had so haunted him since Marianna's passing. As a couple, they made no logical sense. He was attracted nonetheless.

Of course I'm attracted to her; she's fun, youthful, vital, and easy to look at. She is smart, and we share interests in common. Could that possibly be enough to work through the problems looming ahead? Even if she does sense the same emotional pull I am feeling, and there's no reason to believe she feels anything more than curious infatuation, is her interest based on anything of lasting value? Surely no one would accuse me of being youthful. She deserves more vitality than I suspect is left in me.

Many women regarded Grant as intelligent and interesting, even handsome, but mostly what he thought about himself was that he was safe. If Alex had experienced struggles with men, and it appeared that she had, then this might explain her natural draw to him. He was safe, he was experienced, but definitely not a playboy. He was not, laugh-out-loud fun. Mostly he was respectful, kind, and safe.

Breaking the silence, Alex said, "You recall Bishop Diego de Landa, first Bishop of the Yucatan?"

"One of the most fascinating stories of the earliest days of Spanish rule."

"That's right," Alex said quickly. "And he is still a controversial subject. He reminds me of the beginning line in Charles Dickens's classic *A Tale of Two Cities*. You know, where it begins, *"It was the best of times, it was the worst of times…"* Well, in the eyes of history, Landa is known as the best, and the worst. Under direction from Rome, he personally gave the orders for the burning of all Maya records. Anyone not turning documents over to the church was subject to the death penalty. Landa almost single-handedly destroyed the collective library of an entire people."

"On the other hand, in his later years, Landa seemed to recant his actions, and ended up writing the history of the Maya. You remember he said that this land was occupied by a race of people who came from the East? He also said that the forebears of the Maya were descendants of the House of Israel. He must have believed it strongly, as it was an incredibly brave thing to put in writing. After all, the Inquisition was in full force at the time. Landa could easily have been incarcerated, tortured, or even put to death, for such a heretical statement."

"Yes, I suspect he felt horrible for the book burnings," Grant mused, as they walked side by side along the esplanade.

Alex continued her story. "Towards the end of his life, Landa put together a school for Spanish priests to learn the Maya language.

And, he wrote a history of the traditions and cultures of the Maya. He recorded the day and month signs of their calendar, along with the Mayan alphabet. Bishop de Landa is one of those who recorded the prophecy of the Maya's, regarding the coming of the Spaniards."

Couples seemed to dominate the walkways and the areas overlooking the beach. They strolled hand in hand, smiling, laughing, and enjoying one another's company. Young men and women sat on the seawall, arm in arm. Others lay in the grass looking up at the stars. The beauty and romance of the place was infective. Grant put his arm around Alex' shoulders. For a moment, he forgot entirely why they were there.

They fell silent walking slowly towards the harbor. Vendors selling flavored ices, flowers, and candy, held their products up tastefully as couples strolled by. The sea was dark and brooding, at contrast with the lights of the city. A lone lighthouse stood guard on a small islet just offshore, a place called affectionately "Lover's Island." Cars cruised along the beach highway with their windows down and music playing. Friends called out to one another. It was noisy, but peaceful, the sounds friendly and good. Lovers were everywhere, strolling, leaning into one another, occasionally kissing, but mostly just happy to be with their special someone.

As comforting as the setting was, Grant's thinking reverted to earlier concerns. Washington power mongers were after him. Thus, no matter what else happened, he was mature enough to know there was no escaping them. Even if he could get away physically, he could never escape emotionally. All his family members lived in America. If he decided to stay in Mexico, or move permanently to the islands, that would mean disappearing from those who were most important to him. That wasn't an option.

Few people had any real knowledge how the U.S. federal criminal court system worked. The conviction rate in the federal system was an incredible 98.7%! The conviction rate varied over the years, but always ran close to 100%. What this really meant was that if the government wanted to take you out, you were going down. Over half of those being sent to federal prison were for crimes against the state, NOT for crimes of violence, robbery, or any form of offense against an actual person.

Grant reminded himself of the counsel he had so many times given his own clients. *Don't lie to yourself.* Under these circumstances, it would be crazy to fall for someone. It would not be fair for either one of them. He quietly took his arm from around Alex' shoulder.

Grant had argued with himself in the past that Marianna understood he would have to deal with the abject loneliness of her passing. She'd told him to marry again, and marry as soon as he could. "Find someone good. Don't subject yourself to earthly martyrdom to demonstrate your love for me," she'd said. But, how could he even consider developing a relationship when faced with the almost certain threat of serving time in federal prison? He was deeply confused.

"Grant."

"Yes"

"You're very quiet."

"Yes."

"A nickel," Alex said softly.

"What?" Grant asked, still distracted.

"A nickel for your thoughts?" she replied.

"Oh, yeah, seems to me, you offered a peso the last time, and you never paid up," he replied, returning to the present.

"You loved her deeply."

"Yes."

"Tell me about her."

"What's to tell?" Grant said softly. "Perhaps there's too much to tell. I wouldn't know where to start, or where to stop. It's probably best to not get me going."

"Marilia Carmen thought highly of her."

"Who?"

"The maid, Marilia Carmen is her name."

"Oh…yeah, Marilia," he worked at pronouncing her name correctly. After another pause, he said reflectively: "Marianna was good to everyone. She was my best friend, a supportive wife, a dedicated mother, and a committed grandmother. We were high school sweethearts. Once I figured out how lucky I was to have Marianna interested in me, we got married, and stayed that way." He drifted off once more.

"Is it too early for you to talk about her?"

"It's not that, Alex. I can talk about her with people that knew her. It's different with you. You're a woman. You're fresh, spirited, exciting, I'm…," he stalled, and was quiet once more.

A few minutes later, she put her arm in his, as they walked on towards the harbor. "It's nice to know a man who was truly in love with his wife. So many people just bounce around. They're not happy, because they have no real commitment in their heart. For the vast majority of us, love is strictly conditional. It's based on our egos. I love you as long as you do and say what pleases me. Men like you are honorable, predictable, and safe."

She had complimented him. It didn't feel like a compliment. They walked on. He finally spoke with a hint of disappointment in his voice: "Yep, that's me alright… safe."

She didn't understand what had happened, but she could feel the cold surround him. Now, what was that all about, she thought?

They walked in silence. Alex eventually broke the hush, "Where are we going Grant? It looks like the walkway ends just ahead."

His tone softened. "I'm sorry. I forgot to tell you. Veracruz has the most wonderful central plaza. It's close now. I'm sure you'll love it. It's a magical place, one of my favorite spots in all of Mexico."

"Oh, so it's a date! Why Grant Whitaker, I do believe you're taking me on our first date. Unless you count the night, we spent together in Akumal as a date. I suppose spending the night in the same hotel room should count for something, shouldn't it? Maybe this is our second date? Of course, we had breakfast together at the hotel the morning before, so maybe this is our third date. With that, and before he could respond, she leaned into him with her hand still firmly in the crook of his arm, and whispered: "Don't you dare spoil my fantasy."

At the end of the esplanade they turned the corner to thread their way through a menagerie of street vendors. There were puppets, flutes, toy dogs on strings, every kind of handmade toy. It was crowded, but fun. Well-behaved children laughed, arm in arm with parents, or along with older siblings. Families were everywhere. It was Mexico's home grown version of Disney World, or perhaps Epcot Center. Restaurants lined the avenue. Tables were set up on the sidewalks right out to the curbs. They walked two blocks, then turned to the right, and then left again through large masonry arches. They were now in the main plaza in downtown Veracruz. It was strictly foot traffic. No cars allowed.

They had entered a traditional Mexican square, oversized both horizontally and vertically. A huge cathedral with a large bell tower faced on to the square. On the opposite side of the plaza stood a broad, three-story government building with open balconies on all three levels. It was capped with lofty steeples, and bell towers of its own. As tradition required, the two remaining sides of the plaza were commercial establishments with restaurants filling most of the ground level floor space. Tables were set well out into the open, bordering the plaza walkways. A large group of fountains, surrounded by planters filled with palms and bamboo lattice work held center stage. Twinkling white lights had been woven throughout. Small boys chased wheeled wooden toys. Mothers walked with traditionally dressed young daughters.

They chose a table under a large leafy tree and sat mesmerized by the myriad activity. It reminded Alex of the square in Merida.

Could it have been just today? It was similar in lay out, but this had everything in jumbo size and stereo. A uniformed band materialized, and marched four times around the square. Reminiscent of the march of the toy soldiers, they stepped high in unison, then disappeared through one of the arched passageways. Mariachi singers followed close behind, roaming tables singing for tips. Jugglers performed, as vendors respectively showed off their clever toys, and hand stitched clothing.

The trees flashed and blinked, captivating all that walked into this wonderland of lights, music, and song. The magic of the place was thick and tangible. Above it all were the stars shining brightly in the deep night sky. Right there in the main square of downtown Veracruz, Grant Whitaker's emotions cracked, and he dropped his head and wept.

Somewhere in the back of his mind, he thought he should be ashamed, or at least embarrassed. Nothing seemed to matter now. Nothing except the release of emotions held in check for so long. He remembered special evenings here with Marianna. He remembered times he had spent here by himself when just traveling through. This was a special place. Now he had brought another woman here. Was this significant? Was it a test? And if so, was it for him, or for her? Alex reached out and held his hand, knowing something important was happening, having the wisdom not to speak.

Straightening his shoulders, he looked out at the plaza, away from Alex. He wasn't yet ready to look in her eyes. A waiter dressed in fiesta garb, placed a divided dish of nuts, still in shells, on the table. Once Grant got his emotions back under control, they ordered local dishes. For starters, caldo de mariscos, a seafood soup purported to cure a hangover. Alex had pollo encacahuatado, chicken in peanut sauce. Grant ordered fresh gulf snapper with arroz a la tumbada, a succulent rice dish baked with a variety of seafood items. The vegetables included plantains, both yucca and sweet potatoes.

They were seasoned with a combination made famous in Veracruz of saffron, cloves, cinnamon and black pepper.

Time passed, they talked of personal things. Alex told of her childhood, of college, and how she met her husband Daniel. She shared her story of dropping out of college in her senior year. Daniel wanted her to stay home, they didn't need another income. As it turned out, she was unable to have children. For a long while she felt broken and incomplete.

Alex told of throwing herself into her marriage. She worked at being the perfect wife. Daniel was a stockbroker, rising rapidly with his firm. She spoke of their struggles and her husband's affairs with co-workers, the hurt, the shame, and the loss of trust. Daniel eventually encouraged her to return to school. She needed a life of her own. For this she was thankful, but in truth it was helpful for him. He could now be gone more hours without explanation. Dan eventually became a principal for the broker-dealer where he worked. This was in the heady days before the implosion of the banking world. He was a trader; a NASDAQ market maker in two-dozen stocks.

Alex told of Daniel's learning how to coerce payments in free-trading stock from corporate principals. She learned it was a common practice of Wall Street. It was technically illegal; but every market maker was in the game. Corporate principals dutifully turned over private, free-trading shares, as payment to get their firm's stock activities promoted. As with so many stockbrokers in those days, Dan needed a push to stay on top. He needed that extra drive, that extra edge. He was making lots of money, but it was never enough. He began to experiment with drugs. Cocaine was the juice of Wall Street. It powered up brokers to sell, sell, sell. They could work longer hours, think faster, and get more done, but there was always the inevitable fall.

Drug use was the beginning of the end for their marriage. She spoke of learning that cocaine was the strongest central nervous system stimulant known to man. Of how Methamphetamine Hydrochloride, goes by various names, like "Crystal," "Meth," or "Crystal Meth," "Speed," "Go," "Fast," "Zip," and a stronger version called "Ice." She talked of his converting hydrochloride salts into free-base cocaine, so it could be smoked or snorted. This was called "Rock," or "Crack." She learned because her husband was increasingly obsessed with drugs. However, she refused to become a part of it. Believing all the while, that like his prior infidelity, this too, would pass.

For a while Daniel pulled it off. His business grew. He even lost weight, and actually looked better. But, that was only at the beginning. As he stepped further out on the slippery slope of drug use, the two of them grew farther and farther apart. He became almost desperate for her to share in his highs. He wanted her to indulge with him. He was incapable of seeing how crazy he was becoming. His moods began to swing radically. Alex was a prude, stuck in another generation. He was out there, conquering the world. Alex buried herself in the fantasy of past civilizations. She was struggling to suppress the depression that was sure to come.

Finally, it was over. She divorced her husband of eight years after returning home from a night class to discover a harem of alcohol-fueled women in company with her drug-addicted husband. There would be no child support. They had never really begun a family. As part of the divorce settlement she got the house, and enough money to see her through a Ph.D. program, but just so.

It took time for her to find her balance. Her father had died two years prior, and she wasn't really over the loss. Her mother was in a rest home, another victim of Alzheimer's. Alex had become desperate for life solutions. She needed a greater reason to live. Was there purpose to all this pain, misery, and depression?

Alex joined a health club and became a fitness nut. She went to a number of churches, and participated in a Zen program. She began to read self-help books, authors like Ester Hicks and David

Hawkins. As she looked more deeply into the meaning of life, she found herself focused on the Bible, along with eastern authors like, Nisargadatta Maharaj, Ramana Maharshi, and Paramahansa Yogananada. Alex took up running, and became a marathoner. Eventually, she enrolled in a course entitled "Religions of the World," at CSULB. There she met Jose Antonio Vilchez. In the beginning, it was a fairy-tale. He was smitten with her. He seemed primarily attracted to her knowledge and her personality, not just the results of her physical fitness craze.

Jose Antonio encouraged Alex to take a bi-annual pilot's review, to get caught up on flight regulations and take up flying again. She really couldn't afford it, but Jose Antonio had a small plane. Though he wasn't a pilot himself, he had received a Cessna 172 in partial re-payment of a loan. It was perfect, and too good to be true. Yet, it all seemed logical at the time. There was a wonderful release in being in the air again. She was able to fly. To feel the exhilaration in doing the things she'd not been able to do since her youth. She had the thrill of the flight, the fantasy of mysterious ancient civilizations, and the excitement of new romance. Jose was the tall, dark, and handsome guy. He was a cultured Hispanic of high breeding and good manners. She had escaped from the lone and dreary world.

Jose Antonio had Alex fly them to different places. They flew out of Long Beach airport and went to Catalina Island. A notoriously romantic destination, it was but a 26-mile flight over ocean. Their next trip was to Las Vegas, but because it was Class B airspace, and she was not yet used to the stressful approach and clearances needed in this high-traffic zone, they landed at Jean airport just west of the Class B boundary. There was a limousine ready to pick them up, and take them to the Mirage hotel for the weekend. The next trip was to Tucson, Arizona where they attended the world famous annual Gem show at the Marriott hotel.

Each place they went, Jose Antonio had friends drop by. He was smart, fun, and always surrounded by others that seemed to look up to him. He was from a wealthy family, and very good-looking. Even when he introduced her to two of his friends, both DEA agents, she never tumbled. The next trip was to Puerto Penasco, a Mexican seaport at the top of the Sea of Cortez, just an hour's flight southwest of Tucson. They spent the night at the Plaza las Glorias on the seashore. They returned the next day, clearing customs in Tucson.

Another weekend saw them flying to Mexicali, where they went to the horse races. Later, they flew from Palm Springs to Tijuana, and returned to Long Beach. Every weekend the weather was good they took flying trips and saw new things.

Alex had applied to do field work at the Mayan ruins of Palenque. She had been too late. The roster was full. Jose Antonio hadn't wanted her to go, but she needed the field experience for her degree. The fun was subsiding. It was almost like she had to fly. She needed more time for her studies.

One Friday, at Jose's home, Alex told him she just couldn't take him to Guaymas, in Sonora, Mexico, the next day. Only 240 miles south of the border, it was not a particularly long flight. But she was behind in a class, and needed the time to catch up. He was not pleased. Alex was firm. Jose got angry and stormed about. Tensions ran high. Alex told Jose she had stopped her education once before because a man wanted her too. She wasn't going to do it again. He got louder and more aggressive. And then it happened.

In a fit of anger, Jose said something about that crazy husband of hers. He'd been right about her stubborn streak. Up until that very moment, she had no idea that Jose Antonio knew her ex-husband Daniel. It was a shock. What was the connection? Why didn't she know about this? It didn't take long for her to put it all together. It had been a set-up from the beginning. She had fallen so hard she didn't see any of the signs. Devastated, she ran from his house. Alex drove around trying to get her head under control. It finally occurred to her that Jose must be her ex-husband's drug source. Then she realized, she had had been flying him all over the place. What might that mean? Still upset and fuming, an idea began to form.

Getting the list of the students scheduled to depart for Palenque fieldwork, she bribed a young woman at UCLA to give up her spot. It cost Alex most of her surplus cash, but two days later she showed up at the airport and was gone. Alex left her dog and car with a friend. She asked her to take care of shutting down her house. Alex said she'd be gone for a while. She did not explain. Then she took a cab to the bus station. From there, she took a shuttle to the airport. Alex vanished. No one knew where she had gone.

After three months of fieldwork at the Palenque site in Chiapas, Mexico, Alex applied to Mexican immigration for residency. She stated on her application that she intended to stay in Mexico, and work on research projects related to her field of expertise. Five weeks, and a hundred-dollar tip, and she had her FM-2. She could live and work in Mexico. The month after that, she went to Villahermosa, the capital city of the State of Tabasco. It was the nearest major city to the field site of Palenque. At an Internet café, she discovered Jose Antonio had been arrested, the result of a DEA sting.

Alex knew she must be implicated. For awhile she feared someone might spend the effort to track her down. Without notice of any kind she simply left the field site and disappeared. Her life and passion was Mayan archeology, so she headed to the Yucatan. She found work at the Itza, the restaurant and bar where Grant Whitaker had met her. Alex had been working there for almost two years while she tried to gain steady employment at the Chichen Itza ruins. She was able to assist in some fieldwork. But not with an accredited university program, because she was reluctant to have anyone seek a copy of her transcript. It could expose her whereabouts to anyone looking.

It had grown late. They walked back to the Robles. This time they held hands. The way of things had changed.

CHAPTER TWENTY

Veracruz, Mexico

"Senor Whitaker and I would like breakfast in the dining room," Alex rattled off to Marilia in Spanish. Marilia nodded and returned to the kitchen.

"Listen to this one," Grant said to Alex, as he read aloud:

"In 1834, a Spanish padre translated the Totonicapan document from Mayan into Spanish. The said manuscript consists of 31 quarto pages; but translation of the first pages is omitted because they are on the creation of the world, of Adam, the Earthly Paradise in which Eve was deceived, not by a serpent, but by Lucifer himself as an Angel of Light. It deals with the posterity of Adam, following in every respect the same order as in Genesis, and the sacred books as far as the captivity of Babylonia."

Alex was standing behind the dining room table looking into the Aviary. "They must have a hundred little birds in there," she said. "There are little nests all over those rock walls." Then abruptly changing the subject, she commented on what Grant had just read. "We discussed the Totonicapan manuscript the other night. If it is true, the implications are profound."

"Do you get the significance of the captivity of Babylon, reference?" Grant asked.

"Not offhand," she said carefully.

"It's the date. According to Babylonian communications sent by Nebuchadnezzar to his father, who was then the king of Babylon, the conquest of Jerusalem took place right at 600 B.C. I think Judah fell officially in 597 B.C., after which the Jews were hauled off into captivity to Babylon. Nebuchadnezzar later replaced his father as king, and became head of the empire."

"Okay, so what?"

"The 600 B.C. date shows up again and again. There has to have been a transfer of high-culture around that time. It seems to have come from somewhere in the Fertile Crescent to Southern Mexico," he said with enthusiasm. "In fact, I read as much, on a sign near Xel-ha the other day, where I bought this hat," he said while pointing at his head.

"You read what on a sign?" she asked.

"The 600 B.C. date, for the arrival of an advanced culture by boat from across the sea," he replied.

Although interested in what he was reading, it was a distraction each time he looked up, and saw Alex standing there cooing at the birds. She wore white shorts, a white T-shirt entirely too form fitting to ignore, a white headband, and white running shoes. "The lady in white," he said.

"No. It was the Lady in Red," she responded.

"I'm not talking about the movie; I'm talking about you. You're rather distracting. Are you sure you want to go out in public like that?" he asked.

"Most people are not as easily distracted as you seem to be. Have you always been like this?" she teased.

"No. I don't believe so. Guess I'm in a vulnerable place right now," he said firmly.

She smiled broadly, "Well, thank you, Mr. Whitaker. You're certainly complimentary this morning."

"Happy to oblige," he replied brightly, trying to figure out what he was being thanked for. Returning to the paper he was scanning, he read another quotation out loud. "Here's another excerpt from the *Title of the Lords of Totonicapan*:

> "The wise men ... and leaders of three great peoples...extending their sight over the world...came from where the sun rises. Together these tribes came from the other part of the sea, from the East. These, then, were the three nations of Quiches, and they came from where the sun rises. Descendants of Israel, of the same language and same customs as Israel... When they left... the great Father (God) gave them a present called Giron-Gagal... When they arrived at the edge of the sea Balam-Quitze touched it, (the sacred director) and at once a passage opened... for thus the great God, wished it to be done, because they were the sons of Abraham and Jacob."

"Good grief, that's an actual quote from the Totonicapan document?" Alex exclaimed. "They're talking about Israel, and THE Abraham and Jacob?"

"According to this, it is straight out of that ancient literary work. You ever read the whole document?" Grant asked.

"As I recall, it was translated into English by the University of Oklahoma Press in the late 70's," she replied thoughtfully.

"Yeah, I've got a copy of it, and also *The Annals of the Cakchiquels*, the *Popol Vuh*, and *The Books of Chilam Balam*."

Still staring into the aviary, she said: "Look at these little yellow birds, I've never seen these guys before. Do you know what they are?" Then in her characteristic style, and apparently not expecting an answer, she shifted the conversation. "You actually read that stuff? It gets to be a bit much for me. Sometimes I think it's easier to stick with the artifacts."

"Spoken like a true archeologist. Don't let the facts get in the way of interpreting the so-called evidence. Build your own story based on the garbage dump of history," he said laughingly. "You know that Giron-Gagal thing they're talking about in the Totonicapan manuscript? Well that's what a Liahona is, another word for the same thing. Do you remember Jack's house in Cancun? It's Casa Liahona. It means compass house, or house of direction, or some such. He named the house from a term that shows up in the Book of Mormon."

"What shows up in the Book of Mormon?" she said absently.

"The Liahona. It's an ancient name for a compass of some kind."

"Oh yeah, except the concept of the compass didn't appear until well after the time of Christ, and you're talking about a period six hundred years earlier."

"Okay, I get it. But apparently the Totonicapan manuscript didn't know what our esteemed archeologists know. Tongue held firmly in cheek," Grant joked.

"Hey, listen to this one," Grant went on without waiting for her reaction.

"In ancient Mesopotamia, and in Egypt, the serpent motif signified the Creator God, or God of Life. In Mesoamerica, the exact same application existed for Quetzalcoatl, who was also thought of as the Creator God. On both sides of the world, the apparent process by which they arrived at their conclusion was the same. The slightly undulating body of a snake is similar to that of a riverbed, (a riverbed is never straight). A mirror image of the curving riverbed, or body of a snake, is seen in the Milky Way, which is symbolic of the residence of God. It is from the sky that water comes, which in turn is the source from which the rivers fill. Water is the source of all life. Thus, the serpent signified the Creator God. In Numbers 21.5-10, Moses uses the serpent as a symbol of the prophesied Messiah. John 1.3 states clearly that Christ was the "Creator God". The serpent was therefore the symbol of the Messiah."

"Whoa. What in heaven's name are you reading?" Alex asked.

Grant hesitated, as if deciding something. "These are excerpts from this *Archeological Footnotes* paper, from Pepe's library." Redirecting the subject, he went on. "It's in English. You know that business about the serpent? It's actually correct. Throughout the ancient Middle East, the serpent was associated with creation. Western repugnance for the serpent is a result of the Adam and Eve story. Every culture views things through the lens of their own experience. Our cultural lenses include the mythological and legendary stories of our early childhood, and everything with which we've been exposed throughout our lives. All of these things are accumulated in our subconscious. Together they form our internal belief systems."

"So, you're saying the Genesis story is mythological?" Alex asked.

"No. That's not my point. What I am trying to articulate is that all of us color input as a consequence of our political, social, scientific, and religious predispositions. And, every single one of us is subject, in some way, to all the thoughts and feelings we've experienced throughout our lives to date. So, if early on, we were exposed to the serpent as the bad guy, it will likely stay with us most of our lives. Had our earliest experiences been different, we may have felt differently about this philosophical concept. I once wrote a paper on this particular subject, pointing out that even Moses referred to the coming Messiah by referencing a brass serpent."

Alex seemed distracted with her thoughts. Perhaps considering what Grant was sharing, perhaps with other things. In either event, she simply quit talking.

Marilia returned with breakfast. She began by pouring fresh squeezed orange juice, smiling shyly as Grant thanked her, and beamed his best smile. She turned and spoke with Alex for a moment, then looked back to Grant, and nodded her head towards him.

As Alex took a seat at the table she said, "Marilia wants you to know that she is sorry she forgot to serve you flan last night," Alex said.

"What?" Grant replied.

"It seems that Marilia was trained by Anna who told her that whenever Senor Whitaker is visiting, she is always to serve him flan, whether he asks for it or not. Marilia tells me she has some for you now. But it is breakfast, and it seems strange to her that you would want desert. Nevertheless, she wants you to know it is available at your request." Alex laughed, "You have some reputation. The women scramble around trying to take care of you."

Granted smiled warmly, "Please thank Marilia for me, and tell her I will have some flan, if it is not too much trouble." He added conspiratorially, "Better to keep up the mystery, gives the hired help something to gossip about."

"Oh, I don't think there's any shortage of things for them to gossip about. You were still holding my hand when you rang the door bell at the gate last night," she said smiling innocently. "I think our cover is blown." She turned and spoke sweetly to Marilia. She immediately scurried off to the kitchen.

Grant made like he was pulling an arrow out of his heart. "Ouch," he grinned. He dropped his eyes so he could continue reading quotes from the *Archeological Footnotes* paper.

> "Sahagun, an early Catholic padre, who came to New Spain within ten years of Cortez, records: "Concerning the origin of these peoples, the report the old men give is that they came by sea from the north, (down the gulf coast), and it is true that they came in wooden boats... seven ships in which the first settlers of this land came...They came from the direction of Florida, (indicating an Atlantic crossing), and came coasting along the shore, disembarking in the Port of Panuco. Panuco seems to mean: "place where those arrived, who crossed the sea."

Anxious to show off her knowledge of the subject Alex replied, "Sahagun was a great scholar. He may have been the best of all the Spanish priests in the 1500's. His work is still considered the leading authority on the Aztecs. Sahagun wrote a twelve-volume history on them. Early on, the Spanish government forced him to change parts of his original work regarding the Conquest of New Spain. Then the Catholic Church forced him to make additional changes that seemed heretical to them at the time. Nonetheless, his material is still considered to be some of the best."

Grant shook his head. She was a walking bibliography. He smiled to himself. "Just a few more," Grant said, as he continued to read out loud.

> "At the Maya ruins of Uxmal in Yucatan, Mexico, the ancient Jewish symbol known as the Star of David, was found and dated to many centuries *before* Columbus. It is noted that the triangles interlaced, as was common in the Israelite representations. Only in Egypt and Maya lands, is the art style

showing head in profile view with eye and upper torso of human body in full frontal position found. This is a conventionalized, unrealistic, and strikingly unusual art form."

"The Star of David?" she asked. "I didn't know that. Uxmal is right down the road from Chichen Itza. I've been there many times. I wonder where exactly it was found?" she mused.

"As I recall, it was in one of the steps ascending the Temple of the Magicians," Grant replied.

"How come you know all the weird stuff?" Alex asked, with a puzzled look on her face.

Ignoring her comment, Grant continued.

"The Maya's daily functional calendar consisted of 360 days plus 5 supplementary "unlucky" days. The Egyptians had the exact same system. Both the Israelites, and the Mexican ancients, utilized the exact same constellations to represent the primary four directions. Crucifying was a method of capital punishment in ancient Mexico, as it was in ancient Palestine. Leg breaking as part of the crucifixion procedure was practiced in both lands."

"You're killing me Grant. We've not even finished breakfast."

The maid, now cook and server, had brought saucers of flan for each of them. They acknowledged her graciously, and spooned in. Around a mouthful of flan, Grant said, "Okay, sorry, but you've got to hear one more. This is the last one, I promise,"

"Ixtlilxochitl, the Mexican historian of the late 1500's, wrote concerning the earliest colonizers of Mexico: "And the Tultec history tells how man, multiplying after the great flood made a very tall and strong tower....When things were at their best, their languages were changed and, not understanding each other, they went to different parts of the world...the Tultecs...who understood their language among themselves, came to these parts (Mexico) having first crossed large lands and seas...They were of those of the division of Babylon...They say that they traveled for 104 years through different parts of the world until they arrived..."

"I always loved that guy's name," Alex blurted, "I mean what a handle. Ixtlilxochitl, she drew out the syllables slowly (Eesh-toe-leil-sho-cheet-tla.) He is one of the most credible sources of information on the cultures of ancient Mesoamerica. I understand he possessed a library containing paintings and hieroglyphic history of pre-conquest Mexico. He produced numerous manuscripts. After he died, the Catholic Church collected all his original source documents and burned them."

"Now here's an interesting piece of information," Grant began.

"Oh, no you don't; you promised no more for now," she quipped, enjoying the information anyway.

"Okay, but just this quick one," he replied, and went on reading without waiting for her acknowledgement.

"Several ancient paintings of Quetzalcoatl, (the Messiah of ancient America), represent him on a cross with his side pierced with a spear with blood and water flowing from the wound, the same as portrayed in the New Testament. In the Bible, Jesus is known by thirty-five title names that have their equivalent, or close to their equivalent, in Mesoamerica. The cross is a primary symbol of both the new, and old, world Messiah's..."

"Whew, that's pretty curious stuff, you're reading. So, what are you thinking? Perhaps this paper has a connection with why we're being followed? What's the neighbor's name, the one that used to be the governor, and is now in jail?" Alex asked.

"Esteban Morelos. How he fits into the puzzle, if he fits at all, is anybody's guess," Grant said reflectively.

"But didn't Pepe tell you he fit in?" she asked. "It looks like Pepe, your Jose Robles, has disappeared, or is hiding out, and his extended family has apparently gone scarce. This Esteban guy was mysteriously arrested and thrown in jail." She paused as if thinking about something, then asked, "The other brother-in-law to Pepe, the antiquities dealer you told me about. Hasn't he disappeared as well? So, there are people chasing us around. Is it too far a stretch to recognize that whoever is after us must think we have, or know, something that is important to this situation? And, couldn't all this have some relationship to that mysterious gold notebook Pepe told you about? Does that about sum it up?"

"You may be right. It just all seems so unreal," Grant replied.

"So where to next? The mystery is upon us and it would be fun if weren't for the knowledge that some of these guys are NOT very friendly. And, let's not forget that Mario is stuck in the hospital." Before Alex finished her own sentence, she burst out with: "Mario...I forgot to check back on him!"

"Yeah, you'd better follow through. And, we'd better get out of here before our tail figures out where we are. Oh, and before you make the call, ask Marilia if she can give us directions to Miguel Ramirez's house. Who knows, maybe he is still in town?"

Twenty minutes later they were in the car leaving the Robles neighborhood. Marilia was $100 richer...something the Robles would not be happy with. What's worse, Grant had kissed her on both cheeks, a symbolism which caused her to blush right through her dark Indian skin.

Alex called the hospital. Mario was resting. There did not appear to have been a problem with the two strange visitors of the day before.

Alex drove, Grant gave directions. They were headed first to Josie's home. As before, the method wasn't particularly complicated, back to the beach highway, head out of town a couple of miles, then start looking on the right for something familiar. Grant thought he would recognize the house from the road, but it wasn't as easy as he had expected. They finally turned around and backtracked into town before he was able to spot the street. Josefina's was a corner house assessable only from an upper parallel road. The windows were high and designed to look out over a raised area in the backyard and straight out to the ocean without seeing the traffic on the road below.

The gardener was not helpful. But after Alex coaxed him for a while, he did seem to know of Senor Whitaker. Particularly in view of the fact that four of Grant's grandchildren had spent summers there. Eventually, the gardener admitted he had seen Josie just the day before. She had left again quickly, telling him to forget he had seen her. He had no idea where she was headed.

Using the directions given them by Marilia, they tracked down Miguel Ramirez's home. Grant was pretty sure it was the same one he'd been too with Matthew so many years before. No one appeared to be home. He was tempted to break-in. He wanted to see if the secret artifact's room was still there. In the end, he couldn't bring himself to do it. Looking around carefully, they finally left, unsure of where to go, or what to do next.

"Okay, Capitan. Where to now?"

"I suppose there is one other place we might check. The last time I stayed at the Robles home Gualu and Guadalupe were talking. Gualu is the mom. Guadalupe's the oldest daughter. They have the same name, but use different versions, to keep others from being confused."

Alex jumped in, "Lupe is also a contraction of Guadalupe, which also means Mary, Marie, etc. About every tenth woman in Mexico seems to have the same name."

"Yes, it is a hugely popular name in Mexico. Do you know the story?" Grant asked.

"The story of what?" Alex responded.

"The story of Guadalupe."

"Yeah, I think I've heard it before. It has something to do with the Virgin Mary, doesn't it? Where are we headed anyway?"

"Back to the Robles, I have an idea," he said quietly, then launched into the story of the Virgin of Guadalupe. "In 1531, a 57-year old native Aztec Indian who lived in Mexico City, who's Christian name was Juan Diego, said he saw a vision of the Virgin Mary. The visitation became known as the appearance of the Virgin of Guadalupe. The story gets complex, but is perhaps the oldest uniquely Christian story in Mexico. It is held in great reverence. So, Guadalupe, Gualu, and Lupe, are other names associated with Mary, Marie, Marilia and a host of others. All of these names point back to the mother of Jesus."

It was heating up. The air was stagnant. Smog was in the air, but the ocean view was still beautiful from the neighborhoods where the Robles families and their various relatives lived. These were definitely the nicer parts of town. The traffic worsened as they day progressed. It took them almost twice as long to get to the Robles as they anticipated. Alex finally made the turn up the right street. There were two police cars parked bumper to bumper directly in front of the house. Grant ducked down in the seat and Alex drove straight on without turning to look at what was going on. Two more blocks and she turned left and double-backed on the next street going back towards the ocean. Another police car was parked in front of the house whose courtyard probably lined up with the Robles. It might be a coincidence Grant thought. But it seems more likely that the police took the precaution of blocking someone's escape over the back courtyard wall.

"What do we do now?" Alex finally exhaled. "I don't think it would be a wise idea to go back."

"Agreed, so where does that leave us?" he thought out loud. "I'm stumped." A moment later he started to explain. "The reason I wanted to see Marilia again was to ask her about Guadalupe's cottage. It's out of town somewhere. Mom and both daughters were talking about it last time I stayed in the Robles' home. They told me where it was, and for some reason I believe I should know where it is, but I can't remember. All I can recall is it is within an hour's drive of here. It fronts on a river somewhere in the direction of Cerro Vigia. Pepe purchased the property on one side of Guadalupe's river house, and Josie, and her husband, bought the property on the other side. Only Guadalupe and Ramon have built there yet. I remember Ramon told me he was planning to expand their river house, and eventually sell their home in town and move there permanently. It's possible that Pepe and Gualu are there, or at least Ramon and Guadalupe are there," Grant's voice trailed off as he tried to think through other plausible considerations.

"I don't know where I'm going Grant. Do you want me to head back to the airport? At least we could check on the plane," Alex offered. "I'm assuming that the Ramon is Guadalupe's husband?"

"Right, sorry, I forgot, you don't know all the players. Yes, the airport seems our only choice at the moment," he mumbled.

Grant retrieved his U.S. cell phone from the computer valise and called Matthew at his office in Oregon. He was there. A lucky break as he was often traveling. Unfortunately, he was tied up with business guests from Russia. They were on a tight schedule to wrap up and get to the airport. Matthew's calls were being held, but the receptionist told Matthew that it was his father on the line so he picked up. Grant just barely managed to say, "Matthew, I'm in Veracruz, there are some problems here, it is important you call me back."

"Dad, I'm really sorry, I must handle these folks. I'll be back to you within the hour." He rang off.

"I'm not really sure I know how to get back to the airport," Alex said in confusion, as she jigged between traffic jams working her way in the general direction she thought the airport would be located. "Your phone call was short."

"Matthew is in a meeting. He'll call back. I'm sure he will be able to help," Grant said quietly. "I think you're headed in the right direction, that's about all we can do for now. There should be signs when we get closer."

They drove on, each lost in their own thoughts. Grant called his son Ian's office. Ian had also stayed with the Robles in his middle teens. He continued to stay in touch with their boys. Ian was traveling. Something about a boat show in Florida. Grant called his cell phone, and caught him in the middle of a presentation on nautical software. Ian said he would call back.

Grant's daughters had also stayed in Veracruz. All of them kept in touch with the Robles girls. Grant considered calling them, then decided to not get everyone in an uproar. Grant visited Veracruz at least a couple of times a year, sometimes more. Frequently, his route of flight from the islands to Oregon, took him along the southern route from St. Kitts to Santo Domingo for fuel. Then it was off to Montego Bay, Jamaica, to spend the night. The next day, he would typically fly to Cancun, and on to Veracruz, where he spent the next night. He usually stayed in the Robles home. Then it was off to Guadalajara and up to Cabo San Lucas, to the house destined to become his new winter haven. The phone rang.

"Dad! How the heck are you?" boomed Ian's happy voice. "I just sold a large software package to another yachtie with more money than he knows what to do with. So, what's up dad?"

Grant explained some of what was going on. At the back of his mind, a growing suspicion told him his phone might be tapped. He decided not to say overly much.

"What can I do to help?" Ian inquired.

"I suppose nothing. I just thought someone might have contacted you. By the way did you hear that Anna passed away?"

A stunned silence intervened. Once Ian got his bearings, he replied "Dad I…I don't know what to say? His voice began to waiver.

"Marilia Carmen told us that she took sick, went to the hospital, had cancer, and died shortly thereafter," Grant said in a tone that showed he was concerned for his son's reaction. "Evidently, it happened almost two months ago."

Ian reacted as Grant thought he might. "Why didn't someone call our family?" They spoke softly with one another, each concerned for the other's feelings. Ian felt as though there was something odd going on. Finally, he raised the questions. "Dad, ah…, who is this Carmen lady, and who is us?" Grant had slipped using the "us" word without even thinking. Now he had to explain. He was torn between saying something about it being a woman he was traveling with, which would instantly set off a whole new line of questioning, not to mention moving through the family at light speed, and saying the wrong thing over the phone, in case it was being surveiled. After a moment, he decided to say something in between.

"Marilia Carmen is the upstairs maid. Remember? The youngish looking Indian girl that came as one of the nanny's to your wedding." Grant had responded to the easy question first. He paused again; then approached the more difficult question. "I visited the Robles with a friend working at the Chichen Itza site. I thought the family might be able to connect us with someone of influence in Veracruz to get a dig permit," he lied.

Telling something untrue, especially to his son, was extremely hard. Lying did not come easy. Grant wondered for a moment at all the modern movie-type heroes that could tell a lie without any apparent internal conflict. Could it be that easy for some, he wondered?

Grant's attempt at subterfuge backfired on him the minute he said it. "So, you're rekindling that ancient records search at Cerro

Vigia," Ian said. It was a statement more than a question. It was not the kind of thing Granted wanted said over the phone in case someone was listening.

"Er...a...no...not exactly," Grant slurred trying to come up with an appropriate response. "I'm just trying to help someone out." Busted, he thought. "Well, thanks for calling me back Ian. By the way, where are you staying?"

Ian told him, and they made small talk for a while, Grant writing down the hotel name on his pad.

"Love you, dad," Ian said.

"I love you too, Ian," Grant responded.

"Was that your son that called you?" Alex asked after he had rung off.

"Yes. Ian is in Florida working a boat show."

The phone rang. It was Matthew. Grant told him of Anna, and got pretty much the same response as with Ian, although he seemed even more perplexed that no one had contacted him. Matthew was audibly shaken. His voice cracked, and it took him some time to get it under control. It was clear that both of the boys had instantly made the connection to their mother's death. It was still very fresh in their minds.

Matthew seemed to go through a whole range of emotions ending with a brief flash of anger. It was over quickly, and Grant could imagine that he slumped back in his chair struggling to get a grip on himself. Finally, Matthew said, "Father, what is going on down there?"

More soberly than he intended, Grant responded: "Son, I simply do not know. I met with Pepe a few days ago. He seemed stressed and concerned about something, but wouldn't say what. Now, he and the entire family seem to have left town without a trace. No one seems to know what's happening. After a few minutes more, he realized his son was not going to let this go without knowing more, so he said: "Matthew, there's more, but frankly I do not feel safe on this phone. Please call Jorge, Eduardo, and Manuel. See if you can track them down, and find out what's happening. I'll be back to you shortly." He rang off, and sat there for a moment trying to figure out how to make a secure call back to his son.

"You never call him Matt," Alex said as she pulled on to the detour ramp leading into the airport complex.

"Yeah, he doesn't really want to be a Matt. He calls me father. The rest of the kids call me dad. I think he has a need to be a little different, oldest son and all.

Alex drove into the parking area, and was immediately confronted with whether to return the rental car or not. After a brief discussion, they decided no, at least not until Grant was able to speak with Matthew on a secure line. They decided to make a call from a public phone in the terminal, using cash. Alex made the call, and a moment later Matthew was back on the line, asking his father what the heck was going on. There was really no way to avoid the full-story version. Grant launched in. Alex scurried about changing bills for coins. Matthew kept interrupting, seeking a shorter version, but Grant carried on insisting that if he was going to know part, he'd better know it all. Grant left out the part of Alex and his growing closeness, but whether said or unsaid, it was probably clear enough. It was obvious in the tone of Matthew's voice when he asked after Alex. He clearly wanted to know more about her, who she was, where she was from, why she was involved.

After standing at the pay phone for almost an hour Matthew said, "Look dad, I've got people waiting here in my office. I'll call Eduardo and Jorge, as soon as I can, but I don't have Manuel's number here. I'm sure Ian's got it; he met with him in Spain just a couple of weeks ago. I suggest you find a wireless connection and Skype me."

"Good idea," Grant replied. In the end, they decided Matthew would call Grant back on his Mexican cellular, and give him the contact information and numbers he was seeking, along with any other feedback he could muster. Grant turned on his local phone, fearing the battery might be low. He couldn't remember when he had charged it last. The conversation ended with Matthew saying: "Look father, if you're in any trouble down there, or you can use my help, you know I'm on the next plane out of here." Grant thanked his son, knowing these were the closing lines of their phone call.

"I love you, father."

"I love you too, Matthew."

"Very sweet. Touching really, the relationship you have with your boys. I wish there were more of us in my family. It's a very special thing you have going there."

A pained expression passed through Grant's eyes and momentarily showed on his face. He hated all the stress and emotional conflict his troubles were causing his children. The IRS, in concert with the US District Attorney's office, had leaned heavily on his children. Agent's were emphatic that it was in the kid's best interest to come up with incriminating evidence against their father. They had openly threatened to indict every one of them if they were not forthcoming with something they could use. The kids were also told, in no uncertain terms, that if they exercised their 5th amendment rights, they would be sure of being indicted. The entire scenario was engineered to literally rip the family apart. The measure of the family's strength was that they were all still willing to chip in and help one another. If Marianna was only here, he thought wistfully.

Alex sensed his sorrow. She could tell there was a lot going on that she did not understand, and for the present she had completely forgotten about his IRS problems. They seemed so far away and minor compared to what was going on here. In Grant's case, he knew his problems were not minor at all.

Alex and Grant tried to access the airfield through a passenger gate. They were stopped for tickets and scanning. Backing off they went outside the terminal and walked to the back of the tower where they could see the plane through the chain-link fence. It looked okay. No restraints appeared to be around the nose wheel. There did not appear to be a red 320 on the field, at least within their line of sight. Grant would have liked to move the aircraft to a private field somewhere, but a plane could not move without being tracked in Mexico, so it was probably a useless exercise. There were no true private fields anyway.

After some reflection, it seemed best they simply hang around until Matthew called. They waited in the terminal for a while. It was about four times larger than the one in Merida, but still smallish for servicing the 1.7 million people that lived in the city of Veracruz. They talked and thought, and talked some more. Finally, the need to just do something, rather than simply wait around for a phone call, was motivation enough to leave the airport in search of an Internet Café. Driving around in search of a sign indicating Internet service was unproductive. They recalled a Starbucks at a Mall they had passed when looking for one of the houses. It would surely have Wi-Fi. Instead, they found a nice-looking restaurant to kill time within.

"I'll call J.P. and see how he's doing," Grant said. "Perhaps you should check in with Lupe, to see how she is making out with handling the Itza."

Not wanting to use the local phone for fear of missing Matthew's expected call, and in order to conserve the battery, they took turns calling from his U.S. cell phone.

There was no answer at Jack's house, and the call went to voice mail. Grant decided not to mention his return number. Jack should have his number anyway. It was probably a silly precaution he thought, but he'd better start thinking in those terms.

Lupe was worried about Alex. She was not much concerned about the restaurant. No new customers, pretty much locals. Her two friends seemed to be working out fine. The Itza was back to normal. Her brother was to be released from the hospital the next day. Lupe signed off by telling Alex she should be careful wandering around the country with a man she hardly knew. Alex poked back by saying she hadn't been nearly as intimate with Grant, as Lupe had been when the two of them were fooling around on the floor. This knocked Lupe out of her serious mood. She began to giggle, the result showing on Alex's face as she commenced teasing her with greater emphasis. Alex was still laughing when she hung up.

"Perhaps I should call Marilia, and tell her I drove by the house and saw the police out front," Alex offered. "I won't mention you in case someone is listening. I think she'll recognize my voice."

"Nothing to lose I guess," Grant replied.

There was an obnoxious buzzing. It took more time than it should for Grant to realize his Mexican phone was on vibrate. He answered it just in time.

Matthew had caught Eduardo's wife at their home in Houston, Texas. She had the addresses of the Acapulco condo, the Cancun condo and Guadalupe's new home on the Santo Domingo River. The latter was not far from the town of Tlacotalpan. She gave Matthew directions to the river house. She had heard that Anna had passed, and had no explanation for why the Whitaker family was not told. The family members in Veracruz, all seemed to be distracted about something. None of the brothers had said anything to her about significant problems in Mexico. The only thing she had picked up on was some rumor about Esteban Morelos. She had not given it much credence.

Matthew seemed even more anxious. Once again, he offered to drop everything and meet them in Mexico City. Grant thanked him and said he would keep in touch, but he needed to stay on the move for now.

Alex settled up the restaurant tab, while Grant was still on the phone. Shortly, they were out the door making for the car. Alex reported on her call to the Robles home. Marilia was cool and evasive. She simply said thank you, and that everything was fine. She mentioned that the police were still there looking around. Alex didn't ask what they were looking for, and the maid didn't offer any other information. If someone was listening on an extension, it would have been pretty much a meaningless call.

It seemed logical that before they flew to Cancun, or maybe Acapulco, they'd first check out Guadalupe's river place. On the way out of town, they stopped at a Pemex station, fueled, and got a map.

CHAPTER TWENTY-ONE

Tlacotalpan, Veracruz

The road out of the city was clogged with traffic. The air was still, unusual for being so close to a large body of water the size of the Gulf of Mexico. They stayed on the coastal highway until well beyond the sprawling suburbs.

On the outskirts, small farms gave way to sugar cane fields, and the phenomena of barbed wire attached to fence posts in full bloom. When Grant had first observed the fence post marvel, he thought that farmers had planted trees to use as posts. It was just so hard to believe that fence posts had somehow grown into trees. And yet, that was exactly what had happened. The annual rainfall for this area was considerable, and the temperature stayed warm all year round. Wooden fence posts simply took root and grew. Grant had seen the post-to-tree miracle one other place, on the road from Sosa, to Puerto Plata, on the north seashore of the Dominican Republic.

Forty-five minutes after leaving Veracruz, they found themselves driving down a narrow strip of land with the Gulf of Mexico on their left. On the right was the huge Laguna de Alvarado, actually the mouth of the Rio Papaloapan. The river's name meant "butterflies" in Nahuatl.

Conversation was better than quiet reflection. It was generally calming and allowed both of them to better understand the other. When the talking stopped, their respective fears began to get the better of them. Subconsciously, they both understood this, so they kept on sharing thoughts, history, family details, and discussing their personal philosophy.

The drive took them through rolling green hills and past large waterways. Shortly they crossed the junction of the Jamapa and Atyoyac Rivers, and drove on to the charming port town of Alvarado where the Rio Papaloapan finally empties into the Gulf. They followed the road into Tlacotalpan, along the wide placid Rio de Mariposas. Here, the one and two story neoclassic buildings were a riot of color. They were intense shades of emerald and lime green, pale pink, lavender, purple, violet, blue, turquoise, and yellow. There was no unimaginative white in this town. The bold colors were a certain contrast to the town's tranquility. Tlacotalpan was designated a UNESCO World Heritage Site in 1998. The name in Nahuatl means "place between the rivers", something like the meaning of Mesopotamia.

They discovered they had turned the wrong way, and reluctantly reversed course and turned inland along the Santo Domingo River. Eventually they found a gravel road through a tree-lined wire fence that fit the description Matthew had provided. The private roadway degenerated after the first hundred meters. It was not much more than a dirt and gravel track with grass growing down the middle. It wound through stands of trees interspersed with deep grass. Cows grazed peacefully, not even bothering to look up as the car rolled along.

Finally, they crossed a wooden bridge over a slow moving stream to emerge through a border of trees ringing a grassy knoll. Directly in front of them stood a modern stucco home inside a walled area on a bluff overlooking the river. Only the second floor of the house was visible above the high masonry walls. The house was a desert sand color with large view windows. The high, heavy walls were a deep chocolate brown. Shoots of bamboo and newly planted trees, projected above its tiled crown.

"Some cottage," Alex said. "You think this is the right place?"

"I hope so. There are no cars out here, but we wouldn't normally see them anyway. In an upscale Mexican home, they would be parked inside the walled area."

They parked the rental car well back of the wall, got out and walked towards the door to the outer courtyard. Similar to the Robles home, a camera and speaker were mounted at the gateway door. Grant positioned himself so the camera appeared to be focused on him and rang the bell. No response. He repeated the procedure several times. Nothing. Not knowing what else to do they wandered around the outer wall.

The back of the complex faced directly on to the river. It was built of cinder blocks with cut-through filigree. You could see through them when up close. Similar to the hospital in Merida, these were designed to allow air to pass into the inner courtyard. The back-courtyard wall was set about ten feet from the bluff edge. It provided plenty of room for them to see into the main courtyard, or look out over the large expanse of water moving below.

The river was broad at this juncture, perhaps as much as a half mile wide. From a locked gate in the back wall, there led concrete steps halfway down to the water's edge. Wooden steps covered the remainder of the distance to a final platform. The platform was attached to a sliding ramp that ended on a floating dock. No boat was present. Everywhere it was quiet; quiet and green. The air was moist and heavy, birds and insects the only sound. Under other circumstances, they might have found the thick tranquility peaceful and relaxing. Here it seemed to portend danger.

Captured by the atmosphere, both Alex and Grant fell silent. There was a heavy melancholy here. Without realizing it, they were taking care to walk quietly, as if to make a sound would somehow awake forces they dared not disturb. Grant became aware he was hardly breathing…listening carefully, subliminally trying to discern what was wrong with this place. When he spoke, the abrupt change in the quiet caused Alex to jump. "No sign of anyone," he said.

"This place is spooky. Something doesn't feel right," Alex barely breathed.

A quiet one-syllable agreement is all Grant offered in return. They had covered almost three-quarters of the way across the back wall when he stopped, turned, and looked carefully in all directions. No sign of human activity, no boats on the water, nothing. Looking back through the block wall he could see that the house was designed so the upstairs consisted primarily of large viewing windows facing out to the water. He studied the windows for any hint of movement behind the glazed reflection that made seeing directly into the house impossible. Without discussion, Grant climbed the block fence. Alex was caught off guard. When he reached the top of the wall he stood up and again looked carefully in all directions. If someone were in the house they would surely see him now.

"I'm going to drop into the courtyard and look around, you stand at the corner and keep your eye on me, if someone drives up in front, give me a shout."

With that he jumped down into the courtyard and walked around a series of tables clearly designed for entertaining. He skirted a modest pool, and crossed the stone block patio that separated the pool from the house. Tall double entry glass doors stood partially open. He started to enter, but thought better of it. A strong sense of foreboding pulled at his emotions demanding he leave this place. Grant turned and faced back towards Alex. "The back door is open. Something feels wrong," he shouted in her direction.

"What do you want me to do?" she replied in a voice calculated for him to hear, but just so.

"Not sure. Why not head around to the front, I'll see if I can open the gate," he called back.

"Okay. I'll see you there," she said in a voice not much louder than before.

He stood for a moment longer, looking into the house through the partially opened glass doors, trying to understand why the house would be vacant. Perhaps someone is here he thought, someone sleeping, or sick, or ….no…he couldn't bring himself to even consider a more serious situation. *Calm down; don't let the heavy atmosphere get you jumping to conclusions.*

To his immediate right there was a walkway, apparently leading around the house to the front. The edge of the house was about thirty feet from the perimeter wall.

Backing away from the partially open door, he walked around the side of the house, back-tracking the same wall from the inside that Alex and he had walked along. Bushes and shrubs, with occasional stands of bamboo, had been planted along the dark brown outer wall. Similar plantings had been carefully arranged in meandering beds along the house. The walkway was flagstone. It wound around shoulder high statutes, small fountains and slender trees, creating the feel of a narrow Italian parkway shaded by walls on each side. The house could not be more than a few years old, he thought. However, the plantings and vegetation were already large and robust, and the overall effect was powerful.

As the walkway reached the front of the house it turned back to the right and stopped at the beginning of a tile-covered inner driveway. To the left of the driveway entrance was a gate for foot traffic. This was the gate where he had rung the doorbell. Grant opened the latch, and swung the door wide. Alex was standing there waiting, clearly nervous and concerned.

"You okay?" she exclaimed. "It seemed like it took you a long time to get here."

"I'm okay, but I admit this place is giving me the creeps. It's beautiful and serene, but somehow unsettling. The house reminds me of a mortuary for some reason. Come on, let's try the front door," he said with more confidence than he felt. The front door was unlocked. Grant opened it carefully and yelled into the house, "Ramon, Guadalupe, it's Grant Whitaker. I'm worried about you guys. If you're in there, don't be frightened. I'm here to help." There was an echo that would have been louder if not for the tapestries and wall art. Grant turned slightly towards Alex, and said, "Just in case someone else might be here, why don't you yell our intentions in Spanish."

Alex was frightened. Her eyes kept shifting back and forth in the shadowed room ahead. The entry floor was marble, surrounded by dark wood wainscot and crème-colored plastered walls. Two large portraits hung on the wall directly in front of them. One was of Pepe and Gualu, the other presumably the deceased parents of Ramon. A sigh of relief from Grant caused Alex to overreact: "What? What is it," she said with concern.

"At least we're not breaking into someone else's home. The portrait on the left is of Jose and Gualu Robles, and I assume the other is of Ramon's parents."

"Thank the Lord for small favors," she whispered following Grant through the entry way, and towards the back of the house. "Are we looking for anything in particular?" she asked. "I'd just as soon get out of here as soon as possible."

"I have no idea what to look for other than signs of where they may have gone. Of course, they may be somewhere local and will return any minute, although it seems strange. In my experience, no one in Mexico leaves a home of this quality unguarded. There is always a maid, grounds keeper, driver, cook, or someone, on the property. I thought for sure someone would be here." He froze.

Ahead and to their left, on the red tile of the kitchen entry, were the legs and feet of a woman. Probably as a protection mechanism his analytical side began to spin up. His first thought was it must be Guadalupe, followed quickly by the recognition that the sandals and skirt hem, looked more like that of a maid, or cook. It was someone with limited resources. It was not the style of clothing the Robles women wore.

A moment later Alex seized his right arm, and buried her face into his shoulder weeping, "Oh my God, oh my God." She seemed to shrink back partially behind him, as if his body could shield her from what must be a horrible scene ahead. Grant felt his stomach churn. Light-headed, he turned around towards Alex. She interpreted his movement as one to shield her. Alex threw her arms around him with her face on his chest, and sobbed: "Grant, what is going on?"

He could feel the stab of fear moving up his spine. He knew he needed to face the disaster that lay just feet away, but what he wanted to do was run right out the front door. Pulling free of Alex' embrace, almost too aggressively, he turned and walked directly into the kitchen. No one else seemed to be there.

She lay face down. Her head was to one side as if she was pushed into the kitchen and simply went to sleep where she fell. Probably middle-aged, she wore sandals, not the short-heeled pumps Guadalupe wore. Her dress was a one-piece light-colored plaid. A non-descript brown fabric belt pulled around the waist. Short dark hair streaked with gray, was pulled back and tied in a low-slung ponytail. There was no sign of what had happened.

Grant knelt down, conscience that Alex had come to stand behind him. He lifted her head slightly to confirm it was not Guadalupe. He did not know this woman. She was surely dead; there was no sign of life.

Having re-gained some composure Alex said with strain clear in her voice, "Someone has killed her. What…what if he's still here?"

Grant responded clinically, "I see no sign of struggle, no indication of what might have happened. Help me turn her over and let's get a good look at her."

"Grant, let's get out of here. What if someone comes and thinks we did it? I'm scared," she said, stating the obvious. Noting his intentions, she reluctantly stepped to where the fallen woman's feet lay and with a pained expression bent over and grabbed her ankles. Grant lifted her from the armpits and together they turned her over and lay her gently back down.

What had happened here? There was no sign of struggle. There was no blood. There was no apparent entry, or exit wound, either from a bullet, or knife blade. Alex quietly observed, "Her head looks funny. It's turned to far to the side."

"You're right. It looks like someone broke her neck. Probably came up from behind and pulled one of those commando moves you see in the movies. Snapped her vertebrate, and laid her back down dead. My guess is that someone was here looking for Ramon and Guadalupe, or the Robles, or both. Let's check out the rest of the house. Then, we'll get out of here."

They both hesitated right there in the kitchen, reluctant to move. Grant started pulling open drawers until he found a set of carving knives. Without a word. he handed one to Alex and took one for himself. It took a full ten minutes to just walk through the up and downstairs. There was no sign of struggle anywhere. When they came to what was surely Ramon's room, separate and distinct from Guadalupe's, but linked by a common bath and toilet, several drawers of a build-in vanity were partially open.

In the library, Alex pointed out a copy of the *Archeological Footnotes* paper Grant had been reading in Pepe's home. It was about 25 pages in length and stapled at the top left hand corner. Some of the pages were folded over as if someone had stopped in the middle of reading it. Grant picked it up and took it with them. Nothing else seemed to present itself. They walked the back courtyard together to see if they had missed anything obvious.

"Shouldn't we wipe the door handles and whatever we've touched, just in case?" Alex asked.

Agreeing it was a wise course of action Grant grabbed a kitchen towel and retraced their steps. With further thought, they realized there was very little either of them had touched simply out of trepidation. They wiped the front door handle, the kitchen drawer knobs, and the front door gate handles on both sides. Anxiety was high. They were strained and on edge. Grant struggled to convey a calm he did not feel. He wanted to sprint to the car and tear out of this place. Instead he walked slowly, forcing himself to think of anything they may have left behind.

Alex was in no condition to drive. Without comment she handed him the keys. By the time they reached the town of Tlacotalpan, and turned towards Veracruz, the sun had set. The landscape, so lovely earlier, now seemed dark and threatening. Alex was clearly in shock. She sat still in the front seat, rigid, almost unable to move. She was still holding the knife he'd given her earlier. When Grant spoke, she did not comment. When he asked a question, her answers were in mono-syllables.

By the time they reached Veracruz, Grant, too, was exhausted. His neck and shoulders throbbed. Someone should report the death, but he dared not even consider doing it. What was their next move? Where should they go? He drove on in silence, zombie-like, waiting for Alex to return to the present, or for something to occur to him. Grant followed the earlier technique of working towards the Gulf, expecting to eventually find the beach highway. Things looked different at night. Something looked familiar. He couldn't place it exactly, just a feeling. He kept looking around trying to get a fix, and then it occurred to him. He was back in the general area of Miguel Ramirez's home. Grant looked over at Alex. She was stiff and unmoving. He'd have to do something to help her soon.

Perhaps because he had no other plan, or perhaps because he found himself where he did by sheer accident, or perhaps because the ancient gods of Mexico willed it, he pulled to the curb a block down the street from Miguel's house. Grant told Alex to stay in the car. He got out and walked down the street past the house they had visited earlier in the day. This was one of the upscale neighborhoods of Veracruz, and like the Robles district, it had paved sidewalks on both sides of the streets. Tall lamp poles cast light on carefully landscaped common areas. Two teens shot by on skateboards. A light-skinned, well-dressed woman walked a full-sized poodle towards him. Grant nodded pleasantly.

The house was quiet. A light shone through the window. His first impression was to knock on the door, but if something happened to him Alex would be a sitting duck. He returned to the car, trying not to startle her. He needn't have bothered; she hardly reacted. She was haggard, and seemed to have grown older in the last few hours.

"Alex," he said, louder than he intended. Starting again, this time in a softer tone, he questioned, "Alex, are you okay?"

She turned slowly to look at him. Tears filled her eyes as she sobbed, "No. I am not okay."

"I know this is really tough. I do not know what to do, but I need you to talk with me for a minute," Grant said softly.

She tried to respond then choked. She tried again, and only managed a tearful, "What?"

"There is a light on in Miguel's home. I want to knock on the door and see who is there. If I do not come back in fifteen minutes you should leave. Find a hotel somewhere and stay the night. I am leaving you all three of my phones. Call Jack, if you need help. Alex? Alex, are you listening?"

She managed a yes without conviction. With growing concern for her condition Grant pushed on: "Would you please look at your watch and tell me what time it says?

"7:14," she reported in monotone.

"Alex, do I dare leave you here?" he asked patiently.

"I'll be all right. Don't worry about me," she said without conviction.

In thinking through the options now available, his deceased wife's mantra in times of trouble came to him. *The only way out is through. The only way out is through. The only way out is through. Just get on with it!*

Grant leaned over and kissed Alex on the cheek. "I'll be back to take care of you in a few minutes." With that he was gone. He walked to the door and rang the bell. No one answered. No sounds came from the house. It was as if the lights had turned on by themselves. Oh, of course they had! Miguel was probably gone, but he had one of those devices that turned the lights on and off to discourage burglars. It would operate based on a clock, or perhaps be triggered by ambient light levels.

He glanced around to see if anyone was watching. Satisfied there was no one around, he looked for an alternate way in. A courtyard extended from the front of the house, but there were no perimeter outer walls. The place was probably alarmed. Was it turned on, he wondered. It seemed reasonable that anyone who kept the kind of wealth Miguel had once stored here would surely have an alarm on his house. On the other hand, it had been many years since Grant was here last, so it was more than possible, probably predictable, that he no longer dared keep antiquities stored in his home.

Looking closely at the windows, he saw no observable window tape used to sense entry. Infrared motion detection systems had become common worldwide, so that didn't mean anything. Surely anyone concerned about their valuables would install something on that order. Of course, the Mexican upper class usually had staff. Their homes were rarely empty. Standing on his toes he tried to scan the front room from a side window. He searched for the telltale sign of a red or green glow, in one of the upper corners. It was light inside, and dark outside, so straining to see a small colored light was difficult at best. He didn't see anything, but that didn't mean there wasn't something in there.

A sound came from behind him. He froze, sensing movement off to his left towards the front of the house. Tilting his ear in that direction he strained to hear movement. There it was again. He turned around and leaned back against the wall, trying to blend into the shrubbery. Something was moving quietly towards him. He could hear steps, then breathing.

Alex crept right past him. She didn't even see him. "Alex," he whispered. She spun around with the knife raised as if to strike. Then her brain must have processed the words, and she dropped her arm. "What are you doing here?" he hissed.

"I was too frightened in the car. It was worse being alone. Moving around is better than sitting in the car wondering what is going to happen next," she whispered.

Alex sounded better. She must have moved the shock away somehow. "Okay, glad to have you here. But I am about to break into a house, so you would probably be better off in the car."

"No way, I'm sticking to you," she stated flatly. It was clear she was not prepared to broach any argument. *A new side to April Alexandria Jardine has revealed itself.*

"Okay, but I think we'd better get that towel we took from Ramon's. It's still in the car. Do you mind going back and getting it? I'll check-out the rest of the exterior, and meet you back here." He pointed to the ground. Looking up, he searched her eyes, for what, he was not sure, but she gazed back steadily. Grant ventured a small laugh and whispered: "Oh…and I wouldn't walk around with that machete masquerading as a carving knife. Someone on the street may notice, and decide you're out to murder someone."

A few minutes later they met back at the side window to the dining area. Alex confirmed no one was on the street for more than a block in any direction. Holding the towel from the top and letting it drape down the window he turned his face away. With a large rock, he hit the window hard. Really hard. He didn't want to have to do this twice. The glass broke into the house noisily. They both froze and listened for any sign that someone had noticed. After a full minute, Grant reached in, unlocked the window and raised what was left of the lower half of the window. Using the towel, he wiped shards from the sill, and climbed inside.

A minute later he let Alex in the front door, and they were pulling the drapes closed. Someone must have left this place in a hurry to not think of closing the drapes he mused. "Now, help me find the release on the hutch over there," he gestured. It was well hidden and the two of them spent several minutes puzzled until Alex realized it was not on the hutch itself, there was a lever around the corner of the wall at the baseboard. The wall turned out, the hutch was attached.

Light from the dining room reflected throughout the artifact room. The backs of all three walls were mirrored from floor to ceiling, just as he remembered. Loaded shelves fronted all the walls, and there were still buckets of artifacts stacked across the floor. The thought hit him that surely none of these artifacts were anything he'd ever seen before. Those pieces would have been sold years ago.

Alex was pleased by her discovery of the way in, then stunned into silence. The quantity and quality of the pieces stacked in this one room were greater in volume than any single museum might even hope to have. Instantly she recognized there were pieces here that would never be allowed outside of bulletproof, single-pedestal displays.

Alex was a changed woman. Within five minutes of lifting and examining a few ancient pieces of art she was completely lost in her trade. "Olmeca, Middle Preclassic, probably 300 to 500 B.C.E. Zapotec, probably Monte Alban IIA around 200 C.E.," she spoke to herself in growing excitement. She looked like a child at Christmas. There were piles of presents. She was just beginning to explore them. Alex was thoroughly mesmerized by it all. She was happy, and sad, and overwhelmed, and more than a little afraid. "Grant. This is incredible! I never believed it possible. What are we going to do with this stuff?" she exclaimed.

"It's not ours Alex. We're not going to take any of this stuff with us. It belongs to Miguel," he whispered. Instantly she responded, "This isn't Miguel's. This belongs to the world, to the Museum of Anthropology in Mexico City. These pieces belong to the people, to see, to retain their cultural roots, to…"

Grant interrupted. "I hate to rain on your parade, but there are people in the Museum of Anthropology who will sell this stuff into private collections as soon as they get their hands on it. The world isn't perfect. Just because you've been taught that all museums are honorable, doesn't make it so. In my experience, the good stuff is eventually donated to museums in any event. It usually happens when governments allow tax concessions for donations based on their appraised value rather than requiring the donors to prove what they originally paid for a given artifact."

"Remember President Clinton's retroactive tax legislation during his first term in office? Maybe you are too young. Well, one of the things he did was to encourage wealthy contributors to donate artworks such as these to public institutions. And yes, the wealthy got a huge tax break, and yes, they got a lot of public notoriety, but it worked. Many museums were dying on the vine at that point. Immediately after these legislative changes, private collections started emptying into public, non-profit institutions. When it happens that way, the media is all over it. When there's a lot of attention on these kinds of contributions, quality artifacts tend to move into public collections. And of course, the private donors encourage people to visit the museums in order for everyone to see the evidence of their largess."

"Grant Whitaker, you are defending thieves," she almost yelled. "I can't believe what I'm hearing! You can't really believe that nonsense! These artifacts belong to the people. They can't be bought and sold like cars. These are national treasures. Every time a grave robber digs another trench at an archeological site, he destroys valuable information. You're endorsing looting in the name of profit!"

The formerly immobile Alex was now a hissing cat. Her back was up and claws out. He'd certainly found her button, or at least one of them.

Grant began to laugh, "Okay, okay, let it alone. We need to look through the house. Let's see what we can find that may help us. And then let's get moving before a neighbor calls the police; if they haven't already."

"You look. I'm busy," she stated flatly.

Still chuckling he responded, "Yes ma'am. I'll do just that, and I'll do you one better. When this is over I'll bring you right back here, so you can tell Miguel exactly how you feel. I'm sure you two will get along. After all, you like to learn. And, Miguel is the expert's expert."

Alex smirked at him. He could almost hear her thinking she hadn't even heard of him before. Expert indeed!

Responding to her unspoken thoughts he said blandly: "Just because you've never heard of him doesn't make him not an expert. He's been working in this field since you were a baby, maybe earlier. He has to know his stuff. Rather than an egghead professor, Miguel is in the field, touching, working and learning. He is dealing with the real things. Not copies, not photographs, and not by listening to pontificating professors, who're more interested in their reputations than they are the truth. Miguel learns from real live, upfront, in your face, contact with thousands of artifacts from hundreds of locations."

"You're still defending him! He's nothing but a glorified fence. He's worse than a thief; he makes his living selling stolen goods. That encourages even more looting. How can you possibly make excuses for him? There is no way I want to meet this guy. He's the scum of the earth. I..." Grant placed his finger over his lips. Alex fell silent.

They stood unmoving, straining to hear. Grant walked to the front door and opened it quickly. Nothing. He crossed the front courtyard and opened the gate. He looked both ways on the street to see if anyone was watching. It seemed normal enough. Very little foot traffic was about. An occasional car drove by. He returned to the house to find Alex on her knees scooting the lid off a box with symbols cut into it. The lid looked heavy. She was struggling in a tight space to lay it over on its side. Alex withdrew a bundle. It was a wrapping of some sort. She was having trouble lifting it.

Grant was spellbound. *Could it be?* "Alex," he said with growing excitement. "Let me help you with that."

"I've just about got it, she said, through labored breathing. "It's heavy, but not that heavy. There's not much room to move around..., there." She rested the bundle on the edge of the masonry box from which she had withdrawn it. "Looks like you may have been right. A stone box, maybe not exactly stone, but some form of poured cement, which is just about the same thing."

"I knew it. I flipping well knew it," he moaned. "It's for real! They exist." Grant was beyond ecstatic. He couldn't wipe the smile off his face. He was grinning wildly.

Alex looked up to him with some mix of anticipation and admiration. "How did you know?" she insisted.

"It's a long story. Come on, let's see them," he said eagerly.

She began to carefully unwrap the binding. The bundle was oddly shaped, the contents heavy for its size. The last of the leather wrap was removed, exposing a stack of gold colored, metal sheets. It looked to be about eight by six inches in size, bound by three oblong rings. The rings were probably a bronze alloy he decided. The metal plates were literally sheets of gold alloy. There appeared to be a couple of dozen plates collected in a single stack two to three inches thick. The metal sheets were covered from top to bottom, and side-to-side, with cramped symbols. "Oh my god," she whispered. "It's simply unbelievable. It looks like an ancient notebook. Metal pages organized like a three-ring binder, except there's no binder, just the rings."

"I was wrong Alex," he said.

"A man that can admit he's wrong. How unusual. What were you wrong about?" she asked, trying her best to be cute, but still stunned.

"When I said we're not taking anything from this house. This we are taking. And, we're taking it now," he blurted with a mix of exhilaration and concern. "Let's get out of here ASAP."

"You carry the box, I'll carry the plates," she almost yelled. She immediately began rewrapping the leather binding.

The box felt to be twenty to thirty pounds. The plates by themselves were probably over twenty pounds. They did not look that heavy. Lifting them proved differently. He reminded himself that gold was roughly twice as heavy as brass. It was still hard to believe that something that small weighted so much. The plates were not designed to shine, they were made to last. Ten minutes later they returned to the house, having placed the box and writings in the trunk of the car. They agreed that Alex should quickly survey other artifacts in the room. Then close it up as if no one had been there. Grant would search through the balance of the house.

Alex was just closing the wall when Grant materialized with a towel taken from one of the washrooms. "Wipe everything you touched. No fingerprints remember." They left the glass on the floor, but wiped the sill and the pull-tabs on all the drapes. With a heavy drape pulled across the dining room window, it would not be so obvious that it had been broken. They relocked the front door and exited through the front gate.

CHAPTER TWENTY-TWO

Veracruz, Mexico

They drove along the beach highway, lost in thought. Their lives had been turned upside down. There were missing persons, thugs, someone following them, and police at every turn. They'd illegally entered two homes, and broken in to one. They had discovered a murder, and done nothing about it. And yet, there was the thrill of their incredible discovery. Or was it their discovery? They had made a discovery in a sense, but they had broken into someone's home to do it. Most people would probably interpret their actions as stealing.

Now that he began to consider their actions in a more rational light, he was not at all sure they had done the right thing. What had they done? Were they saving an important artifact for the world? Or had they stolen an incredible find for their own benefit? Were they trying to gain leverage against who knows what, in order to save the Robles? Or was it about leverage for them personally? What was the truth? What was driving them? What should they do next?

Things had become surreal indeed. The last few days were more like a bizarre movie, or a disconnected dream. Could this really be happening? In the movies, the main characters never seemed to be bothered about doing something questionable. But it wasn't like that at all. Their actions were, at best, unsettling. What had they really done? Were they simply acting out a self-preservation play, or doing something seriously wrong. Were they now villains along with others in the cast, or the good guys riding in on a white horse to save the day?

Alex broke the silence, "Where are we going?"

Knocked out of his mental preoccupation, he replied, "I'm not sure. I'm trying to figure out what to do."

"We'd better find a place to spend the night," Alex offered. But, it worries me to check into a hotel knowing the cargo we're carrying is so incredibly valuable. Even if the box and plates are a fake, someone is looking for them. Whoever that someone is, they have almost certainly been through Miguel's house before us. They probably had no idea there was a secret room in his house. Didn't you tell me, he typically used a warehouse somewhere?"

Grant seemed to chew on the implications of what Alex was saying. "Yeah, that's right."

"Grant, are you afraid to check into a hotel because someone is out there looking for us?"

"Someone is definitely looking for us."

"Maybe I should drive to a smaller airfield somewhere and you fly to me," Alex mused. "The plane might be compromised, but even if it were not, it would look pretty strange trying to get this stuff through the airport screeners in the morning. In fact, it's probably not possible, at least for people like us."

"Yeah, the guards at the airport search everything going on to the field. They are specifically trained to look for drugs and antiquities. Getting the plane is a good idea, but to go where, and do what? Every field in Mexico has military personnel on it. I've flown into little airstrips where you'd swear no one was around, and some army guy shows up with an automatic rifle, rubbing his eyes."

"Well, they may be thorough at airports, but they aren't at roadside hotels. You can stay the night anywhere outside the tourist area without ID. All you need to do is pay in advance, sign the register, and they give you a single thin towel, a room-key, and a sliver of soap," she said.

They agreed. They would find a non-descript hotel. Grant would check-in, and sign the register with another name. Alex would wait in a nearby restaurant and watch the car. After checking in, Grant would join Alex for dinner. After dinner they would go to the room. If the police were looking for them, they'd be asking after two gringos traveling together. Of course, it would be better for Alex to rent the room, as her language skills were so much better, but a woman traveling alone would be more unusual than a lone American male. They decided to search for hotels on the gulf highway, north of the airport. Well beyond the city. There were no tourist areas north of the city. And, it was the opposite direction from any of the Robles family residences.

The hotel Bonito looked to be about right. It was located in a sleepy roadside township more than an hour north of the city. The town had only one traffic light and two stop signs. All but one of the cross streets were dirt and gravel. It looked adequate, but not nice. They could count five sleepy little restaurant-bars within a hundred meters of the hotel. It had a parking lot with a gate, and a security guard to control it. They drove on past, then turned around and headed back. Alex got out a block before the hotel. Grant proceeded to the hotel security gate. The guard lazily pushed down on the balanced gatepost, raising the horizontal pole. Grant drove in. He immediately felt claustrophobic. Willing his anxiety under control, he walked into the open area that served as the lobby.

Key in hand, Grant Whitaker, aka John Sizeman, walked to the Gila Bar. He took a chair at the table where Alex was already eating. "It's pretty plain, third floor, one double bed. Is that going to be alright with you?"

Responding around a mouthful of enchilada, she said something that sounded like, "Sure."

The Gila was a typical small town Mexican establishment. It was open at the front with three inside walls, a full-length bar, painted tables and chairs. Chili peppers hung from the ceilings along with strings of vanilla, and baskets of flowers. A mirror mounted behind the bar was fronted with shelves of various types of liquors. Alex was nursing her second beer by the time Grant sat down. She was doing her best to knock her stress-level back. As other patrons arrived to eat and drink, it felt a little too close for comfort. They switched tables so they could talk without others paying attention, and noting their use of English.

Alex ordered enchiladas de pollo for Grant, so he would not have a reason to speak within earshot of anyone. She ordered both of them beer without thinking, then called the waiter and added a coke to the order. After four beers, and even though she had eaten, Alex began to slur her words. She seemed oblivious to her condition. Mid-sentence in a discussion about the Mayan long-count calendar, she raised her hand with two fingers extended and waived to the waiter. She ordered another beer. When Alex left for the women's room for the third time, she was off balance. Grant began to worry. This had better stop, or people were going to notice when they tried to leave. He knew it was not his place to moderate her drinking, but unless he did, it could cause them problems. Alex, on the other hand, was feeling better. She actually appeared to be enjoying herself.

When she returned, Grant began, "Alex, I think we'd better go to bed and get moving early in the morning." But before he could finish Alex had broken his concentration.

"What'd you say? You want to take me to bed," she giggled with widened eyes.

Lowering his voice, he whispered, "That isn't exactly what I meant Alex."

She did not let him finish. In a raised voice, she said with a leer: "Tis too what you said. It's what you meant anyway. You been trying to get me into a compromising situvation since we first met."

Arguing with her was not going to work. He tried another tactic. "You're right Alex. I can't fool you. So, you ready to go?"

She sat there looking at him wickedly. "Hold your horses cowboy. I'm just beginning to relax. Kick back a little. You need to learn how to enjoy yourself."

This could have gone so smoothly, he thought. *Now it has all the signs of attracting unwanted attention. I've got to get her out of here.*

He tried again, "Alex, I don't know about you, but today has wiped me out. I really need to lie down. You're free to stay here if you want, but you don't know where the room is, and we can't afford to attract attention to ourselves."

She looked at him blankly for a moment, and then put her finger over her lips. "Shush, we don't want people noticing us. Okay, let's go get in bed," she said with a giggle, "but I'm taking a beer with."

"La cuenta por favor," she spoke up loudly. The waiter nodded in her direction, checked his tab, and came over to the table. Addressing himself to Grant, he spoke to him in Spanish. Grant was stuck. Alex had heard the waiter's question, but was dull enough that she was waiting for Grant to answer. Deciding that the waiter was asking him if he wanted anything else, he looked down at the table and shook his head no.

Like a delayed reaction, Alex put both her hands to her mouth. She began to laugh into her hands. The waiter looked surprised, but Alex pulled herself together enough to hand him some money, and rattle off other instructions. Grant sat looking down at the table, thinking everyone must be staring at them. The waiter returned with an opened bottle, and her change.

Alex needed to lean on him to keep from attracting even more attention. Grant put his arm around her waist, and together they walked off to the hotel. The desk clerk ignored them completely as they walked up the stairs. On the second-floor platform Alex slipped and fell to her knees. She automatically held the bottle high in the air so it would not spill. She laughed again, and told Grant he was supposed to save her from such disasters. After all, she was his knight in shining armor. "Or was it the other way around?" she slurred.

Grant gave a sigh of relief when they finally got to the door of their hotel room. It was dark inside. He fumbled around for a light switch. Finding none, he tried to remember where the bed was so he could feel towards it in search of a lamp switch. Alex stood in the door making humorous, and slightly lewd, comments. Eventually he found a light, and Alex came in without turning to shut the door. The beer almost gone, she sat down heavily on the bed and managed, "Who gets the bathroom first?"

"Ladies first," he offered, thinking wildly about the situation he now found himself in. She staggered off to the bathroom as he got up and closed the door. His thoughts went back to how strange his life had become since meeting this woman. He reflected yet again, about its movie-like qualities. The leading man never had any self-doubts about going to bed with the leading lady. Why was he so plagued about what was, and what was not, proper? Hadn't all such moralistic worries been pronounced dead by the new millennium? Grant Whitaker knew better. He knew who he was, and he knew this was not going to work. Not now, not like this, and definitely not under these circumstances.

He was still debating with himself when Alex stumbled back in wearing only a T-shirt. At least that's what it looked like to him. The effect was predictable. She stood at the end of the bed, mumbled an apology for not being a good date, and fell forward beside him.

He needed a shower. You couldn't function in this heat and humidity and go through the kinds of nervous situations they had endured, and not need at least one. He got up quickly, saying he would take a shower.

The only thing in his light travel bag appropriate for sleeping was his pale green swimsuit. The worry and the self-talk he went through in the shower, and while he shaved and brushed his teeth, was all for naught. By the time he was finished and ready to lie down, Alex was sound asleep. Sleep didn't come easily for Grant. He was tired, very tired, but he was also alert, and unable to shut his mind off. Then there was the problem of an attractive, mostly undressed woman, lying on the bed with him. This very present concern was not easy to ignore.

A noisy truck backfired on the street below. Grant came upright in bed. It was morning. He'd been plagued with dreams all night. They were uncomfortable dreams. He had been chased by killers. A dead woman was on a floor, he was standing over her with a large knife. Strange undecipherable writing kept appearing. A naked lady, holding a beer bottle, was laughing at him. Alex stirred. A thin blanket partially covered her. The way she was turned he could only see her back. He was still conflicted. The need to pee overcame lethargy. He arose and went to toilet.

Light streamed through thread bare curtains. In the bright light of day, he got a better look at himself in the bathroom mirror. His graying brown hair was sticking up in all directions. He looked like he felt, fatigued and worn. Embarrassed to be seen like this, he stuck his head under the faucet running water through his hair. He washed his face, brushed his teeth and generally improved his appearance.

Alex stumbled into the bathroom and immediately sat down on the toilet. While she peed, she looked up at him frozen in place. "Hope you don't mind, I really had to go." It was a natural act. It was not even revealing, other than her tanned legs all askew.

He reminded himself that it wasn't really any different than seeing those legs in running shorts. His libido wasn't buying it.

They were acting like a couple, only they weren't. They were right in each other's space, and they were spending more time with each other than most married people. No one was leaving for work; they weren't running errands. They weren't doing anything apart from one another. There was no relief from each other's closeness. It was wearing on him. The sexual pressure was increasing. At least it was for him, he thought. He recognized that he had become way too sensitive to her presence. Everything she did, the feminine way she moved, what she wore, or didn't, and all the distracting things he hadn't experienced in a long, long time, had taken over his space.

Alex was grumpy to the point of being curt. It was pretty clear she was suffering the effects of her excess. She left the hotel ahead of him, taking her travel case to the car.

They met at the same restaurant, and decided to head back to the airport. He would go to the plane. If no one appeared to be following him, they would rendezvous in the terminal and select a small airport a hundred miles distant where she could drive. They would meet and see if circumstances would allow them to load the box and writings into the plane for a flight to Cancun. There they would refuel, and Grant would fly to the islands where he would be safe. Alex wasn't sure how she would proceed. It was risky, but it seemed like the best course of action for the moment.

An hour later they pulled into the parking lot across the access road from the Veracruz terminal. Alex dropped Grant in front of the terminal, and circled the parking area. Grant was cleared to the flight plan facility located in the base of the tower. He filed a flight plan to Chichen Itza. That was in the general direction of where they would likely meet. He headed off to the base commandant's office to settle up airport fees and get someone to top his tanks.

Leaving his baggage in the plane, Grant grabbed an aeronautical chart and returned to the main terminal. He took a small table in a public area. It was the same place he and Pepe had met a week ago. A few minutes later Alex sat down. Together they looked over the chart and determined where to meet. After a moment Alex whispered, "Don't they have facial recognition programs running behind those cameras?"

"Yes. That stuff has been around since the mid 1990's, but mostly the airports don't talk about it. It's pretty much an NSA-CIA thing. Basically, everyone's face is scanned and run through Washington's database. I don't see where that could be a problem for us. Surely we're not in that league." He wondered if that was true.

They settled on a place to meet. The landing strip at the Palenque ruins in Chiapas. They were both familiar with the area. It would be quite a drive for Alex to get there by nightfall. She would wait in Veracruz to make sure he had actually taken off before heading out. They hoped to meet that night at the Real Palenque hotel, the only property worth staying at in the archeology zone. If he was unable to get a room, they would meet at one of the outdoor restaurants closest to the ruins. She would take his Mexican cell phone, and he would keep his U.S. and Caribbean ones.

A short time later, Grant lifted off for Chichen Itza, but instead of flying back across the gulf he would be flying the more conservative route, staying over land, flying the semi-circle coastline of the Mexican gulf from Veracruz, to Villa Hermosa. At some point, he would turn inland to Palenque. He would change his flight plan in the air with Villa Hermosa approach.

The flight to Palenque was uneventful. Clear and beautiful, the trip was a pleasure. The airport was located on a flat bench, down a hillside ridge, just a few miles from the archeology zone. Pyramids were clearly visible from the air. Set two-thirds of the way up a jungled hillside, the palace of Palenque had an unobstructed view of the valley below. Surely, this is one of the most stunning archeological settings on earth, he thought.

Palenque is positioned about 80 miles straight inland from the Gulf. The site is located on the highest buildable spot in the area. Ensconced in jungle, the view gives way to cultivated pastures spreading out towards the sea. From the air, it was breathtaking.

The small uncontrolled airport had been built to support archeological fieldwork endeavors. An orange weather sock stood straight out on the field below. Grant crossed the strip at midfield, 1500 feet above the local elevation, and banked into a standard left hand pattern to fly with the wind at his back. After passing the end of the runway, he made a descending cross wind turn to final. He landed into the wind. One of two military guards sauntered out to where Grant was tying the plane down. The guard did not speak English. Grant showed him his Mexican transient documents. He looked at them vacantly, and wrote something in a small ledger.

Grant guessed he was a good six hours ahead of Alex, assuming she had no troubles driving. He waved a wad of pesos at the soldier and said "Palenque Arqueologicas," while pointing in the direction of the major ruins complex. The fellow put it together quickly, and motioned him to a jeep. Grant was dropped off in front of a small museum. He gave the soldier a two hundred-peso bill. It seemed to please him.

There was new information constantly coming out of the seasonal field studies now under way at the Palenque site. A bulletin in the museum stated: "…the Palenque Project has been fortunate to excavate a treasure trove of new hieroglyphs." David Stuart, an epigrapher and renowned Harvard professor, had begun the process of deciphering the recently discovered materials. He had already made an exciting breakthrough in renaming the ruler to whom Temple XIX was dedicated. Archeologists had first thought it was a ruler named Chaacal, and then decided it was someone they called Lord Chaac, one of Palenque's greatest lords. Recently, Stuart had shown that the temple was dedicated to a ruler named K'inich Ahkal Mo' Nahb'III.

Of particular interest was the recent discovery of a tomb under Temple XX. The late Donald Marken, had made possible the use of Ground Penetrating Radar, which was providing new insight to hidden caches of information. A project film crew had managed to lower a video camera through a small hole into a supposedly unopened tomb. The camera was lowered at the end of a pole, attached by a harness and a cable with a nylon cord for guidance and security. The museum claimed that no human being since ancient Mayan times had entered this tomb. It was beautifully frescoed, but oddly, the tomb was largely empty. That is to say there were few grave and ceremonial goods. The sarcophagus and the more significant items of value one might expect, were simply not there. *Nothing's changed.*

A water mapping project had come up with some interesting information. Engineers had located twenty-six springs within the excavation site. Of those, thirteen were associated with architecture. There were dressed stone aqueducts, pools, and other curious water features uncovered. Streams were lined with cut stones for artificial channeling flowing through beautifully preserved corbel arched underground aqueducts. Rome in the Americas, Grant mused.

The Mayas actually built structures directly over their underground aqueducts in order to provide water sources to the aristocracy, and pools and fountains for commoners. One of the underground water channels had giant supporting ceiling beams. The water tunnel was ten feet in height. It ran directly under a large temple and several palace structures.

Grant spent several hours wandering around the excavated works of Palenque. He had been here many times, but its giant stone temples, pyramids, plazas, and aqueducts, still held him in awe. Heading back to the parking area, he caught a ride from a local tour guide to the Hotel Ciudad Real Palenque. It was only a few minutes away.

He was in luck. It was off-season and the hotel had a selection of rooms available. He took the master suite. It came with two queen sized beds, and two bathrooms. This was a luxury he had every intention of exploiting. After a swim in the pool and an hour spent in a lounge chair, he headed to the hotel restaurant and ordered an early dinner. Just on cue, an attractive woman in shorts, with a ponytail pulled through a Nike cap, came walking in looking no worse for wear. Given her binge of the previous night, and the hard drive she must have just been subjected to, this was a minor miracle.

Alex walked to him without hesitation. It was as if she had known where he was all the time. "I see you've ordered dinner, may I join you?"

Grant was pleased to see her, very pleased. His old-fashioned chivalry caused him to immediately stand when she walked up. He waited until she sat down and then reseated himself. "My, my, such a gentlemen," she chided.

"Afraid it was my mother," Grant replied. "She was very big on courtesy. It comes out when I least expect it."

They engaged in small talk. Alex talking of the long and wearing drive, made easier by the new toll highway. Grant spoke of his visit to the ruins. Alex spoke of her original field supervisor, and another resident archeologist, when she had been in Palenque doing field studies. When she mentioned Alfonso Perez, it reminded Grant to tell her about the tomb found under Temple XX. Perez was the principal investigator. Hmmm, she said, Alfonso Perez must be someone very much like your Miguel what's his name.

"You mean Miguel Ramirez, the guy whose house we raided?"

"Right. You know, I had a lot of hours to think on this drive. It occurred to me that some of the best field operators I've met down here were people that actually live here. They really do know more about the sites than the visiting archeologists."

"Well, since you mentioned it, let me share with you something else that occurred to me today," Grant said. "When I was reading the reports on the discovery of the tomb, and how they had inserted a digital camera down inside the area before it was opened, the commentary in the museum said it was the first look into the tomb since the ancient Mayans sealed it. I immediately had trouble believing that. True enough, there were some fabulous frescos discovered on the walls. And there were some grave goods discovered, but no mummy and nothing really stupendous. I got the distinct impression that it was just as Miguel had told me so long ago. Local experts catalog the best pieces first, and anything of really significant value is removed before the resident archeologist gets to "officially" open the tomb."

"So where does all this lead us?" she said with some consternation. "I feel like we've got a nuclear device in the back of the car. I don't know what to do with it. I'm just darn lucky there were no military checkpoints on the drive. Can you imagine what would have happened if they caught me carrying ancient artifacts around in the trunk? Do not pass go. Do not collect $200. Go directly to jail!"

She paused for a moment, took a deep breath and then continued. "Listen Grant, as much as I hate to say it, Miguel was probably telling you the truth about some of the good stuff being removed before the credentialed experts were allowed to move in. The stone box and metal records came from somewhere. Of course, we don't know where. But, unless they're discovered at a recognized archeological site, and in situ, their viability will always be in question. What's more, because they do not fit in with current university thought, if and when they do come to light, they'll be branded as a fraud. No one will do serious research on them to determine their viability if that happens."

"Yeah, I wonder how many legitimate findings scholars ignored into oblivion, because they themselves didn't discover them," Grant offered.

"Or, their existence conflicted with current theories," Alex added. "So, if you think about it. We're in a jam. It's not like we can say, "Oh these things are real all right. We stole them from an illegal antiquities dealer."

She paused again, as if considering what she'd said for the first time. "If the Copper Scroll that was found in Qumran, just a dozen miles from Jerusalem, hadn't been discovered by archeologists, no one would have believed it was for real. I mean, who would have guessed? A two thousand year old treasure map inscribed on metal sheets linked together and rolled into a scroll?"

"Good point. So, what do you recommend?"

"I don't know," Alex continued. "But what I *do* know is there are people that know these plates exist. And some of them are willing to kill for them. We're in a very ticklish situation. We can't turn them over to the authorities for several reasons, not the least of which is we stole them. Furthermore, we came across a murdered woman and didn't report it. And, even if we were to turn this stuff over to the authorities, they would probably not believe our story. Just think of the intrigue that surrounded the Dead Sea Scrolls, and the Nag Hammadi manuscripts. Oh, and let's not forget the scrolls of Elephantine. It's downright terrifying when you think it through. We've got to get rid of these things in such a way that no one knows we've ever seen them."

They sat there quietly, each nursing their own thoughts. Alex was thinking about something, but wasn't saying it. She suddenly blurted, "We might try secreting the plates into a burial chamber that's not yet been discovered. Then somehow get a respected archeologist to find them. Other than that, I haven't a clue as to what to do, or where to take these things. My gut says someone is going to track us down, and if we don't tell them where this stuff is, we may pay with our lives. Our lives may be forfeit anyway. I sense we already know too much."

"Alex, you're jumping to conclusions. And the reburying concept is so complicated I can't even think how to respond."

"Come up with another solution then. I've been thinking about this the entire drive here." They sat trapped in their own thoughts.

"Regardless of what we end up doing with these records, I would sure like to spend some time looking at them," Alex ventured.

"I suppose we could haul them into our room, Grant said. "There's a lot more space than last night and we even have two bathrooms. But, if we're going to travel tomorrow, we'd better get these things into the plane tonight. That prevents us from having to do it in the morning in front of a couple of military guys."

CHAPTER TWENTY-THREE

The Pre-Christian World

Their suite included a Jacuzzi in one of the baths. Alex staked her claim, saying she was going to spend an hour in the tub. Grant suggested she finish reading Pepe's manuscript while she was lounging in the water, but she opted for the *Archeological Footnotes* he had been reading. "Pepe's stuff is too much for my brain right now. His manuscript is complex Spanish. At least the *Archeological Notes* are in English, and deal with my discipline."

This section of the hotel was new. Their suite had not been in use long. The new facilities had been built to service the demands of a fresh crop of archeologists, and upscale tourists, who even at the edge of the jungle sought to indulge themselves in the finer things of life. Apparently, universities were prepared to pay the tab for their expanding Indiana Jones' departments. The new breed of senior archeologists stayed here at the hotel, while the students doing field work slogged it out in crummy accommodations that would be immediately condemned in the States.

The bath was constructed in marble tiles from floor to ceiling. The unique gold columns offset the cold feel of marble. Large mirrors faced two sides of the over-sized bath. One was mounted parallel to the Jacuzzi, the other over double sinks. Dropping her clothes in a heap on the floor, Alex stared in the mirror, examining her figure. She was in good physical shape, but the effects of too much sun were starting to show. She sat down on the edge of the tub considering the monumental shifts taking place in her life. It took a long time for the tub to fill.

Candles and matches had been provided. The light had a dimmer switch. I'm going to make the best of it, Alex thought. She picked up the *Archeological Notes*, deciding to leave the lights turned up so she could at least look them over. She lit the candles just because, then settled into the water and began to peruse bullets of information.

- In the recent past, scholars have reported that metal plates were used by the Greeks to preserve important information. Museums in Korea, Iran, Israel, Jordan, Greece, Italy, Spain, France, Bulgaria, Iran, and England, now display artifacts containing ancient writing on metal. The use of writing on metal was not generally known to the world until just recently. Gunther Zuntz, in his two volume series entitled, *A Course in Classical and Post-Classical Greek Grammar from Original Texts*, demonstrated how advanced civilizations in the past, had written their MOST important information on metal plates.

- Dr. Cheesman in his book, *Ancient Writing on Metal Plates*, explores the many similarities in Old and New World writings. He traces the roots of languages spoken by Pre-Columbian Indians, and provides documented discoveries of engravings and other writings found in the Americas. He has compiled extensive evidence from modern research, which demonstrates that ancient cultures throughout the world commonly wrote, and protected cherished records, on metal plates.

- **Phoenicia, 1800 B.C.**
  One of the earliest surviving examples of writing on metal plates is the Semitic Syllabic texts written on bronze plates discovered at the city of Byblos on the Phoenician coast of the Mediterranean, modern day Israel. They are dated to eighteen hundred years before the Christian era. Preserved on metal to stand the test of time, they are almost four thousand years old. The script is described as a syllabary style, akin to a modified Egyptian hieroglyphic system. Scholars consider this the most important link known between Egyptian hieroglyphs, and the Canaanite alphabet.

- Greece, 600 B.C.
  In the ancient Greek world of 600 B.C., Orphism was a major religious movement. The earliest Orphic religious texts were written on bronze tablets. The message of the bronze plates was concerning the fate of the soul in the spirit world. The religious significance and divine source of the material apparently justified having it engraved on metal plates.

- Walter Burkert, in his study of the cultural dependence of Greek civilization on the ancient Near East, refers to the practice of writing on bronze plates as being transferred from the Phoenicians to the Greeks: "The reference to bronze plates, as a term among the Greeks for ancient sacral laws, would point back to the seventh or sixth century B.C. as the period in which the terminology and the practice of writing on bronze plates was transmitted from the Phoenicians to the Greeks." At least two texts claim that there existed similar bronze plates that contained the "ancient sacred laws" of the Hebrews, the close cultural cousins of the Phoenicians.

- **Persia, 500 B.C.**
  The King Darius Plates, one gold, the other silver, date to more than 500 years before the Christian era, and preserve the most important information of the kingdom. Darius was of the royal family of Cyrus. Cyrus was the King of Persia, the man who conquered Babylonia and set the Jews free. The Jews had been held captive in Babylon, after the destruction of Jerusalem in 597 B.C. by Nebuchadnezzar. It was Darius, who founded the line of emperors that ruled Persia, until its conquest by Alexander the Great.

- **Nag Hammadi, Egypt**
  On a December day in 1945, near the town of Nag Hammadi on the upper Nile valley, an Arab peasant digging in search of fertilizer on the east bluff of the river Nile discovered a large red urn. Smashing the jar open with his pick he discovered a thousand pages of ancient papyrus manuscripts bound into thirteen soft leather books. The texts were translations from Greek originals into Coptic, the written language of Egypt from 300 B.C. to 700 A.D. The site of the discovery was across the river Nile from where in 320 A.D. Saint Pachomius had founded the earliest Christian monastery in Egypt.

In 367 A.D., Bishop Athanasius of Alexandria issued a decree banning all scriptures not explicitly approved by Rome. Some of the local monks copied many non-approved writings - including the Gospels of Thomas, and Philip. The entire library was carefully sealed in a large jar and hidden among the rocks. They remained undetected for almost 1600 years. The papyri are now preserved in the library of the Coptic Museum in Old Cairo. Thirty years after their discovery, they were translated into English as *The Nag Hammadi Library.* Together, they represent fifty-two sacred texts, frequently referred to as the *Gnostic Gospels*.

- **The Dead Sea, Israel and Jordan**
  In the spring of 1947, shepherds searching for a stray goat in the Judean Desert, along the northwestern end of the Dead Sea, came upon a long-untouched cave, and found jars filled with ancient manuscripts. The Dead Sea lies 1,300 feet below sea level. The river Jordan empties into this bitter salt lake at the bottom of the deepest valley on earth. The Dead Sea is surrounded by a series of descending cliffs and plateaus.

The story is oft told that a young Bedouin, by the name of Mohamed Abdid, threw a stone inside a crevice and heard the shattering of pottery. The sound prompted him to explore further. Other variations tell of guns strapped to the belly of goats, smuggled close to Jerusalem, to be stashed in the limestone caves that pepper the cliffs along the wadi known as Qumran. The area is only 13 miles east of Jerusalem.

Whatever the real discovery story, by 1948 a Bedouin tribesmen sold seven scrolls to a shoe-maker/antiquities dealer, named Kando. He, in turn, sold four of the scrolls to Bishop Mar Athanasius Samuel, of the Syrian Orthodox monastery of St. Mark. Kando sold the other three scrolls to Professor Eleazar Sukenik of Hebrew University. Bishop Samuel took the four scrolls he had purchased to the American School of Oriental Research, now the Rockefeller Institute. From here they made their debut to the world.

Initially, there were scholars who viewed the scrolls as fakes that must have been produced by antiquities dealers to heat up the trade. Their disbelief that these items could have lasted 2,000 years and still be intact, gave way to empirical evidence to the contrary. For many scholars of the time, the greatest insult to their expertise was that an ignorant goat-herd uncovered this incredible treasure. Scholastic reputations were made and lost based on the findings of a simple Bedouin shepherd.

Archeologists located cave number one, where the first seven scrolls had been found. Pottery, cloth, wood, and other manuscript fragments still littered the site. These discoveries proved decisively that the scrolls were authentically ancient.

Most of the intact writings were on papyrus and leather. They were written from right to left, using virtually no punctuation. One was etched in copper. All were rolled up for easy storage. The term "Dead Sea Scrolls" became the standard designation for the documents found in the general area. The initial discovery launched a search that lasts until the present day. Further discoveries produced thousands of fragments from eleven caves, totaling about 890 separate scrolls. The Temple Scroll was the longest, measuring almost 28 feet in length.

The Dead Sea manuscripts contain previously unknown stories about biblical figures such as Enoch, Abraham, and Noah. The story of Abraham includes an explanation as to why God asked Abraham to sacrifice his son Isaac. Never before seen psalms attributed to King David, and Joshua, were found. Several prophesies by Ezekiel, Jeremiah, and Daniel, been discovered. None are included in the Bible. Every book of the Old Testament, except Esther, plus many other books treated with equal reverence, were a part of the Dead Sea library.

The Dead Sea Scrolls are ancient. They cover a period of roughly 250 years, including the late Second Temple Period, a time when Jesus of Nazareth lived. They are older than any other surviving manuscripts of the Hebrew Scriptures by almost one thousand years. Translation of some scrolls, rendered entire lines of Biblical scholarship mute, and has undermined the authority of many institutions.

Since their unearthing over half a century ago, the scrolls have been the object of great academic attention, as well as heated debate and controversy. Certain religious groups, and a number of entrenched institutions of higher learning, preferred that translation of the scrolls never come to light. Some did their best, to control the release of documentation.

Ultimately, after forty years of effort by politically non-aligned scholars to gain, what the "Biblical Archaeology Review" magazine reported as "intellectual freedom and the right to scholarly access," the carefully erected walls of censorship began to collapse. In 1988, the Israel Antiquities Authority expanded the number of scroll assignments for translation to outside scholars. In 1991, the Biblical Archaeology Society published a computer-generated version, and a two-volume edition of the scroll photographs.

The Huntington Library of California, in late 1991, forty-four years after the scrolls discovery, made available to all, the photographic security copies of the scrolls on deposit in its vault. Under duress, and knowing it had lost the battle to control the scrolls, the Israel Antiquities Authority announced that it too, would be issuing an authorized microfiche edition.

About two thousand years elapsed between the time the scrolls were deposited in the caves of the Dead Sea, and their discovery. The fact that they survived for twenty centuries, that they were found accidentally by Bedouin shepherds, and that they are the largest and oldest body of manuscripts relating to the Bible, make them a truly remarkable archaeological find. Hundreds of millions, perhaps even billions of dollars, have been expended trying to translate, preserve, control, and exploit, the Dead Sea Scrolls.

Certain self-appointed guardians of Orthodoxy, both Christian and Jewish, coupled with politicians seeking fundamentalist support, succeeded in keeping many of the manuscripts out of the public domain for fifty years. Some of the scroll material has mysteriously vanished.

- **The Copper Scroll**
  In 1952, two copper scrolls were found in cave number three at Khirbet Qumran. The text had been incised on thin sheets of copper. Sometime later, the metal sheets were joined together, and rolled up into two separate scrolls. When found, they were heavily oxidized, and far too brittle to unroll. At the Manchester College of Technology, under the supervision of John Allegro, who published their first translation, the copper was cut through with a small saw leaving 23 copper strips, each one curved into a half-cylinder.

  The Copper Scroll turned out to be a treasure map. The first column of the scroll begins with: "In the fortress which is in the Vale of Achor, forty cubits under the steps entering to the east: a money chest and its contents, of a weight of seventeen talents." The scrolls go on to describe the locations of vast quantities of buried treasure, of gold and silver, valuable ceremonial vessels, and coins. Other statements from the scrolls say: "In the gutter which is in the bottom of the rain water tank..." and "In the Second Enclosure, in the underground passage that looks east..." and "In the water conduit of.... the northern reservoir."

- **The Treasure Hunt**
  When the text of The Copper Scroll was made public, it set off a treasure hunt. Israel was not a safe place to be digging things up. The area was in a constant state of war. No one admits to having found the treasure. But,

theories abound. If someone were to say they had found some, or all of the treasure, there is virtually no chance they would be allowed to keep any of it. Hence, the silence is deafening.

The last item listed in the Copper Scroll reads: "In the Pit adjoining on the north, in a hole opening northwards, and buried at its mouth: a copy of this document, with an explanation and their measurements, and an inventory of each thing…" Curiously, Josephus, the Jewish general who became a prolific Roman historian, described the "pit" in great detail. He records it as situated beneath the great Altar of the Temple.

Some believe the scrolls refer to temple treasure, and that it was hidden for safekeeping before the destruction of the Jerusalem Temple. Others believe the treasure belonged to the sect that lived at Qumran, usually identified with the Essenes, a Jewish group mentioned in the works of the historian Josephus.

- **The Knights Templar**
The Knights Templar, whose given name was "The Order of Poor Fellow Soldiers of Christ and the Temple of Solomon," was a monastic order formed at the conclusion of the First Crusade in 1096 A.D. Many believe it is they that discovered the treasure described in the Copper Scroll. The Knights Templar was an Order of warrior-monks who took vows of poverty, chastity and obedience, in the service of the Holy Land, during the period of the Crusades. In about 1100 A.D., the Templar's were granted quarters in the Al-Aqsa Mosque. The mosque

was built on the site of the second Temple of Solomon, which was destroyed by the Romans in 69 to 70 A.D.

When the Knights Templar established their order on Jerusalem's Temple Mount, also known as Mount Zion, they began secret excavations. Directly thereafter they became an enormously rich and powerful Order. After the Crusades were over, the Knights Templar returned to their various chapters throughout Europe. They became known as moneylenders to the monarchs. In the process, many historians believe they invented the Banking System. The Templars became for a time, the richest and most powerful organization in the medieval world. Their network of fortresses became the center of trade and banking throughout most of Europe, parts of Asia and Africa, for 200 years.

By the 1300's, the Templars had their own fleet of vessels based at La Rochelle, on the Atlantic coast of France. The Order's battle flag was the skull and crossbones, later to become a symbol of pirates the world over. The Catholic Church disbanded the Order, and excommunicated its known members on Friday the 13th, October 1307. That same day fifty galleys set sail under flag from La Rochelle and were never seen, or heard of again. The belief that Friday the 13th is an unlucky day, may hail back to this very event in history. Those of the Order not having escaped were captured, and subjected to horrible tortures. The king of France, and the Pope of Rome, seized all the Order's assets they could find, thereby returning France and Rome to solvency after years of being deeply in debt to the Templars.

It is largely held that an influential group of Templars fled to Scotland, under the guise of stonecutters, and established Free Masonry as a covert continuation of the lower levels of their order. It is also convincingly argued that a multitude of Templars fled to Switzerland, where the forest Cantons (states) had recently united into a nation. Switzerland thereafter became the greatest banking nation in all of history. Its banks currently claim to administer over 2/3rds of the wealth of Europe.

Many of the secret temple rites of the Knights Templar are thought to be preserved through the fragmentation of its Order into such organizations as the Rosicrucian's, the Masons, the Independent Order of Odd Fellows, The Scottish Rites of Freemasonry, and other society's that sprang forth from the geographically isolated shards of the Templars.

- **Mesoamerica**
The term Mesoamerica denotes both place and time. Mesoamerica is the name archaeologists call the area of Mexico, Belize, Guatemala, El Salvador, and Honduras. Mesoamerica also refers to a time prior to the arrival of Europeans regarding this geographical region.

Mesoamerica is the only known area in North, South or Central America, from approximately 2700 B.C. until the arrival of Columbus, where a written language and significant cultural sophistication existed. The bulk of the high culture lies between modern day Guatemala City on the south and Mexico City on the north. The halfway point falls in and around the Isthmus of Tehuantepec, the narrow neck of lower Mexico. The Isthmus area is thought to be the originating place of both the Mayan calendar and of writing in the Americas.

- Raul Noriega, the Mexican scholar who discovered the method for interpreting the Mesoamerica calendar and astronomical glyphs, did so by studying the mathematics and astronomy of Mesopotamia.

- The writings and traditions of the Olmec, Maya, Teotihuacan, and other high cultures of Mesoamerica, refer to at least three distinct landings via boat by groups coming from across the sea, each bringing their own cultural identities. One appears to have landed on the Pacific side of Mexico at the Guatemala border, two on the Gulf side of Mexico. There also appear to have been visitors who came by ocean-going vessel seeking trade.

- **A West Coast Landing – Approximately 600 B.C.**
  The Izapa culture ran south along the pacific side of Mexico from the Isthmus of Tehuantepec into the northern part of the coastal plain of Guatemala. This area is within the greater Mayan territories, in other words, within that area of Mesoamerica beginning on the south side of the Isthmus of Tehuantepec. The Izapa culture is different from the traditional Maya, although heavily influenced by the latter, and eventually was absorbed sometime after 350 A.D. Tapachula, Mexico, only five miles from the Guatemala border on today's map, seems to be the original core nucleus for the Izapa culture.

- It is at Tapachula that many scholars now believe that writing, and both the religious and astronomical calendar systems were developed. The original measurement methodology was the cubit, the same as ancient Israel. It is here that the famous Stela 5 is found. It is frequently referred to as the "Tree-of-Life Stone." In a 1987 report to the Maya convention, it was reported that, "For almost a thousand years from 600 B.C., it, (Izapa), seems to have been the largest and most important center on the Pacific Coast, undoubtedly serving both civil and religious functions."

- Izapa influence itself sporadically radiated east and northwest, but its greatest influence is observed southward. One theory gaining traction is that the Tapachula area was the site of a landing party escaping the Babylonians around 600 B.C. It is from here that writing and the calendar seem to radiate throughout Mesoamerica. A short time after the emigrant's arrival, they may have moved inland to a higher, more comfortable climate, where they settled in the Guatemala Highlands. There they began construction of a city that has been continually occupied until the present day. This archeological site is known as Kaminaljuyu. It dates back to approximately 600 B.C.

- The Mexican archaeologist Miguel Covarrubius discussing Kaminaljuyu, states in his book *Indian Art of Mexico and Central America*, that… "Suddenly a highly civilized people arrived and settled on the site and feverishly undertook a vast program of building."

- From the Maya work, *Annals of the Cakchiquels*, we see additional reference to the earliest settlement of the Guatemala highland. The Cakchiquel Maya retain a certain amount of individuality, and they still speak the Maya tongue. The "Annals" were written by Arana and

Diaz, members of the royal Maya Xahila family, in the middle 1500's, and includes the words: "From the other side of the sea we came.... from the west we came.... from across the sea..."

- **An East Coast Landing – Approximately 550 B.C.**
  At about the same time, somewhere between 500 and 600 B.C., another group is reported to have arrived on the Gulf side of Mexico at Panuco, just south of Texas, in the modern state of Tampico. Sahagun, an early Catholic padre who came to New Spain in the early 1500's, wrote extensively about the traditions of the Mexicans. He learned to read and write in the native tongue. He records: "Concerning the origin of these peoples, the report the old men give is that they came by sea from the north (down the gulf coast), and it is true that they came in wooden boats...seven ships in which the first settlers of this land came... They came from the east coasting along the shore disembarking in the Port of Panuco."

- The first Bishop of the Yucatan, Diego de Landa, wrote a history of the Maya in the middle 1500's, wherein he said: "Some of the old people of Yucatan say that they have heard from their ancestors, that this land was occupied by a race of people who came from the East, and whom God had delivered by opening twelve paths through the sea. If this were true, it necessarily follows that all the inhabitants of the Indies (the new World), are descendants of Israel."

- The Phoenicians, who were allies of Judah when the Babylonians destroyed Jerusalem in 597 BC, were perhaps the world's greatest sailors. History confirms they had circumnavigated Africa 600 years before Christ. Archaeological evidence supports at least one visit to the Brazilian coastline well before the time of Christ. It is plausible that Phoenician boats ferried an escaping aristocracy, out past Spain, across the Atlantic, and into the Gulf of Mexico.

- Ceramic storage jars of almost identical style and design are discovered anciently at sites in Israel and Mesoamerica. Further, many ceramics are decorated with collections of wavy lines, produced by the exact same method.

- The Mayan record known as the *Title of the Lords of Totonicapan*, says: "The wise men...and leaders of three great peoples...extending their sight over...the world...came from where the sun rises. Together these tribes came from the other part of the sea, from the East... These, then, were the three nations of Quiches, and they came from where the sun rises; descendants of Israel, of the same language and same customs as Israel."

- **A More Ancient Landing**
  In the state of Veracruz, a colossal stone head was discovered in 1892. Over the years since, other huge stone heads have been uncovered. They appear to be renditions of actual individuals, likely kings or leaders of an ancient society. They have been arbitrarily named the Olmecs, or Olmecas. Quantities of Olmec artifacts have been discovered throughout the Gulf area. They have turned up at widespread sites in Mexico, and adjacent Central America. For decades, these findings were misinterpreted. The Maya were thought of as the "mother culture" of Mexico and the first high culture of the

Americas. Therefore, the Olmecs were either insignificant or some derivative of Mayan themselves. In 1939, a carving was discovered near one of the gigantic heads, with a characteristic Olmec design. It had a date symbol. This revealed a shocking truth, the Olmecs had arrived far earlier than the Maya. It is now believed that the Olmecas represent the first high culture in the Americas.

- The Olmecs recorded in two huge carved stone stela at the archeological ruins of La Venta, the depicting of guests being received from afar. One looks distinctly like a Chinese monk. The other looks Arabic-Persian. Both have beards, dress, and accruements, found only in China and Arabic-Persia respectively. Both are consistent with the time frame when these statutes were carved.

- In a book, entitled *Origin of the Olmec Civilization*, Professor Matt Xu, a Chinese teacher in the foreign languages department at the University of Oklahoma, says that, in his view, the first complex culture in Mesoamerica may have come into existence with the arrival of a group of Chinese. These, he believes, fled across the sea as refugees at the end of the Shang dynasty. The Olmec civilization arose in great influence around 1200 B.C., which coincides with the time when King Wu attacked and defeated King Zhou, the last Shang ruler, bringing his dynasty to a close. Xu has "explosive" evidence in the form of writing. He has found some 150 glyphs from specimens from Olmec pottery, jade artifacts, and sculptures which appear to be Chinese.

- Professor Xu took drawings of Olmec markings to mainland Chinese experts in ancient writing. Most of these scholars agreed that they closely resemble the characters used in Chinese writing and bronze inscriptions. "If these inscriptions had been found in excavations in China," says Chen Hanping, a research associate at the Historical Research Institute, "they would certainly be regarded as writing symbols from the pre-Qin-dynasty period."

If I don't get out of this water I'm going to look like a prune, Alex decided. Setting the papers where they would not get wet, she stood up and let the water stream off her tanned body. Standing, reflected in both mirrors, she studied her naked figure. Not bad for my age. In fact, pretty darn good. So, why is this guy playing so hard to get, she wondered. He likes me. He has trouble keeping his eyes off me. We enjoy the same subjects. I wonder what is really going on inside his head. Is it about his wife's passing? Or, is there more going on?

CHAPTER TWENTY-FOUR

Palenque, Chiapas

While Alex soaked in the tub, Grant emptied her shoulder bag and went to the car to collect the writings. They were too heavy to carry over his shoulder, so he carried them to the room under the crook of his arm. The plates were open on a bed before Alex emerged from her bath.

Grant concluded the metal must be a mix of gold and nickel, or maybe gold and silver, but they must be predominantly gold, because of their disarmingly heavy weight. The plates seemed about twice as heavy as one might expect. Gold is as heavy as lead, he kept reminding himself. Grant didn't' know much about alloys, but he did know a bit about the history of metals. Over the years, he'd written papers and a couple of magazine articles, on the monetization of gold and silver, so he knew something of the physical characteristics of these metals in particular. The most important thing, in terms of the preservation of a text, was that gold was virtually invulnerable to aging. It did not oxidize, or waste away over time, like virtually every other substance known to man.

The plates were relatively slim, yet strong and stiff. He slowly moved each metal page through its rings. Every plate was completely filled with cramped writing on both sides. There were no blank spaces. The writing looked almost Egyptian. Grant supposed the symbols might be modified demotic, a form of written Egyptian in the late classic period. That was before Coptic became the written language of Egypt. He was certainly no expert in this area. And, he couldn't read a word of ancient Egyptian without a translation primer. But, as he recalled, demotic could be translated directly into English. Actually, as he thought about it, there were those ubiquitous copies of the Egyptian *Book of the Dead.* Generally, they showed hieroglyphs on one page, and their English transliteration on the opposite page.

"You have those things translated yet?" Alex asked, as she came out of the bathroom toweling her hair dry. "I must say that stuff in the Arch Notes is all over the place. It ranges from the Dead Sea Scrolls to the Knights Templar. Someone's done a lot of research. The point it seems to be building too, is pretty obvious, but I haven't got to the final summary yet."

Grant looked up from the plates. Once again, he was struck by Alex' easy femininity. She wore a locally made cotton skirt, and a light cotton blouse with hand sewn embroidery around the low-slung neckline. It was disturbingly obvious she wasn't wearing anything under it. Noticing his eyes linger on her top, she said casually, "I bought this at one of those roadside shirt and skirt vendors on the way here. There was no place to wash clothes so it seemed like the right thing to do."

Grant wasn't sure whether she was simply unaware of the effect she was having on him, or she was covering for him, because he was so completely obvious. Recovering somewhat, he looked back down at the plates and mumbled, "Smart move. I'm about out of things to wear myself."

Alex knelt beside him to look more closely at the plates. She smelled fresh and clean, of soap and shampoo. Her blouse was loose and moderately revealing. She leaned forward to study the text. Just a moment earlier he had been completely absorbed by the symbols and deep in thought. A minute later he found himself derailed by her very presence.

"It has kind of an Egyptian feel to it," Grant said quietly, trying to get over the sensation of her closeness.

"Hmmm, seems like a cross of demotic, with some abbreviated pre-classic Maya glyph's thrown in. Those two forms of writing are not all that similar, other than they are both thought to have begun as pictographs."

Looking carefully at the symbols on one plate, she continued, "Some of these symbols seem vaguely familiar. I can't seem to place them. Maybe it will come to me later."

"So, you have some background on Egyptian writing?" Grant asked curiously.

"I took a class on the subject. Daniel and I went to Egypt right after we were married. It was great. The pre-drug Dan was really a pretty good guy. We enjoyed a cruise on the Nile. We saw the ruins, things like that. We were only there ten days, but it is a special memory for me."

Alex assumed the tone of teacher. "Before Alexander the Great, went romping across Asia, and Northern Africa, Egypt had three distinct forms of writing, hieroglyphic, hieratic, and demotic. Hieratic and demotic were merely cursive derivatives of hieroglyphic. Hieroglyphic is the oldest form. It's the one you see in the Valley of the Kings, in the great halls at Karnak, and the inscriptions on temples and palaces throughout Egypt. Formal inscriptions are arranged in columns, or horizontal lines. There are no spaces to indicate separate words, and no punctuation marks. Hieratic, however, uses dots in place of spaces. The signs of both are generally inscribed facing right, and are usually read from right to left, as with Hebrew.

"The signs we are seeing here are not substantially pictorial, or at least I don't think so. Most of the symbols in the hieroglyphic script are recognizable pictures from nature, or things made by man. Some are symbolically color-coded. We think of them as ideograms, like some traffic signs. It's sorta like when we use a picture of a heart to represent the concept of love. Hieratic is an adaptation of the hieroglyphic script. The signs are simplified to make writing quicker. As I recall, hieratic was the ancient business script used throughout most of Egypt's history."

Alex stopped. She peered closely at the crowded symbols spread out in straight lines across the gold plates. She was thoughtful for a while, and then resumed her Egyptian discourse. "By 600 B.C., demotic script shows up. That's the Greek word meaning popular writing. After Alexander, the Ptolemies took over Egypt. By 300 B.C., demotic was the only native writing in use. It is a cursive style, derived directly from hieratic. You remember the Rosetta Stone?" Alex asked. "It included a section inscribed in demotic, along with hieroglyphic, and Greek."

Of course…the Rosetta stone, the crucial breakthrough in deciphering Egyptian hieroglyphs." Grant said thoughtfully.

"Yes, that's right. It was a stone monument of sorts. Actually, it's not all that big. It was found in 1799, in an Egyptian village named Rosette. It contains three inscriptions that represent a single text in three different writing forms. It was a decree by the priests of Memphis. I don't really remember what it was about. A French scholar worked on the translation. He was there after Napoleon conquered Egypt. Because he could read the Greek text on the Rosetta stone, he figured out the other two scripts."

"So where do you think Coptic comes in?" Grant asked, in an effort to keep her talking and gauge how much she knew.

"Coptic was the written language of the Christian Egyptians. It began a couple of hundred years before Christianity, but it is usually associated with the Christian conversion of Egypt. Coptic is, or was, the Egyptian spoken language written in Greek letters. Coptic is considered a dead language today, meaning it's not generally used.

However, it was the official written language of Egypt for about 500 years. The French broke the code for hieroglyphs and demotic, and they began the process of interpreting Coptic. While working with Coptic, they realized the phonetic value of the hieroglyphs. As it turned out, hieroglyphs are both phonetic and symbolic."

"Wow, now if I can only remember all that stuff," Grant said with a respectful smile.

"Thank you," Alex said, while performing a faux curtsey. "You know just the right things to say. I'll have to watch you more carefully, or you'll sweep me right off my feet."

He was becoming terribly infatuated with this woman. Smart, attractive, and fun; not to mention, downright sexy without being overt about it. The mental and emotional war between in his head and heart started up all over again. Couldn't he just "seize the moment," and let things evolve? Even as he thought it, he knew better. Everything affects everything. There is no such thing as casual intimacy, you are either intimate, or you are a fraud, he told himself.

Noting something going on, Alex commented: "You're a deep one, Grant Whitaker. Do you always over-think everything?"

"Meaning what?" he responded defensively.

"I think you know what I mean," she said simply, and went right back to the symbols, without any further response.

Alex continued to leaf through the plates. Without looking up, she asked, "Grant, sometime ago you told me you were looking for metal plates with writing on them. How did you know they existed?"

He hesitated for a moment. "Just a feeling, I guess." A moment later he added, "Let me tell you a story, Alex. This was told to me by Dr. Gary Ames, a fellow enthusiast in Mesoamerican archeology. He is also a pilot, boater, and diver, like me, but unlike me, he has employed all of these hobbies in his research for answers to the great Mesoamerican questions. Gary has spent incredible amounts of time down here doing research."

"I didn't know you were a diver," she said attentively.

"Well, not all that experienced - PADI trained and all that - mostly wreck and reef diving in the Caribbean. My best friend in St. Kitts is a dive master from England. He has a dive boat in the islands. He's a great guy, who is blessed with a terrific wife. She was a good friend of Marianna's." A look of sadness passed through his eyes.

Catching himself drifting, he returned to his story. "Dr. Julio Perez was the stepson of Alfonoso Caso, Minister of Archaeology under several consecutive Mexican presidents. Caso was the guy who claimed the Olmecs were the real mother-culture of Mesoamerica, not the Mayans."

"Yeah, well that's not so clear anymore," Alex offered. "Wasn't Caso the Mexican archeologist that found gold in one of the tombs at Monte Alban?" Alex asked.

"Yep, that's him. So, anyway, as Caso's stepson, Julio Perez was privy to the newest archaeological finds in his day. In that capacity, he became a frequent visitor to excavations, both officially and unofficially. Julio Perez was present at the opening of the tomb of Pacal at Palenque. As I heard it, he was the person who discovered the actual door to the chamber. After excavating a deep narrow shaft for about a year, diggers came to a dead end. Perez descended the shaft, and at the bottom, leaned on a sidewall. When he did, dust fell out of the seal to the door of the tomb. As you know, it is located at a ninety-degree angle to the end of the shaft. Julio was also present at the excavation of many other tombs throughout Mexico."

Alex exploded into his story. "What! Are you kidding me! Perez is the one who actually found Pacal's tomb entrance? You mean right here in Palenque? That's probably the most famous tomb in the Americas! What else do you know you're not telling me," she blurted.

"Wait a minute Alex, let me finish. On one occasion in the late 1950's, Julio Perez was invited to help with an *unofficial* excavation of a tomb. He says it was in the state of Oaxaca. Each of the several people participating in that excavation took a large number of artifacts for their personal collections. Julio took some tiny golden plates covered in writing of an unknown script."

"How do you know this Julio Perez fellow?" Alex asked.

"I did not know him," Grant reminded her. "Gary Ames did. I know Gary. And, remember, Dr. Perez was the stepson of Alfonoso Caso, then Minister of Archaeology. He reported directly to various presidents of Mexico. At one time, his was a very important cabinet position in the Mexican government. Anyway, I've seen the photos of the plates. I've seen the script, and I've seen even more. Gary spent time with Dr. Perez, off and on, for years before Perez died. Julio Perez couldn't make his earlier discoveries known, because under current administrations he would have been jailed for the looting of archeological treasures. However, the process was condoned under prior administrations.

"Gary says that on one occasion, he asked Perez his thoughts about the Maya not having metal tools to carve stone, which of course is what Sir Eric Thomson and his followers taught and what everyone seems to believe today. You recall that at one time Sir Thomson was the absolute undisputed authority on the Maya. No one would dare disagree with what he said, at the risk of losing all professional creditability. Mayanists bought into his ideas, which even today they slavishly regurgitate, notwithstanding considerable evidence to the contrary. Well, anyway, Perez claimed to have a set of metal chisels that came from an old Mayan tomb."

"Grant, what you're telling me is downright absurd. I mean it's not that I don't believe you, it's just that I find it so hard to believe modern day Mayan archeologists don't know this."

"Alex, this information is out there. Think about it. Professors, who've built their entire credentials on staking out technical and historical positions, are not likely to admit that all their books, papers, and lectures, on the subject, are wrong."

"That's one of the reasons these plates are a political bombshell. It is not just about discovering the truth. Eventually much of the truth will probably come out. But, just like the Dead Sea Scrolls, it will take a couple of generations, maybe longer. And in some cases, information will likely go missing. In the meantime, renowned experts will suppress data that conflicts with their work. Or, at the least, they will be very critical of any evidence to the contrary of their written positions."

"I can't believe this! I am sitting here looking at some kind of ancient script, etched in metal, probably gold, and I can see it is real, and I know how we got them, and where. And still, all of my training tells me it isn't really so," she moaned.

Grant tried to lighten the atmosphere by telling a joke. It was not his forte, but it worked anyway. They laughed. They laughed some more, then fell into further discussion, about the plates and their likely source of discovery. Grant shared his reasoning for Cerro Vigia being the logical place. "A long time ago," Grant said, "I was convinced the place to be looking for records, was up in the Santiago Tuxla mountain area. You drove through it on the way here."

"You told me before. What was the hill again?"

"It was Cerro Vigia. It is locally known as Lookout Mountain. About twenty years ago some Mormon anthropologists, and at least a couple of archeologists, put forth the theory that it was the original Hill Cumorah, a place of significance in the history of their faith. That's another story for another time. But, about fourteen years *before* Vigia had become better known, due to a couple of BYU professors, I was convinced there must be a significant cave system inside Vigia. I came to this conclusion for a whole host of reasons, the heavy rain fall, absence of any rivers off the mountain, gurgling fountains emerging around the hill for miles about, and for other reasons which are really bizarre."

"And that would be?" She wasn't letting him off the hook that easy.

"Well, they were metaphysical reasons actually," he said looking somewhat embarrassed.

"Come on, Grant. Quit stalling. You think I can't take another shock?"

"Okay. So, you remember the other day I told you I thought that Pepe Robles and his wife were a bit superstitious?"

"I think I remember you mentioning it."

"Well, about the same time that my son Matthew got to try on the burial amulet at Miguel's house, Pepe and Gualu drove me to San Andrés Tuxtla. That's the town closest to hill Vigia. Pepe was trying to help me locate a site on Vigia from where I could begin my little exploration project."

"You mean your grave-robbing expedition," she sneered.

"Call it what you want. Just because an archeologist has a title, doesn't mean he or she is any less a looter. So anyway, Pepe told me that the Catholic Church at Vigia, in San Andrés Tuxtla, was haunted. That was a strange thing for a guy like him to say. He'd never struck me as interested in the occult. Both he and his wife graduated from U.S. universities. Pepe has a Master's degree in engineering, a rather pragmatic profession, so his comment was a surprise. They wouldn't say much, but neither of them would get close to the chapel at Vigia. I wouldn't have been much interested in the subject, if it weren't for their obvious concern for me being in the area. Recall, I was intending to spend a lot of time, on and around, Vigia. I'd even got myself a local guide up on the mountain, a guy named Carlos Palacio. And, I clearly recall his daughter, who was blinded with severe cataracts. But that's another story too."

"Anyway, the Robles eventually told me that a few years before we had met, they had a frightening experience in San Andrés Tuxtla. They had traveled there to teach a marriage encounter program. Directly after their arrival, and right in the chapel in the middle of the day, some remarkably frightening things took place. They left in one heck of hurry. I don't much recall the details. They were rather fabulous of content, so I immediately discounted what they had to say. Of course, I didn't comment to that affect. However, I happened to call my sister that same evening. Now, at the time, my sister was heavily involved with the occult. I told her the story of the Robles, and she responded that the head warlock for black witchcraft lived in San Andrés Tuxtla. If true, that would mean he was somewhere on, or near, Cerro Vigia. Okay, so don't roll your eyes Alex. You asked me to tell you."

"Come on Grant. You don't expect me to buy into black magic along with everything else? And, you can't be serious…your sister is a witch?"

"No. My sister is not a witch. However, for a number of years, she was involved with psychic phenomenon, which led to her interest in intensely focused groups that attempt to harness zero-point energy. That's also another story, and not important now. Look Alex, I'm not trying to convince you of anything, actually I'm not sure what I think of it. But you asked me to tell you, and now you can see why I was reluctant to share."

"What's witchcraft all about, anyway?"

"I don't know much about it, and in fact I am not particularly interested. I won't even read a Stephen King book. And, by the way, my sister is a terrific woman. The best sister a guy could hope for. On the academic front, she suffered through two master's programs, and two doctoral programs. I suppose she was the perfect child for parents like ours. They were both teachers. Sis is a retired teacher and university professor. She has authored a number of books. She has done hundreds of radio, television, and newspaper interviews. And as a sidebar, she gave a number of public lectures on the occult and psychic phenomena."

"Ouueee…okay, I'm impressed. So, what's with the witchcraft gig?" she guffawed. "I suppose she was casting spells over the radio?" Alex laughed.

"Actually, I doubt many people knew of her occult interest. It was something she was researching at the time. However, the point I was making, was simply that I told my sister on that particular night about what the Robles had experienced, and she told me about the warlock in San Andrés Tuxtla. It seemed more than coincidental, so I began to look into it. The next year, I returned to the area, and met the old warlock. He was a crazy old guy. There were candles burning all over the room, little notes floating in the air, and he tried to put some kind of green slime on my head… nutty story."

"What! You met a warlock! Come on, Grant. Give me a break." She was quiet for a moment. "You're serious?" Without waiting for an answer, she blurted, "What did he look like?"

"Another time maybe, not now," Grant said evenly.

"Okay, I'm sorry for being sarcastic, but you've got to admit you just made a radical turn from science to the weirdly occult," Alex pointed out with a trace of haughtiness.

"Careful, Alex. The so-called science of archeology is simply the study of trash from the garbage dump of history. Archeology is merely a specialized aspect of anthropology, which in turn is essentially the study of people and culture. I would argue, that the underlying question about any specific culture is, what was driving the people's thoughts and beliefs. So, getting a grip on what a given people once thought and felt deeply, has great merit in terms of interpreting the potshards you archeologists spend so much time sifting through."

"All societies were focused on wealth, sex, power, religion, politics, love, and the desire for revenge," she rattled off quickly.

"I am awed with your quick assessment," he said drily. From my perspective, respect and tolerance, or the lack of it, tends to shape and define both people and countries. And, that's as true as historical precedents. For example, consider, that of the fifty-odd predominantly Muslim countries, repressive governments ruled all but two, until the recent Arab Spring phenomenon. In other words, kings, dictators, warlords, and militant clerics, administered virtually all of these nation-states. Tolerance for competing political ideologies or religious views, other than those perpetuated by the state, are almost always condemned in these countries."

Alex started to interrupt, but Grant was too fast for her. "Now, don't get uptight with me. I'm not anti-Muslim I'm just trying to make a point here. Just as Christianity was hijacked by feudal warlords in the Middle Ages, so did Islam become the tool of political leaders to gain and maintain control in under-developed Middle Eastern and African countries. These acts were NOT about religion. They were about power! Black magic, witchcraft, whatever, these are just aberrations on the same theme…the pursuit of power. In other words, anciently it was a mechanism to have power over others."

"You are saying witchcraft was just another tool to control others." Alex said thoughtfully.

"Throughout history, despots of every kind have played on ignorance, and mixed it with the passion of religion, to gain control over the masses. Unfortunately, they have done so, without the average person discovering their deceit. At least that was so until after the tyrant had solidified his or her control. To my mind, it is quite curious, that the state sponsored atheism that Karl Marx preached, bore all the hallmarks of radical religious fundamentalism. In practice, it differed not much at all, from a number of so-called religious countries today."

Shaking her head, Alex tried to interrupt, but Grant pressed on. "Radical fundamentalists of every political, or religious persuasion, tend to have in common a lack of tolerance for the thoughts, ideas and opinions, of anyone who does not think and act the way they do. Note I'm referring to *radical* fundamentalists, those that represent the unyielding extremists of any particular social-political-religious group, as opposed to mainstream "fundamentalists," which generally represent the semi-opened-minded moderates that form the essential core of most stable societies. It seems that no matter how valid, or vital, one's belief system might be, one undermines that system, and ultimately negates it, when one becomes rigid and dogmatic in its adherence." All of a sudden Grant realized how forceful he had become. Embarrassed he stopped talking.

"Whoa.... Where did all that come from?" Alex exclaimed with genuine surprise. "That little discourse just fell out of your mouth. You've got a lot more passion in there than I gave you credit for."

"Sorry. I get carried away sometimes," he said sheepishly. "Really, I'm sorry," he mumbled.

"Every time I think I've got you pegged, you come up with something new. What else are you keeping up your sleeve," she laughed. "Okay. Maybe you shouldn't tell me. I'm not sure I want to know. It's just too much excitement for one night." She paused, and looked up, as if she'd just remembered something. "Speaking of night, if we're going to leave tomorrow, we should probably get the plates into the plane."

"Yes, unless we decide to find someplace to hide the plates around here." Even as he said it, he knew it virtually impossible. Several different study groups were working the Palenque site. And a fresh crop of tourists arrived by bus constantly. There were at least a couple of hundred people wandering around. This was not the place.

Alex realized they had jumped track on their earlier discussion. "Hey, what happened to the story on black magic? I mean, surely there was a point?"

"Hold on to that thought. We'd better deal with the plates right now."

"Okay, so what do we do?" Alex asked.

"We need to secret them away somewhere. Maybe we can get someone with appropriate credentials to find them and make an announcement to the world. It would have to be someone who hasn't already published on the subject. I'm thinking of the publish-or-perish doctrine. Every professor is hell-bent on finding things to support his or her own ideas and opinions. Without publishing, one simply can't gain anything close to top professorships. So, if we get the wrong person, one who has already published opinions that are contrary to the discovery of ancient writings, then he or she might be more interested in suppressing new evidence," Grant ruminated.

"So, you're saying, we've got to get the soon-to-be-famous, non-aligned, archeologist to the site where we've secreted the plates. Then we must figure out how to get him or her to think they've made the discovery. After that, this person must immediately hold a press conference, so whoever is chasing us decides to give up and leave us alone. Is that about it?" Alex observed drily.

"Yeah, I guess it does sound over the top. And there's also the issue that no legitimate archeologist is going to buy into a recently disturbed dig."

"Let's start by figuring out a place to go. It seems like that's the most pressing issue. There's a map of southern Mexico in the car. The one we bought when we were headed out to Ramon's," Alex said.

Two hours later, they were still debating archeological locations they assumed weren't currently a part of any major study program. There must be some place they could skulk around unobserved. The longer they debated the merits of different locations, the more futile the entire idea seemed.

CHAPTER TWENTY-FIVE

Palenque, Chiapas

They agreed. Grant and Alex would stay in the hotel while they looked for an archeological site to hide the stone box and plates.

"No one should know we are here. You filed a flight plan for Chichen Itza, so the base commandant in Veracruz, wouldn't normally know you'd made a change of destination while in the air. If those guys in the 320 are still looking for us, they'd be hard pressed to figure out where we went, at least right away. I spent seven hours driving here, and for sure, no one was tailing me. I think we're safe enough for a couple of nights."

"Let's hope," Grant replied. "I still don't understand why they didn't just throw a chain around the wheels of my plane when it was in Cancun. It would have been easy to prevent us from flying anywhere."

"Maybe they aren't fully official, or someone screwed up, or they don't want to attract attention. Maybe their tracking us in hopes we'll lead them to the plates, the Robles, or whatever." Alex mused.

Grant thought on what Alex suggested. "Either way, we probably ought to get to the plane tonight. In addition to money, I've got a Swiss army knife, a Leatherman multi-use tool, flashlights, and survival gear. I also have a small medical kit on board. If we're going to drive any of those jungle roads looking for remote digs, we'd be wise to have some back-up stuff."

Alex drove the short distance to the airstrip. The airport was paved, but that was about it. Only one small building stood halfway down the runway. It was accessible by a gravel road running parallel to the field. The entire place was dark, with the exception of a single mercury-vapor lamp. There did not appear to be anyone close around.

The field was surrounded by a five-foot high, chain link fence. The main gate was locked. On one side of the airpark, pastures were fenced for cattle, although none could be seen at this hour. After wandering around for a while, they were reasonably sure no one watching. Grant quickly climbed the chain link fence, and strode out to the singular airplane on the tarmac.

Five minutes later, he returned with three bags of chips, a couple of packages of cookies, both stuck into his flight bag. The flight bag was an awkward rectangular case designed for carrying ringed books of instrument approach plates for hundreds of airports. It also contained a hand-held radio, medical items, extra glasses, paper and pens, two pocketknives, a battery-operated magnifying glass for studying aeronautical charts at night, and a host of other miscellaneous odds and ends. Grant had removed all the aeronautical charts so the center portion of the case was available to pack other items. They drove back to the hotel in companionable silence, each lost in their own thoughts. A short time later, they were back in their room considering tomorrow's agenda.

Without much preamble, they both decided to get some sleep, each retiring to a separate queen-sized bed. They were each conscious of the other, and trying to act as though they weren't.

Morning dawned bright with light streaming into the hotel room from around heavy curtains. Grant had awakened first, and headed to the bathroom. When he came out, Alex was already in the larger bathroom. A few minutes later she emerged wearing jeans, running shoes, a loose-fitting T-shirt, and the ubiquitous ball cap.

"I thought I'd dress like a field research person today," she said. "I'll track down data on nearby sites from the archeology research lab. Then we can take it from there."

They skipped breakfast, and went directly to the visitors parking area at the main Palenque site. Grant had been there just yesterday. Alex had not been there for almost two years, yet it was clear from the start, that she knew exactly where she was going, and what she was going to do. While Grant loitered in the on-site museum, Alex walked boldly through unmarked doors into the back section of the building.

There wasn't much to see in the museum. The standard posters were there, discussing the Maya, how long they reigned as the greatest builders and most sophisticated culture, in the Americas. Standard rhetoric, Grant mused. What did catch his eye was a map that included descriptions of nearby archeological sites. One in particular interested him. It seemed to be the closest site to where they were, but it wasn't actually in Mexico. Piedras Negras, was right across the border in Guatemala.

Piedras Negras, he learned, meant "black rocks." It was located on the east bank of the Usumacinta River. This remarkable waterway divides Chiapas, Mexico, from Guatemala. Looking more carefully at the local map, other choices began to present themselves. Places like, El Cayo, La Mar, Yaxchilan, and Bonampak. All these, were on the Mexico side of the river. Seeing all these possible options, Grant's attitude began to improve. Perhaps this harebrained scheme could work after all, he thought.

A young woman, dressed a lot like Alex, seemed to be watching over the self-service museum. Probably, she was there to make sure no one walked off with any of their artistic treasures. She didn't seem to have much to do. She just watched Grant studying wall maps. Finally, she walked over, and offered her services.

"What do you know about Piedras Negras?" Grant asked.

The young woman asked him to wait a few minutes. She returned with a paper entitled *Piedras Negras*, and simply gave it to him. Grant thanked her, and began to read:

> What we know of Piedras Negras is more tantalizing than satisfying. Many of the ceramics from the early excavations were lost or their find-spots garbled. Of forty or more test pits made in the 1930s, only a handful possessed any surviving records. Many of the ceramics from the early excavations, consisted of clearance, sometimes unsupervised by archaeologists, of walls and platforms and edges around buildings. Virtually nothing is known about the more modest settlements at the site. We do not know how the population supported itself, much less how the landscape around the site was used.
>
> The origins of the site, represented by early temples and hieroglyphic texts, are as murky as our understandings of how and why Piedras Negras developed through time. The discovery of substantial burning, and violent destruction of monuments, in the Palace at Piedras Negras, raises important questions about the nature of the Maya collapse.
>
> Unfortunately, the information collected by the University Museum in the 1930's does not allow us to understand clearly what happened at the time. After one year of renewed excavations, the results from the 1997 test digs

raise even more questions. The 1998 season brought studies of the West Group Plaza and the surrounding outlying area. The 1999 season located a mixed cemetery where evidence of a Sahal (noble vassal) burial was found. This lends credence to the change in political structure during the late classic period.

The rediscovery of the largest known cenote of Mesoamerica at Piedras Negras, although now dry, lends credence to why Yokib, a large opening, was chosen for the emblem glyph of this large city-state. Reconstruction of various buildings has commenced but is sporadic.

When Grant looked up, the young woman was still standing there watching him. Apparently, she was waiting for him to ask something else of her.

"Is there anyone working the Piedras Negras site right now," he asked.

"I don't think so. It gets awfully wet this time of year," she replied.

"Has anyone worked the site since 1999?"

"Yeah, just about every year since the late 1990's. One of the universities takes a team in there for about three months of the year. Usually, March through May," she offered. "I've been here almost six months now, but not had a chance to visit Piedras, or any of the other sites along the Usumacinta river. I understand it's not easy getting in there, and it can be quite dangerous."

Making small talk, Grant continued to probe: "Have you been to any other sites outside of Palenque?"

"No, not around here, but on the way to Palenque, I was able to go to Chichen Itza, Uxmal, Coba, places like that. You know; the major tourist attractions. I'm hoping to get to Bonampak before I go home."

"Not Yaxchilan," Grant probed.

"Oh, I'd love to go there. It's supposed to be about the least disturbed and most promising site around. Some research has been done there. I think the woman in charge is named Tate. She wrote a book about Yaxchilan. It's rather remote. The only way there is by boat. Some Zapista's operate a boat service for the Eco-Tourism yuppies. They put in at Corozal, and run down river about 15 miles. Visitors are allowed to wander around Yaxchilan, for a couple of hours, before heading back up river. I hear it only costs about $75 a person."

"Corozal," Grant said, sounding confused. "I thought that was in northern Belize?"

"Oh. I guess that's right. I think the real name is Frontera Corozal. It's up the Usumacinta River on the Mexico side, not far from Bonampak," she explained. "There's a road directly from here to Corozal. It's not very good I've heard. There are a couple of buses that make the run up that direction, hauling tourists to the Bonampak site."

"What do you know about El Cayo?" he asked.

"Bad stuff is happening there. Actually, the same as Piedras Negras, right now. A lot of looting. Some archeologists from Calgary almost got killed. Pretty scary stuff," she said with a shake of her head. "First I heard it was looters, and then I heard it was a whole Indian town that was up in arms. I gather it was because a couple of the archeologists tried to move an altar out of the jungle by helicopter. It turned into a huge mess. There's been political fall-out ever since."

"You didn't mention that when we were talking about Piedras Negras," Grant prompted.

"Guess I forgot. The real problem started in El Cayo. The archeologists barely got out alive. They were robbed, beaten up, and left in the jungle without anything to live on. They finally got to the river, and flagged down a boat hauling supplies to a research group at Piedras Negras."

Alex strolled back out through the doors of the research lab. She walked up to Grant just as his discussion with the curator was winding to a close. He thanked her, and turned to Alex who was already walking out the front door of the museum. Feeling a little sheepish, he followed her out into the moist heat of the morning. When they were far enough away from any one that could hear their conversation, Alex motioned to a large Banyan tree, and sat down on one of its huge, above ground roots. "I think we better find someplace else," she began. "The natives are restless. A whole bunch of intrigue has been going on since I was last here."

"I was just figuring that out myself," Grant replied. "The young woman in there was telling me about some archeologists who ran into trouble."

"Yeah, read this," she said, as she handed him a news release.

Ordeal in Chiapas: Archaeologists Survive Attack During Attempt to Rescue Maya Altar from Looters *by Grant W. Hoopes*

Mathews, an epigrapher of international reputation and an MacArthur awardee, had been excavating at El Cayo, an ancient Maya site on the lower Usumacinta River. The site is located between the Maya cities of Yaxchilan and Piedras Negras in one of the more remote corners of the Maya Lowlands, an area accessible only by boat. Although the site extends on both sides of the river, Mathews' work had concentrated on the portion in Chiapas, Mexico. Mathews' excavations revealed Altar 4, a beautifully preserved monument inscribed with fine hieroglyphic texts and relief sculpture.

Both the carving and the inscription were beautifully executed and wonderfully preserved. While this made the monument valuable for scholarship, it also made it a target for looting. The plundering of archaeological sites in the Maya Lowlands is extremely bad, especially in inaccessible regions of Chiapas and the Petén. Looters regularly tunnel through pyramids in search of royal tombs. They have used chainsaws to strip whole stelae of their carved surfaces, making them easier to transport and sell in fragments.

Mathews and a Mexican archaeologist from the University of Calgary cancelled this year's season at El Cayo in mid-June because it was clear that general lawlessness had made the region too hazardous for a prolonged visit. Most tour companies had cancelled trips to the lower Usumacinta as a result of several years of unchecked robberies and harassment of tourists by local bandits. With looting on the rise, the Insitituto Nacional de Antropología e Historia (INAH) became concerned about the safety of Altar 4.

On hearing of the attempts to steal Altar 4, INAH requested that Mathews and Aliphat remove it from El Cayo and transport it to Frontera Corozal, Chiapas, a town about 40 km upriver, where it could be protected and enjoyed by the community and its visitors. Villagers from El Desempeño and representatives of the Frontera Corozal community had already been consulted about these plans and had agreed to them. Mathews organized a group to reexcavate the monument, remove it, and prepare it for a helicopter airlift out of the site. The group consisted of 11 individuals.

In beginning to reexcavate the monument on the morning of June 26, the group discovered it had been partly excavated and damaged by pick marks in a looting attempt. While they worked, a group of about 30 people from the nearby village of Lázaro Cárdenas appeared, demanding to know what was going on. They claimed that the land was theirs and that they would not allow anything to be taken from it. Mathews and his assistants gave the men copies of the official permits, and all but three, who remained to "guard" the archaeologists, departed.

When the group arrived at the El Cayo plaza early Friday morning, they were confronted by 60 to 70 angry men from several communities. The group was not placated by the explanation that the monument was only being moved 40 km upstream for safekeeping in Frontera Corozal. In a theater of aggressive ridicule, threats, and bluffs, the villagers confiscated all of the expedition's equipment and field notes.

The archaeologists were informed that the local people who were taking over the project. As they hurried toward the river the archaeologists heard gunshots. A smaller group with firearms detained them at the riverbank, ordering them to drop their few remaining possessions and line up at the river's edge.

Mathews was now convinced that they would all be killed. Instead, they were beaten badly with rifle butts and kicked. Mathews' glasses and nose were broken; Arcos suffered broken ribs and a ruptured spleen (which he survived, amazingly, despite his three-day escape); two of the Chol assistants were cut with machetes, one in his face. The assailants then left, threatening to kill the party if they didn't leave immediately. Unable to swim, six of the Chol escaped through the forest. The four archaeologists and Arcos decided to cross the Usumacinta and seek refuge in Guatemala. They found a canoe that was used by the remaining non-swimmers while the others swam, pushing the canoe across to the Guatemalan shore in the cover of darkness.

On Saturday morning, June 28, the archaeologists tried to reach the ruins of Piedras Negras, about 20 km downstream. Injured and barefoot, they hiked all day through thorns and thick forest and torrential rains. They were able to get water from vines, but had no food. According to Mathews, a main preoccupation was with the poisonous snakes that abound in the region. After a hard day of hiking, the group remained lost. They spent another night in the forest, but resolved to continue on toward Piedras Negras the following day.

Meanwhile, some of the Chol workers had made it back to Palenque, where Merle Greene Robertson, Robert Rands, and others, were conducting an archaeological project. The workers described the attack and the archaeologists' flight into the river. They had no idea whether Mathews or the others had survived. Naturally, everyone feared the worst.

In Guatemala, Mathews and his group had made little progress on foot. Injured, exhausted, and hungry, they hid near the river hoping to flag a passing boat to take them downriver to Piedras Negras. They were picked up by a boat carrying supplies to Piedras Negras the next day and dropped off in the Guatemalan settlement of El Porvenir, where they spent the night. The Guatemalan boatmen changed their own plans and arranged to take the group back to Frontera Corozal the next day.

During the first part of the trip back upriver on Monday morning, June 30, Mathews and the others hid under tarps to avoid being seen by their attackers as they passed that section of Chiapas. Their fellow passengers from Guatemala reported hearing that Altar 4 had been disinterred and moved by boat upriver to Nuevo Progreso, a settlement with a reputation for looting and banditry.

The official response to the emergency had been slow and ineffective; it was hoped that worldwide attention would hasten the party's rescue. Through friends and contacts, using both telephone and email, the Canadian press, CNN, the New York Times, the Los Angeles Times, Associated Press (AP), and other major news organizations were alerted. The boat from El Progreso carrying the missing group finally arrived at Frontera Corozal about 3:30 p.m. Monday afternoon.

Grant let out a long sigh. "That's a lot worse than I thought. Guess this area is out. Maybe we should consider Belize. It's probably a lot easier to move around there. Plus, they speak English, or at least most of them do, and there are hundreds of unexplored Mayan archeological sites to choose from. Besides, I'd feel safer outside of Mexico. Maybe these guys chasing us won't follow us to another country."

Shaking her head, Alex replied. "I have a problem with that. There might be a warrant out for my arrest. The minute I cross an International border my name is likely to pop up on someone's computer screen. I don't think I can risk that."

It was midmorning, and Grant's stomach reminded him they had missed breakfast. "Let's get something to eat Alex. We can think this through over food."

Alex half-laughed, "You're a piece of work Grant, first food, then everything else. It's a wonder you're not as big as a blimp. You must have the metabolism of a shrew."

"I just prefer to think at a table, while someone else is serving me."

"I know a lot of guys like you. Most of them are a whole lot bigger though. You'd better watch it," she teased. "Of course, if your kind didn't exist, I probably wouldn't have a job. Speaking of which, I need to call the Itza."

They drove back towards the hotel. There were several stereotypical, Mexican outdoor palapa-covered restaurants, all open, with virtually no guests. They stopped at one that looked about the same as the others, took a table, and ordered eggs, beans and salsa. The fresh squeezed orange juice was excellent. They both ordered another glass.

Grant read aloud from a brochure he had picked up on archeology in Belize:

> *The country of Belize is bounded on the north, by Mexico's Yucatan peninsula, on the west and south, by Guatemala, to the east, by the beautiful Caribbean Sea. The Maya Mountain range is the dominant landscape feature. A small country, it nevertheless includes over 1,000 offshore islands, and the second largest barrier reef in the world. Over*

600 Mayan sites have been discovered in Belize, only six are open to the public. Belize, boasts the oldest known Mayan site; the longest occupied site; and the largest carved jade object found in all of Mayandom.

"Listen Alex, I think I know how we can get to Belize without any trouble. We fly to Cancun, borrow the Zarahemla from Jack, and head south to Ambergris Cay. Ambergris is a beautiful little island, right off the coast of Belize. Almost everyone that goes there is a diver, or fisherman. One more boat shouldn't raise any suspicion. I'm sure we can find someplace to tie-up. It's only about 30 miles over to Belize City from Ambergris. We could either take a small plane (they run back and forth all day), or we take a ferry. There's no customs or immigration between the island and the mainland. Once in Belize City, we can rent a car, and we're free to go wherever we want."

Alex frowned. She did not look at all comfortable with the idea. "That's scary to me. I've never been to Belize. Won't they insist on seeing documents?"

"Well, if we were at the airport, or at the border crossing at Chetumal, sure they would. But taking the boat down, I don't think so. In any event, I could drop you off somewhere along the island, and then go through customs and immigration, with the boat on my own."

"That's a lot of boat for one person to handle, how would you tie up at the dock? Wouldn't it seem awfully weird, for one guy to show up in a boat that size, all by himself?"

"Maybe, but I could just wink and tell them I came down from Cancun to pickup girls. My Mexican papers are in order, so they would probably buy that," he said. "In fact, even if we went through customs and immigration on Ambergris Cay, they're probably pretty laid back at the dock, and likely don't have computer access to the U.S. passport system. Your Mexican FM-2 should be enough anyway. I don't think you'd even have to use a passport if you presented your FM-2," Grant argued.

She sat there thinking, her brow crinkled, clearly not buying it. "I just don't know Grant, where would we go, and how would you carry the stone box, and those plates, on a little plane from Ambergris Cay, to the Belize mainland?"

"Yeah, good point," Grant managed, "I hadn't thought of that. But, I'm sure we'll figure out a way. My call is that Belize is the best place to hide the plates. There are so many archeological settings, and almost all of them don't have tourists. Did you hear what I just read? There are over *600* Mayan sites that have been discovered in Belize, and only six, are open to the public! And, remember, Belize has the oldest known Mayan site yet discovered, which should dovetail nicely with dating requirements. In addition, Belize has the longest occupied site discovered to date. Everything seems to fit."

"How long has it been since you've been there?" she asked.

"Oh, some time ago actually, but I've been to Belize several different times, and most recently flew over the country at low altitude when headed into the Tikal ruins in Guatemala."

"But you've been to this Ambergris Cay place? And you know your way around?"

"Yep, sure have. The town on Ambergris Cay is called San Pedro. It used to be a fishing village. In the 1800s, a bunch of Mestizos fled Mexico and settled there. Before that, it was a Pirate hangout, and of course, long before the pirates, it was a Mayan stopover for traders. It's a fun little place, three packed-sand roads in town, Front Street, Middle Street, and Back Street. It has great ambiance.

"By the way, smart guy," she said with her sense of humor returned, "No one is going to believe you're coming into Belize, from Cancun, to pick-up girls. Cancun is the biggest party-town in the world, outside of Las Vegas. No way is any border guard that dumb."

After another hour of discussing options, they decided to head back to the Palenque ruins, to see if Alex could come up with more information on Mayan sites in Belize. "They have an Internet connection in the lab. It is up-linked via satellite. If I can con my way back in, I'll do a scan on the sites in Belize. You can fool around in the ruins until I'm done."

It was late afternoon when Alex and Grant met up again. She was successful in getting information on Maya sites in Belize. Together, they walked to the center of the main palace. It was humid and hot. They were both sweating profusely by the time they had covered the half-mile distance. They sat down in the shade of the inner courtyard. The papers, Alex had brought, were limp with moisture.

"Altun Ha, is an option," she began. It wasn't discovered until 1964. Excavation work took place through 1970. Nothing has been done there since. It is relatively small, with only thirteen primary structures excavated, so far. The main plaza is enclosed by large temples on all four sides. Apparently, they've mapped another 275 structures, as yet untouched, and 250 to 300 more mounds, have been noted. Seven major tombs have been discovered. One had over three hundred artifacts inside, including the remains of a Maya book! Who knew? It's close to the border, and you can get there directly from Ambergris Cay."

"I've been there, Alex. Marianna and I took a day trip from San Pedro. We went by boat when we were staying at Journey's End, a property at the extreme end of Ambergris Cay. We went directly up the North River, by a shallow-bottomed tour boat. From where we docked, it was only a short hike into the site. Hey, do you remember that old Harrison Ford movie called *Mosquito Coast?*"

"Was that the one where he left the States and took his family into the jungle, and then he went crazy? I didn't like that movie."

"That's the one. *Mosquito Coast* was filmed on the North River, right in the area where Altun Ha is located. There are huge mangrove swamps for the first couple of miles as you come in from the Caribbean. I remember having to pole off in the tourist boat, after we bottomed out a couple of times. Interesting place, it's very quiet. That's a place that might actually work.

Grant laid back and looked up at the famous Palenque tower. It was the only one of its kind still standing in the Americas. Four platformed stories rose above the Palace. The tower was capped with a crowned roof. This place must have been stunning in its day. It's incredible even now, he thought.

Alex shuffled the papers then continued. "Probably the next choice is Cahal Pech, its located on a tall hill, overlooking the town of San Ignacio. The name means place of ticks. What a cheery thought. Can you imagine digging around in a place named for ticks?"

"Strange enough, Alex, I've been there too. It was a different trip. I think I told you, I drove to Tikal, through Belize, once upon a time. The road passed right by Cahal Pech, after leaving San Ignacio, on the dirt road to the Guatemala border crossing. It's all tropical forest in those parts; hauntingly beautiful, but incredibly hot, and sometimes frightening. The main pyramid stands high above the jungle. There were no signs to identify it when we were there. It wasn't open to the public, yet there it was, big as day, out in the middle of nowhere. We saw it again, coming back from Tikal. At that point, we were pretty shook up. We'd had some real struggles in the jungle with both rebels, and military people. The Guatemala side of the border was a very dangerous place in those days. This site is almost on it."

"How many other places have you been in Belize?" Alex probed quizzically.

"That's the only two. You just happened to hit them right up front. I mean it's the only two Mayan ruins I've actually been to, there are other interesting places in Belize. You know, stuff like the Jaguar preserve, cashew plantations, lots of islands, things like that. I do remember, seeing what looked like traces of ancient construction close to the Mexico-Belize border. The buildings were right on the sea, similar to Tulum off the Mayan Riviera. There was no road to them, at least that I could find, no signs, nothing. However, you could see them clearly from the highway."

Alex seemed to take it all in. Then continued with her report: "It says here they've found 34 structures so far at Cahal Pech, seven courtyards, several temples, and two widely separated ball courts, along with a sweat house. The tall pyramid you mentioned is eight stories high, and there's a bunch of unexplored mounds.

Grant was getting more excited about Belize as an option. "Belize has a lot of Mayan ruins with few excavations going on. There's lots to do over there. It sounds like we could find a place, do some work of our own, and seal the stone box and plates back up. Then we call the antiquities department in Belize, and tell them we're tourists, but that we saw looters working the area. We could offer to stand by until someone came to check things out. Maybe we could even get them to search, and find the stone box and plates themselves. They could make the announcement of their find. Then we simply disappear before we get drawn into the media frenzy."

Alex was playing along, but it was clear she wasn't convinced they could even come close to accomplishing all that. There were so many potential complications, and even if they got into Belize without setting off alarms, they could easily be arrested or even shot. Especially, if they were caught fooling around in an unexcavated temple complex and were taken as looters. There was too much that could go wrong. In Alex's mind, there was very little chance of things going right.

"You okay, Alex?" Grant asked cautiously.

"I'm not convinced we're doing the right thing. Seriously, how can we possibly pull this off? Maybe it would be better if we just took the plates back to Miguel's house."

Grant was thoughtful for a few moments before replying. "You're forgetting that there are people out there looking for us. It's a good bet they think we know something about this find. The fact that we found the plates the way we did, was purely an accident caused by their chasing us around."

He sat thinking. "You're right though, we could just return them. But, I don't see how that helps us. And, I don't see how this helps the Robles, or anyone else, except the underbelly of the antiquities business. It wouldn't help at all in terms of getting this fantastic discovery out to the world. And, maybe the plates have something of major value written on them. I mean, it should be pretty clear that someone went to an incredible amount of trouble to find the gold, mine it, refine it, alloy it, fabricate it into sheets, and then go through the laborious process of inscribing on it. Who did all this? Why did they do it? There must be something of immense value recorded on the plates."

"Maybe if I had a demotic primer, I could do some educated guessing," Alex said thoughtfully. "Okay, I have five more outlines on possible sites in Belize. They are Ceullo, La Milpa, El Pilar, Lamanai, and Cerros."

"Ceullo, it turns out, was named for a rum distillery operating right on part of the site. Not a good location."

"La Milpa, was a major ceremonial center in northwestern Belize. About 50 structures have been unearthed. It appears to be surrounded by about 60 more substantial sites and others are being regularly found. The area has been heavily looted. Tall trees and jungle canopy cover most of the grounds. Oh, and it says here that they have installed surveillance equipment to keep down looting. This place is definitely out."

"El Pilar is on the jungle border of Guatemala. It's about a dozen miles the other side of San Ignacio, from where the Cahal Pech ruins, are located. Just recently archeologists have begun to recognize how large this complex really is. The ceremonial center is over 100 acres. The University of California, Santa Barbara, is in its tenth year of working on this site, but by their own admission, they have hardly scratched the surface."

"The World Monument Fund has listed El Pilar as one of the most endangered ancient sites in the world, right alongside Pompeii, the Taj Mahal, and Ankor Wat. With all the current attention it's now getting, it doesn't sound like a good option. But, I have to say, the world is pretty clueless generally, about what's being discovered in Belize. Who knew this site was considered of such significance?

"Listen to this one," Alex continued, "Lamanai is one of Belize's largest ceremonial centers. It is also one of the most important. This site is situated along the New River Lagoon. The central plaza alone covers a half square mile. The site is spread over 950 acres, at minimum. The massive main temple is the largest Preclassic structure known in the entire Mayan world. Lamanai has experienced heavy looting. This site retains permanent guards who circulate along the jungle paths. Oops, I guess that makes it another no."

"The last site is Cerros. It sprawls over 53 acres atop a hill overlooking Chetumal Bay, right across the water from Corozal. This must be the one you were referring to Grant. It sounds like it's larger than you thought." She continued reading aloud, "Tombs and ball courts have been excavated. The site includes three large acropolises, which dominate several plazas, bordered by pyramids.

Two of the structures possess walls, with two and four meter high, masks. Can you imagine coming across masks 12 feet high when you're clearing jungle? Scary stuff, I'd say."

THE SEARCH FOR ZARAHEMLA

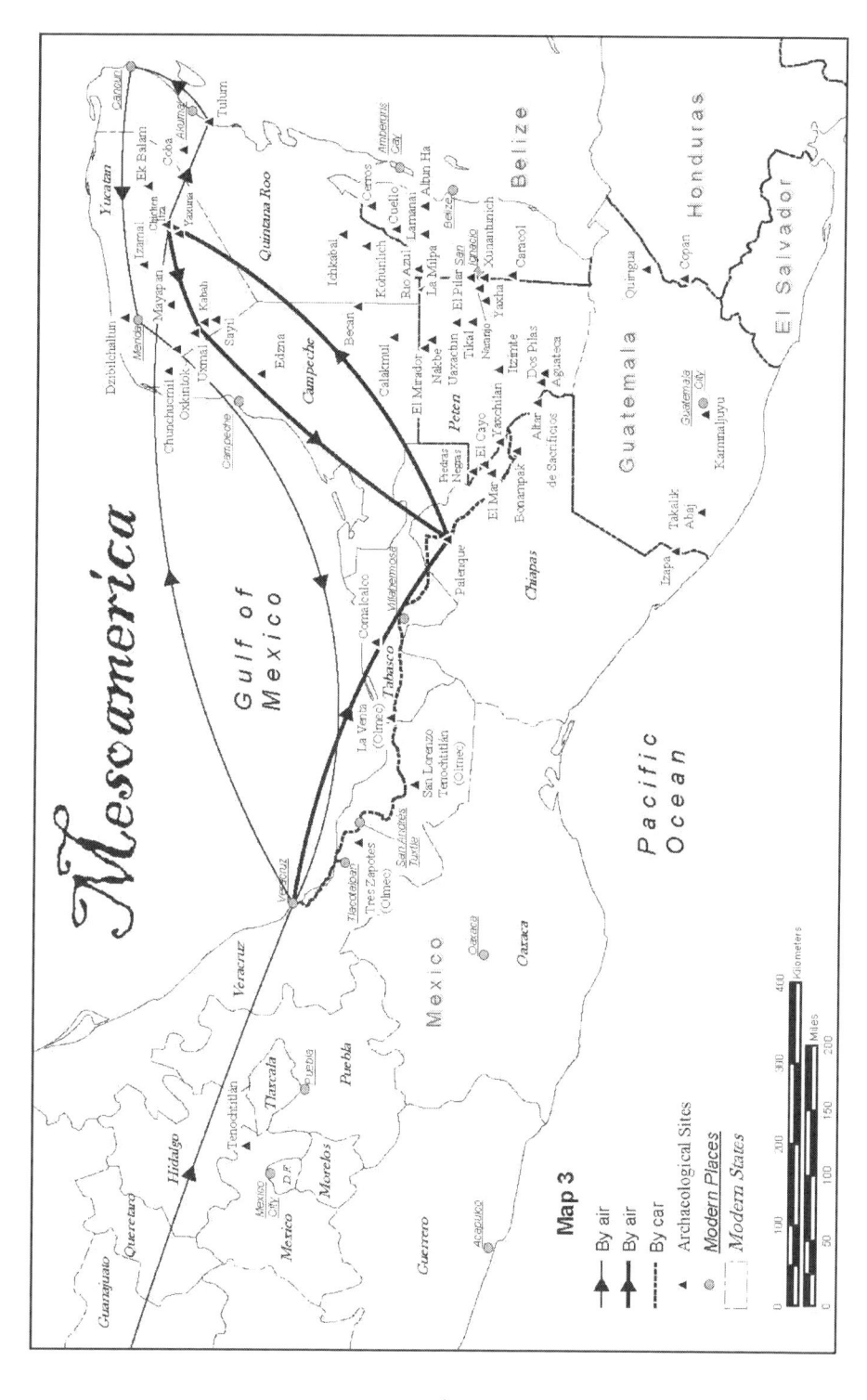

CHAPTER TWENTY-SIX

Palenque, Chiapas

It was decided. They would leave first thing in the morning. The plan was to fly to Cancun, and check-in with Jack to confirm arrangements for taking the Zarahemla to Ambergris Cay. They weren't yet sure how to get the box and records in or out of the plane. No one was likely to investigate the contents of the plane while it was on the ramp, but how they would get the records through customs, was a major concern. Grant suggested that he fly to the small airport just south of Tulum, after dropping Alex off at the FBO terminal in Cancun. From Cancun, Alex could rent a car, and drive the ninety minutes it would take to reach Tulum, where they would rendezvous.

The Tulum airpark appeared to be about the same size as the small airport in Palenque. This suggested that after dark it might not be guarded. Assuming they could jump the fence in Tulum, like Grant had done in Palenque, they should be able to move the box and records out to the car. Alex could then drive back to Cancun, and Grant would fly back in the morning. He would leave the plane, at the FBO terminal. That seemed like the only safe place to tie-down the aircraft for any length of time. Alex would pick him up outside the terminal, and together they would head over to Casa Liahona. There would get Zarahemla from Jack and sail south along the Barrier Reef to Belize.

Satisfied that they had a plan worth pursuing, they headed back to the hotel just as it turned dark. Their headlights illuminated the front of the hotel, as Alex pulled the car into the parking area. A military jeep was disgorging three men at the main entrance. All three reflectively turned towards the incoming lights of their car. Each of them attempted to shade their eyes from the glare of the headlamps. None were able to get a reasonable view. One by one, they turned toward the front door, and walked into the hotel. Each was carrying a simple overnight bag. Alex drove on towards the back of the hotel where the rear entrance brought them closer to their room.

In spite of the clammy heat of early evening, Grant felt a chill of fear run right up his back. "Alex, one of those guys is the pilot of the 320. I'm certain."

"Oh, God, are you sure?" she moaned. "What should we do?"

"Get to the room fast. We'll clear out NOW, before they figure out we're here," Grant spat.

Alex began to shake. It had never occurred to her before that she might be so easily frightened. Even when the revelation that Jose Antonio had known her ex-husband, and she realized her relationship with Antonio was a fraud, she didn't immediately get frightened. She was hurt, depressed, and then angry. All of these emotions passed through her well before she thought to be afraid. Only over time, did she realize the full implications of it all. This time, she had an instant reaction. Alex was shaking so hard she could hardly park the car. "Oh, Grant, I'm scared, I'm really scared," she whimpered.

"Yeah, me too," he said quietly. "You stay in the car. Keep the engine running, and the doors locked. I'll get our clothes and be right back. Thank God, the box and plates are already in the trunk."

Grant ducked in the rear door entrance, and hurried along to their room. Even if the "thugs," as he thought of them, were to discover that he was registered here, they couldn't have got to his room yet. Fumbling with the key, it seemed like an age before he could get the door unlocked. Once inside, he ran about gathering clothes and toiletry items, literally throwing them in their bags. Within two minutes, he was in the hall, both arms full, headed for the rear entrance. He tried to get the thumping in his chest under control.

Alex saw him coming and unlocked the car. She whispering loudly, "Hurry up, let's get out of here."

Grant opened the passenger rear door, and threw the luggage in unceremoniously. He shut the door as quietly as he could; given the surge of adrenaline he was trying to manage. "Drive. Not too fast! Don't attract attention," he commanded. His heart was pounding. Drawing on his limited experience with Zen training, he worked to control his breathing.

"Alex, I'm going to slide down in the seat so there's only one person obvious to anyone observing the car."

Alex was still shaking. She too, was trying to control her reactions by deep breathing.

Driving back out the entrance to the gravel parking lot, Alex fought the desire to speed. Instead, she drove even more slowly than was necessary. She could easily hear the crunch of the gravel under their tires, and the click, chirp, and buzz, of the insects so prevalent here. Everything seemed to have intensified. The swarms of moths circling the parking lot lamps, normally so easy to dismiss, were back in her awareness with a vengeance. She could clearly hear the croaking of tree frogs, and see the flash of swooping shadows, indicating bats homing in on their prey. Alex noted with a new clarity, simple things like the beads of perspiration on the windshield, caused by the high humidity. She heard in stereo, the slap, slap of insects, as they smashed against the glass when she accelerated. Alex's senses had become razor sharp. Yes, she was afraid. But she was also very much alive, and taking direct action for her own survival. The knowledge of it caused within her a giddy sensation, and the determination to prevail.

Grant slid back up into the seat once they were well down the road. The radical beating in his chest began to subside. "Where we headed?" he said, trying to keep his voice calm, and not sound like he felt.

"Airport; maybe we can get out of here tonight," she said, tension clear in her voice. "I know it's illegal to fly at night in Mexico, but what other choice do we have? We could fly straight back to Chichen, assuming the weather is okay. I don't know how we'd deal with the base commandant in the morning, but it would be better than staying here. Those guys had to be here for us, Grant. We know they've killed at least once, and they darn near killed Lupe's brother."

"Makes sense to me. We'll fight it out with the commandant in the morning when we file for Cancun. I suppose we can drop down low tonight, and fly directly there at about 1,000 feet off the deck. If we're able to stay out of the radar space between here and Chichen Itza, we might not even register a bleep."

A moment later something else came to him, "We better be careful at the airport. They may have someone watching the plane."

The main road crossed the end of the runway and continued on. The airport access road was a simple turn-off that ran parallel to the airstrip. It ended at the singular outbuilding that stood at mid-field. The access road came to a dead end at the airport parking lot. Alex and Grant were both nervous about the dead-end road. Grant spoke first, "Perhaps you should drive on past the turn-off, and let me out. Then turn off your lights, and back up so you can see down the airport road. The runway is 4,000 feet, so it's about 2,000 feet to center field. That's less than a half mile. I'll take a flashlight with me. One steady beam means come on down, two flashes means stay where you are; three flashes means get out of town. If something happens to me, and I get the three flashes off, you drive to Chichen. You'll have someone who can look after you there. Check in with Jack, and we'll use him as the contact point."

"Take one of the phones," Alex said anxiously, trying hard to keep her voice from shaking. "That way if we get separated, we can contact one another. If you have to run for cover, and can't flash me, then as soon as you can, give me a call."

They drove slowly by the cattle pasture that lay parallel with the runway on its north side. Rolling on past the airport turn-in, they parked alongside the road about 50 yards south. Grant took his U.S. cell phone. It seemed to be the best choice under the circumstances. Grapping a flashlight, and his Swiss Army knife, he got out of the car, and began to walk towards the airpark turn-in. He hadn't got far, when he turned back and knocked on the window. "I need to change out of this white T-shirt, and put something darker on," he said.

Minutes later, he was wearing a lightweight black polo shirt. Standing by the road, he slipped off his shorts and sandals and pulled on dark jeans and running shoes. Somehow being fully dressed helped him feel more secure. He supposed it was because he could run more easily if circumstances required. He could always head directly into the undergrowth without worrying much about the things that might be crawling on his legs.

Leaning back through the window, he whispered, "Okay, wait five minutes, and then back the car up slowly. Remember, even with your lights off, the brake lights will reflect down the road, so move carefully."

Trying to lighten the moment she laughed quietly. "You know, you finally take your clothes off, and then you get dressed again before we have a chance to take advantage of it." She sniggered nervously, revealing her anxiety. She immediately wished she had kept her mouth shut.

Grant tried to respond with something funny. He wasn't up to it. All he could manage was a smile. With that, he turned, and began the walk to the intersection.

He headed down the airport access road. There was nothing to be seen under the sole mercury vapor light ahead, but still...

It dawned on him that it was just last night he was here doing something similar; sleuthing around, looking for anyone that might stop him from accessing his plane. Grant slowed down to decrease his sweating. With his free hand, he wiped at his neck and opposite arm, trying to keep the mosquitoes from making him the next blood sacrifice, in this land famous for blood sacrifice. He tried to keep the insects off without causing too much movement, but he would probably look like a lunatic to anyone in the shadows watching.

The crunch under his feet was annoying, it would also warn of his coming. He moved off the roadway. There were no other lights around, so with dark clothes he should be close to invisible. Grant had a moment of panic when he thought what he might look like if a car quickly turned down the road and illuminated him in its headlights. He decided the best course of action, would be to drop to the ground before the lights reached him.

Growing more cautious, Grant closed on the chained gate at the empty parking lot. There was no one here last night. It was no guarantee for tonight. He thought back about the three men whose arrival had set off such an emotional chain reaction inside him. Is it possible he had overreacted? Could it have been a case of mistaken identity? No, he told himself. He had surely seen the same guy at the Merida airport.

There doesn't seem to be any other planes in sight. Then it occurred to him, if he couldn't see his own plane, then seeing the dull red twin would be even harder. Grant's plane was high-gloss white with green pin striping and red highlights. His aircraft was new and definitely more reflective than the much older Cessna 320.

He stopped at the gate, looking and listening; willing his pulse rate to drop. There didn't seem to be anything audible above the insects and the electrical buzzing of the overhead light. The still air smelled of rotting vegetation, of life and death. He could sense the swooping bats through the insect spiral that surrounded the light. There must be a couple of dozen of them working this one little area, he thought. It reminded him of the way tuna and marlin worked a school of bait fish. They circle them into an ever tightening bait ball, then dart through and gorge themselves. *Repeating patterns of existence at all levels…fractals.*

Circumnavigating the small terminal building in order to stay outside the light's circle of illumination, Grant strained to see as far down the west side of the runway as he could. He approached the chain link fence, and studied the aircraft parking area. There was a faint outline of what he assumed was his plane. Looking around once more, he climbed the fence and jumped as quietly to the ground as he could. He knelt there, almost afraid to breathe, looking, listening, testing the air, for any sign of cigarette smoke. Nothing seemed to be amiss.

Grant crouched and waited in the dark. He listened to the sounds of the night, resisting the urge to sprint over to the plane. *Better safe than sorry.* How long had he been gone now? He should have checked his watch before he left. How long would Alex wait for him to signal before she panicked and took off? Finally, he stood up realizing he was cramped and strained, and began to walk timidly towards the outline he assumed was his plane. N4876D was sitting quietly in the dark, damp with moisture. Everything seemed okay. Should he signal Alex, or leave her there until he was absolutely sure of their situation? He opted to wait a few more minutes.

Walking carefully around the plane, he disengaged the tie down ropes. He longed to turn on the flashlight, and do a full pre-flight. Caution demanded he hold off. A light on the tarmac would surely raise questions if anyone were close by. He checked the nose wheel carefully. If someone were going to lock him down, it would probably be a chain around the wheel. He ran is hands down the blades of the prop, the other obvious place to detain an aircraft. Everything seemed normal.

The 320 did not appear to be on the ramp…*strange…I'm sure that was the pilot.* He replayed the events of their arrival at the hotel, the three men getting out of the military jeep, his immediate certainty that one of them was the pilot he'd seen in Merida. Could he have imagined it all? Had he jumped to conclusions? Is it worth the risk of having the plane confiscated for breaking the law by night flying? Technically, he supposed, they could be shot out of the air. The Mexican government was serious about halting non-commercial night flights. There were all kinds of reasons not to fly at night in unfamiliar territory, but at the moment the pressing question was the legitimacy of his recollection.

Finally, he made the decision to go. Shading his flashlight as best he could he checked the oil, and drained a small amount of gas from both wing tanks, and from under the engine. He carefully examined the small glass container into which the avgas was collected, for signs of moisture or pollution in the fuel tanks. Satisfied, he turned, and faced where he thought Alex would be watching.

He switched on the flashlight for a steady 15 seconds by the count. He couldn't see a thing down there, but he assumed that

Alex would have seen the light. A beam like this could be seen for miles on a dark night. He unlocked the pilot's door, and the baggage compartment behind it. Inside he shielded the flashlight, and examined the interior. Nothing seemed to be out of place other than the aviation charts he had tossed in the backseat after emptying the flight bag the night before. I'm going to need to find the right aeronautical charts, he thought. Guess I'll leave that to Alex, he decided.

Grant removed the chart he had placed in the windshield to block the sun from overheating the dash. The windshield was covered with heavy moisture. It was completely fogged over, both within and without. Tearing off a couple of paper towels from the roll he kept under the left rear passenger seat, he commenced cleaning the windows. On the outside he cleaned the streaked bugs that had slammed into the windshield on his descent into Palenque. Visibility was going to be a problem, at least until they were off the ground, and the wind pressure cleared the moisture away.

He looked around and saw no trace of Alex. Now where could she be? Perhaps she fell asleep, or wasn't looking this way when I flashed the light, he worried. I can't do it again, or it would constitute two flashes, he thought. A moment later he remembered the cell phone on his hip. Unclipping it, he realized he'd never even turned it on. *Boy, I'd better get it together,* he chastised himself. Stepping back to the tail section he unzipped his jeans. The wisdom of all private pilots is to go while you can. "What you doing there skipper," she spoke quietly. Fumbling and embarrassed he tried to regain his composure.

"Where did you come from?" he managed.

"You flashed me, so I came," she responded. "I didn't see you at the fence, so I climbed in."

"You surprised me," he exhaled, trying to keep his voice at a monotone, and not sound stressed.

"Well it looks like you were absorbed with doing something personal," she grinned.

"Yeah, I was starting to anyway," he mumbled.

So, everything good to go?" she inquired pleasantly.

"I guess so, but something doesn't seem quite right. I mean, where is that twin, and if those guys had been here, why didn't they restrain the plane," he said, confusion clear in his voice.

"Maybe the 320 is down at the west end of the field, pulled off in the grass, or anywhere along the strip, except the apron. Did you notice anything along the east end of the field?" she asked easily.

"I wasn't looking for a plane parked anywhere other than the tarmac. It never occurred to me to look anywhere else," he replied. "Still, it doesn't make good sense. If they knew we were here, why wouldn't they have placed a guard on the plane, or at least, put a chain around the prop. It's as if we're free to go and lose them once again."

"Maybe they don't know we're here. Perhaps seeing them was just a coincidence, or maybe their putting pressure on us, and then following us around, or maybe they landed somewhere else," Alex commented.

"Well, we can address your last thought pretty quickly, climb in, we'll get the aviation chart for the area, and see if there's anywhere else to land close by."

"By the way, I left the car close up against the gate," Alex reported. "I drove it down dark, no lights at all. I rolled to a stop, so as not to use the brakes. I thought I was pretty clever. It must have worked too, because I caught you out here with your zipper down," she laughed softly.

She isn't going to let that go easily, he thought. *But she's right; she did catch me completely off guard, which is odd considering how careful I was in getting in here.*

Grant switched the interior night-light on, it glowed a dim red. He began to flip through the charts in the back seat, when it occurred to him the chart he wanted would be in the front left hand pocket. He had tucked it there, when descending for landing. *Slow down and think.* Grant handed the aviation chart to Alex. She began to unfold, and refold it, to find Palenque.

A WAC chart, (world aeronautical chart) is a large affair. It contains aeronautical maps on both sides. WAC charters cover a large geographical area. The standard VFR (visual flight range), sectional charts, are the same size, but cover only half as much terrain. Therefore, on a sectional chart, everything appears twice the size of a WAC, which makes sectionals easier to read.

The trouble with a standard VFR chart is that it takes twice as many of them to cover the same area. Grant had no sectionals on board. He was used to covering large areas at high enough altitudes that terrain markings, were not that important. There are other, even simpler charts, covering the same airspace, but specific to flying on instruments at high altitudes. These kinds of charts contain virtually no ground terrain information.

Alex needed to study the WAC, but it could be hard to read even in the daylight. Grant reached in the glove box, and pulled out a penlight along with another magnifying glass, and handed them to Alex. "Be prepared," he quipped.

Within moments, Alex said, "There's another Palenque airport just a few miles from here. It's marked restricted," she said.

Grant vaguely remembered seeing the restricted notation on the WAC, when he was flying in. "It must be a government runway. Individuals don't have their own airparks in Mexico."

They fell quiet, considering the implications. "This restricted airport is fairly close to the public one. That may be because it's located on the only flat space available in this hilly region. But, because it is so close to the Guatemala border, it may have something to do with a feared Zapatistas insurrection," Alex offered.

"You are probably right. I'll bet it's an unmarked military installation," he replied.

Grant thought back about what he'd heard of the Zapatistas. They had come briefly to the world's attention when they seized several towns in Chiapas in the mid 1990s. Although the Zapatistas were isolated in the jungles and mountains of southeastern Mexico, their ideas had influenced activists around the world. One of their protests arose at an international conference in La Realidad, Chiapas. The Zapatistas were considered responsible for the 'anti-capitalist' demonstrations of London and Seattle in 1999, and those that followed in 2000, in Washington D.C., and Prague.

Still thinking furiously, Grant said, "I guess that means the 320 is involved in some kind of quasi governmental operation. I mean, assuming the plane is at the other airport. That's actually rather interesting, and ties to the comment you heard from Moises that someone was flashing a badge when they were looking for us."

Mexican charts do not dependably provide the depth of information as do their American counterparts. However, there were no American-issued low altitude charts available. What that meant was, not only must they use a WAC chart for tonight's flight, but it was a Mexican issued WAC chart.

They were going to need exact, low altitude information. It was unusually dark, no moon, low clouds, no ground lights. He would need to fly low, right down on the terrain, in order to avoid military defense radar. In addition, they were going to have to stay outside the more civilized zones, avoiding flat areas that would have airports with approach control radar.

Flying at night was always a bit unnerving, but typically you stayed high, flying strictly on instruments. You simply didn't pay much attention outside the window during a night flight. Tonight, was going to be different, much different. They were within 25 miles of the Guatemala border, flying in hills with high mountains just behind them. They would need to run parallel to the border until gaining the Yucatan, in order to avoid radar sweeps from city airports along the coastline. That meant terrain flying when you can't see the terrain.

Thankfully, they had a good GPS system on board. It would keep them on track. However, local altitude aberrations, such as hilltop mounted telephone transmission towers, were going to be a legitimate threat. There was also a military operations area between Palenque, and Chichen Itza. They would need to dodge around this area. This would put them close to Campeche, and then Merida, approach control. It was going to be an interesting night.

He hoped no cows had worked their way on to the runway tonight. If they had, the airplane was going to be in big trouble. In order to takeoff in the dark, they were going to have to overrun their landing lights. That meant speeding down a blind runway without seeing anything until it was too late to do anything about it.

"Okay, let's get our stuff and load up," Grant said with more confidence than he felt.

It was a struggle getting the box and the plates over the fence. They were more awkward than heavy, but to climb a fence, and lift them over to a woman, even one as fit as Alex, was a chore. Add this to the darkness, and the bugs getting sucked into your nose and mouth, as you're gasping for air, and you have a complicated procedure on your hands. Eventually, they were loaded up. Alex wrote a note in Spanish, regarding the rental car, and stuck it under the door of the Quonset hut. It basically said, sorry I had to leave the car here, charge me what is required to get it returned to the rental company.

Once in the airplane and buckled in, Grant cranked the engine. He was pleased it caught on the first turn. Swinging the plane about, he taxied down the strip to the west end. They turned around, set the brake, and went through the pre-take off procedure.

"It's awfully dark down there," Alex observed.

"Yeah, pretty dark alright. I'm going to get us off the ground by mid-field, just in case there's anything on the runway past center field," he said. "We'll do a short field take-off."

Alex seemed alarmed, "You think there's something down there you can't see?"

"No, but, it occurred to me that *if* there was a breach along the barbed-wire fence that separates the strip from the cattle pasture, we could have ourselves a serious problem. Rather than take the time, to taxi a mile down and back, to verify its safe, I think we should jump off the ground with a short field departure, and leave it at that."

"I thought short field departures were supposed to be done in cold weather. You don't have much lift at this warm temperature. The air molecules are too spread out," she said flatly.

"Right you are, but we've got a pretty powerful airplane, and we're under gross weight. I burned off about 30 gallons of fuel on the way in here from Veracruz. So, even with the gold, and our luggage, we should be okay for a reasonably short field departure."

After a quick run-up and mag checks, Grant added ten degrees of flaps. He stood hard on the brakes, and moved the throttle all the way to the firewall. He released the brakes, and the plane jumped forward on a dash. The aircraft seemed a bit sluggish at first. That was probably the warm damp air, and poor pavement. That and their flaps were down, which tended to interrupt the smooth flow of air across the wing. When the flaps were down it slowed the plane, but it increased lift. Increasing lift was the point.

It was a bit scary speeding off into the dark, not seeing much of anything until it was passing you. When the airspeed reached 50 knots, Grant eased back on the flight control, and the plane lifted smoothly into the air. They were not even half way down the field.

Switching off the landing and taxi lights, he increased the backlights on the dash so he had a better view of the instruments. This was a bit tricky, as Grant needed reading glasses to see the instruments with low light, but he couldn't see forward properly with his reading glasses on. He let them ride low on his nose, and peered over the rims to see forward. They were flying dark. No wing navigation lights, no rotating beacon, no strobe. Their transponder was off, as was anything else that might help someone identify them as an aircraft under way at night.

He leveled off at 1,000 feet AGL (above ground level), and worried that he was already too high. Especially, if that restricted airport nearby was operating radar throughout the night. There were hills all over the place out here. He needed to move towards the Usumacinta River delta to reduce the risk of flying into something unforeseen. They were moving too fast, Alex couldn't even begin to follow their position on the chart, so instead she was studying the GPS map. Grant reduced power to 2400 square, meaning that manifold pressure was pulled back to the same setting as RPM. He leaned the fuel to 13 GPH (gallons per hour), and let it run rich for a while to stabilize the engine, and ensure it didn't overheat. The airplane was slightly dirty, meaning he was flying with his cowl flaps open to increase air circulation around the engine.

Grant finally felt secure enough to glance at the GPS. He reached forward and flicked a button a few times to magnify their position into a 20 mile circle instead of the 200 mile circle Alex was trying to read.

"Whoa…that helps," she said. "I didn't realize you could do that."

"This toggle right here," he replied, while pointing at the correct button. "You can also use this mouse stick to move around on the screen, to help with identifying things. Go ahead, play with it, you'll get the idea. I've got to keep my head focused on the outside, we're dangerously low, especially for night flying, but I don't dare move much higher."

Alex was hesitantly pushing buttons on the viewing screen. Looking at it for a few minutes, she realized there was another smaller screen right below. It was built into the GPS receiver itself. The larger screen seemed to be for improved viewing, and served no other purpose. She mentioned this to Grant, who corrected her saying she was partially correct, but the larger screen also included lighting strike information, night flying color dampening options, and other valuable data, not shown on the smaller screen.

Grant was now nursing the plane further to the north, trying to avoid crossing in to Guatemala airspace. He handed Alex his penlight, and asked her to find them on the chart. She needed to study terrain elevations, and obstacle placements.

"We're flying low and blind, we have no weather briefing, and we can't call anyone, so it's up to us," he said.

Alex was studying the chart with intensity. "I think that everything off to our right, is the area controlled by the Zapatista rebels. It is on the edge of a giant rain forest. It's an almost impenetrable jungle that runs straight east across the Peten, and on to the Mayan mountains of Belize. Piedras Negras is one of the most remote of all the ancient Maya cities, and consequently, one of the least visited. If we weren't heading off to Belize that would be my call for interning the records," Alex said, hoping she didn't sound as stressed as she felt.

"Yes, but with the looting and killing that's going on down there, makes it about as unsafe a place as you can get at the moment," Grant replied.

The forward visibility was poor. It was deteriorating. They flew on in silence, Grant wanting desperately to gain altitude, and fly straight out to the Gulf, so as to be free of obstacles. It wasn't an option. If they did that they would be picked up on radar for sure.

CHAPTER TWENTY-SEVEN

Somewhere over the Chiapas Jungle

Flying at night is disorienting. It is worse when the outline of the land against the horizon is not discernible from the line of sky. This happens on dark nights when the cloud cover does not permit moon or starlight. The rule in these conditions is do not trust your instincts. Lock in autopilot on specific Global Positioning System coordinates, at a specific altitude above sea level. The problem was they simply didn't know what was between where they were, and where they were going. At this altitude, it would be all too easy to slam into a jungled hill.

Grant decided to not have the autopilot track the GPS, but rather manually steer the aircraft through the autopilot by simply turning a knob on the HSI gauge, a sort of directional gyro slaved from a magnetic compass. The knob rotated what was referred to as the "bug," which could be set on any direction around a compass rose. The airplane would hold the directional heading that the bug was set to, allowing Grant greater freedom in the cockpit without having to hold on to the flight control. He refined the direction they were headed by simply rotating the knob and the aircraft would turn accordingly.

On a compass rose, north is always at the top, and considered either zero or 360; the degrees of a circle. Therefore, east would be 090, south 180, and west 270. That, of course, is true of all compasses. They were now on a heading of 030, making their course thirty degrees east of north.

Grant's brain was screaming at him to climb. He knew they were too low. He finally gave in to his fear, and clicked in a shallow climb. One minute later he leveled off at 1,500 MSL. He knew he should be at least four thousand feet higher in this area, but that would definitely put him on military radar. It didn't take a rocket scientist to figure out that the military would be watching this area carefully. The jungle was a major growing and processing zone for narcotics, both in Mexico and Guatemala. The military would be itching for the radar signature of a light aircraft coming from this direction. Chances were that if spotted, the military would scramble a jet and take them out.

"Grant, I'm getting disoriented," Alex said in a quavering voice. "I've done some night flying, but this is really confusing, I can't see a thing, we have no radar vectors, and we're way low." Alex was trying hard to control her emotions. She wanted Grant's respect, but she was a pilot too. She knew how dangerous this flight really was.

Grant tried to sound calm. He spoke as if he did this kind of thing every day. "The main problem here is defining obstacle elevations. We need to clear or avoid them, but not climb up where the military will spot us. This is a drug interdiction zone so we must be extra careful."

"I suggest you reduce the area on screen to a five-mile perimeter so you can spot any obstacles that might be identified on the electronic chart. I'll slow the plane so we have more time to react. Those electronic charts are pretty good about showing towers and things in the States, but here in Mexico I don't know. It may not be very accurate, but it is surely better than nothing."

Grant eased the RPM back to 2200; he had earlier reduced manifold pressure to the bottom of the green arc. Going below that was not recommended. Their airspeed dropped to 125 knots, about 144 mph, still too fast to be running around unseen obstacles, close to the ground in a hilly area on a pitch-black night. He pulled the RPM back further. They were now flying 20 square, 20 inches' manifold pressure and 2000 RPM. This was called slow flight. It provided for better maneuverability, and fuel economy, but was lousy at time for distance. For the present, they would move at a snail's pace.

Trying to replicate Grant's affected calm, Alex asked, "Grant, do you remember when John Kennedy, Jr. crashed his single-engine Piper Saratoga, on approach to Martha's Vineyard? I heard the NTSB issued a statement saying there was nothing wrong with the plane. He apparently got disoriented on a moonless night in ocean haze. I'd say we're in a lot worst situation than that," she stated flatly. "It's both moonless, and starless, we have low cloud cover, and no weather briefing. We've got obstacles sticking up in the air to snag us, and perhaps a military out there hell-bent on shooting someone down. Pretty scary don't you think?"

"Yep, it's an interesting situation."

Maybe he knows something I don't know, she thought. Because if he doesn't, he is either nuts, or has nerves of steel. "You don't scare easily do you?" she asked quietly.

"I wouldn't say that," he replied, remembering how his heart had thumped when he saw the three guys at the hotel earlier. "On the other hand, I readily admit to having more brass than brains."

The tension was palpable. They continued to talk as if there was nothing unusual going on. Pilot ego, she thought, as she remembered when the NTSB had collected black boxes from crashed commercial aircraft. The pilots, and co-pilots, had rarely said anything emotional before impact, other than, AW SHIT. Now here she was, acting the same way. It was weird. Any moment something might loom out of the dark right in front of them, and here they were talking like nothing serious was happening.

"Was Marianna a pilot?" Alex asked, trying to take her mind off their current situation.

"Ah…yes; yes she was," he replied. "Marianna fooled around, flying a bit from time to time for years. She had just got her U.S. pilot's license active the year before she passed. She earned her license in Canada, many years earlier, but quit flying after a minor bouncing incident when landing. Marianna scared herself by asking the question who would raise the children were she to kill herself flying. I guess she figured I was not fully capable of raising the family without her, which I am sure was true. So, as was typical of her, she sacrificed what she wanted, for what she thought was the right thing to do."

"Sounds like a good woman." Alex offered.

"Yep," is about all he could say.

Still in slow flight, Grant punched up a larger area on the GPS map. He was trying to determine whether the manual headings he was giving the autopilot were consistent with where they needed to be. Altitude indications on the electronic map were determined by color variations, but the aircraft was so close to the ground the information was of little help. The GPS reported they were now crossing a small inland town in the State of Campeche. It was known as Matamoras. Looking at the chart, his mind drifted. They were now less than fifty miles from the waterfront property he had purchased twenty years earlier. It was on the Gulf coast a few miles south of Sabancuy. The property had once been a coconut plantation before the state pushed a new road along the waterfront, right through it. This allowed paved access to an incredible white sand beach, cluttered with towering coconut palms. At the time, there had been plans to develop a resort along this beach. Grant had picked up 24 beach lots in a holding trust. The development concept fizzled when Mexican politicians committed greater expansion to Cancun and decided to not expand the runway at the Campeche airport. That meant larger aircraft could not land. Bye, bye tourism.

The sky was still pitch black. They had no forward visibility. Occasionally, they could see lights straight down, which probably represented farms or small communities. Having a better feel now for where they were flying, Grant could visualize the terrain below him. They were out of the mountained area, but there were still hilltops higher than they were flying. From here on out, they would be crossing over a low-lying limestone shelf, covered with hills, jungle, and occasional farms. He dropped down 300 feet, and leveled off at 1,200 MSL.

"You're descending?" Alex said in alarm.

"I know where we are, and I have a fairly good mental map of this area. I think we're safe at lower altitudes. The only thing that bothers me, are those huge telephone transmission towers they've been putting up on the higher hills. I just wish we had better visibility. We'll be coming up on the Yucatan's primary military operations area soon. We need to steer around the extended point of that airspace," he said pointing at the red outline of the military zone on the GPS. "Notice how it projects up towards Merida? We'll be able to see the boundaries on the screen, and simply fly around them, but if we are not low enough, the radar sweeps will still pick us up. After that, it's a straight shot in to Chichen Itza."

"How much longer you figure?"

"Maybe forty minutes. We're heading almost due north now. When we get around that angular military corridor, we'll turn east, perhaps a bit south of east," he said thoughtfully. "My biggest concern is getting below this cloud cover so we can get forward visibility. We're already marginal on elevation."

"It's a quarter to 10:00. We may just make it in before the Itza closes," she said with growing excitement in her voice. "It'll be nice to see Lupe, and find out how Pepe is doing."

The pressure to relieve himself was beginning to make him nervous. Alex had caught him just as he was about to take care of that requirement. Her appearance had stopped him cold. Not relieving yourself before takeoff was the ultimate no-no, at least in his flying book. A full bladder made you jumpy. He had the proverbial pee-pot on board. It was a large Gatorade bottle tucked under the rear seat. He was adept at using it too, but he wasn't going to do that with Alex in the cockpit. He simply was not ready for that level of familiarity. And besides, he had to stay focused. They were low, slow, and in the dark. He needed to be on task.

They rounded the end of the military corridor without incident. He twisted the bug around to 100 degrees; ten clicks south of due east, and watched the small white line extend forward on the map from the nose of his plane. They were still going to be a little north of the field.

The pressure on his bladder was causing discomfort. He wanted to drop down for a straight in approach, like the way he had come in, on the day he'd met Alex. That would easily save them a few minutes in the landing procedure. He was fighting it out with himself, but caution overcame the need to pee.

He decided to fly up parallel to the field at low altitude to see if he could catch a glimpse of the windsock in the dark. With no weather briefing, he simply couldn't tell which way the wind was blowing. The wind couldn't be very strong, or he'd have noticed it in their flight performance. But it didn't take much of a breeze to really screw up a landing if you came in the wrong way. The first rule in landing was you always landed into the wind. This way, you had affirmative control of the aircraft. If the wind was behind you, it could really make a mess of things.

The problem was visibility. They were still in the soup, although they could see straight down. This meant there should be good line of sight, once they descended under the low-lying cloud layer. Any lights from the ground would reflect off the bottom of the clouds, and help with night vision. Ten miles out, he dropped to 900 feet, and broke out enough to have forward angular vision. Things were looking up.

"Alex, are there any tall towers out here, or anything else we should be looking for?"

"There are a couple of telephone antennas. Coming in from this direction we should be clear of them. Let me think a moment," she said reflectively while studying the aeronautical chart.

Five miles out they dropped down to 700 AGL. It was too low for the terrain, and too low for the approach, but he needed to get far enough below the clouds to get a good view of things. He eased the throttle back to 1400 RPM, and increased the manifold pressure to the top of the green arc. He richened the fuel mixture in case they had to do an emergency go round. Grant set in ten degrees of flaps, so they could hold their altitude at this low speed. A moment later, he realized it was going to take at least 1500 RPM to maintain a straight and level attitude. They were now slowed to about 75 knots, and beginning to fly the parallel course just north of the field.

Suddenly, he saw four sets of headlights on the road, just to the south of the field. "Alex, do you usually have people driving around the restaurant at this hour of the night?"

"Sure, we have some guys that close the place up at 11:00. It's only 10:40 now."

"Well there looks to be four vehicles in a row headed to the airport. It seems a bit late for that, don't you think? I could understand it if they were leaving the area, but they all seem to be arriving," he said with growing concern in his voice. "Damn, my bladder is killing me," he belted out.

"Me too," she chimed in. "I didn't know how much longer I could hold it."

"We just may have to hold it a while longer. I'm going to drop down a bit more, and pass right over those vehicles. I'll tilt the aircraft over to the right, so you can look straight down. I need you to tell me what those cars are all about," Grant stated emphatically.

They were still flying dark. No external lights were on. Not even their wing-tip navigation lights. It was strictly illegal, but flying at night in Mexico, was illegal anyway, so it hardly mattered. The airplane was relatively quiet as they were flying slowly, with engine RPM way back of normal. If the vehicles below were closed on top, the occupants would likely not know an aircraft was crossing right overhead. If the vehicles were open, he could sail right over them like a glider, and not power in, until a mile the other side of the roadway. There was no starlight to act as a backlight, so they would be essentially invisible.

Grant angled the plane to cross the vehicles ahead. He turned into a right bank. Alex should be looking straight down on them. He would roll out of the turn, headed back to the west, in the direction the cars had come from.

"Four jeeps, looks like military personnel," she reported in a flat monotone.

"Is that normal?" he asked in the same flat tone.

"Nope, afraid not."

"Suppose they're here for us?" he asked.

"That would be my guess," she stated flatly.

Grant rolled out of the turn, heading west. They were back tracking their inbound route, but this time at an even lower altitude. The good news, they had better visibility down here. They were below the overcast, but way too low for comfort.

"Okay, Alex, I've got to pee, or I won't be able to think my way clear of things. You hold this course, and keep your eyes sharp for obstacles. We're probably not more than 400 feet off the ground. If they're buildings out here, even on small hills, we could be in big trouble," he said.

"Keep sharp. Head around any hills you see. If you must, put this puppy into a shallow turn, and hold your altitude. Lord, I hope there's no power lines slung between these hills. Stay out of those clouds just above us. When I'm finished, you can step into the back seat, and grab the Pringles under the passenger seat," he said quickly.

With that he slid his seat back all the way, turned around, and got on his knees in the seat facing aft. Grant leaned through the separation between the front seats, unzipped his jeans, unscrewed the cap from the Gatorade bottle, and tried to pee. He'd held it too long. It was hard to relax and let go. Besides, he was super conscious of being right next to Alex. They were shoulder to shoulder. Alex faced forward, Grant was facing aft. "Oh for crying out loud," he muttered. This is not the time for a bashful bladder."

To distract herself from listening for his urine stream, which she'd never be able to hear through the headsets anyway, Alex said, "What's the deal with the Pringles?"

Glad for something else to focus on, Grant replied, "A few years before my wife passed, she had a young woman fly to the islands. Actually, this gal was a Capitan in the Air Force reserve. But, you could have fooled me. When I first met her, I thought she was a kid. She was petite, wore unisex clothing, and sported a baseball cap, turned backwards. Anyway, she flew out to St. Kitts, to accompany Marianna all the way back to Oregon. The theory was that Marianna would do all the flying and Delcy (that was her name), would train her on cross-country navigation, instrument approaches, and stuff like that. At the end of the trip, Marianna would have logged enough dual instruction hours to go for her IFR rating. Well, that was the theory anyway."

"As it happened, the day Delcy arrived Marianna had to fly out commercially. An emergency had arisen with one of the grandkids. So, I picked this young woman up from her arriving commercial flight to the island. It was the last flight in at midnight. Once I figured out who she was, I asked her if she minded spending the night with me. She was definitely the quiet type. Delcy didn't respond immediately. She just stood there and looked me over. I could tell she was not feeling real secure about things. After all, she was out on an island in the middle of nowhere, about to spend the night with a man she had never laid eyes on before. She finally said okay, and off we went to my place."

"The next day we took off in my plane returning to the States. We were about two hours out over the Caribbean, with another two hours to go before landfall. Suddenly she said, "I have to pee." That was the first words out of her mouth in two hours. It caught me completely off guard. My response was that we had about two hours to go, but if it were me I'd know what to do. On the other hand, a Gatorade bottle just isn't going to work for a woman. She said nothing for another ten minutes or so, then announced: "I have to pee now." With that, she climbed into the back seat, and fooled around for a while. I didn't know what to think, but I wasn't going to turn around. Eventually, she climbed back up, and said: Better."

"For the life of me, I couldn't figure out what she'd found to pee in. It was driving me a little nuts. But this woman did not talk much, so I kept my mouth shut. A while later she said, "I found the Pringles tube," as if that explained everything. I had a mental visual of her peeing on my chips. It also occurred to me that Pringles came in a cardboard tube, and that it did not seem like the best place to pass water, notwithstanding a larger opening than a Gatorade bottle."

"After a pregnant pause, Delcy spoke up again, "I put the chips in a paper towel. The Pringles tube is aluminum lined. It will hold until we get on the ground. And with that, I learned something about toiletry in the air for women."

Alex was laughing by this time. She was holding her bladder with one hand, and flying the plane with the other. Grant had finished, capped the bottle, and stored it back under the passenger seat. "Okay your turn," he said, as he turned back around in the front sea. "I'll pull my seat forward. You put yours all the way back. That will give you a gap to step through to the rear seat. The Pringles are under the right seat. There's a roll of paper towels under there as well."

Once Alex had contorted herself through the narrow space between the front seats, and was positioned somehow in the back, she asked through the headsets, "So where we going now?" Alex was being cool. She sounded almost a little bored. It was as if there was nothing unusual in what they were doing.

Grant thought for a moment. "We've got enough fuel to get back to where we came from, plus a little more. But it would be fairly dangerous to make an approach around those hills at night. There's no light at the airport, and low hanging cloud cover, so I am not so sure. There are no fuel services in Palenque, so if we return, we're faced with having to eventually truck Avgas in so we can get the plane back out of there. I'm not so sure about that either. When you're back upfront let's talk it over."

A few minutes later, Alex was back in the front seat, miming Grant's story about Delcy, by saying, "Better."

"We've got about two and half hours of fuel on board, maybe a little more. We can fly in almost any direction. Where do we want to go?"

Studying the chart, Alex launched in: "Cancun is less than an hour's flight, but if we go there, we're sure to be detained. It's a big airport with lots of security. They would be certain to lock the plane down and search its contents. When the goodies in the back showed up, it would be major jail time. We could try heading down to the Tulum airport, south of Akumal. Or, there's Isla Cozumel, just off the coast, or possibly Chetumal, on the Belizean border. But, anywhere we go, it's going to cause a lot of questions, and likely get the plane and contents seized."

"Lots of cheery input," he moaned.

"We could go back where we came from. There's a chance no one could prove we ever left, since the airport was closed when we departed. Or, we could fly into Belize, or even into Guatemala. It would require we find a place to land somewhere in the Peten, which is virtually all tropical forest with a high jungle canopy. The coastal cities of Campeche, and Ciudad del Carmen, are easily within reach, but we dare not fly much further. We could make it to Villahermosa without any problem. Going there is about the same distance as returning to Palenque. I say you call it Capitan."

"Okay, my call is we go back to where we came from," Grant stated flatly. "It's the only place we can make a case for never having left the ground after dark. If someone saw the plane was gone during the hours out and back, we can argue we moved it around on the field."

Alex was quiet for a few moments before saying: "The bigger question might be why those military guys were headed to the Chichen Itza airport. Either it was a pure coincidence, or they were sent there to intercept us. If the latter, it begs the question as to whether it was a military radar scan that picked us up, or those guys in Palenque knew we had left."

"If it was the thugs that orchestrated it," Grant said, "They might not check back at the Palenque airport, knowing we had already left. If that's true, then the best place to go is back to Palenque. It's going to be a bit nervy getting down without being spotted. We'll have to turn the lights on at some point."

Rather than risk the hill country, they would fly closer to the coast, and risk radar intercept. By the gulf, the cloud cover would be higher, and the land more flat. They'd be able to see most of the return trip. It would add a half-hour to their time, and use more fuel, but it was the safer bet.

Grant recalculated fuel consumption several times with different burn rates. He was relatively sure they had enough to get back, plus a few gallons in reserve. Under normal circumstances, it would be a pretty scary thing they were doing.

GPS allowed them to know where they were in relationship to where they were going. The main objective was to get down without running into something. Grant climbed the plane to just short of the bottom of the clouds, and flew due west until over the ruins of Mayapan, then turned slightly south to fly right over the Uxmal ruins. The eleven-story Temple of the Magicians towered above the courtyards and plazas. The Nunnery, Quadrangle, the Palace of the Governor, the Great Pyramid, and the House of Turtles, were all clearly visible due to the night-lights that were scattered over the Uxmal ruins complex.

The ceiling lifted as they continued on their westward leg. Soon they were back up to 1,500 feet flying straight and level with good visibility. Grant drew a straight line from Uxmal, to Palenque, and realized they would pass about 25 miles inland of the city of Campeche. That should be enough to avoid radar if they killed off some altitude. The temperature had cooled, dissipating some of the fog that had formed over the jungle undergrowth.

They made a broad semi-circle to approach the airstrip from the west. They would be landing to the east. Maneuvering by GPS map, they let down at the last possible moment, turning their landing lights on just before their planned touchdown. They flew half way down the runway before getting wheels on the ground. The night had created an optical allusion for depth perception. There was a tense moment as they rolled fast towards the fence. The plane stopped a hundred feet from the extreme west end. Grant taxied back to the same tie-downs, having dismissed the idea of moving the plane somewhere else on the field.

It was after 1:00 AM before they had transferred the plates, the stone box, and their travel bags into the car. Alex had left the car unlocked and the keys under the driver's floor mat.

"So, where to now?" she asked rhetorically. They had been discussing options for the past hour, and finally decided they would try sneaking back into their hotel room. They had not checked out. If the bad guys had already been there, it might be one of the safer places to be.

Reaching the hotel, they drove quietly to the extreme end of the parking lot. There was no military jeep in sight. The rear door of the hotel was locked. Alex walked around to the front and through the hotel to open the back door.

Ten minutes later, Grant was starting to panic when the door finally opened. "Sorry, I had to use the ladies room."

At 1:50 they fell onto their respective beds from the night before without saying much of anything.

Grant awoke early. He cleaned up and returned to lie down. He was sure he wouldn't fall back asleep, but he could rest his eyes, and think. Two hours later he awoke to Alex coming out from the bathroom. "Good morning. How are we doing today?" she said pleasantly.

"I had the most interesting dream," he said with a grin. "We were flying in the dark at low altitude close to the Guatemala Peten, and then ended up at Chichen…" his voice trailed off with a small laugh.

"It might as well have been a dream, as weird as it was. And, here we are, right back where we started."

"No one has broken down our door this morning, and I'm hungry. Let's sneak out, and get some chow," Grant said brightly.

Lost in thought, they returned to the same restaurant as the day before. They sat at the same table, and ordered the same food. What does that say about us? Alex wondered. Something seemed different though, the atmosphere was lighter. Grant was unselfconsciously smiling.

"What?"

Lost in his head, and slightly dazed, he looked up. "You know, I forget to pause, and be happy. At the moment, I feel oddly at peace. Pretty crazy, huh? It won't last long given what we are faced with. But, the world seems a bit lighter this morning. I've figured out that whenever I start putting too much focus on the future, my anxiety level soars. Too much time spent on the 'What Ifs of life,' can make one downright miserable. I suppose the lack of joy in my life flows from the lack of balance in my thinking."

Alex was oddly quiet. Grant continued, "It occurs to me, that when we *think* we *feel*. Actually, I am pretty sure we always *feel* our thoughts. Our feelings are a good barometer of our thinking. When we think negative, fearful, critical thoughts, we feel poorly. When we focus on higher, more inspiring, and forgiving thoughts, we feel better." His voice trailed off.

It fell quiet again. Hesitantly, Alex began, "I've learned that it is important to keep reminding myself that without a sense of gratitude, it is impossible to be happy."

"Oh, so that's your secret?" Grant said lightly.

Feeling more confident with the subject, Alex continued. "I think our constant focus on worry, what is wrong with our relationships, the environment, our health, and so forth, acts like a magnet. Worry attracts the things we fear. When we're focused on what's wrong we are not happy."

With no response from Grant, Alex continued with her line of reasoning, "It seems to me, that the world is perfect. It's perfect in terms of the opportunity it provides each of us to become something better than we are. What I mean, is that each one of us will encounter enough struggles in life to aid us in our own personal evolution. Personal growth seems to come as a result of a struggle of some sort. When we are able to back away from our problems far enough, and be completely honest with ourselves, we are able to observe that emotional growth and maturity is a result of our rising in response to the very problems we would prefer to avoid. When we look at life this way, the problems that confront us become our teachers."

"It never occurred to me that the world could be considered perfect," Grant replied. Especially, in view of all the obvious problems that confront humankind. But your point, that our imperfect world provides the perfect setting for us to confront difficulties and grow emotionally, does make a certain kind of sense. And, I suppose our problems can be our teachers; if we will let them. Most of us just complain about our problems."

Alex shifted the conversation to their current predicament. "Perhaps we can figure out a way to get into Piedras Negras. It's the closest isolated set of ruins from where we are right now, but it is in the Guatemala Peten. There are no roads on the Guatemala side of the river. It is strictly jungle. To get to that area from Palenque, would require driving a poor road for a couple of hours or more. Then we'd be faced with a stiff hike through the bush to the river's edge. After that, we'd have to make an illegal crossing of the river, and take a hike through dense tropical rain forest, to get to the site. Oh, and did I mention the river has crocodiles, and the whole area is infested with poisonous snakes?"

"Sounds like fun to me," Grant said with a grimace.

"Of course, we'd have to be pretty exact where we crossed the river, and I have no idea how to accomplish that. And, I'm stumped as to how to get the artifacts across a broad, moving body of water, unless we get a boat somehow."

According to the scant information Alex had gleaned on Piedras Negras, "It is a beautiful site. It is located in pristine jungle. Archaeologically speaking, it is of singular importance, as it is home to the stele that first enabled linguists to decode Maya hieroglyphs. Piedras Negras is situated downstream from Yaxchilan. Yaxchilan may be an evener larger site. Records indicate these two Mayan city states had formed a trading, and military alliance. Both sets of ruins are said to be remote, and difficult to reach.

"You know, Alex, I have a rubber raft in the plane."

"What? What did you say?" she responded in confusion.

"I said, there's an inflatable rubber raft in the plane. It's got all the stuff needed to survive a crash over water. It's even covered, to provide protection from the sun," Grant explained.

"You're saying we could use the raft to cross the river, and make our way down to the site?" she said, attentively.

"I suppose so. We might as well try anyway," Grant, replied.

"Why didn't you say so before?" Alex said excitedly. "Let's do it!"

"Hey, did you ever see that movie with Harrison Ford?" Grant said, in mid-thought.

Alex jumped in on him. "Yes, yes, I saw *Mosquito Coast*. You're getting senile, you already asked me about that," she huffed.

"Yeah, but that wasn't what I was talking about. I meant the movie *Six Days and Seven Nights*, or maybe it was the other way around."

"Oh. Yes I saw it. It was a silly romantic story about a plane crash on an island," Alex replied, still frustrated at Grant's tendency to go off topic.

"Well, there's a scene where the gal, what's her name...I can't remember, anyway, she tries to pull the raft out of the plane. All the while, he keeps saying, don't pull on that. She was angry and not listening, and was sure she knew what she was doing. Whereupon, she pulls on a cord and the gas canister fires off, and inflates the raft inside the plane. The scene ends with her face squashed up against one of the windows."

"Yes, I remember. Okay, so?" she said irritably, frustrated with his detour from the topic at hand.

"Well, that's my raft. What I mean is, that's the same kind of raft I have in the plane. Except with mine, it has a little tent top. We don't even have to blow it up. All we have to do is pull a tab when we're ready."

What he'd said hadn't yet sunk in. Alex was only half listening. Her mind was somewhere else entirely. She ended up asking, "Did you see his movie *Hollywood Homicide?*"

"Yes. But the only line I remember is something about, how he had to find his Ginko in order to remember where he put his Viagra."

"Oh? And..." She started to make a smart remark when what he'd said earlier registered. "Did you say the raft is automatically inflatable?" The question was rhetorical, as she immediately called to their waiter, and asked where to buy supplies for spending a couple of days in the bush.

It wasn't long, until they had a box of supplies including, candles, matches, bug spray, and canned goods. Canned food seemed to be the only way edibles were preserved in these parts. They picked up a couple of cameo tarps, some heavy rope, and a new hat each. They also managed to acquire two rucksacks, machetes, collapsible shovels, and a collapsible pick.

Reluctant to return to the hotel, they decided it was necessary to check out properly, so once again Alex went in, while Grant stayed scarce. A few minutes later, she walked boldly back to the car. "Okay, let's go," she said hurriedly.

"So, we're taking the road towards Bonampak?" Grant confirmed.

"Yes, as soon as you get the raft. And, guess what? I asked about the guys that arrived last night in the military jeep. The woman at the front desk did not check them in so she didn't know too much, but apparently, they turned around and left about 10:00 PM, even though they had already paid for three rooms."

"I'd say that pretty much confirms they were on to us. It also tells us they have major connections in government," Grant mused. "Let's get going."

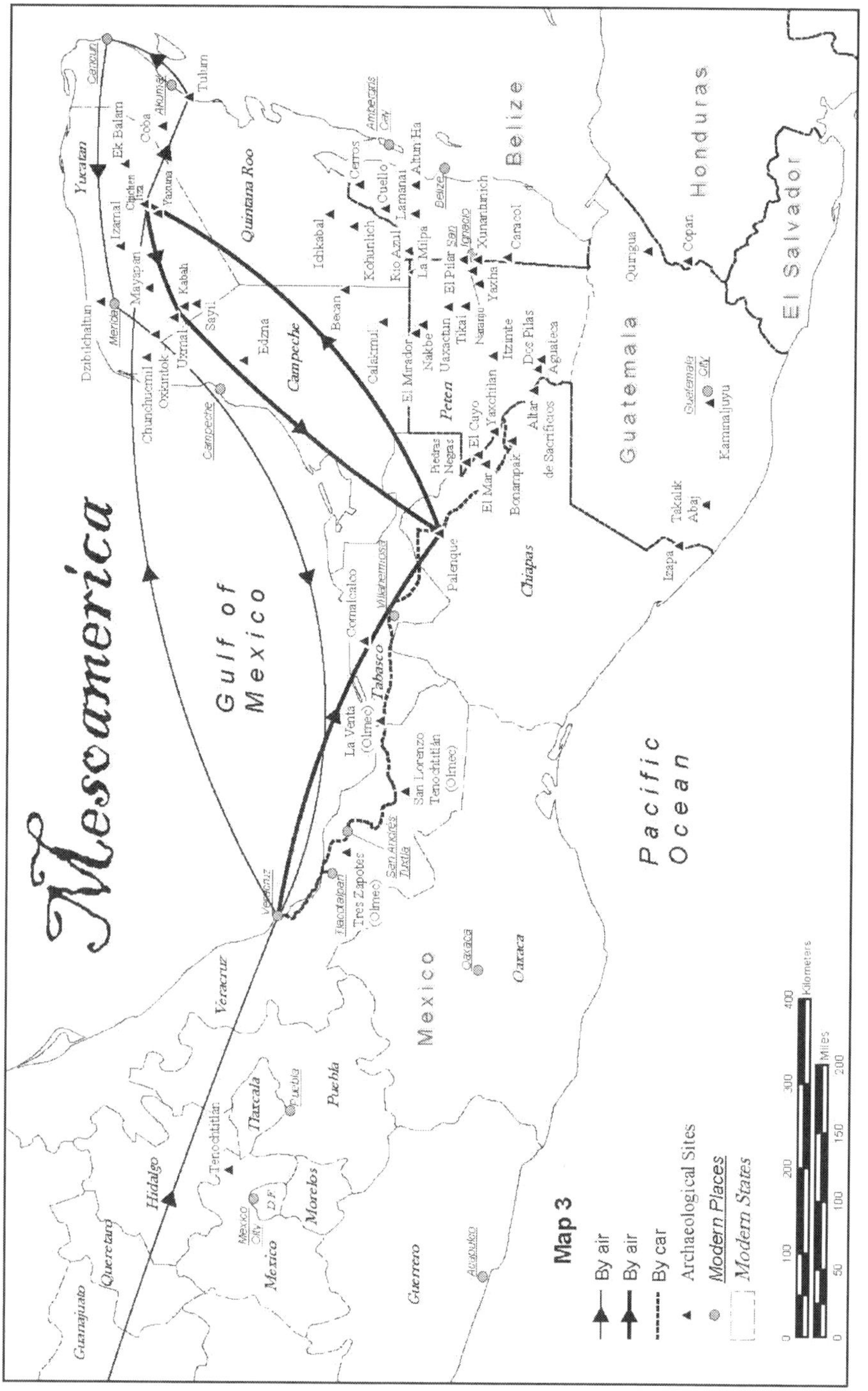
Mesoamerica
Gulf of Mexico
Pacific Ocean
Mexico
Guatemala
Belize
Honduras
El Salvador
Yucatan
Quintana Roo
Campeche
Tabasco
Chiapas
Oaxaca
Veracruz
Puebla
Tlaxcala
Hidalgo
Queretaro
Guanajuato
Mexico
Morelos
Guerrero
D.F.
Peten
Cancun
Tulum
Akumal
Coba
Ek Balam
Yaxuna
Chichen Itza
Izamal
Mayapan
Merida
Dzibilchaltun
Chunchucmil
Oxkintok
Uxmal
Kabah
Sayil
Edzna
Campeche
Becan
Calakmul
Ichkabal
Kohunlich
Rio Azul
Cerros
Cuello
Lamanai
Altun Ha
Ambergris City
Belize
La Milpa
El Mirador
Nakbe
Uaxactun
Tikal
Naranjo
El Pilar
San Ignacio
Xunantunich
Caracol
Yaxha
Itzimte
Dos Pilas
Aguateca
Altar de Sacrificios
Yaxchilan
El Cayo
El Mar
Piedras Negras
Bonampak
Palenque
Villahermosa
Comalcalco
La Venta (Olmec)
San Lorenzo Tenochtitlán (Olmec)
San Andrés Tuxtla
Tres Zapotes (Olmec)
Tlacotalpan
Veracruz
Oaxaca
Tenochtitlan
Mexico City
Puebla
Acapulco
Quirigua
Copan
Guatemala City
Kaminaljuyu
Takalik Abaj
Izapa
Map 3
By air
By air
By car
Archaeological Sites
Modern Places
Modern States
Kilometers
Miles

CHAPTER TWENTY-EIGHT

The Road to Bonampak

By noon, they were negotiating the ruts of a recently repaired road. They had been told this was the road that paralleled the Usumacinta River. It ended at the mysterious Mayan ruins of Bonampak. The river was not in sight. It was a mile or more to their left through dense overgrowth. But they knew it was there, and somehow that was comforting. Their loosely concocted plan was to go about halfway to Bonampak, and look for a trail, or turn-off, leading to the ruins of El Cayo. No road was indicated on their map, but El Cayo was on the Mexico side of the river. It seemed logical, that there might be a road cut through the bush directly to this archeological site by now.

If they did not spot a turn off to El Cayo, there might be one for the La Mar site. It was just a few miles further up river. It was also close to the road. In any event, they planned to park the car, and hike to the river, where they would inflate the raft, and float down stream bound for the Piedras Negras ruins on the Guatemala side of the Usumacinta. The drive, at this point, was largely about reconnaissance, after which they could refine their plan.

For over an hour they navigated a gravel road through sparsely populated savannah, eventually arriving at a small town not on their map. They stopped and inquired of the only person they had seen. They had to go further. The distance between the river and the highway would narrow just a few miles ahead.

They passed through isolated farms, and a few cleared areas. Torrents of dust shot up behind the white Nissan rental car. Chunks of gravel flew in all directions as they negotiated the twisting corridor of road through an increasingly dense jungled area.

The forest walls grew higher and thicker. All that was visible was the road surrounded by jungle, and a narrow strip of blue sky far above. They arrived at Busilja, a clearing littered with great stacks of mahogany and ceiba. The logs were awaiting shipment to a lumber mill far to the north. There was a village here with a small wooden schoolhouse, two miniature dry goods shops, and a meager scattering of thatched huts. The shops were tiny, only about 6' by 8' overall. Customers didn't go inside. They stood outside making purchases across a small counter top.

By mid-afternoon, they were pressed between giant walls of dark green. The heat was intense. The inside of the car doors were hot in spite of the air-conditioning. No rut, or pothole, seemed to elude them. Car and road repeatedly diverged.

"Grant, you've got to slow down. If the car gets damaged we're going to be in a real predicament," she blurted irritably. "Couldn't you miss a few of the holes? It looks like you're steering right into them."

"We're only going 25 miles per hour," he replied, defensively. "It's hard to avoid these ruts. It feels like we're going faster than we are." He slowed down anyway. How far had they come? It seemed like they'd been driving all day.

"I don't know how we're going to figure out where we are, if there's no turn-off to El Cayo," Grant worried out loud. "It would be impossible to hike through this stuff. It could take us a week to go a few miles."

"There might be a turn-off somewhere ahead. If not, I guess we just keep going until we find something we recognize on the map," Alex replied. "We have enough gas to get us to Frontera Corozal. If worse gets to worse, we can go to Corozal rent a boat, and drift all the way back down the river."

"Be pretty hard to conceal what we're doing if we rent a panga," he mused. "I doubt they'd let us spend a night at the ruins, or even board the boat with the gear we've got. Not to mention, the stone box and metal plates."

The jaw-rattling continued, knocking them both back into stressed silence. Time and distance seemed somehow meaningless. There was nothing to identify this mile of road, from any other. It was now, just hundred-foot walls of vegetation. It evoked the strong sensation they were driving through a hot, living tunnel. Insects smacked the windshield with regularity. Some were frighteningly large. The density of green was claustrophobic. Suddenly, they broke out of the forest, and were looking at cleared land. The ground here was raw dirt, and rock. Grass was beginning to take hold in patches. Everywhere, life struggled to reassert itself. "Now that's more like it," he muttered. "But where are we in relation to anything else?"

"I don't know, but let's drive a little further. If we haven't come across anything in another half-hour, we'll get out and take a hike," she declared with more confidence than she felt.

They continued rumbling along the gravel road, sending up huge plumes of dust, signals that warned anyone ahead or behind, of their presence. Then as quickly as they had emerged from the halls of green, they were back in the undergrowth. Even in the dim light, filtering down through the forest canopy, they could see the jungle ahead was joined at the tops. It was a gigantic arboretum through which they must drive. There were fluttering things all around. The impact of their bodies against the windshield reached a frightening crescendo. The glass was thick with the bodies of smashed insects. The window washers were no longer able to sweep them away. Grant pulled to a stop, and waited for the dust to settle. "I've got to clean the windshield."

At a standstill, they could more easily see what they had been driving through. It was a huge swarm of golden butterflies. They formed a thick cloud in front, through the side windows, and all around them. It was eerie. For some reason, it reminded Grant, of the old Hitchcock movie, *The Birds*.

"They're actually quite beautiful," Alex breathed out softly. Grant was reluctant to get out. They sat there waiting until the swarm was well past.

Cursing himself for not thinking to bring paper towels, he took a bottle of water from the backseat and a dirty T-shirt from his bag. He left the engine running, so the air-conditioning could keep the interior of the car cool. He opened the door, and stepped out into a tropical oven. The change in temperature was dramatic. He could barely breathe. Grant quickly set about cleaning the windshield. He rubbed as vigorously as he dared. It wasn't working very well.

The damp heat was so thick and close, it was hard to think. It's just too dangerous to keep driving when you can't see, he thought. He wandered around the car looking for a piece of wood, or anything to scrap off the quashed carcasses. Finally, he pulled out his wallet, and removed a credit card, using the edge as a scrapper. The card, plus water, seemed to do the trick. "What the hell am I doing out here?" he muttered to himself.

Back in the car, Grant collapsed in stunned silence.

"Pretty hot out there," Alex offered.

"Yeah," he was exhausted by even this minor exertion. Grant wanted to complain, he wanted to complain a lot, but something about Alex's presence made him check himself. He controlled his desire to whine. Had he thought about it, he would have recognized then, that he wanted to come across stronger to Alex. The simple truth was he wanted her to believe he was more together than he was.

"You know," he finally said, once the car was in gear. "You're not going to get a chance to try your hand at translating those records. Does that bother you?"

"More than you know," she said with some gravity. "I've been trying to figure out how I could make copies of some of the pages. I think they will reflect light too much for good photographs, but it's worth a try anyway. I could do rubbings, if I had the right kind of paper. What do you think?"

"If we manage to get these things hidden away properly, and even if someone else finds them, if we're found to have photos or rubbings, we're going to be in big trouble. Maybe if you could do something, and get it mailed out to somewhere safe, but frankly, I'd be afraid to risk even that," he said worriedly.

If there were signs to El Cayo or La Mar, they had missed them. Grant kept reminding himself that you simply don't make that much progress on a dirt road doing twenty to twenty-five miles an hour. They stopped two more times to clean the windshield. The last time his credit card cracked and tore in half.

They decided to continue until the road intersected the river. On the map, it was somewhere close to Bonampak. They drove on. The jungle occasionally giving way to cleared zones. Heavy equipment stood in three different clearings, they had recently passed. These were log-harvesting operations. Occasionally, they would see a pick-up, and twice they saw parked logging trucks, but there were no cars out here. Sporadically, they came across areas where they could see that vegetation had been burned. "Pretty hard to understand how they get that stuff to burn," Grant said thoughtfully. "They must throw diesel fuel on the ground cover in order to get the vines hot enough to evaporate the moisture stored in them."

"There are times during the year where the forest is dried out more than others," Alex replied. "The ancient Mayans pursued that exact same method for clearing ground to plant maze. The slash and burn process is as old as recorded history. It clears the ground, and produces a fertilizer of sorts, to stimulate new growth. I'd say the loggers harvested some of these areas, and once they left, the jungle immediately began to reclaim the cleared zones. At that point, local subsistence farmers stepped in and burned the new growth. I doubt they'd burn old growth. The timber is too valuable."

They had purchased eight large bottles of water. It might not be enough, he worried. "I can't imagine carrying this stuff overland. What were we thinking?" Grant asked, while shaking his head in disbelief at their naiveté.

"Yeah, back at the hotel it seemed it was going to be pretty easy. Maybe not finding somewhere to actually hide the records, but it never really occurred to me how impossible it is to cut through the jungle. The only chance is to find a trail, and then it would still be a horrendous task," she added.

Finally, a small hand-lettered sign on the right of the road said, Bonampak, with the number twelve. "Looks like it's about twelve kilometers that way," Grant said, pointing down the access road. So, do we want to check it out as an option, before heading on to Frontera Corozal?"

He brought the car to a stop, causing a huge cloud of dusk to rise and swirl around them. "Let's see, twelve kilometers, I think that would be about seven and a half miles. It's not terribly far," he said.

"It's going to be dark in a couple hours. I suppose we can sleep in the car if we must. It would probably be tomorrow before we could get a boat to take us downstream anyway. Your call," she replied.

"No. It's your turn to decide our fate," he sniggered. "I did that last night and look where it got us."

"I've always wanted to see Bonampak. Since we're here, we might as well take a look. They turned off the air-conditioner, rolled down the windows, and made the turn towards Bonampak. The heat settled in, but it was not nearly as bad as it had been.

Recent rains had washed great chasms out of the sides of the roadway. Some of them were a good ten feet wide, and just as deep. It was impossible to walk from the road directly into the jungle in places due to the size of the ruts. Fallen branches littered both sides of the road. Huge rotted tree trunks lay where they had been pushed by clearing equipment. The forest to either side of them was a tangle of ceiba, mahogany, and zapóte, trapped in a mesh of thick woody vines.

Of necessity, they drove slowly, listening to the crunch of gravel, and the cracking of small branches under their tires. Ubiquitous swarms of insects hummed and buzzed. The songs and cries of birds, added to the strangeness. High overhead, the foliage ruptured into weird and wonderful colors. Macaws flitted about, their plumage breathtaking. The delightful toucan, with its characteristic beak graced the treetops in several places. The keel-billed motmot, with its distinctive drawn-out call, "kawaa, kawaa," was visible in lower branches. This bird was thought to be extinct at one time, until re-discovered here, in the Usumacinta river basin.

The dang smell of the forest was heavy in the air. Orchids grew high up in the canopy, adding their gentle scent to the odor of rotting vegetation, new growth, and damp dirt. Twenty minutes later, the jungle widened into a substantial open area. The sky seemed larger, after hours of their catching only glimpses through the natural awning formed by the tropical rain forest.

Several huts, a few burros, and some grazing horses, stood in a pasture. Across a grassy strip appeared another larger clearing, the entrance to the ancient ceremonial center of Bonampak.

"I think that's a grass landing strip," Alex gushed enthusiastically. "Hey, and look there," she pointed in the direction of the field. "A paved road is coming in. It runs parallel to the runway. That's odd. I wonder what's down that way."

"Yeah, that's a runway alright," Grant agreed.

The ruins of Bonampak, were not nearly as impressive as many Mayan sites. Although a number of richly carved stele stood amongst the ruins. A tall steep pyramid, a ball court, several plazas and temples, along with some smaller pyramidal structures, had all been cleared of vegetation. Hundreds of ancient buildings were hardly more than mounds of rubble, waiting to be reclaimed from the jungle's grasp.

The great treasure of Bonampak is the brilliant colored murals painted on the sides of the interior walls of a three-room temple. They are the best preserved, and most colorful in all of Mayandom. A war is depicted between a dark, and light skinned people, literally blacks and whites. The dark-skinned warriors the victors, leading their captives to ritual sacrifice. The question usually asked by those non-archeologists, who saw photographs of the murals, was where did the white people come that were so carefully depicted on these walls? The ruins were already hundreds of years old by the time of Columbus. No one had a reasonable answer. Anthropologists tended to ignore the issue, saying they had probably painted white people in the murals to differentiate them from the victors...not a terribly satisfactory answer.

There were two guards at the site. One was charging a fee to enter the ruins. According to treaty, the Lacandon Maya owned the property. The guard collecting the entrance fee made it clear the site would be closing within the hour. Alex suggested Grant slip him a few dollars to ease his hurry to leave. That done, they walked amongst the ruins by themselves. No one was anywhere nearby. A sign introduced the frescos:

> These were painted on wet limestone cement with more than 270 figures. The frescos show the story of a battle and a sacrificial ceremony. The first room has jaguar-skin robed lords with elaborate headdresses and ornate scepters, mustering their warriors for battle while musicians and dancers parade before them. The middle room shows the actual skirmish, with a lot of blood and brutality. A second fresco in the same room shows prisoners being judged by the lord of Bonampak. The third room shows a prisoner being sacrificed by being beheaded.

Standing inside, moving the light across the walls of the frescoed temple, the colors were so surprisingly intense that some looked as though they'd recently been painted in high-gloss enamels. "I can hardly believe how stunning and sharp these murals actually are. It's incredible that we're really here and seeing them in the original. I've seen full scale copies in the museum of Anthropology, in Mexico City, but somehow they do not do them justice." Alex said, shaking her head in wonder.

"You notice how no one comments on the obvious? They never mention the prisoners are all white guys, and the victors are all black," Grant observed.

"Yes, that is interesting No one has a real answer for it." She turned and looked at him for a minute, seeing what she assumed was a smirk on his face. "And, why do I think you have a theory on that?" she asked.

"Got me," he said, as he walked off feigning interest in another structure.

Following along, she mumbled, "You are a strange one, Grant Whitaker."

"What do you think Alex? Any chance we can secret the box and records around here?"

"I don't know how. I gather there are people here all the time. The place is probably never really deserted, and the eco-tourists, and bird-watcher types, arrive without much warning," she said with reservation. "This would be a great place, but we'd have very little privacy. We need to be more remote," she said evenly.

Returning to their car, the guard Grant had tipped was hanging around smiling broadly. He was, nodding his head towards them, probably hoping to be of some further service. "Maybe you should ask him who he would recommend we hire for going downriver for a couple of days," Grant suggested. "Here's a $10 bill. Let him see it when you're asking the question."

Alex walked towards the guard, who could easily see the money in her hand. He was all smiles. Grant headed over to the car. He had parked it under a tree with the windows down about an inch. A mango fell and rolled off the top of the car. He idly looked up into the tree, noticing it was heavy with fruit. With food like this in abundance, even were they to run out of canned goods, and get lost in the jungle, they probably wouldn't starve if they were careful.

On the island of St. Kitts, where he lived part of each year, mangos were prevalent. They were a favorite of the verdant monkeys, who would sweep in and collect all that they could gather. There were so many monkeys on the island, that the official estimates placed the ratio at two and a half monkeys, per person. The verdant monkey is the one prized by the organ grinders of old. Here in the rain forest, it was the spider and howler monkeys that controlled the forest canopy.

Staring out at the grass airstrip, he thought how he would make the approach for landing here. He concluded the strip was built for light singles. I sure wouldn't want to bring a twin in here, he thought. Once again, he noticed the pavement coming in from another direction. "A mystery," he said out loud to know one.

Away in the distance, he heard a blood-curdling growl. It sounded like a large male lion on the Serengeti. Had he not been in these jungles in the past, he would have assumed it was a jaguar, or what the locals called tigers. The jaguar in the Lacandon tropical forest was not nearly as common as it once was. It was over twice the size of its jaguar cousin in Africa. Grant had seen them several times in Africa, but only once in Central America. He was pretty sure that horrible growl he'd just heard, belonged to a male howler monkey. Once a troop of them got to howling, it sounded like lions at war. It sent shivers up your spine.

Grant thought back about his previous experiences in the Lacandon jungle, deciding that his favorite animal was the coati, actually the coatimundi. A member of the raccoon family, it has a cat-like body and long upright tail. It's cute little masked face, and inquisitive nature, give them a unique personality. They are friendly, and will frequently come up close, and beg for food. They seem to trust people and even perform tricks of a sort. A delightful creature, it could be quite charming.

Standing there lost in thought he was oblivious to Alex's return. "That was a good call," she said, "Enrique Lopez, that's the guard's name, will get his brother Alfonso to provide a boat tomorrow. Enrique will take us down river. He says we're not supposed to spend the night inside the ruins, but we can set up an overnight camp outside the archeology zone."

"Enrique will take us to Yaxchilan, and then all the way down to Piedras Negras, by passing El Cayo. He won't stop at El Cayo, because he says the looters control the area. He was reluctant to go as far as Piedras Negras. In fact, he was amazed we would dare spend the night there, but as long as he didn't have to do it himself, and he could come back, and pick us up a day or two later, it was okay by him."

"What did you tell him we were doing?" Grant asked suspiciously. "It seems he's being awfully helpful to a couple of lone tourists. I get the feeling this is really going to cost us."

"Oh, we're not tourists Grant. We're archeologists, working on a private project. I told him we were here to refine a conceptual system of ancient civilizations, and make them comprehensible across cultural barriers by identifying the categories of order regarded as appropriate by the people under study."

"What did you say?" Grant struggled to mentally replay what he had just heard. He finally decided it was gibberish. "I'll bet you can't say that again," he chided her.

"Oh, I can say that again. That was the mission outline of our field study group," she laughed. "We had to learn it in Spanish, so we would look like we knew what we were doing down here. Language is important. Especially in areas like this. A local will not acknowledge they do not understand what you've said, but just like the British, if it sounds intellectual, or high-class, they will instantly acknowledge your superior position by how you speak, ergo…"

"You're just full of surprises. But for real? You were actually taught to exert your intellectual vanity," he said grinning. "Why does that not surprise me? Ergo, I gather Enrique thinks he is helping someone of note?"

Assuming an air of casual sophistication, Alex replied, "Well, that might be your conclusion, and it might be his, but I certainly didn't say such a thing. It is too bad we don't have a real camera though, taking his picture a few times would probably be a good idea. Frankly, I don't think the cameras in your phones will make much of an impression."

"I have a camera," Grant said brightly.

"You do? Is it with you? I haven't seen it," she said incredulously.

"It's fairly small, but larger than a cell phone. It's in my aviation bag," he said smiling broadly. "I can take his picture, and show it to him in the display window, which is darn near the size of the camera itself. That should please him."

Grant opened the trunk, dug around in his flight bag for a moment, and materialized a Canon Sure Shot. He turned it on, took a quick photo of Alex, turned it around and showed it to her. "Just like our phones, only more options and more pixels," he added.

"Okay, so you probably ought to act like you're taking important photos from time to time tomorrow. Just make sure you get a really good one of him. Show it to him, and write down his address, so you can send him an enlarged print. Uh...I don't suppose you have a copy of the National Geographic in that mysterious bag of yours," she laughed. "That might do wonders."

"Sorry. No magazines. We'll ham it up, and make him out to be an incredible guide. And, what is all this going to cost?"

"Not too bad. He wants $200 for going down and another $200 to pick us up. No pesos, and no Guatemalan quetzals, only U.S. dollars," she said lightly. "I was pretty sure that was fine with you considering all the money you're carrying around."

"Okay, it's a descent price. But I'd feel safer if we were paying him $100 on the way down and $300 for the pick-up," he groused. "Something might happen to dampen his motivation to retrieve us."

"Okay, let me work on that," she said with a dismissive gesture. "Perhaps we'll offer him a substantial tip when he picks us up. I wonder if he can bring us some cold beers or something," she mused.

Her mood changed, and her voice became serious. "One thing is bothering me Grant. Things must be pretty bad when a local armed security guard won't spend the night at the ruins for hire. He won't even stop at El Cayo."

Shaking his head slightly, "Yeah it doesn't sound too good. But we're not going to be gone that long, and hopefully we won't be attracting attention to ourselves."

Brightening up, she remembered, "Oh, and Enrique said that overnight visitors usually stay at the Hotel Escudo Jaguar. I gather it's the only hotel in the area. It is located next to the river at the boat launch. We should meet him in the morning at 9:00, on the dock. He also mentioned there was a campground. But he warned it was lousy with mosquitoes."

They intercepted the paved road, still wondering where it was coming from. They arrived at the little village of Frontera Escheverria, which turned out to be the official name for what most people referred to as Frontera Corozal, or simply Corozal. Because it was a border crossing, between Mexico, and Guatemala, there was a military checkpoint a mile before the town. Even though they were not crossing into Guatemala, at least yet, they were asked to present their passports and tourist cards. Alex and Grant handed over their Mexican residency documents. It was a surprise for the military personnel standing guard, but they duly logged the entries, and waved them on.

There was nothing modern about Corozal. It typified a classic Third World village in the middle of a non-civilized area. It had been established in the late seventies as a resettlement project for local Indians displaced from northern Chiapas. The displaced Indians had initially settled inside the Lacandon jungle, but were forced to move again, after the area was declared the "Montes Azules Biosphere" at a world conference of some sort. Corozal eventually became the launch point on the Usumacinta River, for visiting ruins along the river

The hotel was empty. The desk clerk mentioned that a bird-watching tour group had just left. They had apparently rented the entire hotel for the prior three days before returning to Palenque.

When Alex shared their good fortune, Grant said reflectively, "If that's true, then there must be another road from Palenque to here. There were certainly no tour buses or mini-vans that passed us today. You know, something tells me we weren't on the main road. I vaguely remember hearing something about the Mexican government paving a tourist access highway to Bonampak a couple of years ago. I'll bet the main road loops around, and comes in from the other direction. That would explain the paved apron at the ruins near the landing strip."

"You mean we really didn't have to endure that horrific drive through the jungle? If you're right, I wonder how we got messed up," she said with a look of puzzlement on her face. "Oh yeah, I was asking about a road that ran parallel to the river on the road to Bonampak."

The next morning, Enrique was at the dock as promised. He was alone. The riverboat was wider than a canoe, and twice as long. Working together, it took Alex and Grant several trips to move all of their supplies to the boat. On the second trip from the car, Grant wrapped the empty stone box in one of the tarps, and loaded it without raising any suspicion. The metal records were stored in Grant's knapsack. He wore them on his back while carrying the collapsible shovels and the pick wrapped inside the other tarp. Enrique was content to visit quietly with another boatman during the loading process. He showed no interest in helping.

The trip down Sacred Monkey, the local name for the Usumacinta River, was just a couple of hours to Yaxchilan. This was one of those times where it felt very much like they were modern Indiana Jones types. Having a local guide take you to remote ancient ruins down a huge deserted jungle river, has a rather unique flavor to it. There were no tourists and no signs of modern civilization as they moved down river. Occasionally, they spotted crocodiles, lounging at river's edge. Although they didn't see them, they were also aware that giant river snakes plied the river eddies. Grant decided he wasn't interested in swimming here, no matter how hot it got.

Alex was thoroughly engaged in conversation with Enrique. Finally, she turned to Grant and said, "It seems awfully deserted here, even for this remote location, so I asked him why we weren't seeing at least a couple of other boats. He told me that the military had established two checkpoints between Palenque and Bonampak yesterday. The rumor is they're looking for a couple of American looters. Evidently checkpoints have tied the road up so completely that the scheduled tours for today didn't arrive. Everything is cancelled until the army finds who they're looking for."

Even though they were speaking English, just in case Enrique understood more than he let on, neither of them would discuss what they both surmised. What had begun as a pleasant morning, and a beautiful ride down the Usumacinta, turned into a gut-churning set of scary possibilities. They fell quiet, each trying to interpret this new information in light of where they were, and what they were planning to do.

Enrique put in to a beach, just below the ruins of Yaxchilan. He encouraged them to stretch, take a break, and look around. There was a guard shack and small thatched hut overlooking the river. No one seemed to be there. The three of them headed roughly southeast along a winding path towards the lowest ceremonial site. Enrique led them up a hill to a rustic dining hall. It was nothing more than some benches covered by a palapa roof. It had had been built to service field archeologists, and the university students who joined them. It now served as an interim picnic ground for the handful of explorers that were brought here on day-trips by riverboat guides.

They weren't hungry. But the setting seemed to call for food, so before exploring the site, Alex passed out soft-shelled tacos that had been provided in a box lunch prepared by the hotel. She had a bottle of beer for Enrique and herself, an old-fashioned bottled Pepsi for Grant.

There was no such thing as Diet Coke out here, causing Grant to think back on his encounter with the Guatemala military of many years earlier. The army seemed to be constructed of fifteen-year old boys with automatic rifles. The entire event might have turned out differently had he not started passing out cans of Diet Coke, from the large ice chests in the rear of his van. The soldiers were clearly skittish, especially after Marianna started lecturing one of them in English about gun safety. She was shaking her finger in young man's face after one of the soldiers had pushed the barrel of his gun into Grant's stomach.

Perhaps the only reason they didn't get shot when she pulled her mother-lecture routine, was that about a dozen soldiers were in a perfect circle around them. They all brought their AK's up when she started in, no one could fire without endangering the other soldiers. It was tense, but finally a couple of these kids started to snigger at how Marianna had faced down the boy-soldier holding the gun to Grant's stomach.

Although the young soldier didn't know what Marianna was saying to him, she was taller, older, and instantly represented what she was: a powerful mother of many children. She was not going to tolerate disobedience from a youngster, even one with a gun.

The boy's tough facade broke. It showed on his face, and the mood shifted when the other young men caught his look. He tried to reassert himself, but Grant had immediately walked to the open rear door of the van, and begun passing out sodas with a big smile. You could literally see the struggle in the young men's faces, as they tried to decide whether to lower their weapons so they could free a hand to take this precious gift, or follow whatever procedures they had been trained to pursue.

In the end, the sodas held sway. It became immediately clear that they were all puzzled by the cold cans, and pop-top lids. None of them had ever had an iced beverage in a can. Cokes in the Guatemala Peten were still smallish green bottles cooled by sitting in tepid water. Grant had opened a pop-top can to the astonishment of all the soldiers. But, when he went to open others, none of them wanted their treasure to be opened and consumed.

Grant had thought back on this encounter many times over the years. Perhaps the most important lesson he had gained from the event was his realization of just how differently we may view things. Our individual ways of interpreting events are a consequence of our own cultural prejudice. We assume things are so, because they seem naturally correct in light of our past experiences. That's what we think of as *common sense*. Yet, the lesson that had become so obvious to Grant was how easy it was to be absolutely wrong in our assumptions, and simply never know it.

All of us view the world through our own cultural lens. The way we view life undergirds all our beliefs, both known and unknown. This is how we perceive things, or subconsciously translate everything in our personal reality. Every experience, every sensory input, and all the information coming into our brain, is first filtered, and then compared, through the lens of our past conclusions. This process is automatic and unconscious. Yet, it ultimately governs everything we think, feel, and say. Do I dare examine my internal beliefs more deeply? Do I even know what the beliefs are that underlie and shape my moment-to-moment response to everything in my world?

"Hey. What is going on?" Alex demanded, realizing he was somewhere else entirely.

"I'm sorry, just thinking back about a little encounter with the Guatemala military."

"And...," she said, hanging a verbal question mark in the air.

He told her the story. Then he told her more. Just talking about the experience somehow reduced the dread lingering at the back of his mind surrounding their current predicament.

It was immediately clear that Yaxchilan was more enveloped by jungle than any other archeological site either of them had experienced previously. The undergrowth, and the forest canopy, together seemed somehow more extensive than that of the Mayan city state of Tikal; a place notorious for the density of its jungle surround.

"This place is overpowering. It feels as though the forest is about to close in and cover everything. And yet, it's vibrant and alive," Grant almost whispered.

"Yeah," Alice whispered in return. "It's probably because there has been a distinct lack of tourists here. It's hard to even find photos of Yaxchilan in the outside world. There are no site guides, or postcards. While I've seen some digital photos posted on the net, none of them even begin to capture the feel of this place."

Finishing their tacos, Alex told Enrique they would be back within the hour. They set out to explore the site before moving on down river. Grant carried his camera conspicuously. The trail leading to the ceremonial center's sole entrance was a stimulus to the imagination. It conjured up images of a great and ancient kingdom. Surely it had been a royal realm of profound and extensive influence. The humid path was framed by enormously tall trees intertwined by walls of vines. The ground was covered with slippery stones, many fallen from ancient temples that loomed high in the trees. The first glimpse of a structure at ground level, was an elevated stonewall. It ran parallel to the trail, receding in steppes as it rose.

The trail came to an abrupt end at a narrow entrance through the heavy stonewall. The portal to the city above was flanked by a pyramid and temple. To enter required one to pass through a dark archway into an even darker corridor. Together they ducked into the pitch-black tunnel. Bats swooped; the stone steps and ramparts seemed to move. The lichen-covered walls were even more disorienting than the jungle they had just traversed. They fought off the tendency to reach out for support. Life crawled, buzzed and slithered everywhere.

A right turn brought them to a set of steep upward steps. Light barely filtered down into the labyrinth of stone. Warm, moist air, carried the fetid smell of decay. The narrow exit at the top of the staircase framed the access to an immense outdoor chamber. Heart-shaped leaves, the size of dinner plates, dominated the courtyard. Trees were wrapped so tightly in dark green vines it was hard to spot even a swatch of bark.

They had entered a place of jade and emerald. An indescribably lime on olive world. The sun pressed down from high above, heavily filtered through the forest canopy. The air hung thick and still. They trudged along in a veritable steam bath, barely able to talk.

Horseflies and mosquitoes moved in large swarms. They walked on with leaden feet, moving around the broken ruins of ancient palaces. Breaking out into an open space they saw steep hills that formed the pinnacles on which sat strange temples. Standing there open mouthed, they gawked unabashedly at the bizarre landscape of this ancient ceremonial place. They were alone, dwarfed by the silent cloying jungle, surrounded by the relics of a mysterious past.

Yaxchilan stood out from other Mayan sites due the number of decorative artworks still intact on its buildings. The door jams, lintels, and other carved artworks, had survived the passage of time much better than other locations they had seen.

Alex was obviously more fit than Grant, but it was she who finally called the halt. "I really don't care if I see this place, if we have to do it at this pace," she gasped. "Let's sit, and figure out how to proceed."

Grant hadn't realized how hard his heart was pounding. "It's amazing how little exertion it takes to run out of breath here," he managed. "Yet, the air is heavy with enriched oxygen because of all the growth. It seems strange."

Without addressing his comment, Alex went straight to what was on both of their minds. "Grant, you think those roadblocks are about us?"

"Good chance," he said sullenly.

"What are we going to do?" she whimpered. More dread was apparent in her voice than she had intended to reveal.

"I think we need to finish what we started. Let's bury the records somewhere as soon as possible. There's plenty of privacy here, and this site should be safer than moving further downstream. We'll end up with several more hours to work, if we stay put. Why spend more time on the river? Maybe we could get back to Corozal by tomorrow evening, drive across the bridge into Guatemala, and make our escape that way," Grant said more forcefully than was necessary.

"But what about your plane?" she worried.

"If they're setting up roadblocks to catch us between Palenque, and Bonampak, they may be doing the same thing in every other direction out of Palenque. Other than the waitress at the restaurant, and the outfitters, no one knows we were headed into the bush. And, neither of them, actually knew which way we were headed," he said, thinking frantically.

"What did you tell that research student at the museum?" she asked.

"Not much. I asked her for information on Piedras Negras. She gave me a flyer. We talked about the problems with looters, and the archeologists from Canada. I guess we sort of talked about all the various ruins out this way."

"So, if the police, or the military, or whoever they are, have interviewed field staff, they may have surmised this is where we are headed," she concluded. "Assuming the roadblock is about us."

"I think we have to assume it's about us," Grant stated flatly. "That means we need to take rather drastic actions to prevent their getting close, even if that means abandoning the plane."

They headed back to find Enrique. He was sitting under a banyan tree smoking. Alex spoke with him for a while. He began to frown. His grimace deepened, as she continued her explanation.

Eventually, he shrugged his shoulders. Alex talked on, and this time, he smiled broadly, and shook his head yes. She leaned into the boat, and said quietly to Grant, "Help me get this stuff out of here. I promised him the full fare if he could pick us up right here tomorrow late afternoon. I also told him that if he brought me a couple of cold beers in an ice chest from the hotel, there would be a big tip for him."

Five minutes later, their gear on the dirt beach, Enrique was pushing off waving goodbye. Five minutes more and it began to rain. They hurriedly stored the supplies on top of the monstrous exposed roots of a tree, and sat under the branches watching the water pour down. "Where did this come from," she said. "I never even saw a cloud approaching."

CHAPTER TWENTY-NINE

Frontera Corozal, Chiapas

The rain was coming down much harder now. It didn't take long before the river was moving more swiftly. The high water mark was obvious along the banks, but the water level was still a good fifteen feet below that. Rain or no rain, they had to start moving their equipment further up into the ceremonial site.

Alex and Grant worked steadily away in a drenching downpour, slipping and sliding, thoroughly soaked. The cascading rain on the dense vegetation drowned out the constant cacophony of the birds and insects. Or perhaps the frogs, insects, and birds, all kept silent when it rained.

Stepping under a tree for protection, Alex pulled her T-shirt off, and tried to wring it out. She stood there in bra and jeans, then turned around and sat on the woody root of a tree. She bent over and took off her shoes, then unbuttoned her jeans, and pulled them off. "Sorry she mouthed. Too much water, it's weighing me down."

Sitting there in bra and panties, she was about as dressed as when he'd seen her run down the beach in Akumal. But something was vastly different this time. His body instantly responded, ignoring the pouring rain, the wet and miserable conditions, and the exhaustion he had felt just moments earlier. Damn, he thought, why am I so blasted vulnerable? He stood there trying not to stare, struggling unsuccessfully to tear his eyes away from her. They couldn't really hear one another without yelling, and now didn't seem to be the time, but she noticed his attempts to regain control. Alex turned around, and began to dig in her knapsack looking for her shorts. That act was as hard on him as the immediate shock of seeing her wriggle out of her wet jeans.

Unkempt and soaked, and generally a tired mess, he hesitated then walked towards her in the mud. He stopped behind her bent over figure. Her undergarments were modest, but wet as they were, there was not much to them. Sensing him, she straightened up and turned around. She stood looking up into his eyes.

There was a moment's hesitation. Alex wasn't stopping his advance. She wasn't encouraging him either. The intermittent, quasi-romantic dance they had been playing these several days, made it clear to Alex that it was Grant that must initiate the next step. It wasn't that she was reluctant it was simply that all her instincts told her it must be him. Whatever internal conflicts with which he was dealing, made him somehow different than many of the men she had known. This was a difference she respected. She even admired it, at least to some degree. But it made him difficult to read. More than once, it had left her confused, frustrated, and even irritated. Yes, it was up to him to decide when, if, and where.

It wasn't the most graceful embrace. They clung to each other as much in desperation as affection. When he pushed her back to look at her and say something, she leaned up and kissed him hard on the mouth. He wanted to swing her up in his arms and carry her away. But, there was no safe place. And even if he lifted her while standing in the mud, he'd probably just embarrass himself by falling down. Somewhat awkwardly, he stood there holding on to her, feeling the press of her breasts against his chest, willing there to be a place they could become more intimate. And glad there was not.

He finally took her hand and led her to one of the above ground roots of a banyan tree. They sat down side by side, the only way they could. For a moment, she was embarrassed as he removed his shoes, and then his soaking shirt and jeans, and draped them over another root, turning his pant legs up so they would not hang in the mud. The rain was lessening now. They could speak and be heard. But, neither was prepared to talk. She leaned into him again. They embraced, much more intimately. Eventually, with barely controlled passion.

Thoughts of how unfair it was to pursue Alex had somehow vanished. In some way, the rain had washed away his fears, his guilt, his concerns, and his overriding sense of responsibility. Those thoughts would return. He knew they would. But for the moment, life was all about his need for her, and their desire to be together.

It was awkward and almost funny, but they couldn't seem to get enough of each other. There was no place to lie down and no place to be comfortable, but just as all life struggles to survive and procreate so it was with them. Their survival might be seriously in question now, yet the moment was too powerful, and their passion once unstopped, continued to consume them.

Ever so reluctantly Grant whispered, "Not like this. Not now."

Alex simply nodded her head. At some level, she recognized his need to find balance with whatever it is that he felt so deeply. There were things going on within him she did not, probably could not, understand. She began to push back, saddened, fighting a feeling of rejection. Grant tightened his hold and pulled her closer.

The rain reduced to a soft drizzle. Insects began to emerge and declare their mating intentions. Very soon Alex and Grant would of necessity have to get moving on their intended objectives. They held on to one another for another moment, thoroughly intertwined, willing the rain to continue, and hoping that it would stop.

"I had just about decided you didn't like me that much," she said quietly.

"It had nothing to do with like," he said more loudly than he intended. "I," he fumbled. "I don't know what to say." She put three fingers against his lips and whispered, "Don't talk. Feel." Grant looked over her shoulder at the dramatic increase in the river flow. He felt as though he were on the raging water being carried, he knew not where. It was dangerous. It was frightening. It made no real sense. Yet, he did not want to quit. Something greater was at play. He shuddered briefly, squeezed her again, then got up to change and spray them down with repellant before the bugs came out in legion. "Summer cologne in the tropics," he said smiling.

"Come on, beautiful, we've got to find a place to secret these records." His compliment got a wonderful smile. She struggled up wiping ants off her legs.

Digging around in her knapsack, she brought out her only spare pair of jeans. "I sure hope our clothes dry before the next deluge. I'm going to have to wear socks to keep the insects off my ankles, and I only have this one pair."

"With the ground so wet, I'm not sure what we can do without making a huge mess. On the bright side, if it rains again, all trace of wherever we work should be washed away," she said.

He reached out his hand to pull her up from where she now sat fully dressed. She jumped up. Kissed him boldly, then turned and walked back towards the dark stone archways and the labyrinth that formed the entrance to Yaxchilan. "Hang on there just a minute," he said, "at the least we should take the shovels with us."

"Oh," she said spinning around like a ten-year old, her arms in a windmill. She threw him a disarming smile.

Within an hour, the world of wet and green had changed again. The dirt was firming. Water still sat in puddles in the giant leaves sprawled open on the ground. The relentless sun began to raise the moisture in a fog. The affect added mystery to an already mystical place.

They began the hunt in earnest. "So, tell me about this Zara-whatever? You said it was probably somewhere along this river the other day," Alex asked with interest.

"It's a long story. It begins in Judah over 2,600 years ago," he began. He stopped and thought for a moment. "Maybe we had better stick to the hunt for now, and save the story for after dinner conversation."

"Good for me," she smiled back, "But you have a habit of not finishing your stories."

As they looked for a place to conceal the records, he argued with himself about how easily Alex had moved to a state of childlike happiness. She had done this right in the midst of the calamity that faced them both. Aside from the physical discomforts they were experiencing, and the proximity of aggressive looters, they were being sought by both the military and the police. And, if they were able to escape Mexico, each of them still faced serious problems with the U.S. government. Not a bright future, all in all. So, Alex knows all this and yet here she is choosing to be happy. So, is that naïve, or is that intelligent, or what?

I suppose happiness is an effect of our state of mind. It is a feeling, not a situation. The minute we look for happiness anywhere other than our own thoughts, we are lost. That's because we're focused on the outside, in search of something that comes from within. Happiness is an emotional response to the way we are thinking. It is not a circumstance. And, at least in theory, we can choose to feel differently.

Once again they experienced the extraordinary passageway through the corbelled arch, down the shadowy corridors and up the narrow stairway so dark they were forced to feel their way up the steps. Once again, the arrival at the plaza created a remarkable transition from the outside world into the ruins of a dramatic, lost world.

They agreed to split up. Alex began reconnoitering the ceremonial city for a place to intern the stone box and its precious contents. Grant began to search for a place to setup a camp for the night. The labyrinth structure that formed the unusual entrance to the city, also closed off the northwest corner of the main plaza. This particular building was large and strangely laid-out. It had already been substantially excavated so it might be a good place to find shelter. Doomed to count things, he noted that this particular construction was composed of nine vaulted chambers connected by sixteen vaulted passageways constructed on three levels. The bottom two levels were essentially subterranean and filled with bats and slithering things. He changed his mind. He wouldn't be spending more time down there.

On the top level of the southeast side of the labyrinth, there was a small doorway leading to an interior chamber. A carved limestone bench was in the center of the room. Another was cut out of the wall at the far end with an adjoining large niche. They had not brought hammocks. One did not sleep on the ground close to the jungle. Luckily the two benches within the interior chamber would do nicely as narrow single beds. They'd be hard, but they were off the ground, and in a relatively clean place made of stone.

Feeling rather pleased with himself for his rapid discovery of a good place to spend the night, Grant set about moving their gear from the river's edge, up into the city. He removed his small high-powered binoculars from his aviation bag and stuffed them into the rear pocket of his jeans. The knife went into his right front pocket. Rather than carry the yellow life raft and the rest of the equipment up into the city, and then back again tomorrow, he wrapped them in one of the two cameo-colored tarps, and pushed the package high up in the branches of a nearby tree.

By the time he was done moving the rest of their gear to the top of the labyrinth, he was exhausted again. He stood there on the edge of the plaza with his hands on his knees gasping for air. Is this a sign of age, or am I in such terrible shape, he wondered.

Everything here was built vertically. There were steep pyramids at the top of equally steep hills in all directions. He wanted to find Alex and discuss this with her. It didn't feel right to start yelling. You never knew who, or what, might be hanging around. From where he stood in the main plaza he had limited lateral view. However, he could see at least three hills directly behind him. Each hill had cut-stone stairs leading up to a temple on top. He picked the closest and headed up to gain a topside view and look around for Alex.

Grant reached the bottom of the first hill and started up the broad stairs leading to the collapsing temple on top. There were four tiers of steps, each about three-stories in height. At each level there was a small plaza or courtyard of sorts. The higher he went the more buildings came into view. He stopped to catch his breath and look around. This ancient city was much larger than it first appeared. The size of the place surprised him. Yaxchilan is not well known, so he had assumed it must be a minor ceremonial site. Now he could see that this assumption was wrong. His next thought was that they would be lucky to even walk to all the excavated structures by tomorrow afternoon, much less determine where and how to secret their treasure.

As with most ancient Mayan cities, the natural surroundings were extraordinary. Situated in the heavily forested hilly lowlands of Chiapas, Yaxchilan was surrounded on three sides by the Usumacinta River. Judging from the high water marks along its banks the river would be moving very swiftly much of the year. He reminded himself, they don't call this area a rain forest for nothing. Gaining the temple at the top of the hill, it became obvious why the city had been built where it had. It was on a thumb of land jutting out into the river providing steep banks on three sides that would naturally thwart aggressors. In addition, the steep hills contained within the city walls allowed for spectacular viewpoints and those all important sky alignments that were so much a part of the Mayan philosophy. Behind him were even higher hills. He walked to the southern edge of the temple platform. Here he could see another impressive temple at the peak of the highest hill in the area. Whoa, that would be a hike just getting up there, he thought.

From his perch at the top of the first hill, he had a good view of much of the ceremonial layout. He sat down to study it, and think it through. The Usumacinta River, flowing from northern Guatemala into Mexico, formed the biological backbone of the largest tropical rainforest north of the Amazon. It was just a remnant of the lush jungle that once blanketed all of Central America. This amazing river drained an area of almost 80,000 square kilometers, and yet virtually no one outside this place even knows of its existence, he thought.

Surely, this is one of the most interesting places on earth. Hidden temples, gigantic pyramids, and ancient tombs are all about us. We're surrounded by a largely unexplored tropical forest, saturated with exotic wildlife. Howler and spider monkeys abound. Toucans, macaws, crocodiles, jaguars, ocelots, and a myriad of tropical and migratory birds are all right here. It is an amazing place, he thought, not for the first time.

His mind registered movement off to his right at the top of a pyramid, just below him. He knew he had seen something. He wasn't sure what. There were a variety of eagles here. In fact, the Harpy eagle, the largest eagle in the world, was thought to be entirely extinct until discovered very much alive, right here in this tropical river basin. He sat and waited, hoping to see the movement again.

Something flapped off the side of the pyramid below. Just as he was turning away to scan the other 80 or more structures in his line of sight, Alex stepped out and around the temple complex at the top of the same pyramid he had been watching so intently. Dropping his reluctance to shout, he yelled out, "Hi there." Watching her look around in confusion he was certain she had at least picked out the human quality of the sound. She turned around and looked up at the highest hill with its impressive temple. Her eyes eventually wandered over towards where he was waving at her. There was a moment's hesitation, and then she recognized him and waved back.

All of the pyramidal structures were faced towards the river; most were oriented to the east. Some faced on an angle to the south where the river swung around the city boundaries. Both of the structures that Alex and Grant stood upon faced the same easterly direction. There was no way for her to come directly to him, or vice versa. One of them would need to dismount the pyramid they were on, and then climb down, and up the other. Or, he supposed, they could meet somewhere in between. Perhaps that was the best bet at present. He signaled Alex he was heading down and motioned for her to do likewise. She apparently got the message and disappeared from view.

Grant walked down the stairs of the temple, and then descended the groups of steps built into the hill. The massive engineering effort it took to build this place struck him once again. The natural hills of the site had been carefully incorporated into the ceremonial city's building plan. It had been done to great effect.

They met on the large flat area they were calling the main plaza. Alex was smiling.

"Anything hit you yet?" Grant questioned. "I've got us a little camp set up on the top level of that confusing building you pass through on the way into the city. You don't mind sleeping on a sacrificial altar, do you?"

"Whatever you think," she replied, not really getting his attempt at humor. Alex was enthralled with her surroundings.

"I'm convinced we'll figure something out," Grant tried again. "Anyway, the stone beds will get us off the ground. It's in a reasonably clean area without a lot of insects."

"Grant, this place is amazing! I'd heard of Yaxchilan before, but I had no idea it was this incredible. Look at the friezes. They're everywhere. The placement of the temples high on natural pinnacles, it demonstrates the architect's interest was not strictly in the river, but also in the view of the eastern horizon. They must have used these remarkable vantage points for astronomical observations by using the v-shaped cleft formed by those two high mountains in the distance. You can see just about where the sun would have risen. It's staggering to contemplate. This is a great place to intern the records. We've got to find somewhere reasonable that has not been closely reviewed and documented."

"Okay, let's get on with it," he said. Turning around he looked up to the highest temple structure on the steepest hill, the one that had caught his attention earlier. "I really don't want to go to the top of that thing," he said as he pointed up to it, "but the logic of the place is compelling."

"Let's go," she said, almost bouncing with enthusiasm. "It is surely the principal edifice, outranking the others in perceived power."

Age does make a difference he thought. Here I am dreading to walk up that hill in the middle of the day in this energy-draining heat, and she's raring to go. I guess I've got more miles on me, he grumbled to himself. Angling to what seemed to be a west by southwest direction he wondered out loud where his compass was. Oh yeah, safe in my aviation bag where it's doing me absolutely no good, he crumbled.

Together they walked towards the base of the highest hill. The bottom of this steep rise was well up behind the pyramid that Alex had just been on. A trail wound up in that direction. It made their assent a bit easier. It was a significant climb nonetheless.

"Let's sit for a few minutes, I need to cool down," Grant said sheepishly. All along the trail they had seen collapsed stone architecture, partially buried by the accumulation of dirt and vegetation. Some areas had been partially cleared. It was likely the work of the last research group that had been here. They saw ancestor cartouches marked with celestial signs on steles long since fallen to the ground. Round carved stone altars seemed to be randomly scattered about. In places, sculptured lintels still remained affixed to the tops of temples, or what might have been the equivalent of government buildings.

They sat under the shade of a large tree and looked down at the Usumacinta. Anciently, the river had served as the great royal highway to the magnificent ceremonial centers of the Maya.

Choked with emotion Alex managed, "It's really indescribable. How could you ever explain this to anyone? How could you do it justice?" She let out a deep sigh. "This is it, you know. This is where I want to be for a long while. I want to make the jungle my home and live like Jane," she said wistfully.

"I'd love to be your Tarzan, but unfortunately I don't fit the bill," he said, a bit too self-consciously. "I mean, I like the place too, but there are practical things to consider," he tapered off lamely.

"Yes, yes, but the day is only half over, and we can walk until we are worn out. You know Grant, the jungle reminds me of how tenacious our lives are, how short, how precarious, how precious. I feel so alive in this place. This is a spiritual refuge. That's the only way I can explain it. It is a spiritual refuge, a safe haven, a sanctuary."

They headed up a long steep trail. Only traces of an ancient stairway remained here. The ascent was breathtaking. They tried to imagine what it must have been like to approach the governing palace at the height of its glory.

Gaining the top of the hill, they continued to climb up another three terraces to reach the base of the uppermost building.

Here were carved stair treads before each of the doorways. In the center top sat two thrones of carved stone. Over the central doorway to the throne room was a corbelled arch. It appeared likely that on summer solstice day, the sun's first rays would pass through the center corbelled doorway, to shine directly on the thrones at the rear wall. Life-sized figures depicting the king and his consort may have sat here. The figures were gone, but stucco pieces from the originals lay scattered on the floor. Friezes on the walls were seriously corrupted and hardly distinguishable, but at one time they would have been bright with bold colors like those mysteriously preserved in Bonampak.

The walls of the supreme palace were massive. The interior chambers were small. Alex and Grant looked about for a way to intern the records. Nothing presented itself. They would never be able to lift the stones that formed the floor of the throne room in order to secret the plates underneath. The thought had occurred to both of them about the same time. The famous Temple of the Inscriptions in Palenque had turned out to have a stairway leading down underneath its throne room to a burial crypt. It hadn't been discovered for a long time after work had begun on the site. It required lifting floor panels with pulleys and a winch to see what was underneath. The Palenque Temple stairway had been entirely filled with rubble. It took an additional two seasons of field work to clear the passageway down to where they found the most famous sarcophagus of the Americas. There was no indication that anyone had previously attempted to lift the floor stones here. That process would likely not happen for years to come.

"It really makes you wonder how they got all these carved stones up the hill and set in place," Grant mused. "They must have had some kind of block and tackle system going for them."

There were two more structures atop the hill. One seemed to be almost a duplicate of the throne room. It was built beside it and faced out in the same direction. Several other buildings far below appeared to assume the same alignment.

"What now?" he asked, deferring to Alex's expertise.

Looking around in wonder, she managed quietly, "I don't know Grant, I just don't know."

Alex was defocused, and seemed slow, and a little high. It was as if she'd had too many beers, or was stunned from lack of oxygen. He recognized the signs from having flown too high with an occasional passenger that was not using oxygen. But they were in the jungle at low altitudes in an extremely oxygen rich environment. Perhaps it's heat stroke, he thought.

"You okay?" he asked worriedly.

"Sure," she responded without much emotion.

"You got some water in that pack of yours?"

"I...I...think so," she said.

"Alright, let me help you with that," Grant said, as he slid her knapsack off her back, to see what she was carrying. It was not particularly heavy, but she had been exerting a lot of strain in the humid heat, so she probably needed to sit quietly and drink plenty of water. So do I. There was a full bottle of water in her pack, along with a coil of rope, a flashlight and one of the small collapsible shovels. He took out the unopened water bottle and encouraged her to drink.

"I'm not really thirsty," she said as she shrugged her shoulders.

"Okay, but humor me a bit, will you? I really want you to drink some water. We probably don't have any idea how much we're losing in this heat." With that he encouraged her to sit back in the shade. Once she got started she drank quite a bit. Convinced he'd been right, he took the bottle and drank deeply himself. Together they finished off an entire large container. They sat quietly starring out into space, stunned, seeing little. He tried to get a sense of their mental clarity. He probably would not have known they were flirting with dehydration if it wasn't for his being so interested in Alex. The water worked. Her spunk was coming back.

"Did you know that the Mayan calendar, when correlated to our modern-day calendar, began in the year 3114 BC, on August 13th, and that it ended on 2012 AD?" Alex asked.

"Yes, I heard that. Wasn't it supposed to end on December 21, 2012?" he asked.

"Sort of, that was the end of a cycle. The Mayan Long Count gets pretty complicated. It counts forward from the August 13, 3114 date. It is reconciled with two additional interlocking cycles, a 365-day solar year, and a 260-day lunar ritual cycle. The calendar was supposedly developed around 600 B.C., when the spread of sophisticated civilization was extending throughout Mesoamerica," she explained.

"The ancient Jewish calendar was similar. It was a 365-day solar year, and a 260-day religious calendar based on lunar observations," Grant observed. "As I understand it, the oldest known Mesoamerican calendars were found in Izapa, near Tapachula on the Pacific border of Mexico and Guatemala."

She turned and starred right into his eyes. For a moment, he was worried she was worse off than he thought. The moment passed and she turned away saying, "You know too much about this stuff for someone that's not taken this as course study."

"Well, thanks. It's been a hobby for a long time."

"Old world history or Mesoamerican archeology?" she asked suspiciously.

"Both I guess. I've only spent time at the archeological sites in Mesoamerica, but I suppose my hobby is really ancient history. You know, ancient religions, warfare, battle strategies, that kind of stuff. That's about all that was recorded in the pre-Christian world."

"And why is it, I think there is something going on with you, that I do not fully understand?" she observed.

Laughing a little uncomfortably he replied, "Alex, there's all kinds of things I don't know about you. Why would you expect to know so much about me?" Then, with a small laugh, he added, "I mean after all, we're just getting to know each other."

She turned and hit him on the shoulder, smiled, and said, "Okay I'm feeling better, let's look at these other two buildings while we're up here." With that she stood a little shakily, and marched off. For another half hour, they walked around the top of the pointed hilltop that sported three, almost identical, structures.

"I think this hill must have been a cinder cone at one time," Grant observed. "The shape is pretty unusual for anything else." She didn't respond. Her focus was on studying what looked like a Maya royalty matrix. It was covered with dating glyphs and a ruler's cartouche.

Grant wandered around to the back of the structures and looked to the landlocked side of the city complex. A series of even higher jungled ridges surrounded the land area. This coupled with the river on three sides, each with steep banks and rushing water, would have made the city virtually impregnable. The backside of the hill where he now stood looked to be almost straight down. It was much steeper than the approach from the riverside. Without the stone steps, even the front of this hill would be a dangerous place to climb. The back was virtually a cliff. Tall grass grew at the back of these buildings right to the edge of the drop-off. A gentle breeze moved the grass about. His eye caught some kind of stone work right at the cliff edge.

Grant had seen something like this before. It was on an exploratory day-trip with Pepe and his son Jorge. Grant's son Matthew was also there, as was Miguel, and two of his antiquities suppliers. It was Grant's one and only trip to a ruin site with known looters. Fearful that new offerings might be fakes, Miguel had insisted on seeing the source of some new pieces he had purchased. He invited Pepe and Grant along for the experience. As it turned out, he was also concerned about being alone with the looters. The rest of us provided some bit of security. It was a day he would probably never forget.

Curiosity overcame Grant's concern about getting too close to the cliff edge. He unclipped the machete from his belt and got down on his knees. Moving forward slowly, he began clearing grass towards the edge of the drop-off. There it was, a narrow stone threshold that looked to be supporting steps going right over the side. It was both disorienting and frightening to consider that someone, at sometime, had climbed straight down over the cliff edge. He lay flat on his stomach and scooted forward to the rim, looking over. The cliff fell straight away for at least a hundred feet before sloping steeply into a narrow gorge. The first hundred or so feet consisted of rock with little growth having caught hold. Once the back side of the hilltop began to slope away, the jungle held sway. There was no real way to know how far down lay the actual bottom.

The cliff face had likely been caused as part of the hill gave way and slid to the bottom of the trench far below. So how was it that there were stone steps leading over the edge? He pushed himself further out. He was afraid to lean on the steps themselves. They were not more than 10 inches wide. They hugged the cliff face and appeared to go down at a steep angle. Scooting back from the edge he cleared away some more grass in the direction the steps were turned. Once again, he scooted out and looked down the cliff face to see where they went. They seemed to stop about twenty feet down. He was getting dizzy. It's strange, he thought, I can fly under almost any circumstances and it doesn't bother me, but hanging over a cliff like this takes all the self-control I can muster.

He pushed back carefully until he felt safe to stand, then turned around, and went looking for Alex. She was right where he had left her; she seemed transfixed on the glyphs, and was clearly not thinking about finding a place to hide the plates. "Hey," he tossed out.

"Oh, Grant, this is wonderful. I suppose it has all been worked out by someone else who's been here before, but from what I can tell, it seems to be a lineage history of a guy named Bird Jaguar, or something like that. I so want to stay here and explore," she whined.

"Bring your pretty little self out here, and look what I've found," he said, "and bring your backpack."

Obediently, she followed him out, and around to the back of the structures. Seeing the steep drop-off within thirty feet of the backside of the buildings, she instinctively reached for the stone construction that comprised the back of the temple complex. "Whoa, that's some drop-off," she said.

"Yeah, that's what I thought, but check this out." He pointed with the machete at the area he had cleared.

"What? I don't see anything," she replied.

"Look carefully. I cleared some of the grass away," Grant pointed again.

"You went out there?" she said shaking her head. "You must be crazy. How do you know the ground won't give way?"

"I suppose I don't, but I was pretty careful. Do you see what I'm pointing at?" he asked.

"What," she said again, with slight irritation.

"That," he said patiently, "that little stone platform."

"Good grief Grant, you brought me out here to see that? This entire area is full of cut stone. What's the big deal?"

"If you scoot out to the edge, you'll see," he replied patiently.

"You're nuts if you think I'm going out there."

"Listen Alex, I'll tie the rope around your waist and stay back here. You just crawl to the edge and look over."

"No way am I going to do that!" she said in a huff. "What's the big deal anyway?"

"You need to see this Alex, and tell me what you think. Otherwise I'm going to do it, and I weight more than you. I can hold you with the rope if the ground starts to give way, but I doubt you could hold me. Humor me and be a brave little girl, and do as I ask."

"You're really serious?" she said in amazement. "What has gotten into you?"

"What's gotten into me is that foundation stone out there is the beginning of an extremely narrow stairwell going down the backside of the cliff face. I can't tell, but it looks like it stops about twenty feet down, which leads me to believe the rest of the steps have either fallen away or there is a cave directly under us. A cave makes sense to me because this hilltop is probably a volcanic cone of some sort."

"Oh. You really think so?" she said neutrally. "Well, why didn't you say that to begin with? What do you want me to do?" she asked reasonably, as if she hadn't just been thinking he had taken leave of his senses.

"Let's get a bowline tied around your waist, and you crawl out there to the edge on your stomach. If the ground gets a little shaky, or starts to give way, I'll just reel you in," he said calmly.

"What's a bowline?"

"It's a sailor's knot. Do you have to know everything?"

"Just curious. Are you sure it will hold me?"

"The knot will hold. Come on Alex, let's get going. You're not all that heavy. I can hold you."

"Actually, I'm not heavy at all."

"Yes, of course, that's obvious. Can we just get moving here?"

"I'm scared," she said flatly.

"That's okay, you'll survive it," he said, a little too flippantly.

Before she would continue he had to teach her how to tie a bowline. She wanted to see how and why it would work. Grant finally gave up and showed her how to sling a line around her waist and tie it blind. "We used to practice doing it with our eyes closed, so in a serious offshore blow we could tie ourselves to the boat without looking."

"Who's we?" she wanted to know.

"Family, and close friends. Before the Zarahemla we had a blue-water cutter. That's an offshore sailing rig with a single mast. And before that an ocean-going yawl, that's a twin-stick rig. Two masts, both forward of the helm. So, are we ready yet?" he said impatiently.

"I suppose so," she replied, with a slight upward tilt to her head.

Alex got down on all fours and crawled out to about the same place Grant had first felt giddy. She flattened out and scooted forward. Slowly, she inched out to the edge. She seemed to be talking to herself, trying to get up enough nerve to actually look out over the cliff face. When she did, she wasn't far out enough to see where the steps ended. "Come on Alex, you've got to get out there a little further," he chided.

"Don't push me," she snapped. "I'm doing this at my pace. It's me out here, not you." With that she mustered more courage, and extended herself over the edge, from the shoulders out.

"Hey, you're right. There is a cave down there," she said, overcoming her fear a bit more. "I can't believe anyone ever actually went down those steps, there's not even a hand-rail or anything to hold on to."

"There may have been at one time. So, what do you think?" he asked.

"What do you mean, what do I think?" she said grappling with her lightheadedness.

"Can we get down there? It could be the perfect place to intern the plates, and we wouldn't have to do any digging."

"You are crazy," she muttered as she slid back towards safety. "How on earth would we ever get in there, and how could we possibly get a stone box and gold plates down there? It's simply not an option," she stated flatly, as if that ended the discussion.

"We've got a couple of good ropes, and a pick and two shovels. It seems like we could rig something," he said thoughtfully.

"Yeah, well I think you've been out in the heat to long. That's just too spooky for me, and I for one, am not up to it. I did what you asked, and that's it. If you want to kill yourself, that's up to you."

"What's that?" Grant said as he cocked his ear to the air.

"What's what?" she said, irritated with him.

"Don't you hear it?" he asked.

"Hear what?" But just as she said it she heard it, too. A whomp, whomping sound was echoing off the hills and getting louder.

"Alex, that's a helicopter. My guess is, it's coming here," he said, anxiety clear in his voice.

CHAPTER THIRTY

Yaxchilan, Chiapas

Not knowing what else to do, they walked around the edge of the throne room and crept inside to the back wall. Having collected the items from outside, Alex lay her knapsack down on a stone bench. Grant was mentally running a rapid inventory of their resources. Realizing they were out of water he immediately felt thirsty.

"Look Alex, if this is someone coming for us, they're going to be all over the place pretty soon. We have no water and the rest of our gear is back down at the labyrinth. I think maybe it would be wise for us to head down to where our gear is stashed. Let's get what we can, and come back up here and hide out. If you don't want to go, I will try to get back as fast as I can."

"Let's get moving," she said mildly, showing no visible sign of fear.

"Scared of heights, but not guys with guns," he muttered as they began to hurry down the stairs.

"Something like that," she managed. Besides, I don't think these guys want to kill us. My guess is they want us very much alive.

"If that helicopter comes in low, let's make sure we're out of sight," he shouted. They moved quickly down the steps of the first terrace. The noise was getting louder. It sounded almost on top of them, but Grant was pretty sure it was the echoes from the limestone cliffs along the river. They scrambled down steps and made it to the trail where it was safer to gain speed. "Be careful! We don't want to complicate things with having a bloody incident up here," he called to Alex. She was already several yards ahead.

Alex runs like a gazelle, he thought. She's graceful and sure-footed. It irked him that he was not above being slightly jealous of her athleticism. They reached the bottom of the steepest hill. Here was a fork in the trail. One headed back the way they had originally come. The other angled around the hill he had spotted Alex from earlier. A moment's indecision and they took the unfamiliar trail. It looked as though it would take them behind a pyramid and keep them out of sight of the main plaza. It was the right choice. They came out at the bottom of the hill he had first climbed. They could now clearly see the labyrinth building. Not wanting to get caught out in the open they put on speed and crossed the main plaza in record time. They climbed up to the top tier of the labyrinth and ducked into the southeast doorway leading into the interior chamber. A moment later, the helicopter arrived overhead and began circling the area. Grant was so out of breath he couldn't talk. He managed to get back to the carved limestone niche in the adjoining room, cracked open a bottle of water, and gulped it down aggressively.

"Hey, you better go easy there," she said. "Take it from a runner. Don't drink too much water too quickly after running hard in the heat."

He couldn't respond. His chest was heaving. Grant stumbled back in to the entry chamber and sat down hard on the limestone bench. After a few minutes, he could hear the helicopter above the pulse thumping in his ears. Whoever they were, they were doing a careful reconnaissance before setting down. Willing his heart rate under control, he said, "I think the chopper will put down on the beach. It's about the only place that would be marginally safe. The main plaza is covered with stone pilings, steles, and other clutter. If whoever has come here is familiar with the place, they'll be up and through that dark passageway pretty quickly. If they haven't been here before, we may have time to get our stuff and move out before they get this far."

Alex nodded. She was listening to the helicopter pause at the opening of various temples and palaces on the tops of pyramids and the steepest hills. The men in the helicopter were being careful to exam the highest spots first. "I think we better head back where we came from as soon as we're able. They have hovered at those upper hilltops several times. I suspect they'll focus on the lower plazas now. There are hundreds of places to hide down here. It would have been virtually impossible to not have been spotted had we stayed up there," she whispered.

It sounded as if they were setting down on the beach. Grant quickly stuffed the canned goods and bottles of water in the remaining knapsack, and swung it on. He grabbed the stone box and headed straight out the door, saying over his shoulder, "Get the plates, they're back in the niche wrapped in one of the tarps. He wasn't half way back across the plaza when she caught up to him, her arms loaded.

They retraced their steps from the earlier run. When they reached the back of the lower pyramid, they fell down panting. Out came the water again. They drank deeply. After catching their breath, they headed off towards the foot of the highest hill. Grant was winded. He had over-exerted himself once again, and this time he knew it. Although he thought of himself in pretty good shape, at least for his age, these vertical climbs, fully loaded, moving rapidly in the suffocating heat, were knocking him out. He had to figure out a way to conserve energy by doing things smarter.

Grant and Alex were now out of sight of anyone coming up through the darkened corridor to the main plaza. It would take a few minutes for anyone coming through that maze to collect their bearings and organize a careful search. At the moment, Grant was more concerned about his arms and legs failing him. The knapsack was heavy with water and canned goods, but not really the issue. The larger problem was the stone box. It was awkward, and hard to carry. Running uphill in the heat, carrying a load, was causing his arms to quiver.

He stuck out his right hip and balanced the box there, like carrying a baby on your hip, he thought. This allowed his left arm to regain circulation and was more comfortable. However, carrying the box like this, he could only walk. They began to climb the steep trail moving up towards the throne room. Unless the helicopter pilot chose to take-off and do another reconnaissance sweep, they should be out of sight all the way to the top.

It took a lot longer to get up this time. Carrying the gold records had seemed easy at first. But Alex had ended up with the same problem as Grant. Gaining the hill top temples, they moved all the gear around to the outside back of the throne room. They would not be visible to someone below. By design, the interior of the throne room would be pretty much open to view from lower levels.

Creeping around the south corner, away from view from the main plaza, he lay quietly on his stomach with his small binoculars scanning the city complex. He tried to ignore the insects that had determined he was an item of interest. It was close to fifteen minutes before he saw the first movement. A camouflaged team was moving quietly amongst the ruins using hand signals. Each person carried a blackened automatic rifle. This was not a bunch of looters. This was a well-trained military unit. So, it was true. The military had been called in to support whoever was tracking them.

Staying flat on the ground, Grant slithered backwards until he was safely behind the throne room once more. It was a couple of hours till dark. He supposed there was a chance the searchers would not climb this hill until they had exhausted other options. The helicopter had carefully examined this area so it was even possible that no one would come up here at all.

"Alex, there is a military unit in full cameo down there. They're methodically working through the ruins as a team. It may take them a while before they head up this way, but I think we should assume they will do that before dark. If we can stay hidden until then, we might figure out how to get back down to the beach, get the raft out of the tree, and float down river during the night. In the meantime, our best bet is to get over the side of the cliff, and into that cave. I know that's frightening to you, but I simply have no other suggestions."

Alex sat quietly with her back against the carved limestone wall. Her knees pulled up almost to her chin. She nodded, "Okay, what do I need to do?"

"We've got two good ropes. Each is about thirty feet long. I'm going to tie them together and you're going to get a bowline around your waist. I'll let you down over the side. You face the cliff and feel your way down the steps. We should be able to speak and hear each other easily enough. Take your back pack. Include one of the shovels, a flashlight and a bottle of water."

Grant, are you sure this is the right thing to do," she said miserably.

"I think it's our best course of action at the moment. I can hold your weight. We're limited in what we can do right now. This is our best option."

They decided to open a can of beans and eat them cold so they didn't complicate things with low blood sugar. The beans weren't much good. When they finished Grant tossed the can over the cliff edge. Alex, a die-hard environmentalist, didn't say a word.

Grant crawled around the side of the throne room to check on the men below. It didn't take him long to spot them working their way along the largest grouping of buildings situated on a bluff above the river.

Directly in front of him a large stele, essentially a stone post, lay on its side. If he could just figure out how to slide it back to where they were located, he would have something to anchor the rope around. He crawled out further and reached around and tried to move the large carved rectangular stone. It moved some, but not much. He scooted back to where Alex had packed her knapsack and was sitting with her head down.

"I've got an idea," he whispered. Before you let yourself over the side, let's get the stele lying at the front corner pulled around here to use as an anchor. If I need to join you down below, I'll be able to tie a line around the stele and use it to support me."

"If we can slide it around here, why do you think it will hold you?"

"I'll wedge it with small rocks and other debris to anchor it. It should take at least twice my dead weight to move it further," he said reasonably.

"And, how pray tell, do you know that?" she retorted sarcastically.

"Well, I guess I don't know for sure. But something tells me it's worth a try."

Keeping low they crawled around to the stele. Grant reached around and pulled the top corner. It slid along the dirt turning towards him. Alex pulled the other end. It slid back towards her. They had to clean the area multiple times over which the stone would slide, but over the next few minutes they were able to crab-walk the large block of stone to where it could be wedged against rocks embedded in the ground.

Grant splice-tied the two lengths of rope together, then putting his arms around Alex's waist he tied her to one end. He looped the other end of the line around the stele taking up the slack.

"Okay, you're secure, I know this is scary, but you can do it. I am in a good position to hold you, no matter what happens. The rope is plenty strong."

Alex nodded, trying to be brave.

"Scoot out to the edge. Allow yourself to slowly drop over the side until gaining your footing on one of the steps. If the steps give way you're still going to be okay. If they hold, it will make this a lot easier. Once you are over the side and out of my sight, keep talking so I know what to do. You understand?"

She nodded again. "Alex talk to me, I need to be sure you're able to function."

She nodded again, but still did not speak.

"Alex, please." He knew she was struggling. He leaned forward and kissed her. Some little bit of emotion flickered behind her eyes. He kissed her again. She swallowed hard.

Alex scooted backwards towards the edge. "Okay, a little to your left." She moved the opposite direction. "Your other left," he said as patiently as he could. She shifted her hips and legs slightly the other way. "Move back some more. We'll do this in easy stages so I can manage the line."

When her feet were extended over the ledge and she hadn't yet reached one of the steps, she froze. "Come on Alex, you've got to keep pushing yourself over the side. I've got you.

Exerting determination, she pushed back a little faster than was comfortable for him. Her legs were projected out into space. "Alex, you need to shift further over to your left. Swing the line over and stretch down until you can touch a step with your foot."

She froze again. This time she was in a bad place where he couldn't do much to help. "Come on Alex you've got to do this. Swing your legs to your left. Just hold the line tight and do it." Slowly she began to move again. This is taking way too much time he thought. Those military guys could be half way up the hill already. "Hurry it up Alex, we're running out of time."

He could tell when she got a foothold; the tension on the line released some. "Keep your face into the cliff and give yourself some slack so you can stretch down to the next step."

"That's right. Now take a little more tension off the line and see if the step will hold." She was over the side and out of sight.

"I...I'm scared Grant, I'm really scared," she sobbed.

"It's okay to be scared. Just keep talking to me. Remember a couple of nights ago when we were flying to Chichen Itza?"

"Yes," she said, her voice faltering.

"Well I thought you were incredibly brave. I mean you're a pilot, and you knew how dangerous that take-off and low altitude flight was. You didn't falter. I need you to do this now. Please keep talking to me so I understand what's going on."

"Okay," she said, her voice still shaky. "I'm on a step of some kind, its....oh my god," came a gasp.

"Alex, you okay?"

"Ah, yeah, I...I guess so, I...ah...looked down to see what I was standing on. It's really a long way to the bottom. It scared me," she mumbled.

The sun was moving lower on the horizon. It was directly in his face now. Even if she'd been standing there in front of him, unless he shielded his eyes, he would have had trouble seeing her clearly.

"Describe the cliff face," he said.

"It's mostly rock, relatively firm, some dirt, not much, shale below."

"Alex, you need to take another step down. Put some weight on the step and test its strength. You have about twenty feet more to go. Just release enough line to let you gain the next step down, and keep telling me what you're doing."

Once she was a few steps down with her face pressed into the rock, he asked her to describe how the first step, almost level with her face at this point, was anchored to the cliff wall. "I don't know," she called up, breathing heavily. "I can't tell. It narrows somewhat. It looks like cut stone that's been pounded deep into the wall of the hill. The steps are not connected to each other. They appear to be separate."

"Those steps are there for a reason. We can assume they're headed someplace important. It was no easy task to build them into the cliff face. Maybe this was an escape route for the king in the event of an attack. Or perhaps it allowed a priest to magically appear somewhere without being seen in the transition. Whatever it is, it might be of value to us. Make sure you warn me each time you are taking the next step."

"Yeah, maybe human sacrifice," was her sour response.

As she worked further down she was harder to hear. "Grant," she called up, "Grant," she yelled with unmistakable fear in her voice.

A moment later the rope went slack, his heart literally jumped. "Alex, Alex, speak to me," he spoke as loud as he dared.

"You were right, she called up. There's a cave down here. Maybe it would be better to call it a secret room. It scared the bejesus out of me when I stepped in. The setting sun lit the whole place up and there are wall paintings of life-sized men in full regalia. Some of the colors are as brilliant as those we saw in Bonampak. This is a major discovery," she said excitedly."

"Alex, we're going to be out of light within the hour. Are you safe to stand by for a few minutes while I check out the military?"

"Yes," came her much more confident reply.

With that he put another loop in the rope, crossing the first loop so there was holding friction on it. He turned and crawled to where he began to scoot on his stomach around the outside edge of the throne room. He scanned the area with his binoculars. Nothing revealed itself. He checked his watch and then continued to glass everything in the arc of his vision. There was no movement in his line of sight. He finally decided they must be working an area he couldn't see from where he lay. Either that or they were on the trail coming up to the throne room. From where he was located he would not be able to see down the access trail without scooting a lot further out. He decided that would serve no particular purpose, but just the thought that they might be closing on him started to grind on his thinking. He was jumpy with premonition.

Returning to the stele he went close to the edge and called down, "Alex, you okay?" The hairs on the back of his neck were almost standing straight up.

"Yeah, pretty good, interesting place."

"Alex, we're running out of time here. I need you to untie the rope and let me pull it back up, I'm going to tie the plates on, and send them back to you in a couple of minutes. If that works out okay, I'll tie a sling and send the stone box down. You with me?"

"Grant, if the rope goes back up, how am I going to make sure I can grab it when it comes back down."

"Snag it with your shovel and pull it to you." He could almost hear her sigh, then she tugged twice on the line and said, "Okay it's ready to come up."

Five minutes later the plates were down and she was able to grab them on the first try. Another five minutes and the stone box was on its way. He sensed someone's presence coming up behind him. Each time he looked, no one was there. Get a grip Grant. Steady on. You've got to get this job done and get the heck out of here, he told himself.

"Hey, you're swinging wild," she called up.

"Sorry, I was looking to see if someone was up here," he replied. It took her three tries to snag the line and pull the stone box in. Grant stowed their remaining gear behind the stele. On his knees, he scraped up some of the grass cuttings from earlier and piled them on top so they would not be obvious. Even if someone looked behind the prone pillar, nothing would look out of place. The problem was going to be the line wrapped around the stele and going over the side. Careful scrutiny of this hilltop would reveal the rope, even though he piled rubble and grass around it. "Hey Alex," he called down in a controlled voice.

"Yes?"

"I'm going to leave for a few minutes to see where those military guys have gone. I'll be back shortly." He started to crawl towards the front, his binoculars at the ready. He needn't have bothered. He could hear the heavy breathing of several men struggling up the trail where the access steps still survived. The only thing he could think of was to head over the side and join Alex in the chamber.

Without further thought, he grabbed the line, uncovered his knapsack and put it on in one swift motion, then piled as much grass and dirt as seemed natural over the wrapped line and scrambled over the cliff edge. He knew the friction wrap on the line was not sufficient to hold his weight if he actually fell, but the line should give him some stability and help him from falling backwards due to the weight of the water in his backpack.

With his heart in his throat he desperately sought a step with his extended toes. I should have unloaded some of that water, he thought. It is definitely screwing up my center of gravity. Grant pushed his face into the rock trying to counterbalance the weight in his pack. The knowledge that someone might discover the line and loosen it drove him to get down as quickly as possible. The steps came right down the cliff side to the cave opening. All it took was for him to step in. Alex was unaware that he had climbed down and was on her hands and knees in a corner about twenty feet back in. Drawing deep breaths to regain control, he headed towards her, and said quietly, "Alex, men on top."

She jerked, spun around and gasped. "My god you scared me!"

He held his finger to his lips, pointing up. The chamber was well lit for the moment. The late afternoon sun was shining directly into the opening. Soon the sun would set behind the higher hills to the west. It would get dark fast.

"They can't hear us if we're not too loud. It will probably be a few minutes before they head around to the back of the buildings. On the other hand, I suppose they may split up and do them both at the same time," he said nervously.

"How many of them are there?" she whispered.

"Don't know. I could hear them coming up the last terrace, heavy breathing. I thought it best to drop in and see you instead of hanging out up there."

"What are we going to do?" she said anxiously.

"My guess is we're going to be spending the night here." He began to look around for some place comfortable to settle in.

"Where's the rest of our stuff?" she asked with a worried look on her face.

"I piled grass on it. Maybe that will work, maybe not. It's the rope twisted around the stele that will catch their attention if anything does. I tried to cover it up. There's not much we can do about it now."

Trying to come up with something positive Alex said, "The setting sun would be right in someones eyes if they were looking towards the ledge. There's a good chance they will miss the rope."

"Let's hope."

The first third of the chamber was covered in bird droppings and nesting material. The walls had been beautifully finished at one time. The areas where the light did not strike directly still retained life-sized paintings of Bird Jaguar and a queen figure of some sort. Alex called her Lady Chuen, apparently having worked out something about the dynasty of Yaxchilan. The rear wall artworks were virtually gone. The setting sun had apparently faded the frescos until they were essentially indistinguishable. Alex pulled out her flashlight and began to study the artwork towards the rear corners of the chamber. "Look at this," she said with emphasis.

Her light revealed a false wall constructed with a small doorway behind it. Alex walked carefully towards the shortened arch. Still very much concerned about the military team above, Grant whispered, "Alex, wait a minute, let me listen topside." He went cautiously back towards the cave opening and tried to hear movement or conversation from above. Hearing nothing for several minutes he headed back toward Alex, just as the light reduced to semi-darkness. The sun had dropped behind the western hills.

"Whoa, that was quick," he muttered. "Where's the light switch."

His eyes began to adjust to the dimness of twilight. They probably had less than fifteen minutes before it would be pitch black. Fumbling around in his backpack he materialized the other flashlight and walked cautiously back to Alex. "I suppose we shouldn't use both of these at the same time to conserve batteries, but let me at least get a look at what you've found."

Alex was already squatted down shining her light into an interior chamber. "Looks empty, there seems to be a stone bench at the back. I'm a little nervous about going further, no telling what we'll find."

He sensed what she was referring to. There are all kinds of things that inhabit the jungle floor, and although they were in a cliff side cave, they were definitely in the jungle. Scorpions and the highly poisonous Barba Amarilla vipers came to mind. Then there were the poisonous insects, usually not able to kill, just make you wish you were dead. Kneeling down beside Alex, he scanned the small alcove. The interior was draped with old spider webs, "There must be a lot of insects around to support those web builders," he mused.

"It's not funny Grant. They can be very dangerous," she replied solemnly.

He laughed nervously and ducked through the door and moved into the center of the room. He stood partially upright, carefully shining his light on each wall in turn, rotating slowly searching from top to bottom. "No artwork in here," he said. "There's a few creepy crawlers and a couple of spiders in the corners. Not much really."

"Are they poisonous," she asked quickly.

"Beats me. I might recognize an Amarilla viper if I saw it. The other stuff I know little about. Oh, did I tell you the story about...can't remember its name, but anyway a couple of large poisonous spiders, about the size of your hand decided to do a mating gig on my pant leg. One jumped off my shoulder to pounce on the one on my leg. Actually, now that I think of it, maybe they were fighting over who gets to eat me. One of the looters I was with took a swing at them with his machete. At first I thought he was trying to kill me. He turned the blade just before impact and hit them with the broadside."

He started to go on, but Alex whined, "Grant, I don't want to know about that right now. As it is, I'll be afraid to sit down tonight, much less lie down or sleep anywhere."

"Yeah, I hear that...well looky here," he said curiously. "There's a drain hole going somewhere. Maybe this was the royal toilet or something," he said half-jokingly. He moved closer to the hole when something blew up right at him. He lurched backwards slamming hard against the stone bench. He slid to the floor in pain. At the same moment, he heard Alex scream. Her light went out.

The room filled with noise, the beating of a thousand wings. It was so loud there was no sense in even calling out to Alex until the cave was empty of the nighttime predators.

It finally fell quiet. "Alex, you okay?" he grunted.

"No," she said flatly. "I was just scared right out of my wits, and I bruised my butt. The flashlight is probably broken."

"Yeah, I hurt myself, too," he groaned. "At least we've got one light. If yours is broken, let's make sure we retrieve the batteries."

"I don't know where it is," she whined. "I dropped it when I fell, and I am not going to feel around for it."

"Just a minute," he replied while trying to straighten up. "This is going to hurt for a while," he mumbled. "I think I may have broken a rib or something. It hurts like hell." He sat down hard on the edge of the stone bench.

"Grant, I really need you to come out here," she said, an edge of desperation in her voice.

"Am trying Alex, give me a minute. It's hurting pretty hard."

He tried to stand up again. Okay, he could deal with it. Before going to Alex, Grant shone his light down the bat hole. It was smaller than a standard manhole cover, but just so. "Hey, there are steps going down inside the toilet bowl."

"I don't care about that right now. I need you here before I lose it," her voice panicky.

"Alright, coming," he said, as he turned and crept out through the half-sized archway. He swung his flashlight around till he found Alex sitting cross-legged holding both elbows with her opposite hands, trying to touch as little as possible. About four feet away lay the flashlight. He picked it up and toggled the switch. It came back on. "Got lucky on that one," he said, as he limped back into the middle of the chamber. Grant was literally bent over with pain. He was trying not to say much.

Grant slowly gathered their backpacks and brought them to the rear wall where the paintings had long ago disappeared. It was the only area in the cave that looked reasonably clean. "Come on over here," he said. "This looks to be about the best place for hunkering down for the night. Make sure you don't shine your light towards the mouth of the cave. If those guys are still up there they might be able to spot it."

A lightning flash lit the room. Thunder and rain were not far behind.

Shaken, they leaned into one another, and sat back against their packs in the dark. Each quietly wondered if someone had discovered the rope and gear above.

They shared a can of cold processed raviolis. It wasn't much, but it helped.

"You know, I haven't had to pee all day," Alex observed.

"Neither have I," he said. "We must be sweating so much water our bladders never get full. Guess that's a good thing to some degree. This isn't the best place to setup for a toilet facility."

"Guys are lucky. You can just head over to the cave entrance and water the jungle below. Things aren't so easy for women."

Alex was having trouble sitting. Grant was having trouble taking deep breaths. "I guess my ribs aren't really broken, but a couple of them are definitely out. Can you shove them back in for me?" he asked.

"How do I do that?"

"Let me empty my backpack. I'll use it as a cushion and lie down on my stomach. Feel your way down my back until I tell you where to stop. Put one hand on top of the other and with the heel of your palm, shove hard when I am exhaling. Don't be easy. Push fast and hard."

It took three tries before he felt the familiar click as the ribs moved back into place.

"Whoa...I heard that!" she exclaimed.

"Yeah, it happens all too often. They feel like they're in now, so it should heal in a couple of days. Nothing I can do for your bruised butt, except maybe rub it for you."

"And where do you think that would lead," she groused half-heartedly. The first trace of humor he'd heard in a while.

Their legs were stretched full out on the floor with their upper back, neck and head propped up by the backpacks. After a few minutes, Alex turned towards Grant and leaned into his chest groaning, "I've got to get the pressure off my butt. Mind if I use you for a pillow?"

CHAPTER THIRTY-ONE

The Cave, Yaxchilan

It was a miserable night. They were constantly flailing at their face or neck to whisk away real or imagined insects. The sound of mosquitoes was distracting, and more. They got out the remaining tarp, the other having been used to wrap the raft and aviation bag left in a tree by the beach.

For awhile they were awake and talked. By morning neither of them could remember anything of their conversation. Just before dawn the bats returned, a surge of living things flying on sonar straight through the chamber interior. Briefly, Grant remembered reading somewhere that a bat eats its weight in insects every night. Probably the reason the chamber was relatively clear of them.

The exhaustion of the previous day had taken its toll. Sleeping on rock hadn't helped. A mist shrouded the jungle, a welcome change from the sweltering heat. They got up, and began moving around stiffly. Grant took his flashlight and headed back into the interior room to get a better look at the bat hole. It was almost round. Someone had constructed it a long time ago. Shining his light into the lower chamber his eye followed the steps, he had seen before. They descended straight down a wall, disappearing in the dark below. He decided to make the descent and see what was down there. "Alex, I'm going down the bat hole."

"Wait a minute. I'll join you," she called back from the next room.

Grant stepped into the hole and worked his way down, feeling for steps, and looking for hand holds long since eroded. The floor was closer than he expected. The steps stopped within ten feet where he found himself standing on a rock landing of some sort. "This is where we want to store the plates," he said, an echo almost instantly returning.

"Can I come down?" she asked.

A minute later she had joined him. They cautiously began to examine their surroundings. It was another room built into the interior of a natural cave. "I wonder what they did down here," Alex mused. "They've discovered underground caves all over the Yucatan, where structures were built over the top of them. Apparently, this allowed certain priests access to the underworld, where they performed special ceremonies. It's not really clear what they were doing in the caves. But as you probably know, the Maya were very superstitious about cave openings, especially where water was present. Caves like this were considered conduits to the netherworld, the residence of the Maya's equivalent to the Judaic-Christian's Satan."

"What a cheery thought," he mumbled. "That reminds me of the story I started to tell you about Cerro Vigia and the Santiago Tuxla mountains. You remember? That was when we got sidetracked on my sister's thing about witchcraft?"

"Save it for later, along with the story about that mythical Zarahemla place on the river. Oh, and while you're remembering things, I want to know what you were doing with looters," she said rather forcefully.

"What do you mean?" he countered.

"You told me last night about some poisonous spiders that were on your leg, and that a looter knocked them off with a machete,"

"Ah yeah, well that's pretty easy to explain," Grant was saying when she interrupted, and said, "Not now, stay on point."

They hadn't used the flashlights much during the night so they felt safe enough with both of them on for a while. Nagging at the back of Grant's mind was the issue of how much he may have used these in the past. He wished he had his solar recharging flashlight. Oh well, we'll only be here a few minutes, he decided.

They followed the sculpted cave in the direction the chamber was tapering. It looked like a passageway ahead.

"These walls have been worked by masons," Alex commented, "I wonder where they lead?"

They walked another hundred feet, descending to a division in the passageway. "Okay, which way," Grant asked. "We'd better stay together. It's probably best if one of us shuts off their light."

"You shut yours off," she stated flatly, heading off towards the larger of the two avenues that opened ahead of them.

That wasn't what he had in mind. He was used to leading not following. Grant took hold of her free hand, and watched the play of light in front of her.

Another couple hundred feet sloping downward and they entered a large cavern. Alex shined her light up and around. To their surprise the whole room started to brighten up as the beam from her flashlight reflected from what looked like a thousand chandeliers hanging from the ceilings. "Wow," was about all she could muster.

"It's incredible," he managed. "I can just imagine what the Mayan's thought about this place. One fire in here and the room would light up like magic." He glanced at his watch. They'd been down about twenty minutes. "We're going to need to head back soon. I wouldn't want to run out of light down here."

Reluctantly they turned and headed back the way they had come.

"This is where the plates need to be," Alex said quietly.

When they got back to the divided passageway they decided to take another few minutes to see where the other tunnel led. They had no sooner made the turn than the passageway became much smaller, shrinking to the size a person could only negotiate on hands and knees. Grant did not like tight places. He supposed he must be claustrophobic. Most of the time he could deal with it, but down here was another matter.

"Well, this doesn't look like it's heading anywhere. Let's turn around."

"Just a minute, let me crawl ahead. You stay here," Alex replied.

"Okay, but please be careful. That tunnel floor may disappear without warning." There is no predicting this woman, he thought. She's afraid of heights, but not a black tunnel under tons of rock. She's afraid of thugs, but not the military. The thought triggered memories of his deceased wife. She had been seriously afraid of cockroaches. You couldn't even say the word around her. Something from her childhood he supposed. And yet Marianna had been one brave woman about a whole lot of other things. Especially when facing her impending death.

Alex ducked in and crawled off. He could only see flashes of light off the tunnel walls ahead. Then she disappeared and all there was for him to see was a slight glow down the tunnel corridor. Another minute passed, it felt like ten. He was getting nervous. Come on Alex, speak to me, say something, he thought.

"You know you're beginning to scare me, Grant," her voice echoed back along the rock walls.

"Yeah?" he said, relief washing over him just to hear her voice.

"How did you know the floor would drop off?" she called back to him inquisitively.

"Just a guess. It happened to me on Cerro Vigia crawling down a similar kind of tunnel," he said nervously.

"Hey, not so loud, this place is an echo chamber. There's another one of those vertical shafts back here. Just like the one above, it also has steps in the wall. They're cut right in the rock. I'm going to head down and see what else there is to see." She wasn't asking.

"Maybe I better crawl back there and shine the light down on you so you can stow your light and use both hands as you descend."

"Good call," her disconnected voice came echoing back along the walls.

He carefully took out his light, turned it on and began to crawl forward. It was all he could do to overcome his sense of dread at the rock walls closing in on him. He tried not to think how much solid rock and stone was directly above him. It's hard to decide to not think about a thing, he reflected. The very act of acknowledging it as something you don't want to think about strengthens its presence in your mind.

He arrived at a small circular room where Alex sat with her back against the wall waiting for him. She had turned her light off and was sitting quietly in the dark. Pretty brave, pretty smart, he decided.

"Hey," she said without thought.

"Hello to you, too," he declared.

"Okay, let's take a look down this hole," she said, pointing at the top of a vertical shaft in the middle of the small inter-chamber. She crawled over and lowered herself feet first and started to feel her way down. "There are hand holds here, this is going somewhere for sure," her voice came echoing up the shaft.

"Okay, I'm down. It's about a twenty foot ceiling here. The chamber is small, but not nearly as small as where you are. You want to come down or give me a few minutes on my own?"

He didn't want to go down. He wanted to go back up. He knew he could not leave, so he decided he would rather be with her than waiting, and not knowing what was going on. "Headed down," he said carefully, trying not to reveal his growing anxiety.

He reached the next level and looked around. They were in a natural chamber, maybe 10 feet by 20, with perhaps a fifteen to twenty-foot ceiling that sloped down to crawling height at one end. "So where does it go from here," he wondered out loud.

"That's what I was thinking. It's been cleared out, and access brought specifically to it, so it must be connected to something else or why all the effort?"

"There...there," she flashed her light towards the edge of a dark corner of the room. A false arch had been chiseled out of solid rock to allow entrance to another space.

"They must have had rock masons in here for some time clearing and finishing up inter-chambers," she observed. "The air is good. They surely used torches for light."

Cautiously they walked towards the shortened archway. "Me first," she said, as if trying to prove her courage after her quasi-breakdown the day before while flaying about on the cliff edge. Alex moved on, talking as she went. "Another down-sloping corridor, if I'm not too turned around, it's heading into the center of the hill. You okay to back track us out of here?" she questioned.

"Hope so. But if we keep this up much longer we're going to be pretty confused. Let's not run the risk of our lights giving up." Just the thought of it made him nauseous.

He clicked off his light, hoping to save battery again. "I've got my light off so tell me what's going on, I can't see a thing in here," he said a little too loudly. "Just keep talking."

"I'm walking along a corridor. It looks like it has been widened for easy access. It's starting to open up some more. Oh, I'm back in an open cavern, it looks like the cavern we were in earlier. When I turn the flashlight towards the ceiling it illuminates the whole place. I think I'm below where we came out when we first hit the crystal cavern."

It was too eerie sitting in pitch-black listening to her voice echoing off the walls. "Okay Alex, we need to get back. We've got a lot of things to do. Let's ditch the box and plates in the first chamber below the bat hole. Then we can travel light, and figure out what to do next."

"I'm sure there's more to this place, she called back. We have not even found the bat cave yet. But, you're right, we'd better get back up on top," she said, almost reluctantly.

Even though returning to the original chamber required they climb, it was much faster because they knew what to expect and how to get there. They used only one flashlight on the return, feeling comfortable having no light on at all when climbing up the vertical shafts. When they emerged at the inner room, just inside the first chamber, their eyes were so dilated they could see without a flashlight. Ducking through the archway and gaining the cave entry, the light was so bright they were forced to sit down and let their eyes adjust before doing anything.

"Okay, first off, let's move the box and plates down one level, and secure them for a future find," Grant said with authority.

"You know our fingerprints are all over these things. We're going to have to wipe everything down carefully, then collect dust and sprinkle it in amongst the plates, before we secure them in the box. Then do the same thing to the exterior of the stone box," she said reflectively.

"Yeah, I suppose it wouldn't do well to have someone checking up on things like finding recent fingerprints all over the box and its contents. Is that a test you'd normally make on a new find?" he asked, a bit surprised.

"No, it's rare when things are found in situ. But when there is any question about the integrity of the find, any number of tests might be performed," she replied.

It was a bigger project, and more difficult than either of them had thought. They had to manhandle the stone box down the vertical shaft. They ended up having to use both flashlights. They lay them on the floor turned on, casting reflective light, rather than directly on their work area. They each needed both hands to get the box down safely. They were afraid to use their candles. Wax, even a little bit, would not go over well, if found. Once down, Alex set to work cleaning things with a dirty shirt, and then examining everything twice to make sure there were no threads, or traces of any contamination, in or on the box, and in or on the plates.

Grant collected cave dust from the anterior room and together they finished the project storing the box unobtrusively against the opposite wall from the direction of the passageway that led off towards what they were now calling the top level of the crystal cavern.

Back up in the external chamber, they were discussing the best approach regarding moving out of the cave. "I'm going to head up the stairs and look around. I'll call back down when I've completed some reconnaissance," he said, as if there was no sense discussing it further.

A moment later he had snagged the line hanging down past the cave opening with an unfolded shovel. He mounted a backpack and was on the rock steps reaching for the next one up. Now that he could see exactly how these things were constructed, it was much easier going. You could reach about three steps up and hold onto one step while climbing. Something like a rock ladder he thought. He was conscious of the fall off behind him, and was careful to not look down. It only took a minute for him to reach the upper ledge. He crawled over the top and lay there listening for anything unusual. A minute later he was crawling quietly to the corner of the throne room, searching carefully for any sign that someone was watching the area.

Grant removed his backpack and scooted around the top of the hill to the front corner of the throne room. Lying flat on his stomach, he surveiled what he could see of the ancient city below. Birds swooped and called, insects buzzed, in the distance he could hear other jungle sounds, but nothing human seemed to be around.

Behind the back wall of the throne room, he walked along the first two buildings. He was blocked from sight in almost all directions. Getting back down Grant crawled out and around the third building which faced directly towards the labyrinth. He couldn't actually see the labyrinth as a hill and pyramid structure were in the way. However, from this vantage point he had a largely unobstructed view of the city complex below. Grant sat on the steps of the third building and surveyed everything he could see with his binoculars. The military was gone, but it was possible they left a spotter/sniper somewhere out there. If that were the case, they would surely be seen before long. He went back to get Alex.

"Don't look down this time," he instructed as she was preparing to step out and climb the rock steps to the top. He had already pulled up the rest of their things. Alex had been careful to remove all trace of their having been in the chamber. Cinched in the rope, she climbed right up the steps. The problem with getting up or down to the cave entrance was primarily psychological. It was not particularly hard once you knew what to do.

They sat talking for a while, their backs to the stele and their feet almost to the cliff edge. How different it was from yesterday. They had overcome their fears, and were chatting comfortably within a few feet of a significant precipice. Grant shared his concern that the military might have left a spotter somewhere. It was also possible that a soldier had seen the rope around the stele in the early evening and there was now someone sighted in on the place just waiting for them to materialize. They discussed this likelihood and then came to the conclusion that they were prepared to take the risk. With the rope coiled up and stowed, and the other gear retrieved, they swung their packs and headed self-consciously around to the front of the throne room.

Seeing and hearing nothing unusual they headed down the stone steps and the dirt trail below.

"We haven't had a chance to see the majority of the ceremonial center," she observed.

"Save it for another time," he said tensely.

"Hey, lighten up. You're making me nervous," she fired back.

They dropped their bags at the labyrinth, on the top level in the interior chamber where Grant had originally expected they would spend the night. Now they were going to negotiate the blacken stairwell, the dark stone corridor, and exit the archway along the bottom of this same building on the way to the beach. They'd seen no sign of anyone. It was as if yesterday were a complete fantasy, a dream of some sort.

Carefully they made their way down to the beach. The dark corridor was now child's play compared to wandering around in the bowels of the hill. Before they exited into the open air, close to the river, Grant signaled Alex to stand still. He crept out ever so slowly, hoping to spot anyone along the beach. After what seemed an age, he signaled Alex to come out.

"So where do you think they went?" she asked. "If they knew we were here, why didn't they stay until they found us?"

"I don't know. It depends on whether they arrived here out of logic and didn't actually know we were here, or perhaps they had a discussion with that young lady at Palenque, and they're checking multiple sites. Maybe they tracked the rental car to Corozal. Maybe they spoke to one of the guards at Bonampak. If they had spoken with Enrique they would not have left so quickly. Either that, or they expect we'd be back to meet him this afternoon, and they'd grab us then."

A minute later, Grant offered another explanation. "I'll bet they saw the logbook from the military gateway before the border crossing. Remember, we cleared that small guard post outside of Corozal? They wrote down our Mexican residency information."

"That's right. They cleared us into town so that anyone there could simply cross over to Guatemala without any further departure approval," she said excitedly. If the military determined we had passed through the Corozal checkpoint, they would expect that we had gone downstream or crossed over into Guatemala. If they did not speak to Enrique, he may just show up here, and we'll have our ride back. If he doesn't show up, maybe we should use the raft and float downstream, and see where it takes us."

"Maybe they interviewed the regular boat charter guys. Enrique is a guard at Bonampak; he just borrowed his brother's boat. There's a possibility that he may get here without knowing someone's after us," Alex said. "Either way, our best bet is to stand-by and see if he shows."

Grant checked the tree limbs where he had packed the raft and aviation bag. Everything seemed fine. Rolling his wrist to read his watch, he added, "We've got a few hours before Enrique is supposed to be here. Let's go see more of the city."

"Good for me," she said brightly.

They returned to their packs, unloading two of the four remaining bottles of water, and most of the food. They kept the rope, and took along the flashlights, then headed off towards the large complex they had not yet visited.

Full-sized carved stone caimans, Central America's version of the crocodile, were scattered in various locations. It was a reminder that the river was a dangerous place. Sculptures and frescoes were in great abundance. Yaxchilan was not yet stripped of its treasures. Here there were still breathtaking works of art, right where they had been last placed by the Maya themselves.

The sun burned off the morning mist leaving the plazas and surrounding jungle hot and muggy. After about ninety minutes, Grant's knees were buckling, and his mind was a fog of exhaustion. Alex was looking beat as well. Water helped, but they decided to head back and wait for their ride to Corozal anyway. Enrique would show up they reasoned, simply because he wanted the money. The underlying question was whether or not he knew they were being sought by the military, and whether or not he had made a deal with someone to turn them in.

Alex suggested they risk greeting Enrique at the landing, provided no one else arrived with him. She would question him, and tell him they'd seen a military helicopter. If he didn't seem to know anything, so much the better, if he did, then perhaps she could weasel some kind of information out of him. If there seemed some likelihood that he was looking to turn them in, they might be able to pay him enough to get him to help them out. It was a risky call anyway you sliced it.

As they emerged again from the arched passageway that formed the entrance to Yaxchilan, there were three boats pulled up on the beach. A fourth was just landing.

At least a dozen men were lounging about waiting for their comrades to make the shore. Straight black hair fell long down their backs. These men were carrying an assortment of older rifles, the two youngest, actually boys, had bows and arrows. Their dress and hair identified them as local Lacandon Indians. They probably lived in the rain forest, very possibly on the Guatemala side.

Until recently the Lacandons had lived outside the influence of Mexican society. Never discovered by the Spaniards, or the Catholic missionaries, their daily life remained much as it had for hundreds of years. They grew maize, beans, and chilies. They worshipped the ancient gods of the forest and nature. Now they hunted with rifles. Bows and arrows were produced mainly for sale as souvenirs. Some of the men traveled to the outside world to sell necklaces, deer and lizard skins, and the bows and arrows made from the strange American Quayacan shrub.

The Lacandon tribal collective had some form of recognized ownership for the vast areas of the jungles they inhabited. They were paid money from mahogany lumbering operations. Unfortunately, the timber harvesters were notorious at shortchanging the Indians. The amounts they received did not come close to the loss in wildlife, and the herbs and foodstuffs they gathered for their survival. The Mexican side of the river was under full siege by industrialists. The Guatemala side remained largely untouched.

Grant had seen satellite photos of the area. There were vast logging operations under way all along the Mexican side of the border. But the Guatemala side was so remote, that logging was not economically feasible, at least yet.

The largest source of hard currency for the Lacandon Indians came from the sale of ancient artifacts. They collected and stored them, awaiting antiquities brokers who frequented the area in search of product to resell to recognized wholesalers. An entire network of buyers, sellers, and transporters would ultimately move the product along to final retailers. By that time, each artifact would have documents of legitimacy, validating their authenticity. They would also include a story of where, when, and how, a particular artifact was discovered, and why it could be legally sold on the private auction block. It was widely understood that the more sensational the story of an antiquity's retrieval, and the more mysterious the location, the higher the price that could be demanded for it.

"Looters," Grant whispered.

"They're just local Indians. Why do you think that?" she whispered back.

"They're here. No one else is. Why?" he said simply.

"That reminds me, where are the guards? Aren't there supposed to be guards here?" she asked.

"That's what I thought, too. There is no one at the guard shack so they must only come down river when there are tourists, or when they are expecting arrivals for some reason. Maybe they are here, and we just don't know it. My guess is, the reason those Indians are here is because the guards aren't."

They were standing very still, well back of the beach. They hadn't been spotted. The Indians were focused on the last arriving canoe. "What do we do?" she said, in a worried voice.

"We ought to duck out. They might rob us if the opportunity presented itself, or turn us in if they were benefited somehow. We'd be better off to stay out of their way. Let's move back to the archway and get back up to the labyrinth."

They eased themselves back out of sight and returned the way they had come. Grant decided to climb to the extreme top of the third level of the labyrinth. They had a base camp of sorts. He reasoned that if he could get into position he would be able to watch the activities on the beach and spot Enrique when he arrived.

The Indians did not seem to be in any kind of hurry. It took them quite a while before they headed into the city. Most of the men left their rifles with a boy standing guard at the beach. Two kept rifles with them, probably for protection within the city from other looters, or possibly the Yaxchilan guards. Maybe they were one and the same. Who knew? The Indians seemed to know just where they were headed. They moved off in single line.

Grant whispered down to Alex from the roof of the labyrinth. "They're headed through the passageway. Step back in, and stay quiet until I come to you."

He watched them emerge in the plaza. Without any hesitation they turned left, heading southeast towards the area of the city complex Alex and he had just been exploring this area thirty minutes earlier. He felt rather fortunate they had decided to move towards the beach a couple of hours before Enrique was due to arrive. Now that he thought about it, it made more sense to stay where he was and watch the river for any sign of Enrique. He crawled to the edge of the roof just above where Alex would be standing inside. "Hey," he whispered loudly.

"Yes?"

"I think I ought to stay up here and look out for Enrique," he said.

"Want some company?"

"Sure, as long as you've got some water. It's always a good idea to be nice to the water boy."

"So, I'm a boy now," she said playfully.

"Well, no. There is no one blind enough to make that mistake."

They sat in the shade of a roof comb, a piece of masonry work affixed to the very top of many Mayan structures giving it additional height. Roof combs once served as a kind of billboard. The roof combs here were originally covered with a thick white plaster, as were all the structures at the site, then they were painted in multiple bright colors with scenes depicting things of importance to the rulers and priests of the city. What remained of this particular roof comb provided protection from the direct rays of the sun. It made their perch on the roof more tolerable.

"You know," Grant said thoughtfully, "I've heard that there is only one rule of law along this river border. Whoever commits murder on the Mexican side crosses to Guatemala, whoever kills someone in Guatemala crosses the river to Mexico."

"You're kidding."

"I'm not," he said softly.

Now that they were at a lower elevation, the sounds of the forest canopy were louder. Sitting quietly seemed to amplify the hum and music of the millions of super-sized insects, and the flocks of multi-colored song birds. Spider monkeys yammered in nearby trees, occasionally screeching at one another for real or imagined offenses. It was actually pretty wonderful here, notwithstanding it was miserably hot and fraught with danger.

"I can't decide whether this is a spectacular place and we should be thrilled to be here, or give-in to the wretchedness and misery of the jungle, and conclude this is a living hell," she observed somewhat philosophically.

"I suppose that both statements are true. It reminds me of something I heard once. Apparently, about 90 percent of how we feel about a thing is determined by our attitude towards it."

"Our thinking is not something that happens to us. It's something we create. Thoughts can either work for us, or against us. It all depends on the thoughts we focus upon. Positive uplifting thoughts equal positive uplifting feelings. The reverse is also true. When random thoughts arise, we need pay close heed to which ones we empower with our attention."

"Wow! Where did that come from," Alex asked. "You believe that?"

"Yes. Yes, I do," he said gently, not wanting to disturb his reverie.

"You're a strange one, Grant Whitaker."

The air was still. The heat was damp and overpowering. It was steadily sapping their clarity and strength. It felt almost as if they might suffocate were the air to not freshen soon. Grant drifted off in semi-sleep. When the rifle shot rang out, he was instantly alert nonetheless. "Shit!" He jumped up, and stared in the direction the sound had come from.

"What! What was that?" Alex sat up startled, and confused.

"That Indian boy down there, the one who stayed with the boats, he just fired a shot in the air. It looks like he's trying to warn the others that someone is coming downriver."

"Look! There's a boat just upstream. It might be Enrique. If it is, he's probably not real sure about landing now," Grant said, trying to overcome his mental confusion.

"We've got to let him know we're here," she said in desperation. Alex jumped up, waving her arms and yelling towards the small boat fighting the current to hold position.

The young Indian hearing the shouting turned around, and seeing someone waving erratically on the rooftop of the labyrinth, got scared and fired off a shot in Alex's direction. The bullet careened off the roof comb knocking bits of rock and plaster down around them. Alex immediately hit the deck, swearing and shocked beyond reason. A moment later, having gained a modicum of composure, she fumed, "That immature little brat shot at me."

"Yes, he did. And that little exercise of yours terrified him," Grant spat back irritably. "What's the matter with you?" he ranted. "We've lost our only edge. Now these guys know we're here. If they think we're going to rat on them, or that we represent either an asset or a liability to them, we're toast."

With that he pulled her up in frustration, urging her to head for the corner where they had climbed up. "Come on," he said gruffly, "we've got to get out of here!"

If it was Enrique, he had decided to turn around and head back up the river. The small craft disappeared around a large sweeping bend. "Shit, shit, shit," Grant growled. "We've lost our ride AND we've got looters after us." Somewhere in the back of his mind he knew he was being unfair. He was just too hot and worn out to care about anyone but himself. How had he descended so quickly into such a dark and angry mood, he momentarily had the presence to wonder?

Alex seemed incapable of understanding the rapid change of events. "Wait a minute. You just wait a minute. I'm not leaving here until we clear this up," she shouted at him as she climbed off the roof.

"You can hang around and clear things up if you want, but my guts are screaming at me to get the hell out of here," he barked. The heat had made them both uncontrollably irritable. They were both exhausted, and miserably tired.

He resumed his rant notwithstanding questioning his own conduct. "Listen, young lady, I've lived long enough to know to trust my instincts, and I'm NOT staying here now," he hissed.

She glared at him with a terrible expression. For a moment, he thought she was going to lunge at him. "Oh, so now I'm a young lady, am I? What are you trying to say? I'm just a giddy girl? You can runoff if you want. I'm staying here."

Regardless his exhaustion, and seeming inability to control his aggravation, Grant's mind was racing to assess their situation. The looters would be back to where they now stood within a few minutes. Depending on how far away they were when the first shot was discharged. Chances are the two men with rifles might start shooting when they saw them standing between them and their exit passageway. This was definitely not the right place to be at the moment.

He tried to calm down and reason with Alex, but he was in no mood to be nice. "Alex, you've got too listen. We're in a jam, and your hanging around to straighten things out is not the right thing to do. We've got to grab our stuff, and get the hell out of here, before those tribesmen come around that corner and start shooting."

Grant was speaking through clenched teeth, as he ran into the inside chamber where their packs were stowed. He was mumbling to himself. Somewhere in a more objective place in his brain he knew there was no point in being rude and severe. It really wasn't like him. Yet, he just couldn't seem to exercise enough control to stop being nasty-tempered.

"You're not getting off that easy," she started up again as she followed him into the vaulted room. "What happened to that philosophical bullshit you were spouting earlier? Huh?" Alex was just warming up, when suddenly he lunged at her, threw his hand over her mouth and yanked her struggling to the stone floor.

Right on cue, several men rounded the corner of the raised platform two hundred feet to their east. They were headed straight for the passageway. Holding his hand over Alex's mouth he leaned his head back around one of the two columns that marked the entrance to the chamber and counted the men as they went by.

"Listen, Alex," he whispered sarcastically, "I'm sorry this isn't going your way. Thirteen of those guys have gone on down into the maze, that means there's two more slinking about. I'm telling you the only wise thing for us to do is get moving, and I mean now." For some reason, he still couldn't be nice.

Alex went limp. She nodded her head, and he let go. She immediately jerked away from him and began to sob quietly.

"Grab your stuff. You don't want to be hanging out with a bunch of looting Indians."

"So, now you have it out for Indians," she said angrily. Unchecked fury shone in her eyes.

"That's ridiculous. Don't go turning PC on me. We're in trouble here, and this just isn't the time." He had his backpack stuffed and swung onto his back, and was headed through the arch. "Don't be stupid, Alex. I'm crazy about you, but I won't force you."

Alex wasn't going to be nice to him. But it was as close to an apology as she was going to get right now. And, she too began to realize something was wrong with both of them.

He ran down the steps and slightly west of south to a smallish raised structure, about ten feet high and twenty feet square. Following him at a full run, she easily overtook him and went right on past until she was around the corner. The other two looters would surely be east and south of them. Ducking behind this raised platform put something between them and the looter's approach path. Assuming they were headed towards the passageway.

Breathing hard, Grant said, "Once those guys talk to the kid on the beach, there's a good chance they'll be headed back here looking for us. I can promise you they'll all have their guns with them this time. Let's circumnavigate around to the west. Then we can make our way south to pick up the trail to the throne room.

I say we head back to the cave. It's probably the only place we're going to be safe. They probably won't quit looking until they've found us, or it gets dark, whichever comes first. These guys know we're here. And, they know the jungle. We don't. Here is where we better stay."

She nodded her assent without looking at him. They made another dash across the open plaza running south by southwest planning to pass on the west side of the pyramid that Grant had first climbed when looking for Alex the morning of their arrival. They were out in the open, and completely exposed. Everything depended on where the missing two men were located, and which way they might be looking. Running in higher temperatures is not a good idea. Running in sweltering heat was close to insanity. Alex made it behind the hill. Grant made it shortly thereafter. He couldn't go on. "Hang on a minute, I've got to rest," he said as he lowered his pack and took a drink of water. "Give me a couple of minutes."

The two minutes he'd said he wanted was closer to thirty seconds. His heart was racing so hard he was sure two minutes had passed. "Okay, let's go," he said. They pressed on to intersect the trail that let up to the throne room. Field research groups had cleared this area, probably more than once, but plants had grown up covering the route, and there did not appear to be any recognizable trail.

As they slowed to a walk, it was easy to see up to where they were going, but hard to see right in front of them. Alex tripped over a large round altar stone lying flat in the undergrowth. She pitched headfirst straight over it. Something slithered away as she lay sprawled out breathing hard. Grant stopped and pulled her up. She jerked away from his help, trying desperately to assert her independence.

"How bad?" he managed.

"It hurts," was her only reply. She struggled to her feet, limping badly. Five minutes later they intersected the trail headed to the hilltop throne room. They began to climb. Their exhaustion forced them to stop twice on the way up just to catch their breath. They rounded the throne room and lay down, sprawled between the prone stele and the cliff edge. Grant materialized the water once again. After drinking deeply, they sat stunned. Each tried to grapple with their fear, irritation, and anger. What had really happened back there? Neither of them was absolutely sure. Both were ashamed of their own conduct. Rather than deal with it maturely, they each were projecting it on the other.

As their breathing returned to normal, Grant tried to lighten the mood by quipping, "We're beginning to make a habit of this." She didn't respond. He didn't say anything further.

Leaving all but his binoculars, he scrambled back out to a forward observation position and scanned the ground below. The natives were definitely not a military unit. Yet they knew a whole lot more about tracking than the men who were working the area the day before. It wouldn't take them long to see the route they had taken. That didn't necessarily lead them up, because once he'd intersected the trail at the bottom of this rise, there were other ways they could have gone, and other trails they could have followed, never the less...

CHAPTER THIRTY-TWO

Acapulco, Mexico

"They returned and filed a flight plan to Merida," General Botia was saying. "Had a flight plan been filed to leave the country they would have been stopped immediately. At that point, our agents were south of Cancun checking hotels between Playa del Carmen and Akumal, so they were delayed in following them to Merida. However, when they arrived there, Whitaker's plane was on the ramp. Agent's Vargas and Soria went to a local hospital expecting to find Whitaker and Jardine there. While they were gone, Whitaker and Jardine filed a flight plan to return to Chichen Itza."

"My dear general…Can we skip forward to their current status?"

"Certainly. Whitaker's plane is in Palenque at the civilian airport. They may have crossed into Guatemala at the border town of Frontera Corozal."

"And you know this because?" Garcia said without emotion, although he was sure he might explode at any minute. Probably not a good idea, he thought to himself, the old buzzard was in pretty good shape, and probably ate nails for breakfast.

"Our military checkpoint is before the town of Corozal, which lies exactly on the Usumacinta River. Whitaker and Jardine were recorded as passing through the garrison there, presumably with intentions to cross into Guatemala. However, Corozal is also a disembarkation point for small boat tours going down river. The Guatemala checkpoint is similarly recessed on the only road that transverses the jungle in that region. This allows the local Indians who live on both sides of the Usumacinta, to work with one another without the complexities of constant border examination."

"And..."

"The Guatemalan check-point did not record their passing," Botia replied.

"Meaning..."

"We are not sure. The Guatemalan's are not dependable about recording transients, and Whitaker and Jardine may well be on the road to Guatemala City, or they may be working their way across the Peten to Belize. We considered that they might have rented a boat and gone to one of the archeological sites along the river, so we dispatched a military squad by helicopter. They searched sites down river as far as Piedras Negras, and up river to Altar de Sacrificios. Our military unit questioned the boat operators at Corozal, but, as you know, they do not trust the government, and many are sympathetic with the Zapista's, so they were of little help."

"So, if their plane is in Palenque, they must have rented a car somewhere close by," Ramon Garcia observed.

"That is a reasonable assumption, Senor Garcia, but we checked everywhere they could have rented a car in the area, and even further, including Tabasco, Campeche, Chiapas and the Yucatan. It is our opinion that someone must have been standing by to provide ground transportation. We have also obtained further background information on our suspects.

Whitaker is the author of the paper that makes the case for the transmigration of high-culture from the middle east to the

Americas. He has also authored numerous articles and several books on business and economics. We were able to determine that he is on the Board of Directors of the Caribbean bank that issued the credit card he uses, that he has Mexican residency, and a house in Cabo San Lucas. On his Mexican residency application, he is listed as married to Marianna Whitaker with two other homes: one in Portland, Oregon USA, and one in St. Kitts, West Indies. Senorita Jardine is 41. She came to Mexico with a university study program. She did field research at Palenque and appears to know the local area. She applied for, and received, an FM-2. She lives near the ruins at Chichen Itza. She works for the Itza restaurant."

"So, if you have narrowed their location down to Corozal, why the roadblocks in a half-dozen states?" Garcia asked irritably.

"Senor Garcia, you asked me to skip ahead, and not give you all the details. Suffice it to say there was good reason to believe they might have been in any of these areas earlier, so proceeding on the side of caution we established roadblocks wherever they were known to have traveled recently. Once we were certain that they had crossed through the Corozal border stop, we began calling off the roadblocks in other areas."

"I see," Garcia said thoughtfully. "Where does that leave us?" he asked more of himself than the general.

Botia assumed he wanted a response. "We are concerned that both of these persons are U.S. citizens, and we are reluctant to lock down the aircraft in hopes that someone will try to fly it once more. It is under 24-hour surveillance in any event. We have no real evidence of wrongdoing, so we must be careful taking them into custody. The Guatemalan military has been advised, and an appropriate reward quietly offered the officer in charge of the Peten area. An alert has been given to the international airport in Guatemala City, and we are continuing to check vehicles in the Bonampak area. Roadblocks have been withdrawn outside the Usumacinta region. Whitaker and Jardine cannot stay hidden. We will have them soon."

There was no immediate response from Ramon Garcia, so Botia continued. "It is unfortunate that this has become such a difficult and unwieldy problem. Perhaps the political inquiries that have concerned you will drop away now. Obstruction to traffic has been removed, and citizens are allowed to move about freely once again."

"Perhaps," Botia said, not at all convinced.

The meeting was over. General Botia excused himself to return to Mexico. Acapulco was too hot for him. He failed to grasp the obsession with beaches, and he abhorred the entire idea of clubbing. Mexico, the city, was a mile and a half high. It provided pleasant temperatures year-round. Here on the ocean, the humidity soared, and it was frequently hot. No, he'd rather be back in the city.

CHAPTER THIRTY-THREE

Yaxchilan, Chiapas

The Lacandon looters had dropped out of sight. Grant scooted back to where Alex leaned against the stele with her feet outstretched to the cliff edge. He took a rope and began to prepare a safety line for her. "Okay Alex, grab on and head down," he said attempting a cheerier voice than he felt.

Alex expertly tied a bowline and pushed herself out over the ledge without comment. A minute later she was in the cave's outer hall. Once she was down he lowered their packs and what was left of their food and water. He untied the rope from around the stele and went down without a safety line. He felt unusually vulnerable on this descent, even though he knew what to expect and believed he was relatively safe. Gaining the entrance, he stepped in with the rope tied around his waist, the other end already in the cave, secured to nothing. She noticed what he had done, but said nothing.

Alex was propped up where they had slept the previous night. He sat down beside her.

"Let's eat something."

"I'm not hungry," she barely mumbled.

"What?" he said more loudly.

"I'm. Not. Hungry," she said angrily.

"Neither am I," Grant replied, trying to sound reasonable. "But we really don't know when we'll get a chance next, so it's probably the best thing to do. I feel dizzy and disoriented, maybe food will help."

"Then you eat," Alex replied.

Grant opened a can of corned beef hash, the smell made his stomach roil. He ate his way through half the can and passed it over to Alex. She took the can, looked at it and set it down without eating.

"You need to eat," he finally said.

"It smells revolting."

"It doesn't taste as bad as it smells," he said quietly.

A full five minutes went by before she picked it up, made a face, and silently began to eat.

"We've got some chips and candy bars in my aviation bag in the tree by the beach. Maybe I can get my hands on that."

They sat in silence. Both were conscious of their bad conduct. Grant particularly so.

"I wonder how much farther the cave network goes down," he said, trying to make conversation. "It may go down to ground level, or even lower," he continued. "It might even provide some kind of backdoor exit into the jungle. Maybe it was some sort of escape hatch for royalty."

Alex was not interested in talking. She sat unusually still.

He tried again, "You know, I have a penlight in my aviation bag for reading charts, I've got matches, and a couple of emergency candles, and extra batteries for our regular flashlights."

Alex did not respond.

"I even have some extra survival gear, and a small medicine kit. Oh, that reminds me. What's the status of your knees?" he asked politely, as if there was nothing wrong between them.

The question required a direct answer. She muttered an unintelligible response.

"Excuse me? Say again," he responded in pilot jargon.

"I said, they hurt," she said irritably.

"Okay, let's have a look." He was trying to mend the argument of earlier, with no success.

"You're not serious," she said incredulously.

"Yes, I am," he said with a forced smile. "If you need medical attention I need to know."

"I'm fine," she said.

"Seriously, Alex, is there a chance the skin is broken? If there is, you know what the jungle can do to an open wound. And, let's not forget the kind of critters it will attract."

"I don't think so," she managed, realizing of a sudden that what he said was true.

"Better have a look see," he said moving in front of her to unbutton her jeans. Leave your shoes on. I just need to know whether or not it's important that I sneak back down the hill and get meds," he said, struggling to sound reasonable.

She didn't stop him. But when he told her she needed to lift her hips so he could pull her jeans down, she looked him straight in the eyes and said, "You think you're pretty clever don't you?"

"What?"

"Get off it, Grant; you're insulting me…again."

"I'm being serious here," he said trying to hold a straight face.

"You really upset me," she blurted, her chest heaving. "You frightened me. You turned into some kind of crazy man."

"I'm sorry. Alex. I don't know why I was so out of control. I am ashamed, embarrassed, and confused. It really isn't like me. I mean, everyone gets grumpy, but, well, I don't understand it. About the only thing I do know, is that I don't want you angry with me." He was responding without much internal censorship.

"I'm seriously falling for you. No, that's not right. I have already fallen. It doesn't make sense. I don't know how it could ever work out for us. But what I do know is that I need you to not be mad at me. We're in a really tight jam here. We can't afford to be at cross purposes with one another," he finished lamely.

"That doesn't give you the right to yell at me, or put me down," she stormed.

"You're right. I was wrong. I'm sorry," he said again, while internally justifying his actions as no worse than what she had done. Over time Grant had learned that the best way to end a conflict was to apologize early, and often. Life was just too short to waste it on hurt and bad feelings. Besides, he was in the wrong. And, he might as well admit it again. "Alex, I was wrong. Please forgive me," he said sincerely.

"Now, are you going to let me pull those jeans down so we can see what we're faced with here?" he said attempting a smile.

"What is it you are trying to be faced with?" Alex grouched without much fire. "You're such a bad actor. I can't believe I'm letting you get away with this," she said, as she placed her palms on the stone floor and braced up so he could ease her jeans down her legs. She winced with pain as they slid over her knees.

He was concerned for her. He was also very attracted to her. "You really are beautiful," he breathed out.

"Will you shut up! This isn't the time. I hurt, and I'm angry, and you're trying to fool around," she moaned.

"Sorry...I am sorry...I can't seem to control myself."

"You and every other guy I've ever known. Life must really be hard on you men. Ouch, that hurts. Be careful," she whined.

Alex had scrapped both knees. Dried blood went all the way into the sock of her left foot. "Not good Alex. We need to clean you up and get some antibiotic cream in there. And, we've got to get those abrasions covered up. Infections come fast, and are extremely virile in this neighborhood. I'll head out just as soon as the sun drops a bit more. Hopefully the looters will have taken off by then. I doubt they want to hang around after dark."

Grant dreaded the thought of going down to the beach and back again. Aside from the danger of being robbed, shot, or captured, he was bone tired. He was clearly having trouble with focus. The constant heat had sucked the life out of him. Yet, here he was ready to head out again. Only two bottles of water left, he thought. *We're extremely dehydrated as it is. We don't have much more to keep us going.* He was sinking into worry and there wasn't a lot of hope to hold on to. *If I sit here thinking like this I'll never get the energy to get moving.* "Guess I'll go now," he said out loud. He stood up unsteadily.

She watched him getting ready to leave, knowing full well how terribly tired he was. "You really don't need to do this for me. I'll be fine until morning. We can deal with my knees then," she offered. "Both of us need rest now. It would be safer to wait until morning."

Grant steadied himself against the cave wall. "Let me drink some more water, and then I'm gone." He drank a half a bottle, knowing he should be more conservative, but recognizing he was going to be useless without hydration.

"We need to find a clean water source. Our systems could hardly stand drinking river water. If we had something to boil water in we could sterilize it," Grant said mechanically. With that he turned and headed up the cliff wall steps dragging a line with him. Once at the top he tied off the rope. No one would be trying to use that resource to follow them after dark.

Once again Grant crawled out to an observation position and glassed the area vigilantly before heading down. He went slowly, walking cautiously, listening, watching, careful to not overstress himself again. The water had helped, and probably the cold hash helped too. He felt better. And, now without the sun beating down on him, the air was not nearly so suffocating. Once again it occurred to him, just how fouled up one can get by simply not getting enough fluid in this kind of fatiguing heat.

He saw no one. Just to be sure, when he reached the labyrinth he climbed to the top and studied the beach area. The boats were gone. Everything appeared to be quiet. Passing down through the stairwell and corridors was still frightening, especially at this hour. The place seemed to be moving of its own accord. He tried not to think of all the bugs and slithering things that were moving about. He hesitated at the archway before stepping out into the waning light. It looked clear.

Slowly Grant moved towards the beach, alert to sound and movement. Stepping clear of the protective lower walls of the labyrinth, he felt exposed. He had to force himself to keep moving.

Gaining the tree where he had left the tarp and its contents, he pulled himself up to a large limb and sat quietly hidden inside the branches. He was there much longer than needed. He took time to observe everything around him, slowly, carefully. This must be how the Indians do it, he thought. It felt strangely inappropriate to make any sound. He was as silent as possible.

Securing his aviation bag Grant dropped noiselessly out of the tree. He moved stealthily, exuding care and patience, observing everything thoroughly, endeavoring to blend, to become one with his surroundings.

He had learned something here tonight. He hoped not to forget it. It sounded like some understated kung-fu wisdom, yet it was surely true. It was knowledge he might need to draw on. When he returned to the cave he was somehow revitalized of spirit. He tried to explain his experience to Alex. It was lost in translation. It sounded strange. Even to him.

Grant encouraged Alex to drink deeply, explaining how they weren't aware of just how close to hallucinating they had become. There was not enough fresh water in their systems. Neither of them had needed a toilet in almost three days…a bad sign. She drank and within a few minutes felt better. "We can live out here for a while if we must. There is food to gather. Clean water is the challenge."

In the morning, his concerns proved to be mute. It rained. It rained for hours. They were able to collect clean fresh water by using a tarp strung up from the edges, and weighted in the middle with a stone. They filled their bottles, undressed in the cooling rain, and washed away the grime. The band-aids on Alex's knees made her look innocent, even more youthful than she already did. They washed their clothes and hung them out waiting for the drying sun. A simple thing like getting enough water was all it took. They were grinning from ear to ear. Their anger and frustration with one another had passed.

Life slowed. They were living in the moment. Finding enjoyment where they could. Yaxchilan was theirs. No one came, not Enrique, not the military, there were no looters, no bird watchers, no eco-tourists, there were no tour boats, no one. The river swelled, and the current began to move more swiftly. Dangerous eddies and dramatic whirl pools formed as the rushing water circled Yaxchilan on its long run to the sea. No one dared be on the river when it rained this hard, they decided. The low clouds and heavy precipitation was pretty certain to keep helicopters and spotter craft grounded.

They ventured into the jungle, following narrow game trails while it was still raining. The continuing showers were refreshing and held the insects at bay. They gathered fruits of varying kinds. There were poor quality bananas, plantains actually, and tree ripened mangoes. They found wild lemons and a dwarf orange of some kind. They drank fresh water until their urinary systems were fully functioning. They gorged on fruits along with the chips, and candy bars they had brought with them. Life was suddenly so much better.

They finally felt clean. The difference was amazing. They talked and played, teased and flirted, and thoroughly enjoyed each other's company. Their lives had been renewed. The pressing problems that seemed to surround them were put on hold. Alex was back to pining about becoming Jane of the jungle. Grant felt years younger, stronger, and considerably more energetic.

After dark, they sat listening to a symphony of frogs and insects while watching the jungle's equivalent of a laser light show, a remarkable display of super-sized fireflies zooming about. The smell of a refreshed tropical forest permeated the outer chamber of the cave. It was a powerful aromatic aphrodisiac. It was not lost on either of them, yet something held them at bay. Maybe the stars were out of sync, or the planets were not yet fully aligned. Whatever it was, they both sensed the timing wasn't right. So, although they were deeply attracted to one another, they each reached for balance, and delayed the sealing ritual of physical intimacy.

Morning dawned. Today they would need to decide how to proceed. Before noon, a long narrow boat arrived with six visitors. Alex and Grant sat on their hilltop perch beside the throne room, and took turns watching the tourists through the binoculars. "Still no guards," Grant said thoughtfully.

"Maybe they're on their way," Alex offered.

The tour boat had left by 2:00. At least half the time the small tourist group had been there, they had spent eating. "Hard to understand why they came at all," Alex observed. It seems like they would have at least tried to come up here, just so they could look around."

"Yes, it does seem odd," Grant said reflectively. "You know, if I were Enrique, and was intent on getting paid, I'd show up today around 4:00. It would be a worthwhile experiment for him, even if he did think the Lacandons had robbed us."

After discussion, they decided to stage their equipment down to the beach once more, and wait to see if Enrique arrived. If he didn't, they would speak to the next tour boat that dropped in. It might be a few days, but at this point, neither of them seemed to care. If a tour boat operator revealed concerns about them, or suggested that they were still being sought by the military, their backup plan was to inflate the raft and float downriver.

About 4:00 P.M. Enrique arrived. He held offshore, studying the area carefully before he ran the boat up on the beach, lifting the outboard motor before its propeller fouled in the silt.

Alex and Grant walked out casually from their perch near the foundation of the labyrinth. They greeted him as if nothing unusual had happened two days earlier. He had a puzzled look. Then seeing they looked no worse for wear, broke into a broad grin.

Alex immediately engaged Enrique in dialog. After the first few minutes, Enrique reached in the boat and produced two bottles of beer. There had been ice in the pot where six bottles were stacked. The ice had already melted, but the drinks were cold, at least by tropical standards. Grant wasn't a beer drinker, and was generally of the opinion it should go back in the horse it seemed to have come from, but this time he made an exception. He greedily drank the first bottle without ever tasting it. It was cool and refreshing, a genuine blessing.

He immediately opened a second bottle, and drained it almost as quickly. Alex watched him. She smiled broadly as she continued to visit with their ride. Minutes later Grant was feeling lightheaded. It wasn't from a lack of fluids.

The three of them sat on the roots of a banyan tree. Grant wondering if Alex was aware that this was the place they'd had their moment of passion, directly after their arrival to Yaxchilan. Alex was still in deep conversation with Enrique. When she looked over at Grant with a knowing smile, he knew, she knew.

Alex turned to Grant and gave him an update. "It seems there was quite a stir in Corozal the other day. The military was searching for someone they claimed was engaged in smuggling stolen artifacts. They had no photos. However, they apparently described you fairly well."

"Why didn't they hang around and grab us?" Grant asked, surprised at how direct Enrique and Alex's discussion must have been.

"Nobody here likes the military. This is the land of the Zapista rebels. Locals wouldn't take two steps out of their way to help the government. And, just for spite, they would give them wrong information. However, given the circumstances, Enrique feels that we should be happy to double his fee, plus pay him for the extra trip when he was shot at."

"Oh, come on. He wasn't shot at; you were the one who was in danger. The first shot was just a warning to the other men," he said laughingly. "So, do you trust him?"

"I think so. He wants the money and is happy to be of service, and he remembered to bring the beers. I hinted about the car, he didn't seem to know anything. I say we head back," she summarized.

"Okay, then, let's get going. If they're up there waiting for us I hope they'll allow us a real meal before they haul us off," he laughed again. *Must be the beer working on me. That wasn't even funny.*

Enrique seemed almost jubilant. He even helped them load the boat. This was worrisome to Grant, but Alex felt certain it was because of how much money he had been promised. In less than three hours they had made the return trip and were pulling up to the dock. Nothing seemed particularly unusual. There were other boatmen visiting with friends nearby, or at least that's what it seemed like to Grant. No one paid much attention to them, other than a casual glance to confirm who had the fare and whose boat had been employed.

The car was right where they had left it in the hotel parking lot. Apparently, no one had tumbled to the rental car. But then again, she had rented it hundreds of miles away in Veracruz. As he thought about their predicament, it occurred to him that the military might have posted a reward. The logical place for them to check first would have been the hotel. He began to have second doubts and shared them with Alex.

Alex took the matter up with Enrique, their new best friend. He was emphatic that no one in town would dare go to the military. Anyone who did would be in serious jeopardy within the whole community. Enrique grinned broadly as he explained the facts of the area to Alex. He was quite cavalier about the entire matter. Grant reminded her that Enrique had nothing much at risk here, so they should think things through carefully. Watching him strut about the docks, it reminded Grant of an old film where Errol Flynn played the part of a swashbuckling pirate. It was seriously overacted.

In the end, they decided to eat first, and then make a decision on where to stay. Alex invited Enrique to join them, which he was more than pleased to do.

Reluctant to let Enrique see where he kept his money, Grant spent some time fussing with loading the car. Half way through dinner he asked Alex to confirm again how much he was supposed to pay in order to settle their obligation. She told him and he materialized from his pocket the correct amount plus another $50 as a tip. Enrique had probably never seen that many U.S. dollars at one time. He tried to be serious, but he just couldn't wipe the smile off his face.

Enrique was obviously smitten with Alex. He was busy pursuing a highly-animated conversation with her. They both seemed to be enjoying themselves so Grant left the table looking for a men's room. He decided to walk the perimeter of the grounds. It was dark. The mosquitoes were out in force. He wandered around, flailing off insects, trying to put his mind at rest. He was nervous about the military. He was struggling to make sense of things. The whole matter was confusing, nothing seemed to clear up. One thing he knew for sure. Someone was searching for them. Yet the whole affair seemed inconsistent and haphazard. Either that, or Alex and he had been incredibly lucky.

When Grant returned to the table, Alex was on her fourth beer; an obvious conclusion, as there were three empties beside her plus the one she was nursing. Exercising unfelt patience, he waited for a lull in the conversation, and then suggested that Alex have Enrique find out if the military checkpoints were still in place between Corozal and Palenque. They spoke for a few more minutes and Enrique excused himself. He went to the bar and made a call, making an issue of tipping the barman for use of the phone. The bartender was so surprised his mouth dropped wide open. A few minutes later he returned.

Enrique addressed Alex without even looking at Grant. Alex turned to Grant, "You okay?" she asked. "You look pretty unhappy about something."

"Not really, just trapped in my own thoughts," he struggled to recover by smiling broadly.

Alex looked at Grant strangely and continued, "Enrique called his cousin who comes in and out of town through the additional checkpoint, established the day before our arrival. He says they're still stopping traffic and searching vehicles, but no one is checking the logging road to Palenque, which was evidently the road we arrived here on by mistake."

"What are you thinking? Is it wise to check-in and spend the night here?"

"I don't know where else we'd go, and I don't want to spend the night in the car, so yeah. Let's check-in and spend the night here," she decided.

Alex offered Enrique another $20 tip on top of costs if he would rent a room for the night in his name, pay cash and give them the key. He was happy to accommodate. It had been a valuable day for him.

When they got to the room they argued playfully about who got to take the first shower. There was an embarrassing moment as they both considered taking it together. They blushed simultaneously, instantly recognizing the other had thought the same thing. Grant deferred, sweeping his arm towards the bath. As it happened, Alex still had shampoo in her roller bag from the trunk of the car. The fragrance of lilac, fresh soap, clean hair and skin, was both invigorating and inviting.

The singular over-soft bed, afforded their first comfortable opportunity for a romantic interlude. Neither of them really understood why they were still holding back. Perhaps it had become their habit. They lay on their backs, starring at the ceiling, lost in their own thoughts. Sleep refused to come. Both feigned slumber. Powerful emotions were at work. Grant felt oddly uncomfortable sleeping with this beautiful woman. He wanted to be alone. Yet he feared loneliness, almost more than anything. He had been lonely for too long now. He lay quietly, staring at nothing.

Alex sat up, grasped his head, and turned him towards her. She had known all along he was awake. Looking deep into his eyes she said simply, "I do not want to lose you. I know you feel the same. Figure it out."

Grant tried to respond. Hot tears streamed down his cheeks. He pulled her close. With her head on his chest, and thoroughly conscious of the swell of her breast against his side, he finally let go and drifted into restless sleep.

Just before dawn he woke. Frustrated and concerned, he wandered about the room. Worries for their future came rushing in. What would come of them? What was right and fair for Alex? What about her legal problems? What about their safety, his family, the business, the IRS, the Grand Jury, the golden plates, the military checkpoints, his plane? The list seemed endless. He was worn out by the time Alex stirred. She stretched drowsily, and headed to the bathroom. His entire focus changed. She's alluring, even when she just wakes up, he observed, while arguing with himself once again about the foolishness of building a relationship on sex appeal and physical attraction. When she returned, he abandoned the argument and joined her back in bed. He fell deeply asleep.

They awoke again. This time he felt more at peace. For a short time, he had forgotten the things that so deeply disturbed him. He was happy to be right where he was, doing just what he was doing. They got their things together and headed for the restaurant. Alex ordered a morning lunch box for their trip to Palenque. They enjoyed a casual breakfast, neither wanting to spoil their precious moments together. Both of them knew things would change soon. Each of them avoided the questions and issues that circled about, demanding their attention. It was getting easier to ignore their problems, to lose themselves in just being together. And, it was deeply satisfying to have someone with whom to share their past, to reveal themselves too, to discuss things both funny and sad. They could even talk about their immediate present, but neither dared discuss a future together.

Finally, Alex said innocently, "Grant, where are we headed?"

"I thought we'd agreed to go to Palenque," he stammered, surprised at the question.

"That's not what I meant," she said softly. "Where are *WE* headed?"

Grant was instantly on guard for some reason. He looked into her eyes, searching for hidden thoughts. "Where do you want to go?"

The issue of their relationship was on the table again. Neither wanted to be the first to discuss how crazy it was, why it couldn't work given their circumstances, what the problems were that loomed so large. How could they even contemplate the implications and complexities of a romantic involvement?

Alex didn't respond for a long time. Not able to maintain eye contact, she stared down at the table. "I don't know exactly. I think I want what you want."

"What I want isn't really possible," he blurted out before realizing the implications of what he'd said.

"Alright then," she stood. "Time to get going."

"It's rather curious just how many of life's decisions are influenced by one's libido," he mused out loud. Thirty minutes later they were on the road.

A quote by Matthew Baldwin kept running through his head, *"Money, it turned out, was exactly like sex. You thought of nothing else if you didn't have it, and thought of other things if you did."* Well, he didn't have it, but he was definitely thinking of other things right now, none of them good.

"It's nice out here in the early morning," she offered, trying to get a neutral conversation going.

He hadn't noticed. In fact, he was worried that they would be lucky if they were actually on the right road. Enrique had told them how to get around the border checkpoint just in case. Grant wasn't entirely sure the dirt track winding through the edge of the forest would end up connecting to the gravel road back to Palenque. His mind was locked on problems. They were spinning circles in his brain.

"I…ah…right," he stammered, actually looking around for the first time. "The jungle mist adds a mysterious feel to the place," he managed.

"I suppose if you lived here, you'd do your heavy work in the early morning, before the sun was high enough to drain your energy," she said trying to force him out of his head.

"Probably so," was all he could manage.

The dirt track arrived to a gravel road and he turned right as he had been directed.

"Okay Grant, you're upsetting me. What's going on?"

"I'm sorry Alex. It's just…well, it's just everything."

Intuitively she said the right thing. "Grant, I need you to be strong for me. I am tired of being scared. I am tired of looking over my shoulder. I want you to protect me. We've got something special developing between us. Please let's hold on to it. Don't let the worries of what might happen, ruin what is happening."

Once again, he was impressed with Alex's intuitive wisdom. *Every time I think I have her worked out she comes up with some new insight. It's amazing we've met under such difficult circumstances, and yet, I wouldn't change it for the world,* he thought.

"You're right, Alex. I just can't figure out what we're going to do, I mean seriously, I have no idea."

"Then let's enjoy the moment and not waste time. Whatever is going to happen is going to happen, regardless of how much we worry. Don't you think that's true?" Alex asked gently.

"Perhaps...I guess I'm not sure exactly what I think about that. I am not really a fatalist. We must have some control over our destiny. I'm searching to discover what cards we have to play in this complicated game. There are so many things up in the air right now. I don't know what to do, or even where to start."

Grant paused; then continued in a more neutral tone. "You know, I once memorized a little saying to help me when I was feeling overwhelmed and distraught, it went something like this:

> Happiness is always an effect of our state of mind. It cannot be found in circumstances. The minute we start looking for happiness anywhere other than our own thought processes we are lost. That's because we're focused on the outside, in search of something that can only arise from within. *Happiness is a feeling."*

Alex sat considering Grant's cryptic analysis. "You seem to have a penchant for philosophy. I think your nickname should be Thoughtsy."

He smiled and instantly felt better. "So, what do you think, Alex? Is our capacity for joy and happiness simply an effect of our state of mind?

"It seems true in some abstract way. But, when you're dealing with real threats and legitimate fears, what then? In some ways, it's hard to even consider the concept of happiness, given what faces us in our immediate future."

"Yeah, I hear that." Grant replied softly. "I suppose there is nothing we can do about some of the issues that confront us. Perhaps we should just ignore them until they unfold further. Yet, if there IS something we can do to influence outcomes, we should be thinking about them."

They drove on, lost in their own thoughts. The road seemed less severe than when they had arrived from the opposite direction. It's probably because I know what to expect, and I'm driving more slowly, he thought.

"Alex, if I head back to the States would you go with me?" Grant asked.

"What would that accomplish? I might be arrested, and we would be separated," Alex said flatly.

"Maybe we could figure out how to cross the border without being caught," Grant offered. "I have a couple of ideas."

"Even if you could get me across, what would I do? Where would I go? How would I live?" Alex asked, clearly frustrated.

"Yeah, I suppose you're right. And, I suppose I'm in the same boat. If the Grand Jury indicts me, there will be a warrant out for my arrest. I just can't see any easy way forward. I suppose that means I must proceed straight ahead, and deal with whatever comes. After all, I can't just leave my children and grandchildren, and never see them again. And besides, there is really no way to ignore a warrant for any length of time. Even if I could ignore the warrant, life would be horrible living under the constant threat of discovery. What could I do? Where would the money come from? Sure, I have some resources not yet seized, or frozen, but wires, and money movements, are all transparent to the U.S. government since 9-11."

"What does 9-11 have to do with your money?" Alex asked.

"After 9-11, all U.S MLATs were rewritten. So now, any country using any source of American money process, like VISA, MasterCard, American Express, bank wire transfers, etc., have all been forced to re-sign their MLAT with the U.S." Grant was still explaining when Alex interrupted.

"What's an MLAT?" she asked in confusion.

"Oh, sorry, MLAT stands for Mutual Legal Assistance Treaty," Grant replied. "All the current U.S. MLAT agreements require that foreign governments, along with their various financial institutions, report on all U.S. persons. No exceptions. All financial activities, both foreign and domestic, are transparent to the U.S. government. The rationale for this forced reporting by non-U.S. institutions on U.S. persons was supposedly related to terrorism. The reality of most of these policy changes was related to *taxes*. A U.S. person cannot do anything of consequence without their government being told. Therefore, any funds I might manage to pull together from whatever sources that have not already been seized, would eventually lead straight to me. No matter where I was. There is really nowhere to run. There is no safe way to hide. And, I don't want to do that anyway."

They drove on quietly for a time before Grant continued. "The only way we could get away, would be to change our entire identities, and then we'd lose the resources we have, right along with all our family relationships. What possible kind of life could we build under those circumstances?"

It was the first time he had used the "us" and "we" seriously. And as bad as things seemed to be, they had begun to explore how they might make a life together.

"If there's a will there's a way," she said gently.

"Easy to say, hard to do," he said a little too sternly.

"How much effort you want to put into it, is your choice," she replied softly.

"Come on Alex, it can't be that easy. Is it that easy for you? Besides, how long would you be happy with a guy my age?"

He'd finally said it. It was bothering him more than he realized. Alex didn't say a word. The conversation hung there, each of them waiting for the other to say something.

Just ahead was a logging truck that completely blocked the road. A huge timber harvester with its gigantic semi-circular claws was placing logs onto the truck. They sat and watched the harvester in silence. When the claws closed, they looked like giant handcuffs clipped around the center of the logs. It was a jarring visual. The mental association caught Grant off guard. He sat there stunned by the implications of actually being arrested. It seemed an impossible thing. How could that really happen? He didn't even get traffic tickets. Hadn't he always conducted his affairs as a model citizen, and taught his children to do the same?

Grant had known there were powerful people who wanted him neutralized. Nevertheless, he had still been outspoken and public in his criticism of federal agencies he saw as seriously abusing power. In retrospect, he had been crazy to think he could get away with calling out people in powerful places. It was his own uncontrolled hubris, his inflated ego that had gotten him into so much trouble. Why couldn't I have just kept my mouth shut?

Anyway, I slice this, I am to blame, Grant thought bitterly. He had once thought of himself as a do-gooder, an honorable whistle-blower. He had busied himself with pointing out obvious conflicts of interest by high-ranking federal personnel that saw themselves above the law and conducted themselves accordingly. Look what it has brought me. Why didn't it seriously occur to me that I was playing with fire? What was happening now was much worse than just being discredited publicly. Federal agencies were rapidly seizing all his assets, threatening individual family members, terrifying his friends and neighbors, and moving to indict him. Sending him off to prison would neutralize him completely.

Like so many before him, it had been the IRS that was selected to take him out. Trumping up charges from other agencies required more effort, and added to the risk that legitimate litigation might allow him to go free. With an IRS indictment, one was put in the impossible situation of having to prove one's innocence. Not technically true, but surely it was the truth in current reality. You were guilty as charged, unless you proved otherwise, and that was essentially impossible. One cannot prove a negative.

So, it's come to this, he thought. I will be held in a federal prison somewhere, no longer able to legitimately call for the investigation of those responsible for so much corruption in high places. What could he do other than submit? There was no way clear.

Alex misunderstood his silence. She thought he was still thinking about their age difference. She exploded. "What is with men? Aren't you guys supposed to be tough, and rise above your insecurities, and all that stuff? Men are such babies," she griped.

Surprised out of his thoughts of prison, he responded, "Where did that come from?"

"Get off it, Grant. You know where it came from. Why all the insecurity? You don't think I'm capable of integrity, loyalty, or trust, is that it?" Her frustration was feeding her angst.

"No, no, I didn't mean to infer that. Geez, Alex, I was thinking about being arrested. Okay, I suppose that is insecure of me, but well, I'm confused," he stammered.

Alex wasn't listening. And she wasn't done. The volume was turned way up. "Men! You're all a bunch of apprehensive children. You act tough, but you're not. Sure you can be hard and dangerous, and fight wars and bully people, but inside you're still just a bunch of timid weenies. If it's not jealousy, it's how much money you make, or don't make, or how much stuff you have, or how good you are at sports, or how fit you are, or the size of your penis. OR, how OLD you are, or something else equally as stupid."

They were stopped, but he still had both hands on the wheel. He turned with his mouth open. He looked at her, and said nothing. She was passionate and angry, but she was also speaking from her experience. He had to admit, at least to himself, it was rather refreshing. It was also a tad intimidating. He started to grin. She was red in the face and getting madder. He couldn't stop himself. The smile kept getting broader. She folded her arms across her chest and fumed. He began to laugh out loud. Alex turned away, and looked out the window. He laughed louder.

"There is nothing funny about this," she shouted at the passenger window, not daring to look at him.

"Yes, there is," he said, continuing to snicker.

"What is so funny?" she hissed.

"What's so funny, Alex, is that you're absolutely right! I've never heard anyone put it so succinctly."

It took a moment to sink in. She turned towards him and said suspiciously, "You really think so?"

"Yeah, I do. It's a rather sharp knife your tongue wields, but you're spot on. Although I would like the opportunity to defend myself, I mean really, I don't give a flip about how I do in sports anymore." He laughed again. "Well, maybe that's not entirely true either."

Alex tried to stifle a giggle. She didn't want to laugh. She wanted to be mad. She laughed anyway.

Funny, he thought. I feel better. The problems have not gone away, but laughing is somehow cathartic.

CHAPTER THIRTY-FOUR

On the Road from Corozal to Palenque

It didn't seem as hot and forbidding headed back towards Palenque, but once they were past the log harvester and moving again, he realized the gravel road had not improved. The constant jarring from the inescapable ruts and potholes were once again putting them on edge.

They entered one of those long tunnels of rain forest canopy. The walls of the jungle seemed impenetrable within feet of the roadside. It immediately went from bright to semi-darkness. Grant couldn't identify why, but something did not seem right. He argued with himself that this was a natural reaction to the change in light, but he was nervous and on edge. Alex also had a premonition. She sat silent and tense.

Grant glanced in the rearview mirror just before the road swerved to the left into what appeared to be a reversed S curve. The road had been rebuilt where the ground had collapsed around a sinkhole. Just into the first curve, he saw men with guns dressed in full camouflage stepping silently out of the jungle behind them.

"Shit," he exclaimed, as he braked to a stop well after the curve. "What," Alex exploded nervously.

"Either military, or well-equipped Zapatistas. They came out of the jungle behind us as we passed. That means we'll run into another squad ahead."

"How do you know?" she asked in desperation.

"Standard protocol for trapping a vehicle on a lonely road. It happened to me in Guatemala once. There will be a roadblock ahead. If we reverse course there will be one behind. The squad behind will have called the one forward to advise them we just passed. When we don't show up, they'll both start moving towards us. We probably have less than two minutes."

In desperation she whispered, "What do we do?"

"Check for cell service…now," he almost shouted.

Within a second, Alex had leaned over the backseat, and was struggling with Grant's fabric briefcase where all three cells phones were clipped to an inside pouch. Grant reached over the seat and jerked it forward. They each grabbed a cell phone and powered up. Alex, always quicker than Grant, was already trying to get a signal. Grant looked first to the road in front, then in back, expecting any second to see a military squad approaching. "Damn, damn," she was muttering in frustration impatiently waiting for a signal. "Who do we call," she blurted.

"J.P."

"Mexican cell is working," she said excitedly.

He grabbed the phone and referenced the outbound call log. Finding Jack's previously dialed number he pushed send. It seemed an age passed between each ring of the phone. Four rings and it went to voice mail.

Grant spoke rapidly, "Jack, this is Grant, I'm with Alex. We're on a back road coming from Corozal, a town close to the Bonampak ruins on the Usumacinta River headed towards Palenque. We're trapped on a jungle road. A squad of military just stepped out behind us. I assume there is a roadblock in front. When you get this message, call the U.S. Embassy in Mexico City. Advise them that we have been detained by the military. We need the U.S. State Department's intervention to get us out. Tell them we heard Alex was being sought as a material witness in a federal case, and we were headed to contact them regarding this matter. If you do not hear back from me within fifteen minutes, assume the worse."

They could see no one on the road in either direction. Their view was limited by the curves in the road, the dense vegetation, and the lighting. While Grant searched the call log for the Robles phone number, he told Alex, "No matter what. We know nothing of the gold plates. We met, fell for each other, have the same interests, and are both lonely. I introduced you to my friend in Cancun. After that, strange things began to happen. Everything went down as it happened EXCEPT we did not see a dead person at Guadalupe's. We went to Guadalupe's but no one was home, the same for Miguel Ramirez. We went both places trying to find Robles family members, and figure out why someone seemed to be chasing us".

He looked around in frustration. "We came to Palenque to see where you used to study. We decided to visit Bonampak and Yaxchilan. We made the decision to go to Bonampak after taking off for Chichen just before dark. We flew for a while, and then returned after discussing our possible future together. Alex, remember this, government agents will lie to you. They will say anything to get you to admit something. They will tell you I have confessed and ratted you out. Do not believe them! Stick to your story. No matter what they say.

The phone was ringing with no answer at the Robles. He got switched to voice mail. Grant left a similar message as before. Alex was handing him his U.S. phone saying it was ringing the last number he had dialed to the States. "Should be your son's office," she said. A receptionist for the software firm was giving her a canned spiel. Grant interrupted, "Ian or Matthew Whitaker please. This is an emergency. Tell them their father is calling."

"I'm sorry Mr. Whitaker, both of your sons left for Belgium this morning. I can put you into one of their voice-mails if you like."

"Right…either one, but whoever's voice mail it is, track him down and make sure he listens to it." Some clicks and the voicemail message for Ian came on. It seemed to take forever. When he finally got the chance, Grant spoke quickly and clearly, leaving a message similar to the ones for Jack Morgan and Pepe Robles.

The engine was still running. The air conditioning was still on. They were sweating nonetheless. "Where are they?" Alex said, barely able to contain her anxiety.

"Not sure. They're probably trying to figure out why we didn't show up at the roadblock ahead. It was bad form for the rear squad to be spotted. They are probably arguing about it via radio."

"Any chance there is no roadblock ahead? Couldn't it have been a military unit searching for Zapatistas?" Alex asked uneasily.

"Anything is possible. It just seems too pat for me. I don't guess there is anything to do but move ahead and find out." With that he put the car into gear and drove. As they came out of the second curve entering a straight section of road, soldiers were crowded on either side in the form of a deep V. They had to slow, and were finally forced to a complete stop. They were thoroughly surrounded by men holding guns at the ready.

Putting on his best smile, Grant rolled down his window and asked innocently of the only man with a drawn handgun, what was going on. A wall of heat flooded the car. He had forgotten how uncomfortable it was to be outside. The man, who appeared to be in charge, spoke authoritatively in Spanish. He motioned with his gun that they get out of the car. The message was clear. Both of them opened their car doors and stepped out in the heat.

Judging from his dress and manners, Grant was pretty sure the man with the hand gun was an officer. The officer kept demanding something from Grant. He was speaking in Spanish. His motions and tone of voice were a clear threat. Grant kept repeating, "No hablar Espanol," while shrugging his shoulders. Alex, standing on the opposite side of car spoke rapidly to Grant saying, "He wants to know what you were throwing out of the car. He believes our delay was due to our hiding something." She had hardly spoken when the man in charge yelled at a soldier next to Alex. The soldier shoved the barrel of his rifle hard into Alex's stomach. She doubled over trying to catch her breath. While she was bent forward another soldier shoved her shoulders down. She immediately fell to her knees. Alex was out of sight.

At almost the same time a soldier struck the back of the joint of Grant's left knee with the butt of his rifle. Grant collapsed on to his knees. He gasped to Alex, "I love you."

A gun barrel was pressed against the back of Grant's neck while the commandante, if that was what he was, shouted at him in Spanish. Grant again declared, "No hablar Espanol." His neck was bent and his head faced towards the ground. Evidently none of the soldiers spoke English. A moment later he felt a sudden flash of pain and everything went black.

He awoke to his head throbbing. It was probably the pistol. He was hot, thirsty, and unable to move. As he slowly gained more consciousness, he realized his hands were tied behind his back. He was lying on the bed of a troop carrier truck, the kind with a canvas top. He squirmed, trying to get more comfortable. His feet were tied. All Grant could hear was the sounds of the jungle. It seemed no one was around.

Okay Grant, this is where you're supposed to break out and rescue the leading lady. The plastic ties that secured his wrists were tight. For the life of him, he couldn't imagine getting free without outside help. What would he do then? There was nowhere to run.

The soldiers would be at least somewhat versed in jungle tracking, and they would likely find him even if he could get away. Time passed, his tongue was swelling, his head pounding. It finally occurred to him to yell out for Alex. "Alex, are you alright," he shouted feebly.

The canvas was swept aside from the rear of the truck. Two soldiers looked in. Grant tried to ask for water, "Aqua por favor." They simply stared at him. He tried again, "Aqua por favor." He must sound pathetic, he thought. One of the men climbed in the truck. He opened a canteen and helped him slurp some water while he lay on his side. He could hardly swallow, but what a blessing the water was. Grant rolled his eyes, and nodded his head in thanks, whispering, "Muchas gracias, senor." The soldier looked at him without expression. In English he said, "Woman okay."

Grant was surprised and appreciative. "Muchas gracias, amigo," he said. He meant it. His head dropped back down on the truck bed. He either passed out from the heat, or his head injury.

More time passed. He awoke again. Grant became more conscious of his predicament. Soldiers began climbing into the truck. They sat facing one another, their feet lined up on both sides of him. The truck started and lurched forward.

If he had thought the previous drive on this road was difficult, it bore no resemblance to the radical jarring he was now experiencing. He would have preferred to simply escape back into unconsciousness, but the jolting was so aggressive his head was being slammed against the steel floor.

One of the soldiers stuck a booted foot under his head as it whipped up and down. Another sign of mercy. A simple soldier had kept Grant's head from banging viciously against the truck bed. He tried to look up. It was too hard. Eventually, two soldiers propped him up against the forward bulkhead. With his hands tied behind his back, the strain on his shoulders showed with every bump. He may have been better off where he was.

There were eight military personnel in the truck with Grant, four on each side. They seemed to be discussing something. The soldier, who had given him the water earlier, moved forward in the jostling truck. He cut the plastic band that bound his wrists behind him. One of the other soldiers tossed him a folded tarp to sit on. Another handed him a canvas bag to put behind him. He was offered more water. He greedily accepted. These guys were just doing their job. It was clear they saw no reason for him to be subjected to this kind of discomfort. Thank God.

The soldier that spoke broken English asked him why he had stopped his car before coming to the roadblock. Grant told him he had seen men with guns come on to the road behind him. He assumed there was a trap ahead. He stopped and called his influential friends. He asked them to warn the government, in case it was Zapista's trying to capture them and hold them for ransom. Once translated, this explanation caused a flurry of discussion in the truck. There were a number of angry comments. These soldiers had been forced to search the almost impenetrable jungle, for three hours in extreme heat, while they looked for what their officer assumed Grant and Alex had tried to hide.

Several times thereafter, soldiers offered him a drink from their canteens. Once or twice, he was offered a cigarette. He declined, but was appreciative of the offer. It was dark when they pulled up to another roadblock. One of the soldiers hurriedly bent forward and strapped Grant's wrists lightly. A few minutes later the truck came to a stop. The engine was turned off. The previous stop had been the gate to a military compound.

Grant's ankles were untied. Two soldiers helped him out of the truck and across a gravel parade ground. He was locked in a small cell. A bucket with a closing top was in one corner; the toilet. Bars began one foot off the floor and ran all the way to the ceiling on two walls. The other two walls were concrete block. A steel bench ran along one wall. A soldier provided him with a jar of water.

He gave Grant a one-inch thick mattress and pointed to the steel bench. It was about five feet long. Short for his 5'11" frame. There was no sign of Alex.

By noon the next day, his interrogator had arrived. Three soldiers came to his cell. One stood outside, two stepped in. They locked him in ankle irons. They placed a chain around his stomach. A separate chain ran down behind from the belly chain. It was locked to the ankle irons. His wrists were cuffed. He could only make small shuffling steps.

Grant was led into a cinder block room. He was immediately claustrophobic. Traces of pale green paint stained the walls. The floor was poured concrete. The place smelled of insect repellant and disinfectant. A collapsible desk was in the center of the room. A single chair faced the desk, its back to the door. A black rubber nightstick was the only item on the desk. His wrists were uncuffed. He was pushed down into the chair. His hands were re-cuffed behind the chair. He was left to consider what he was about to endure. Time passed. He was having trouble keeping track of the most mundane things. Probably a result of his head injury, coupled with exhaustion, and the anticipation of the pending interrogation.

A voice came from behind him, "Senor Grant Whitaker?"

"No hablar Espanol," Grant responded evenly.

In heavily accented English, "You are Grant Whitaker, are you not?"

"Yes," he responded. *What a ridiculous question. They could hardly be mistaken as to my identity. They have my luggage, passport, residency documents, my wallet, everything.*

"You have stolen valuable artifacts that belong to the government of Mexico. This is a serious offense. You will spend much of your life in prison," the voice stated without emotion. "You will now tell me where you have hidden the contraband, or I shall be forced to take strong measures."

"I have no idea what you are talking about," Grant replied, hoping he sounded appropriately confused.

The interrogation had begun. His accuser stood behind him. At first he spoke quietly, in monotone. Later he cajoled. Then he began to shout. The threat of physical abuse hung heavy in the air.

Grant struggled to sound like an innocent traveler. He claimed to have recently fallen for a woman he'd met in Chichen Itza. He talked on and on, literally dumping information, trying to seem as compliant as possible.

Just as he thought he was making progress, he caught a glimpse of movement from his side. He was struck hard across the stomach with a black rubber nightstick. He rocked over on one side and fell to the floor. The chair spilled out from under him as he struck the concrete. His arms were stretched back to their limits. There had been no warning. He'd had no time to tighten his stomach muscles. His digestive system revolted violently. He began to wretch.

The pain was exquisite. He lay there on the floor in a puddle of his own vomit. He gagged, trying to catch his breath. His arms were stretched back so far, they were literally being pulled from their sockets.

The voice was yelling in Spanish. Two guards came in. Two buckets of water were poured over him, washing much of his vomit to a center drain in the concrete floor. His wrists were uncuffed, relieving the incredible stress on his shoulders. He lay there unable to move, still gasping reflexively. The smell was foul.

One of the guards kicked Grant to get his attention. A bucket and a scrub brush were set next to him. He was to clean the floor of the remaining mess. Grant couldn't think straight. He was lightheaded and dizzy. He tried to drag himself up. His arms had no feeling in them. He couldn't support his body. A lifetime of being in control had ill-prepared him for the position he was now in. The immediacy of his world had shrunk to the guards, and the voice from behind. He was incapable of doing almost anything. He drifted in and out of consciousness.

A guard continued to push him with his foot. Grant could move his legs slightly, but the ankle irons were still chained to his waist. He simply could not shift in such a way as to brace, and get up. A moment of clarity, and it occurred to him that he must look absolutely wretched, squirming around on the floor. He tried to right himself unsuccessfully. His head was throbbing. He was racked with dry heaves. The choking was putrid. More than once he gagged and thought he would be unable to breathe. The guards grasped his situation. They stood the chair up, took hold of him, and sat him back down. His wrists were cuffed in front and secured to the belly chain.

He sat there stunned, sick, and immobilized. He was completely at the mercy of others. This isn't like the movies he kept thinking. It only took one heavy slam to my gut to render me useless. *Am I that weak? Am I that unable to protect myself? Is this the way it has always been when sadists control their victims?* His gasping for air finally subsided. Circulation was returning to his arms. But, the pain in his shoulders and the burning across his stomach, were still intense.

The voice was calm. "Senor Whitaker, we are not playing a game. You will tell me what I wish to know eventually. The only question is how much you will suffer before doing so." The questions began again. Grant couldn't quite understand them. The effect of the heavily-accented English and his own confusion blurred the words. When his interrogator asked why he had stopped on the road before reaching the roadblock, Grant gave the same explanation he had given to the soldiers in the truck. He had been making phone calls. He tried to explain the gist of his calls. He couldn't think clearly to explain. Finally, he shouted that they could see for themselves by referencing the call logs on his cell phones.

Grant was drifting in and out of consciousness. He vaguely realized he had hit his head when the chair went over. The pistol strike to the back of his head on the Palenque road had been exacerbated by his head banging in the truck. Now his head had slammed the concrete floor. He vaguely understood he was suffering a concussion. He was delirious. Time passed. Soldiers drug him back to his cell. Dimly he realized he had never seen his accuser. Squinting up from his too-short bunk, he regained some mental clarity. It was light. It must be late afternoon. Someone was listening to his heart. He drifted off into semi-consciousness.

The sun was setting. A guard arrived and left two flour tortillas with a bean paste, and another jar of tepid water. Grant cautiously got to his feet. His head was bandaged. *When did that happen?*

Swaying, he braced himself against a wall. He drank and tried to think. *Strange, I would have thought I'd be going wild worrying about Alex, worrying about how my children were dealing with my disappearance, worrying about my business, the grand jury, the plane, and a hundred other things. I am so dull, nothing seems to matter. It's just too hard to focus.* Grant sat down heavily. He lay on his side with his knees pulled up to fit on the bunk. He tried to sleep.

Morning came early. His jail cell faced the rising sun. Grant struggled, trying to remember what that meant. Two large cockroaches scattered from off uneaten tacos. He swung his feet to the floor. I've got to get some energy and exercise, he thought. The cockroaches had not eaten much. He gagged the tortillas down. He tried to distract himself by doing push-ups. He got to the floor but was unable to do a single one.

Grant was on the floor when a soldier appeared with a tray. He could see a hard-boiled egg, another bean taco, and more water. Embarrassed for some reason, he got up swaying. He attempted a smile at his jailer. The soldier momentarily returned a tight-lipped smile on reflex. He motioned Grant away from the bars of the door. He opened it, and handed in the tray.

Grant tried to speak with him. He asked after Alex in English and then tried his limited Spanish. The jailer just shook his head, leaving Grant to wonder what he meant. The day passed. The sun went down. He saw no one until dark. A different soldier arrived with a dinner of beans and rice on a tin plate. There was a mango and water. No utensils were provided. He either ate with his fingers, or lapped the food like a dog. The smell from the toilet bucket was ripening. It was hard to eat with unwashed fingers, three feet from a stinking bucket.

Another day dawned. A new jailer came. It was the soldier that had helped him when they were taken into custody. "Hola, amigo," Grant said soberly. His head was improving, the throbbing was reduced. "How are you doing Senor Whitaker?" the soldier asked carefully. "I am Alvaro Salazar."

Grant attempted to pronounce Alvaro correctly. "Alvaro… do you know what happened to Senorita Jardine?"

"Woman gone."

"Where?"

He shrugged his shoulders. "Are okay? You sleep two days."

"Not very happy, but getting better," Grant replied. "What is happening? Why am I being held? The man who asked me questions would not even let me see his face. Am I being charged with something?"

Alvaro Salazar had a blank look. He couldn't process all the questions. He finally responded, "I think you in trouble with government, also Museo Nacional de Antropologia. Person from Museo call many times. Angry you sleep." After a brief pause he continued, "No trouble talking you, por favor," he said worriedly.

"I understand. I will not say anything. Can you find out anything else? I am worried about Senorita Jardine. Oh, and can we get this bucket emptied? The smell makes me sick."

"Try," Alvaro turned and walked away. Sometime later he quietly approached Grant's cell and whispered, "Senor Whitaker, you have mucho dinero." It was a statement not a question. "You help my family, I help you?" he asked, just above a whisper.

"Yes, I will help you and your family, after I am released. What can you tell me?"

"Jorge Ramon Garcia Peron calls. He presidente Museo Anthropology. Do you know?"

"No," Grant replied, as he racked his confused brain for any association with the man's name.

Alvaro seemed disappointed. "Him ask mucho questions you. He angry. Colonel Torres no happy. He not like Senor Garcia speak to he. Colonel Torres call general Botia."

Grant assumed the colonel must be the base commandant. "Who was the man that questioned me? Is he still here?"

"No," Alvaro said quietly. He stepped back from the cell bringing a finger to his lips. He stood there and listened for a while then left without any further discussion.

Alvaro returned again before noon. He unlocked the cell door and passed in a clean pail with no lid. "Take top other bucket," he said. He handed Grant a jar of water, and motioned for him to return the empty one. Looking around to confirm no one else was within earshot, he said, "Man question you Capitan Armando Vargas. Military intelligence. Colonel Torres afraid Vargas. Vargas gone. Come back for you."

"Have you any news about Senorita Jardine?" Grant asked in a whisper.

"Si…she go with man come with Capitan Vargas." He shook his head with a dour expression, as if this was not a good thing. "I think take Mexico."

It took Grant a moment to recall that when locals refer to Mexico, they are referring to Mexico City. Perhaps this Vargas fellow, or his superiors, would try to gain favor with the U.S. government by turning Alex over to the American Embassy in Mexico City. They would question her first, of course. He shuttered involuntarily thinking about the implications.

"Alvaro, anything else you can learn about the senorita would be appreciated."

Another guard arrived with the same uninteresting food at evening. Alvaro was not to be seen. It could be worse, he tried to tell himself. Yet, he had to admit, he was in fear of the next interrogation.

Alvaro was back in the morning. "Soldiers talking about you. Many peoples calling. Mi colonel is worried. He say men here soon to take you." Alvaro looked around, and then whispered, "How you pay me, senor?"

"I promise to find you as soon as I am able. There is money in my flight case," Grant responded.

"Si. Si. Every people knows money your bag. You very rich man, senor.

Everything is relative, Grant thought. There's about $5,000 in that bag. Not enough to accomplish much. But from a Mexican soldier's point of view, it was apparently a fortune.

CHAPTER THIRTY-FIVE

Portland, Oregon

It was a fashionable restaurant on Broadway, just a block from the Schnitzner Performing Arts Center. They were two blocks west of the expansive Federal District Courthouse, one block south of the Justice Center. The setting was more like New York, than Oregon. The tablecloths were starched linen. There were too many forks. The walls played host to various forms of modern art. Expensive suits and dresses, high heels, leather satchels, and trim cases, were huddled all about. This was downtown lawyerland. There were places like it in every major city in America.

"You're a very lucky man, Grant. Your family stood by you, and fought hard to get your release. At the same time, they were being subjected to constant harassment by the USDA's office. It's rare to see that kind of unified effort these days. It clearly affected the Appeals Court judge, who has allowed your release prior to trial.

Your family and friends filled the courtroom as a show of support. That wasn't lost on the prosecution," Grant's lawyer, John D. Stanhope, was saying. "It's rare to see people endure the suspicion of a swarm of investigative agents. Both your friends and family have had to endure overt threats from the prosecutor's office. Nevertheless, they still rallied to your side, knowing there was risk to them personally. I doubt you have a clue as to how fortunate you are." He was shaking his head, muttering, "Very unusual indeed."

"It was a huge surprise when they took the cuffs off, and ushered me through a side door into the courtroom, and I saw everyone. I didn't know anyone knew what was going on. Other than hearing from you yesterday, I was cut-off from the outside world for more than eight weeks. Even after I was transferred to Oregon, my children were barred from visiting me. They couldn't call in, and I was blocked from making outbound calls."

Grant was quiet and submissive. He was still very much stunned by it all. The constant deprivation of the past eight weeks had taken their toll. He struggled to keep up with Stanhope's dialog.

His lawyer shrugged his shoulders, "Well, you know, they're convinced the rules are for the bad guys, and that the rules do not apply to them. Of course, the bad guys are anyone they're after, for whatever reason. Be careful, Grant. Never underestimate the arrogance of those who work in the Justice system. I know. I spent ten years there."

"Oh, and another thing, quit talking about what's right, moral, or true. No one cares. It won't provide a lick of merit to your case, and you'll only come across weaker than you are. You must face it Grant, you've been openly critical of federal agencies in the media. They will always make you pay. No exceptions. You do not have enough juice to keep them at bay."

John Stanhope paused a moment, shook his head, and added, "You are so much more fortunate than you realize. You could still be stuck in a Mexican jail for starters. I'd suggest you keep that in mind."

Not able to help himself, Grant muttered blankly, "Power corrupts and absolute power corrupts absolutely."

"Come on, Grant, you're smarter than that. Playing the victim won't get you anywhere. This is not about what's right. You've got to stop thinking that way. The government has the power. According to the Department of Justice's own website, just 3% of those charged by the various U.S. District Attorney's offices will ever go to trial. The accused is always forced into taking a guilty plea. If they don't, they stand no chance at a reduced sentence."

John Stanhope had been lecturing Grant for more than an hour. He wouldn't let up. "Judge Panner, one of our federal court judges in Portland, was quoted in a front-page article in the Oregonian, as saying, that a lawyer that does not plea his or her client in a federal criminal case, could be considered guilty of malpractice. Do you get that? There was nothing there about innocence. He was addressing the very real understanding that the government gets its way. Always! Look, Grant, I'll stay with you if you go to trial, but I'm telling you right up front, you'll end up much worse off than if you plea. It's the only reasonable way forward."

They were quiet for a time. Grant was still not able to reconcile himself to all that was going on around him. He was dizzy. He was out of touch, and unable to find the energy to even consider what his lawyer was saying. Stanhope resumed his lecture, "You're going to prison. This is something you've got to face. You're on the government's shit list. You're going down. Period. One way or another they will lock you up. For those few who stupidly attempt to fight the federal system, the percentage that actually win, is so low that you could say it offers you *NO* statistical chance at all. And, even in the event we could launch an adequate defense, and in the very remote chance we prevailed, you will be financially broken, emotionally spent, and your family will be forced to desert your side in order to preserve themselves and their children. The truth is you don't want to put your family at any more risk than they already have been forced to endure. Deep down in your heart, you know you cannot allow your children and grandchildren to be dragged through much more."

"Grant, you, more than most, recognize what self-empowered bureaucrats can do to disrupt lives. Do you want them to ramp up their focus on your children, grandchildren, and close friends?"

Grant sat there dully, hardly able to follow what he was being told. He dropped his head and shook it no. It had been a rhetorical question in any event. They both knew the answer.

"Grant, even if we were to surmount all the odds and prevail, the government *WILL* come after you for something else. They *WILL* get their piece of you in the end. The only way to win in this situation is to think in terms of negotiating the lowest sentence you can. You must plea. Any other action will cause you, and the one's you love, more grief than you can imagine."

"It is so wrong," Grant mumbled to himself.

"Yeah, well, if you had simply murdered someone, or committed a crime against another citizen, you'd stand a chance. But you're a target of the U.S. government. So, even if you were to prevail at trial, and I give you less than a 5% chance under the best of circumstances, they'll never quit coming at you until you cease to be threat on any level. Come on. You're a businessman; start thinking like one. This is about *negotiation*. You have to grasp that you're going down. That's all there is to it. The question is how hard and how many you take with you. So, what can I bargain with to help in reducing your sentence?"

"I'm sorry counsel, call me naïve, but this is America. The government is supposed to be here to protect us, not destroy us," Grant spat angrily.

Grant's defense counsel was a pragmatic man with little interest in blather. For ten years, he had served as a United States District Attorney in a southern federal district. He had turned down a judgeship. Stanhope was now considered one of the top criminal defense lawyers in the western United States. He was based in Portland, Oregon, by choice. He had been in private practice for over twenty years. "Yeah, yeah…give me a break…you and I both know better. That's why you wrote about the abuse of power to begin with. You had to know this was going to happen. Now it's happened. Deal with it."

Grant was still having trouble thinking. He looked around, stunned by the fact he was now out of jail. He was back in his home town of Portland. He tried to respond intelligently. He simply couldn't think clearly. His lawyer was speaking so quickly, and so forcibly, it was hard to track. Finally, he managed to reply. "I never thought they'd come after the people who exposed their deceit. But, after the Patriot Act was enacted there was no practical means to halt any federal enforcement agency, no matter how extensive the abuse. Then Patriot II got shoved through as a rider on a defense bill, right after it had been quashed in the legislature. Now, I suppose, there is really no stopping those holding bureaucratic power."

"That's right, Grant. There isn't any chance for you now. Maybe the populace will get wise to the loss of liberty in America, and quit listening to all the crazy reasons they should give up our forefather's great ideals, in exchange for what they think is safety."

"Has there been any publicity regarding the other authors indicted and arrested on various charges?" Grant asked weakly. "It seems so patently obvious that the government is silencing every single one of their serious critics. Why is it, no one seems to know?" Grant asked nervously.

"Right. No one knows," Stanhope responded bluntly. "And you better not be the one to tell them. If you so much as utter anything to the media, the prosecutor will make a motion to have you returned to jail pending trial. Remember, you're dealing with a federal court judge whose office is in the same building as the prosecutor's office. These people work together every day. You have no pull with them. To make matters worse, the judge that was assigned to this case was originally a legal intern with the IRS. He's also infamous for tough sentencing."

"Surely that would disqualify him from presiding." Grant offered faintly. "Shouldn't he recuse himself?"

"This isn't State court. In Oregon State court, we can disqualify a judge for no reason at all, and get another judge assigned. There are a lot of judges in the state system. In federal court, it takes a full-blown hearing, and then you rarely get a judge changed. If you do, the next one is gunning for you. There are only five federal court judges in Portland. They meet together every morning to review their collective cases. You've got to get it through your head, this is the Fed. They control the system."

"What happened to freedom of speech and freedom of the press?" Grant asked, not really expecting a reasonable answer. He was having serious trouble processing the shift to his new reality. Grant looked around the restaurant once more. It was just the kind of place he had once felt comfortable. Now he was feeling incredibly awkward. An air of self-importance permeated the room. The haughty sophistication of the powerful coupled with the trappings of authority, suddenly felt stifling to him.

John Stanhope saw the glaze in Grant's eyes. He vaguely recalled hearing that Whitaker had banged his head in Mexico. "Grant, are you okay? You look like you're in a trance." Without waiting for a response, he went on. "Look, it isn't about what's fair. It is what it is, and we've got a major uphill fight ahead of us. Count your blessings, you're not rotting away in that Mexican jail, and you're on the outside. At least for while." John Stanhope stopped, scribbled a note on a legal pad, and continued. "We have a few months before trial. We've got to prepare a reasonable defense, otherwise we have no negotiating strength. Go home. Get your head together as soon as possible. I want a full written response to the allegations in the indictment. It's for my eyes only. That's the place to start. Go get busy."

"I still don't understand. If the federal court system doesn't take bail, why did they insist on taking title to three of my children's houses, in addition to picking up my passport and seizing everything in sight?"

"Okay, Grant, I know you've been out-of-it, and not following the details. But the DA's office was insistent that you were a flight risk because you knew too much about international affairs. The prosecutor actually argued that you know how to make your way in the world outside the United States. That's actually rather rare for most Americans. I have to admit though, in my ten years as a prosecutor, and all the years since in handling criminal defense, I have never heard such a bizarre argument to keep someone in jail pending trial. The DA's office actually said in open court that you knew too much. Unbelievable! What a crazy argument…your honor the defendant is too smart! Unfortunately, the judge was briefed by agents sent out from Washington D.C. He sided with their argument. So, you simply had to stay in jail until we were able to get you out on appeal, pending trial. What was it, another twenty days you spent in the Multnomah County jail after you were transferred here?"

"Twenty-one days. Three in the Justice Center in solitary confinement, at the special request of the prosecutor and the IRS, I was told. The deputies at Justice refer to the IRS CID agent's as the "bad boys." No one likes them. Everyone is afraid of them, especially the federal Marshalls. They call them America's SS. The federal marshals were descent guys, overall. Anyway, I spent another eighteen days at Inverness County jail in a dorm with 85 guys. I heard there are about twelve hundred inmates at the Inverness jail. I only saw the ones in my dorm. I was locked up at all times. There was no recreation, no access to the outdoors, nothing. But, at least Inverness was better than the hell hole at the Justice Center. And, that place was a cake walk compared to the three weeks I spent in Mexican jails, and the two more weeks in the federal prison transient system, before I got here," Grant moaned.

Stanhope was digging around in his pockets looking for something. He wasn't listening. He'd heard these things many times before. "So, Grant, the bottom-line is: the federal appeals court judge, after seeing your family support, decided he would bind you to Oregon State by putting you in the position of destroying your children's financial lives if you decided to expatriate. Having the federal government take title to their houses was the only way the judge would let you out of jail pending trial. Look, you should be darn thankful. The appeals court judge really upset the prosecutor and that gaggle of rogue agents that work for the criminal investigation division of the IRS. They were hopping mad you got out at all, even for a short time."

"I wouldn't have asked the kids to do it, if I had known," Grant said quietly.

"Well, you're out. So, even with your restrictions on travel, you are now in better shape to work on your defense." After staring at him for a moment longer, Stanhope went on, "It's pretty obvious you're spacey right now. Take a few days and get yourself together. We'll talk again." The lunch was over. Counsel picked up the tab. The cost would be passed on of course. Paying for lunch was an easy way for a lawyer to keep track of legal work done during mealtimes.

"Uh...one more thing, Grant asked. "Did you find out anything more about Alex, I mean April Alexandria Jardine?"

"We're checking on it. Jordan Grover, a new associate in our firm who just joined us from the DA's office, heard she was being held for questioning in San Francisco. We should know something specific within a couple of days." As the waiter handed Stanhope back his charge card, he continued, "Someone in my office will call you just as soon as we know something. I get that this of importance to you."

Grant's mind drifted. I wonder who found the murdered maid, he considered dully. *Did I really hold those plates? What happened to the Robles? Who were the people that had Alex, and I arrested?* He vaguely remembered that he had promised to help a soldier's family. There were so many unanswered questions. There was no closure on much of anything. Grant pulled himself out of his thoughts to see John Stanhope staring at him quizzically.

"Sorry, counsel. I keep drifting."

Together they walked out to the sidewalk. It was a truly spectacular day. The kind of day that kept Oregonians committed to their State notwithstanding the gray cloud cover that hung over western Oregon over half the year. There was good reason Portland was known as the Rose City. Roses were in bloom everywhere. In the distance, to the east and northeast, Mount Hood and Mount St Helens were clearly visible. The air was clean. It was washed the night before in Oregon's ubiquitous drizzle. But regardless the beautiful weather, streams of grim-faced, well-dressed people moved swiftly by, trapped in their own realities. It seemed to Grant they were all rushing about climbing their respective ladders of success. Something flitted through his mind about climbing the ladder of success only to discover it was leaning against the wrong wall.

John Stanhope and Grant Whitaker stood together on a street corner ready to cross at the light. Stanhope seemed to remember something. He looked over at Grant, saying, "You sure had the Mexican government riled up. What was all that drivel about ancient records? And, what on earth were you doing in the jungle?"

"Some other time counsel," Grant said sullenly, as he oriented himself to look for the daughter waiting to take him home. "It's actually quite a story and I'm pretty sure it's not over yet."

So many loose ends, so much unfinished business, he thought. *I wonder if I'll be able to get through what now confronts me, reunite with Alex, and return to Mexico. God help us.*

The End

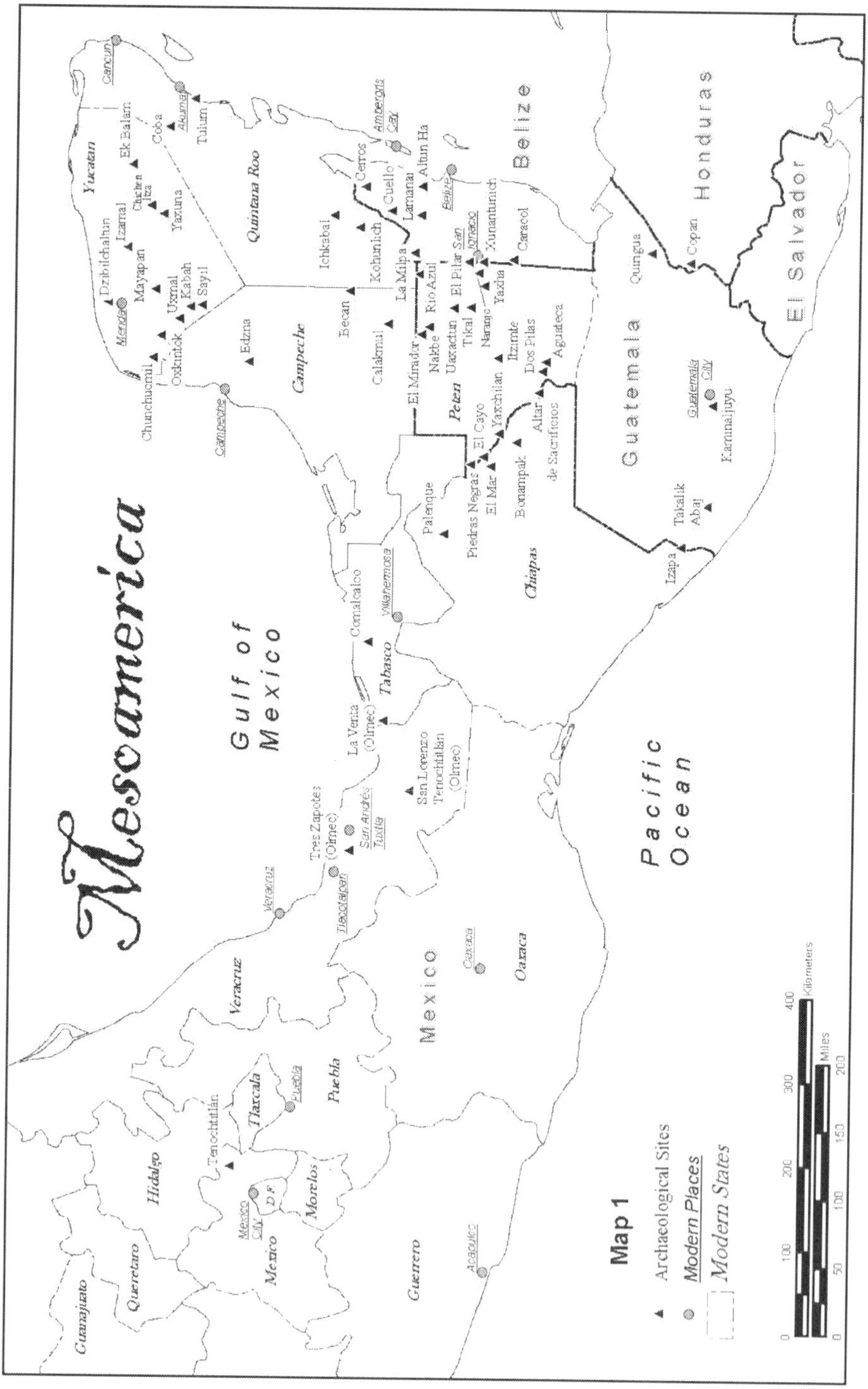
Mesoamerica
Gulf of Mexico
Pacific Ocean
Map 1
Archaeological Sites
Modern Places
Modern States
0 100 200 300 400 Kilometers
0 50 100 150 200 Miles
Yucatan
Quintana Roo
Campeche
Belize
Honduras
El Salvador
Guatemala
Peten
Chiapas
Tabasco
Veracruz
Mexico
Oaxaca
Puebla
Tlaxcala
Hidalgo
Queretaro
Guanajuato
Guerrero
Morelos
D.F.
Cancun
Akumal
Tulum
Coba
Ek Balam
Chichen Itza
Yaxuna
Izamal
Dzibilchaltun
Mayapan
Uxmal
Kabah
Sayil
Merida
Oxkintok
Chunchucmil
Campeche
Edzna
Becan
Calakmul
Ichkabal
Kohunlich
Cerros
Cuello
Lamanai
Altun Ha
Ambergris Cay
Belize
La Milpa
Rio Azul
El Mirador
Nakbe
Uaxactun
Tikal
El Pilar
San Ignacio
Xunantunich
Caracol
Naranjo
Yaxha
Itzimte
Dos Pilas
Aguateca
Altar de Sacrificios
Yaxchilan
El Cayo
Piedras Negras
El Mar
Bonampak
Palenque
Quirigua
Copan
Guatemala City
Kaminaljuyu
Takalik Abaj
Izapa
Comalcalco
Villahermosa
La Venta (Olmec)
San Lorenzo Tenochtitlan (Olmec)
Tres Zapotes (Olmec)
San Andrés Tuxtla
Tlacotalpan
Veracruz
Oaxaca
Puebla
Tenochtitlan
Mexico City
Acapulco

ABOUT THE AUTHOR

Terry Neal is a life-long student of ancient history, and a recognized authority on money and economics. He served as a consultant to the governments of several island nations, and was formerly an economic advisor to clients in sixteen countries on five continents. He is the retired founder of an international business with 250 offices worldwide, has been the CEO of multiple public and private companies, a venture capitalist, trust manager, public speaker, and syndicated radio show host. Neal has authored multiple newsletters, magazine articles, two lecture series on CDs, and seven prior books.

Terry Neal is a widow, has eight children, twenty-seven grandchildren, and four great grandchildren. He has led a fascinating life, as all who know him agree. Terry loves to fly, he loves to sail, and he loves to travel, read, and talk. Author of five books on economic strategy, Neal served three years in prison on an IRS charge of conspiracy to defraud the government of taxes based on the principals outlined in two of his books. Two books on science and philosophy followed. *The Search for Zarahemla* is Neal's eighth book; his first novel.

Made in the USA
San Bernardino, CA
04 September 2017